BROTHERS
Two worlds, one destiny

A book by
Ariel Mauricio Egber

BROTHERS
A book by Ariel Mauricio Egber

Original Title: *Hermanos*
Author: Ariel Mauricio Egber
Production: Ariel Mauricio Egber
Orthographic and Style Revision: Ettel Fontana
Literary Advisory: Carolina Alcalá
Design: Carlos Gabriel Tamez
Layout: Carlos Gabriel Tamez
Cover Illustration: Antonella Trovarelli
Drawings and Images: Antonella Trovarelli
Marketing: Janett Egber

Kickstarter Project
Production: Ariel Mauricio Egber
Design: Carlos Gabriel Tamez
Video: Carlos Gabriel Tamez
Music: Joycee Egber
Voice: Ariel Mauricio Egber
Marketing: Janett Egber

English Translation
Production: Ariel Mauricio Egber
Translator: Michael Chartand
Editor: David Gaskill
Proofread: Sahar Shavit, Nicholas Lewin, Hamda Noorie
Design: Carlos Gabriel Tamez

BROTHERS

Two worlds, one destiny

a book by

Ariel Mauricio Egber

Dedicated to Marina Egber, who left us early.
With fond memories of our colourful childhood.

To my parents for their guidance.
To Janett, Joycee and Hayley, you are oxygen.

ACKNOWLEDGEMENTS

Seventeen years ago, while I was still living in Israel, a story began to emerge. During that period, the story had started to bubble in my mind, but I was yet to even come close to putting it down on paper. My first year in Australia was very difficult, characterized by a cocktail of languages, cultures, and lifestyles. Clinging to my original language really allowed me to strengthen myself and look to the future, and in that regard, I began writing this book, a product of my imagination.

At first, I wrote only 50 pages, but soon became engaged in other things and the novel was archived for almost five years. When I finally decided to get back to it, I went on to write another 100 pages, but the file was so old that it hardly matched with the latest technological advances; even Word had advanced two versions forward.

And so the book was put aside yet again, but, like a fine bottle of wine, it needed time to mature, and remained on my computer and in my head for another 10 years, without a single word being added. That was when inspiration struck. As I began to consider what had happened, the words and ideas that had been maturing inside me flew out one after the other and in just six months, the novel was finished.

The characters are all figments of my imagination; some were defined with features that I have come to appreciate in people I know, and others less so, but all somehow exist inside me. The ambitious, the daring, the conservative, the pragmatic, the determined, and even the anxious, are all part of my being. The places are real, too; they exist and some are latent in my memories, but I've changed the names of the restaurants and cafés. The Israeli–Palestinian conflict, a part of history, lives in my consciousness, having experienced it firsthand as a resident, and I still have my parents and sister in those lands.

Technology and security are my passion and my current job. When I wrote about the virus, I knew I was walking along a narrow and dangerous path that could easily get away from the readers, so I tried to be plain and as uncomplicated as possible. My goal was that anyone with the novel in their hands could easily understand what I wanted to convey. I hope that I have succeeded.

I deeply desire peace in the world, but I know it is difficult. I also firmly believe that if you follow the wars, the next will be based on the cybernetics capacity of each nation. If a virus can reprogram turbines or centrifuges with disastrous impacts on nuclear power plants (as did Stuxnet), the future is uncertain and dangerous. I must admit I spent more than three months studying the anatomy and parameters of this destructive malware that in reality actually exists, and I shuddered at its annihilating power.

The book opens many facets and questions, and there are many unresolved issues. I wanted to achieve something different, so I tried to keep the reader thinking, walking along the path of his imagination and deciding for himself how the book would conclude.

When I finally finished building the story, I knew the text was raw and needed revision. Many things had changed in those 17 years between the versions, and I had spent more than 30 years without really speaking Spanish, and so my linguistic wealth had fallen away. Upon immersing myself in the first review, I recognized fragments and expressions that didn't sound right or that weren't clearly understood.

After the third reading, the book began to take shape. The plot became something so intense, that it kept me awake across many sleepless nights. Eventually, I realized I needed to speak with a professional and that's how I met Ettel, the Spanish teacher, who gave the book the nuances it was missing. Pauses, punctuation, spelling, but mostly just her opinion and wisdom, both of which have been essential in the publication of this novel. She was the first to read the book and I owe her more than thanks and admiration at the same time. Afterwards, in my search to find someone to polish the book from a literary perspective, I came to know Carolina Alcalá, a person erudite in the written word. In the short time we collaborated, I learned many things from her. She challenged me by questioning my work and noting inconsistencies. Ultimately, she helped finalize 'Brothers' as a professional novel. Her work was impeccable and deserves my appreciation.

As I decided to self-publish the book instead of waiting for a publisher, I needed someone who could do the design and layout of this swirl of pages, and on that front, I met Gabriel Tamez. Gabriel impressed me with his creativity and flexibility, and his ideas and imagination helped transform the book.

Finally, I can't leave out Antonella Trovalleri, who took care of all of the artwork including the cover illustration, and all the images in the book. When I saw her first sketch I was shocked; it was so much more than just a nice drawing. It described exactly what I wanted and, indeed, each image was a fundamental part of the puzzle that is 'Brothers'.

A Hispanic cocktail of Ettel of Uruguay, Venezuelan Carolina, Gabriel of Mexico and Antonella of Spain, has turned a bunch of words into a book and so, I owe my thanks to all of them.

For the past 18 years, I've lived in Australia and I'm truly humbled by so many friends interested in reading my creation. That's where the idea to translate this book started... It certainly took some time, but following the initial self-publication in Spanish, I knew what it would take to make this a reality; so I started looking for the right people that would help with the English version.

Again, I ended up finding the right people all around the world: Michael Chartand, a Canadian based in Colombia –an editor & manager of a newspaper in Barranquilla Colombia, with a strong Spanish background who translated the entire book. This was just the start; I then needed an editor that would help polish the dialogues and add literal value, so I was fortunate to find David Gaskill, an American editor with over 37 years' experience working in a Newspaper. David added a lot of value with his comments and advice. After reading this novel again and again to ensure the story and nuance remained as the original version in Spanish, I needed help with final proofreading. A very talented young man that I know for some time, Sahar Shavit took this task very seriously and added the last bit that the English version was missing. Nick Lewin from Australia and Hamda Noorie from Pakistan added a very valuable outcome to the general review.

Last, but not least... Gabriel, my designer had done an amazing job again in making this version as professional looking as the original. I am so thankful that I found all of them, as without them, the English journey would not have been possible.

There weren't many more people involved in the creation process, but there were quite a few people who gave me the necessary space and understanding, and who accompanied me all the way to the end. I give heartfelt thanks to my wife Janett, who on many nights helped me maintain focus and allowed me to work by managing the house with so much going on, especially given that we have two adolescent girls. She has always given me the space I need.

Thanks to my daughters Hayley and Joycee for being interested in how I am doing all the time. They are the light that enlightens me (and are waiting for the English translation to read).

Thanks to all who love me and appreciate me.

Yours truly,
Ariel Mauricio Egber.

INTRODUCTION

February 10th, 1992

Two different kites rose in the thick, Middle Eastern air. One sported dark shades of black and grey, while the other was a rainbow of vibrant color, with brighter tones of red and yellow glaring against the sun's thieving rays. The dark kite was tethered to a little boy in Bethlehem; the other, to another boy, in the North of Jerusalem. Suddenly, a strong gust of wind grabbed the two kites and yanked them upwards simultaneously.

The boys bolted forward, desperately trying to hold on, but the strings had already slipped from their hands. Caught by surprise, they had no option but to follow the kites with their eyes and they began running, heads to the sky so as not to lose sight of their toys, while the kites whipped and twirled, forming shapes in the air.

The boys raced ahead, quickly losing track of where they had been playing, and it wasn't long before they found themselves in unfamiliar territory. The boy from Bethlehem stopped dead in his tracks, met by a harrowing scene: a human barrier of green-garbed soldiers stood before him, a wall of authority preventing him from advancing any further. He dared not to move, as these men leveled their machine guns at his lost eyes. At more or less the same time, the boy from Jerusalem encountered an identical scene as he approached the Western city.

Both boys kept their eyes on the sky and, together, lost sight of their kites. They couldn't see that the kites, after a long trajectory, had become entangled in a knot above the Wailing Wall, ending their voyage lodged in one of the walls that protect the old city. A white dove alighted from its perch and, in landing on the wall, became caught in the fine lines of the kites in such a way that upon taking off, it became more ensnared and rapidly fell back again.

Its wings fettered by the entangled kites, its body thudded softly against the roof of the old church, on the Road to Calvary — the same that Jesus had traveled en route to his crucifixion.

As the two children stood, watching the same sky, a single, silent tear slid down each of their cheeks.

1

Teherán - Irán
End of August, 2011

The experiment was about to begin. The turbine was running norma-lly. It had been installed exactly one week ago by two Russian industrial engineers. Pressure, temperature, speed; all parameters were being monitored, and the same process was being performed with the valves and the piping. Two senior generals from the army stood back, next to a man dressed in a black suit, with a long beard and dark complexion — one of the leaders of the Iranian intelligence service, who had been authorized to oversee this complex operation.

All information concerning the variables involved could be seen on a wall screen, silent and unmoving. A Russian technician nodded, gesturing to Rohan, who sat in front of his laptop, intensely focused on the task at hand. Rohan typed some commands, activating the program that had been in the system but dormant for over a week, doing nothing but studying industrial control systems. Suddenly, on the verification screen, the parameters began to change. At first, the changes were moderate, and then came the rapid and radical transformation. The turbine also began to change its movement, and its rotor started turning inconsistently, far outside normal parameters. It began to speed up to 1450 Hz, more than a thousand miles per hour, then slow back down to 2 Hz, and then repeat itself. After three continuous cycles of sudden acceleration and deceleration, the material began to show signs of weakness. After an hour and a half of fracturing and warping, the turbine was completely out of control. In no time at all, the fractured turbine crumbled, and cremated itself in front of the astonished eyes of those gathered in the room.

"Wow!" exclaimed the Intelligence chief, watching as a group of fire-fighters who had been standing by, began to extinguish the flames.

"How did you do that?"

"We 'reversed engineering' all the protocols of the industrial system of our targets."

"Can you translate this to simple languish?"

"We understand now, how the industrial controllers of our enemy working from A to Z, then we created a new code to modify the critical parameters, we can manage and change their functionality, until we destroy them."

"I'm impressed. Everything indicates that we're prepared."

"Affirmative. The attack program is ready; we just have to finalize some details in the worm's encryption and test them together."

Rohan was excited! The project of his life, as he had been calling it for the last six months, was on the verge of achieving perfection.

"We need the exact timings to prepare ourselves," the intelligence chief instructed him.

"Two months — maximum three," came Rohan's reply.

"Do you need anything else?"

"Yes, it would be useful to have experts in cryptography."

"Don't worry about it; look for them, give me their names, and I'll get them. This time we shouldn't have any margin for error. We'll give it back to the Zionists, an eye for an eye. We will never forget *Stuxnet*[1]."

---

1 Stuxnet: a software-based worm that affects Windows-based equipment, discovered in June, 2010 by VirusBlokAda, a security company based in Belarus. It is the first worm known to spy on and reprogram industrial equipment such as SCADA control and monitoring systems, and can affect critical infrastructure like nuclear control stations. Symantec has confirmed that the majority of the equipment infected with Stuxnet is in Iran and the principal suspects for having injected it are the United States and Israel.

2

Jerusalem - Israel
October 22nd, 1982

The mist had almost encased Mount Olivet, one of the great summits of Jerusalem and, indeed, of the whole world. Shaarei Tzedek Hospital emerged at the top, poking through the haze as if it were a tall tree emerging above the canopy of a rainforest. It seemed as though the hospital's dilapidated and paint-stripped walls were more affected by the rain than by the passage of time.

Inside, on the fifth floor of the maternity unit, the day had been far from normal. Since early that morning, three women had already given birth, and it was only 10 a.m. The rooms were full, which had led to a line of beds in the hallway, accommodating a multitude of women who were waiting to give birth. In the delivery room, five women in active labor kept the nurses buzzing from one woman to another like bees in their hive. There were only four nurses on shift and it was blatantly obvious that they were struggling to cope with the situation; one of the two doctors present in the hospital was working on caesarean sections while the other one was on call.

David Levi, a tall and blonde doctor, grumbled his discontent in that peculiar Hebrew-American of his, which sounded rather confusing to anyone who happened to be listening in. He had known for some time now that the hospital was about to collapse, and even though he had complained many times to the authorities, his warnings always fell on deaf ears. What bothered him the most was the fact that he had reluctantly changed his shift to go to a wedding — the kind of wedding where attendance is not really optional; the kind you're almost forced to attend. In the face of such tumult, he knew it wasn't going to be an easy day, and so he waited in the dimness, where the dull drone of the radio could be heard coming from a small speaker in the corner of the room. *"This is just the calm before the storm,"* he thought, intently staring out the window. The views of Jerusalem could always cheer him up and calm him in times of stress.

Meanwhile on the radio, an announcer passionately described a recent attack in Lebanon with an unfortunate outcome: a bomb explosion on the side of a road that had intercepted a passing armored column from Tzahal, had resulted in 10 dead soldiers and 16 wounded. The army had been operating in the depths of the Lebanese lowlands, looking for PLO terrorists. Ten kilometers from Beirut, they stopped to regroup. *"That country was an ally without meaning to be,"* David thought, outraged at the devastation that was being broadcast.

Rachel Mizrachi, one of the hospital's midwives, uncharacteristically burst into the room, and without stopping, shouted, "David! Two at the same time!"

David put on his white gloves and surgical mask and sprinted to the delivery room, where he discovered two women in labor, each experiencing rapid contractions: a thick-lipped, brawny Muslim woman with brown hair and skin; and an Israeli woman, white as snow. Their medical histories, as well as the petrified looks on both of their faces, made it apparent that the two of them were first-time mothers. The Muslim woman was alone — and as the tradition went, the Israeli woman was accompanied by her husband, who was paler than she was. In a moment of great pain, the Israeli woman screamed and squeezed her husband's hand so tightly, that he, too, let out a yelp, and the ends of his fingers momentarily became white. Surely she would have preferred he didn't see her like this — so disheveled, so defenseless, and in so much pain. The man seemed quite bewildered, and he began to shiver, giving free reign to his own fears. The doctor came around just at that moment to see the women, and routinely looked between each of their legs, which had by that time been positioned in stirrups to keep them apart. The sight that met him scared him for a moment — both of the babies were in the exact same situation, their heads already beginning to emerge from their mothers, almost like a twist of fate. Each woman's cervix was reddish and dilated. David took a deep breath and nodded to signal Rachel, who, although hadn't expected it, understood that she would have to play the role of doctor for a few minutes and assist with one of the deliveries.

"I will guide you; don't be afraid," David reassured her, attempting to calm both Rachel and himself at the same time.

David took over the Palestinian woman, as he believed she would be more difficult, but both women were screaming and groaning from the pain. They'd been through a lot together; each one had been having contractions since five in the morning, and the nitrous oxide —laughing gas — just wasn't cutting it; it had no effect at all on their lacerating pain. A few minutes later, after the big push, they gave birth at exactly the same time, in immense pain, as dictated by the Torá. David cut the umbilical cord of each woman and took the Muslim baby in his hands. Rachel wrapped the Jewish one in hers. Both babies were brown-skinned with black hair, and their first indescribable cries happened almost in unison.

Suddenly, another Palestine woman on the bed next to the window began having rapid contractions and called out in pain. Without hesitation, Rachel and David placed each of the tiny babies into small cribs and David contacted the pediatrician, who was just a few meters away in another room, but unfortunately far too busy to come himself. Instead, he sent an assistant to collect the babies for examination and to clean them up, but the assistant, Tal Elad, apparently didn't notice that the names were missing. By the time Rachel realized she had forgotten to mark the names, the babies were gone. It was her responsibility to identify the newborns in the delivery room and to put their names on their wristbands from their charts — a highly important task, especially on days like this one, when so many children were born. She was in despair over her mistake, but snapped back into focus as the Muslim woman in front of her broke water and became the center of her attention. In an instant, she stopped thinking about the name tags for the cribs.

The pediatrician, a young man named Rafi Segal who had come to the hospital just a week ago, took the babies from his assistant and, with remarkable skill, checked, cleaned, and wrapped them up, almost automatically. When he weighed them, the scale showed the same number;

they were exactly the same. They had the same birth time and the same weight. *"What a coincidence!"* he thought. Noticing there were names scrawled on the wristbands that were different from those on the charts, he switched the charts without thinking, and continued with his work.

3

LEONEL
Tel Aviv - Israel
End of August, 2011

Toward the end of summer, a Saturday in Tel Aviv is a delight that is very difficult to reproduce. The sun beat down on the golden-hued sand, the coastline crowded with people — primarily tourists — and the women strutted their bikini-bronzed bodies as they went around the beach. The sun used to slipped away every night to the rhythm of samba and salsa, and the nights were an endless flood of beer, music and rhythm — characteristics that gave the city its name: Tel Aviv, "the city without rest."

At about four in the afternoon, I left the coast and walked up to my apartment to take a bath and rest before diving into another night of music and alcohol. Only three blocks used to separate my house from the sea; and I had found my refuge in the heights of the Sheraton Hotel on Mapu Street. I called it that because, in fact, it was on the basement floor, underground. It had only one window; the only indication of day and night. Beside my room, a heavy, stainless-steel door gave rise to the true "shelter" that every residence in Israel had. The shelters were built for protection and evacuation in times of belligerence. I loved my apartment, because it was well-located and mainly because it had its own parking spot — something very hard to find in the heart of the city. Often, I gave access to my parking spot to some of my friends.

It was my free Saturday and I didn't have to work. My job as a security guard at a bank helped me to pay for my studies and I worked every other weekend.

I was studying in my fourth year with the Faculty of Medicine at the University of Tel Aviv, but I was also attending an advanced course in security systems. I was part of a group of people who were interested in computers, and we got together once a week to try to undermine a website — hacking, as we called it. We did it for pleasure and competition, and that world of indecipherable codes, encryption and denial of service attacks (DDoS), both challenged and fascinated us.

The reality was that I was interested in studying — and I did it with ease, but it was very difficult to combine both studies and work at the same time. I preferred working at the bank because I could bring my books and study. The shifts at the bank during the week were usually very difficult, but I didn't have a choice; I needed to work to survive.

My parents had fought their way through life exactly like me, and could offer little more than moral support during that stretch of their lives. Sometimes I try to remember my childhood, but no matter how hard I try, I can't evoke moments full of happiness. My mother continuously lived under a fog of distress and worry, and my father was always consumed in his work. I never understood why Mom was like that, but perhaps that's why she never had any more children. Don't get me wrong — my mother devoted everything she had for me and the things that were important to me, but those moments of candid happiness, filled with joy — they just didn't exist. Perhaps time had erased them, or I had experienced such disconnect, that they were simply furthest from my current state of mind.

Nevertheless, I felt proud of the path I had chosen, even though that option sheared many hours off my sleep and I missed many of the pleasant moments a typical boy of my age would have enjoyed.

In college, I managed very well. I was very interested in my career and we were working three times a week at the Ichilov Hospital in Tel Aviv, where the real action was. There in the hospital, I felt that I was in the best position to learn and, at the same time, to help others.

But these hadn't always been my only interests. I studied during four years of military service in Unit 8200 of the army — one of the most prestigious units, because besides being a high security group, it was within the Central Intelligence body of the Israel Defense Forces, whose main mission was to capture signals intelligence and decipher secret codes. At that time, during our days, we managed strictly confidential data. We spent whole days decrypting programs, codes, and messages; and listening to conversations, so we were all the time extremely committed to our tasks.

When I finished my mandatory service, I was offered a two-year, paid contract; it was a good salary and the work was of my liking, so I accepted it without hesitation. At that time, I had already started studying computer security, forensics, cryptography, and message encryption. With this added knowledge, my position and my performance came together well. Two consecutive years in a row, I was given an award as a top soldier, and I was involved in many classified projects — most of which were so secret, I couldn't even speak about them with other soldiers.

That time in the IDF sparked my love affair with espionage and research. All of it fascinated me and I so readily devoured science fiction, that in my last year of paid work I completed my training along with a special course in personal investigation which I took at night. The army tried to keep me with them as they wanted the best and didn't want me to quit. But I didn't care for the life of polished boots, pressed uniforms, and having to shave every morning. Instead, I decided to leave.

A distant cousin got me a job with an old investigator in Jaffa. Then there, I participated in various investigations, although almost all of the cases the old man gave me involved distrusting spouses, missing children, and even a few lost dogs. It wasn't long before I realized that I couldn't hack this life either. Since I had always been a good student and always been very interested in the human body so I decided to enroll in the Faculty of Medicine.

After just a year in college, I received a letter from the Mossad asking me to join their ranks — typically something offered to only the best recruits from the intelligence service of the Army — but I was so excited about my medical studies that I dismissed the Mossad option. Sometimes I wonder how my life would have been if I had made a different choice.

These memories came to me without meaning, but then as I thought of the commotion, and with a bit of nostalgia, I led myself to review everything that I had lived.

At the entrance to the stairs leading to my apartment, I was surprised to see that the old man from the first floor wasn't at his window, as he normally was.

"What happened to him?" I asked myself.

I went downstairs, and noticed that the lights were still on. The trepidation I felt was not surprising - I was the only one who lived on this bottom floor. Maybe someone was looking for me, or maybe someone took his bicycle from the miklat and forgot to turn off the lights.

I opened the door cautiously. My cat, Jony, circled the kitchen counter — something she usually only did when someone approached the house. Then she lunged at me, letting me know that her dinner time had passed and she expected a feeding.

On the floor, I found an unmarked envelope. Jony had already trodden on it and licked it curiously. I took it in my hands and looked it over, nervously considering who might have delivered this on a Saturday afternoon, when the post office is close. I pulled out the sheet of a paper inside. As I read the strange script, I felt my pulse quickened, and the strong pounding I felt within my chest each time my heart beat left me feeling anxious and out of breath. "THE WORLD IS NOT WHAT YOU THINK. IF YOU ACT FAST, YOU'LL HAVE THE OPPORTUNITY OF A LIFETIME," it said in untidy, capital letters. On the back there was a phone number; #02 Jerusalem code area...

4

Tel Aviv - Jerusalem
29th of august, 2011

One week had passed since that strange Saturday. The faculty kept me very busy in the year-end exams, the hospital, my work. It all merged together in one. But my entire life squished into "nothingness" at the thought of the immensity of the words in that note. It's amazing how the unknown — the inconclusive thing — can impact our lives. Ten thousand and one times, I thought to myself that maybe it was a bad joke — but then, whose?

I tried to discover whether it had been any of my friends, and over the next week, I strategically queried each of them, one by one, including those with whom I had no common thread, but I found neither information, nor trace of the author of the anonymous message. The only possible witness who could have shed some light on the situation — the old man on the first floor, who is always in his window — had coincidentally decided to go for a walk that day, something he almost never did. Was it a trick of fate?

Eventually, my life went back to normal. I didn't want to bother my parents as they had their own problems and I didn't want to give them more stress. So why hadn't I called the number on the note? May be it was the fear of what I might find or may be I was just trying to forget about it.

A week or two later, while I was nodding away with half-closed eyes and an anatomy book in hand, the phone rang, and absolutely scared the hell out of me! It rang out like thunder, violently shaking me from my torpor in the most crucial time of the day. The old clock, which had been a gift from my parents when I had moved out of home, pointed to 9 p.m. I picked up the receiver and a husky woman's voice asked for me by name.

"Yes, this is Leonel. Who is speaking?"

"I'm the one who wrote you the note. You didn't call me ... I don't know why. I want to meet you."

"B–but ..." I stammered, "Who are you?"

"For now, it's not important who I am. You will know at the right time. Let's meet each other tomorrow, at 6 p.m., after your shift in the bank. We'll meet on Ben Yehuda 106 in Jerusalem, Café Yosi. I'll be wea-ring black."

"But ... Jerusalem —" I said, and the voice on the other end of the line instantly went silent.

That night, Morpheus[2] for me had no resemblance at all to the mythical Greek god. A whirlwind of strange sensations raged inside me; my heart pounded with a new intensity I had never felt before, and any questions I had, were answered with only a perplexed furrow. How did this woman know where I worked and at what time my shift ended? Perhaps I was being followed? Everything was cloudy and there were few answers. After what seemed like several endless laps in my bed, and with the heat of late August evaporating my latest thoughts, I decided to take a sleeping pill. It was 3 a.m. when I swallowed it, and I soon slipped into a deep, but troubled sleep.

---

2 Morpheus: is the Ancient Greek god of dreams.

5

Tel Aviv - Jerusalem
30th of August, 2011

At 4:30 p.m., my shift ended at the bank. That day I hadn't had anything to study or do and on days like that, the boredom of my job would push me into a daydream and with such a feeling of heaviness, I often felt like I could simply die like a vegetable behind those glass doors that separated me from the public. When I saw that people were hesitant to enter, it always made me crack a smile. I often thought they put me in that job because of my unique stature. I'm 182 cm tall and I have a dark complexion; perhaps they thought my appearance could generate fear.

While I consumed another eight hours of my life inside that place, the outside world rolled on by, but on that day, the peace and quiet helped me contemplate the meeting. Should I go? The uncertainty led me to ruminate more and more about the issue, and curiosity began gnawing inside me.

"Come on, come on!" I told myself. "You need an adventure."

I fired-up my white, '92 model Daihatsu. I've never questioned its loyalty, but a trip to Jerusalem could present a risk for any old car. Hills into the Holy City are precipitous, with sharp curves, and are usually crowded with old motors grumbling all the way up to the top. However, the 70 kilometers from Tel Aviv to Jerusalem passed in silence, although under a cloud of impatience as to what would transpire.

Ben Yehuda is one of the main streets in downtown Jerusalem. "It's impossible to live in this land without at least having heard of it, except perhaps for some kibbutznik[3] in the Golan," I thought. Everyone also knows that getting into this place with a car is complicated, and to find parking is a nightmare, especially after 6 p.m. Nevertheless, I made that mistake, and began spinning up and down the streets looking for a place to park my car. I ended up stopping near the Wailing Wall and went rushing to my meeting because I was running late. Cafe Yosi was a very small bar, mainly for bohemians who come to this blessed city. I knew from a previous visit that the interior was dark, with black curtained windows, comfortable chairs and tables which were so low that they could be used for a conference of dwarves. At that hour, the bar was completely full and I wondered how I would recognize the woman I wanted to meet. All of the women in the bar were wearing black — a perfect color to shape their bodies and all the fashion in those days. I lingered at the door for a while, until a heavy hand patted my forearm.

"Rachel Mizrachi," the woman said, huskily, putting her hand out in greeting, hoping to shake mine. "Are you Leonel?"

"Yes," I answered, and grabbed her hand in mine. Her palm was sweaty — as, I presume, was mine.

She smiled and sat down. "The noise will force us to raise our voices," I thought. Why would she have chosen such a crowded place?

"Who are you and why are you being so mysterious? What do you want from me?" I shot out the three questions at once, trying in vain to calm my nerves.

"As I said, I'm Rachel Mizrachi, a retired nurse. I need your services. I know you currently working on personal investigations. Moshe Cohen of Talpiot gave me your name and he recommended that I reach out to you."

Moshe Cohen. For a moment I didn't remember who he was, but suddenly, the memory became crystal clear in my mind. One of my first jobs had been investigating a very pretty woman from Ramat Gan[4], whose husband suspected her to have a lover. One day, waiting in the parking lot at Kenyon Ayalon, camera in hand, I spotted a black car behind mine. The driver of the car was spying on me and had been for a while. I looked in the rear-view mirror; there was no doubt that he was staring at me. After 15 minutes, I got up the nerve, left my car and went straight to the dark vehicle. Old Moshe Cohen was sitting there with a mocking smile on his lips.

"I think we're working on the same case," he informed me, baring some brilliant, golden molars.

"How? The same case? Did the man also hire you?"

"No, I come from the other side — the woman hired me. The two are at Kenyon now, but nothing is happening, neither are adulterous you know; they're rich, they have lots of time, but they have no idea how to have fun."

I remember we laughed for a long time and eventually he introduced himself and told me his whole life-story, a saga of 30 years in the police force, an institution where he had come up through almost all the ranks, and then 10 more years as a private investigator. He intended to retire soon. He lived alone, and he told me he had a son, but left most of the details unsaid. We closed the case on that couple with an agreement between ourselves, and I remember seeing him on one other occasion, when we helped each other with information. We always kept in touch. Unfortunately, Moshe wanted to take advantage of everything; there was nothing trustable about him. In our circles, he had a reputation as being an unreliable person. The only thing in common that I found then, between us was our surname, Cohen was not a rear name for a jew.

I speculated why old Cohen would recommend this woman to me. Why doesn't he deal with it himself? What would he ask me this time? I didn't want to get dirty in something illegal... or, who knows, maybe I was wrong and I didn't really know his personality as well as I thought.

"Look, ma'am, I don't work in investigations anymore. Now I study medicine and, as you well know, I do shifts as a security officer at a bank, to pay for my studies."

Rachel wasn't surprised at all by my answer. Clearly, she knew all about my life and was prepared for whatever I had to say. She rested her hands on the table, forming a triangle with her elbows. It was the first time I had stopped to look carefully at her. Two almost straight lines graced her forehead, and her hair looked slightly tinted and well kept. The pupils of her eyes unmasked those of a sad woman, and neither the heavy makeup nor the raised eyebrows detracted from that downcast look. She didn't look nervous. She spoke slowly, and that impressed me.

"Leonel, I didn't expect you to answer yes. I know your situation and I understand where you're coming from. But let me tell you what it is, and then you can decide. I want you to know I'm willing to pay a lot of money; in fact, I am willing to spend all I have."

"A lot of money?" I raised my eyebrows in anticipation.

"Yes, a million shekels."

A million shekels! Immediately, I wanted to pinch myself to see if I was dreaming. I could feel my heart racing in my chest and small droplets of sweat began to accumulate on my temples. I thought where would a single nurse get a million shekels?

"Listen, Leonel. I have to find a person — in fact two, but let's start with the most difficult things first."

"Yes, but I ..." I protested, but any attempt at refusal was abruptly cut off as Rachel began her lengthy explanation:

"Twenty-eight years ago, I was witness to a terrible tragedy. It happened when I was working in the maternity unit at Shaarei Tzedek Hospital. Working as a nurse there was one of the main sources of encouragement for me at the time. On an extremely heavy day, there could be more than 20 women in the labor unit, five of whom would have advanced dilations. At such times, we worked with only four nurses and of course our efforts weren't nearly enough to cater to all the women.

One day, two of the women were in labor, one a Muslim and the other Jewish, and they began to give birth at the same time. The obstetrician on duty, also overwhelmed, asked me to take care of one of them. I had never attended a birth on my own, but it was OK because it was under the doctor's supervision.

Strangely, the two women gave birth at exactly the same moment. Both newborns were very similar, but on closer inspection, I noticed that the Muslim had a small mole on his back at the waist. Just at the moment when the doctor and I were walking to place the babies in their cribs, another woman who had just begun labor cried out in pain, snapping us to attention. We hastily left the newborns in their cribs and called the pediatrician to take charge of them, and then went quickly to support the new patient. It was right there in those few seconds that I became aware that we had made a vital error, one which would haunt me for the rest of my life.

I had forgotten to identify those babies with their respective labels — my sacred duty in the delivery room, and when I turned anxiously to see them, they were gone. In that moment of deep trance, the woman who was in labor lost her water almost in my hands and I had to give my full attention to her. I remember while handling that birth, I looked at the pediatrician and saw that he was busy too. I assumed he'd be attending to the newborns, because they were no longer in their cribs. As soon as I was free, I rushed to the nursery room to verify that the identification process had been completed successfully, but the babies were no longer there. The pediatrician told me they were with their mothers, so I went straight to the Muslim quarters. The whole family seemed to be there and the entrance door was full; it was almost impossible to get in. I pushed my way through the crowd and saw that the baby was already nursing in the arms of its mother. I approached, congratulated her, and stood alongside. When the child finished eating, I took it in my hands, mumbling about routine checkups. I rolled his body in my hands and looked him over carefully. I almost froze when I didn't see the mole. I had no doubt that the boy in my hands was the Jewish baby.

Without saying a word, I went to the room of the Israeli. The baby was there, pleasurably enjoying food from its mother, and so I did the same as in the other room; I congratulated the mother and waited for the baby to finish eating, whereupon I held it in my arms and reviewed it covertly. The mole was clearly visible. This was the Muslim baby.

Exhausted, confused, my mind unable to think, I was petrified. My shame and guilt wouldn't let me act. I feared the wrath of both families and the negative consequences that my mistake could have for me in the hospital. I finished my shift and I went home shaking. It was done.

That night (and for many more afterwards), I couldn't sleep, and although I took pills, I just couldn't rest. The next day, I took the plunge and decided to confess everything to both families, no matter the consequences. I went straight to the hospital, but when I arrived, the Muslim family's room was empty. I asked where they had been moved to and was informed that the family had checked out of the hospital just two hours prior to my arrival. On the way to administration to get their contact information, I paused outside the open door of the Israelis and looked in. It was a beautiful sight; the mother was lying in absolute calm, her baby folded in her arms. But it wasn't her baby. Should I tell her? How would she react?

I quickened my step towards administration and there I found the details of the Muslim family. The mother's name was Fatima Asad and she lived on 30 Ararat Street in Bethlehem. I didn't hesitate for even a moment. I looked at a map to see how to get to Bethlehem, and without considering the inherent danger of entering the occupied territories, I began my journey. When I got to the town I found the entrance blocked by the army. A soldier explained that since that morning a curfew had been in place and no one was allowed to enter or leave the city because the army was looking for a terrorist group, which was suspected to be barricaded there.

Neither my explanations of urgency nor my pleas to be allowed to go through; not even a mention that it was a case of life or death, nor my credentials as a nurse — nothing I said, had any impact on the soldiers. It took another week before I could enter the city, after the terrorist group had been dealt with, but I never found the Asad family. I located their house, but neighbors told me they had gone away for a while, leaving no address or means of contact. In the days that followed, I did everything in my power to find them, but I wasn't successful. Nor did I ever tell the Israeli family who also believed that the son they had was their own.

This burden has followed me for many years; a constant reminder weighing me down, and keeping me from living a free and normal life. I have never been able to accept a partner; my friends became scarce; and I reduced my trips — my contact with people. I live each day tormented by the thought of what I did that day.

Recently, I received an inheritance from an American uncle. He had never married, had never had children, and had always felt a great affection for me, enough to consider me his own daughter. I had no father left, so his affection helped me a lot. A girlfriend of his came out of nowhere and tried to dispute my inheritance, but in the courts, the matter ended in my favor. I decided right there, right then, that all the money from that inheritance — a million shekels — would be earmarked to telling the truth about those two children of the past, who today, are likely to be men.

***

Her eyes had welled up by the time she finished speaking, and I offered her my handkerchief, although I felt sure her cheeks had become accustomed to the sobbing. I was shocked. So much pain and so much time; the story was enveloped in cruelty. I felt sorry for those two boys who today are no doubt young men, unaware of their true identities, identities that are the embodiment of such dissimilar traits. I also felt a deep sorrow for Rachel and her torment after hearing it from her own mouth.

Rachel wiped her eyes and reached into her black handbag. She pulled out a check book, wrote a check for 10,000 shekels endorsed to my name and put it in my hand.

"Rachel I can't ..." I blurted.

"Think about it and call me. Only you know this history now. Only you can help me do what's right."

She took her purse, cried another tear, and quickly left the café. I went to the window and as I watched her go, I felt a very deep pain. With the check in my hand, I stood motionless for quite a while, unaware of the passing time.

Throughout the trip to Tel Aviv, I couldn't get the woman's story out of my mind. Her face full of pain; the two babies; the families and their customs; the current confrontation between Muslims and Jews — it all hung out in a whirlwind too difficult to decipher. There are mistakes and injustices in the world; we're human and, as such, we make errors, but this case was totally different. She had changed the lives of two people simply as the result of a failed identification. To save my sanity, I tried using a tool I had learned in a private investigations course — separating personal feelings from work feelings — but it wasn't possible. I always thought that I'd be prepared to take on a case like this, where the issues can so easily become personal and bring you down. In this woman's case, I wasn't confident that I had enough experience to take it on, but on the other hand, I craved the money. I pulled up my accounts and concluded it would take me many years to reach a million shekels. Even 10,000 was almost a fortune in my wallet, and that represented only one percent of the total. Then again, the money wasn't mine yet, because I hadn't accepted the case — and I probably wouldn't, either, because I didn't think I'd be able to work on it.

6

LEONEL
Tel Aviv - Israel
Beginning of September, 2011

The following days were different. It had cost me to make up my mind, but once I had, the most difficult part was behind me. Now it was time to get my things in order to be able to follow through with my decision. I liked medicine and I knew that to leave it would disappoint some people, but what persuaded me was that this was one of those calls that only come by once in a lifetime, and I knew that it had to be answered immediately. I'd be damned if I would allow myself to miss the opportunity, and then spend countless days, weeks — even years, wondering, "What if?" I considered it a test 'from above," and although I wasn't a believer, I couldn't shake the sense that somehow, for reasons unknown, I had been chosen for this task.

I had the option to stop my studies for a while and take them up again upon finishing the case, but that would be difficult, as I would have to re-apply to the Faculty of Medicine to enroll for my degree — something virtually impossible in Israel since, at the time, only just over 100 positions were made available across the entire country each year.

I knew there was only one person who could help me with this: Professor Dr. Jacob Lachman. He was like a godfather to me, a man of absolute integrity who understood and explained medicine in a very human way, with a style quite different from the rest. His wisdom was never questioned, and the way he conveyed it humanized all of us, making us better professionals and even better people. He always said to us that diseases start in our minds, and that we should always talk with our patients prior to examining them.

I can say I was truly lucky, because Dr. Lachman accepted and valued me. He knew I was not just another student; he knew how hard I had fought and worked to take my place at the University of Tel Aviv. I was lucky to meet him when I was in my second year, and from that point on, we maintained a very special relationship. Sometimes we ate together, talked politics and philosophy; we were both soccer fans, so we often went to the sports field together, and to one bar or another for a drink.

Lachman was 85 years old. His gray hair and the lines under his eyes revealed a history that could only be described as grueling and laborious. He had been separated from his partner for many years. One day while talking over drinks, he confessed that he never wanted another, and had, over the years, clung to his loneliness much like a child might cling to a warm blanket. I knew he had a son, but he never told me about him; in fact, he avoided the subject altogether. Many times I thought he treated me like the son he had wanted to have, or had had but never saw. Of course, he always kept his distance and acted very professionally when he referred to me in our college classes. Jacob was an older person, but his passion for medicine and teaching kept him active and lucid. His human quality was an invaluable contribution to the faculty, which considered him to be at the top of his profession, one of those human beings who are irreplaceable regardless of age. I thought about how to explain the matter of the babies to him, but then realized that I could not, because Rachel had sworn me to silence and absolute secrecy if I aspired to take the case.

I was sure that Jacob would understand the story, which was very human, but the duty to keep silent prevented me from telling it to him. So I started thinking about how to produce a credible story, close to reality, that would convince an intelligent person like him on why I would need to interrupt my studies. I hadn't found a solution for that yet.

I considered different options: one was making my mother sick, but I quickly dismissed it. Faking the death of a relative was also out of the question, because he knew I had almost no family in Israel and that my relatives in Argentina were very distant. Assigning some disease upon myself would be in vain, as he would simply insist on examining me himself. Suddenly, like a lightbulb snapping on in my head, I remembered Rachel's inheritance money, and it became clear that this would be my reason. I would simply explain to him that I had been designated for a very large inheritance, which would require me to make inquiries both locally and abroad. After all, it wasn't entirely untrue.

As I developed the idea, I formed responses for every eventuality, making sure that my story could not be faulted in any way. And so, one day, I found myself eating with Dr. Lachman in a canteen in Gevirol Iven Street, in the center of Tel Aviv. We loved eating kebab there; the hummus was a culinary delight that is difficult to describe, one of the specialties of the place. We sat at a table near a window that overlooked one of the noisiest streets of Tel Aviv. The smells of cooked meat could destroy any thought of dieting or fasting. We started to eat and talk normally. I was nervous and didn't enjoy the feast that usually delighted me so much. Lachman quickly noticed this.

"Leonel, what is it? Do you want to tell me something?"

"Actually ...yes. Look, Jacob, I have to put my studies on hold for a while, I have a problem – let's say ... a complication, but it is something I must resolve for the sake of my family."

"Well, tell me, tell me what is so important that it will stop you from studying," he said, signs of anxiety beginning to appear across his furrowed brow.

I hesitated a little, because I knew it would be difficult to lie; Jacob knew me very well and I couldn't let my gestures and behavior betray me. I put all my creativity into play.

"A brother of my grandfather died in Argentina; he never married or had children, nor did he leave a will. We, the relatives ... we never suspected that he was in possession of such a fortune. We knew that he had two houses and a small factory in Entre Rios[5], but we never imagined that he possessed much money and other properties beyond that. His direct heirs would be my grandfather, who lives in Argentina, and my father, but there are other lawyers pushing for the money and I'm not sure what excuses they are using. My father is asking me for help,

---

5 Entre Rios: province in Argentina.

because he doesn't know how to proceed. He is pleading with me to handle it. And the truth is, that he is an old man who no longer has a head for paperwork - and we are dealing with a lot of money."

It was a relief to finish my story. Jacob, meanwhile, was moved. I must admit, the story had many weaknesses and many question marks, but it was believable.

"How can I help you?"

"Jacob, you know that studying medicine is everything to me, and you know how much effort I've put into it over the last few years, but now, I feel I have to devote myself to this inheritance issue, especially because my family needs me. Also, let's face it — that money could change my life."

"Is there no other option? Would it not be better to hire someone to do the job? You don't know that much about legal issues."

"Yes, I know that, but my grandfather is not well; his health is very delicate, and my father is not in a position to take care of this either. It is not easy in a country like Argentina to find someone honest to take charge of everything. I've thought a lot about it and I think it's best I take control of the problem."

"Well, that seems reasonable. But ... how can I help you?" he asked again, raising his thick eyebrows.

"I would like the university to keep my place for me for whenever I can come back."

Jacob took his right hand and put it on his forehead as a sign of disquiet, taking a meager sip of beer as he sat, ocean-deep in thought.

"Look, Leonel, I understand your situation and know you well enough to believe that you have evaluated all the options. I do not want to start an interrogation; you know that I try to handle everything related to studies and university objectively and without favoritism. But I think very highly of you and I value your honesty, so I will try to help, although I can't be sure what the results will be."

At that moment, I felt like a huge weight had lifted from my shoulders — not only because it would be possible to reserve my spot, but particularly because of Jacob's attitude. I realized once more just how highly he thought of me. We were saying goodbye in the street, when Jacob asked:

"And if they don't hold your place for you, would you still go on this mission?"

I should not have hesitated, but I did, and Jacob noticed. I felt, suddenly, that my place had vanished; everything had been for nothing.

"Yes," I asserted, trying to convey all my supposed conviction.

"Have a good night," Jacob bid me farewell, and he gave me his usual handshake — but somehow it seemed weaker in grip than the handshake to which I had become accustomed.

7

There are decisions that can take years: getting married, buying a house, having a child… but there are others that only take us seconds, and are no less important and can mark your life forever. In the meeting with Jacob, I had answered yes to his question of whether I would continue with my mission even if it meant losing my spot in the university. It wasn't until later, after I really had time to think about it, then I realized the severity of my decision: I would be throwing away four long years of study in exchange for something uncertain, without recognition, and that would surely carry with it many hardships. Nevertheless, I had made my decision and I moved on.

In the following days, I tried to organize the tasks I needed to complete. I started by preparing a list of the information I would need and for which I would have to consult Rachel. The first things that came to mind were the names of the people involved, their actions in the hospital on the day of the deliveries and afterwards, in their homes. I organized all the ideas into a new folder called "Brothers," which I had created on my laptop. A call to old Moshe Cohen could perhaps broaden the panorama; maybe the old man was aware of the case, or had at least heard of it and could be of some assistance. After all, he had been the one who recommended me.

I dialed his number and when he answered, he didn't sound surprised by the call, even taking into account the time that had passed without us speaking. It seemed like he had been waiting. We agreed to meet at Yootbata, a restaurant that belonged to a kibbutz in the south end of the country. The place is located on the coast of Tel Aviv and specializes in salads and delicious, natural juices.

Moshe was 20 minutes late, but I was ready and waiting for him. In all the meetings we had ever had, he had never come on time. He apologized, which was part of his routine, and we sat at a table on the second floor, from which we had a unique view of the sea. The sun shone brightly; it was a beautiful day — but perhaps not the most appropriate on which to meet this arrogant codger.

"How are you, Leonel?"

"I'm good … I hope things are well with you, too," I said, trying to rush through the unnecessary courtesies. "You know why I called you?"

"No, I don't." He smiled, illuminating me with his golden teeth. "I referred Rachel to you on a matter, I imagine you might want to ask about that?"

"Something like that," I responded, "but clear something up for me — why don't you accept this task yourself? I presume you know that there is a lot of money involved."

"Look, Leonel, I'm retired. This case is going to require plenty of dangerous incursions, travel, and surely, difficulties will arise. I'm too old for all of that."

I figured he probably wasn't telling me the truth, but, undoubtedly, had created a good excuse that was difficult to question. It was also undeniable that he had already made inquiries that gave him the knowledge of related dangers and travel.

"How much do you know about the case? What do you know about this?"

"Look, I know everything. I've known Rachel for more than 25 years, but until four months ago, she hadn't told me anything. And then one day, she just unraveled her story completely, looking for help. I did some preliminary research and decided it wasn't for me."

"Because it involves danger?"

"Perhaps. So you've already accepted?"

"No, I haven't yet, I'm going to think about it; you know... I study now and I have my stuff."

"Yes, I understand, but this is huge and will help you more in life than medicine ever will."

There was something in the way he spoke that gave the impression that we were talking about a reward that was more than just money.

"Think carefully," he advised. "If you decide to take the case, I will give you more details. It's quite confidential, so until you accept, I can't really give you any more information."

When we shook hands to say goodbye he said, "Every person has a chance in life; this is yours — don't waste it. Ah! Another thing: remember, people are divided into two kinds, those who will use you and others who will let themselves be used, but there is a tiny little circle populated by people like Rachel Mizrachi; she wants to do good."

Things weren't any clearer after my talk with Moshe. I clung to the idea that it was an opportunity that shouldn't be wasted, but I couldn't vanquish the thought of losing my place in the Faculty. At the hospital, I visited some doctor friends to see if they knew of precedents where students had suspended their studies and were allowed to return afterwards. I didn't get a favorable response: almost no one had heard of a similar case and nobody believed that the Dean of the School of Medicine would reserve a spot for an unlimited time.

That day I was helping in maternity. In practice, we changed areas according to the needs of the hospital, although really it shouldn't have been that way. More than helping, it was learning by doing, as I called it, because we couldn't really do much. Those hours distracted my thoughts from all my earlier ideas.

In the delivery room, there was a Palestinian woman in labor, and quite close to being fully dilated. She had been lying there for four hours, pushing. She was without her partner and her chart informed me that she was 16. I figured she would have been married at 15, which was a common marrying age among Muslims. Because of her youth and fragility, the nurses were compassionate with her and, for a moment, I doubted whether her fragile, skinny body could possibly endure the wrenching pain of giving birth. Her mother, grandmother, and sister were there, but there was no male presence in the room.

Suddenly, the grandmother began shouting something in Arabic. As I approached, I saw that the young girl was trembling and as she suffered the contractions, it seemed that she would split in two. The scream also brought a nurse and when I looked at the womb, I shuddered: before my eyes, two little feet protruded. The baby was stuck, facing the wrong way, and I knew at once this wouldn't be a normal delivery; a caesarean section was needed. When the obstetrician checked her out, he gave orders to prepare for surgery and an urgent transfer to the surgical unit.

When the doctor asked me to help deliver the baby, I didn't think too much about it; there really wasn't time for fear or nervousness. So, once I had observed the appropriate hygiene and donned the required dress code, I was soon with her in the operating room. The surgeon took his scalpel and slit the lower part of the girl's abdomen. He inserted his hand inside her body, followed by a moment of silence. Upon his request, I helped to open the wound with spatulas, and then with a sudden movement, he cried out, "Life!!" and as we watched, the baby, which was now in the doctor's hands, began to voice his first cries. The pediatrician looked at him briefly, and then a nurse tucked him into a blanket and placed him on his mother's chest, where he curled up tightly, resuming the position he had grown accustomed to over the past nine months.

Impacted by what I had just experienced, and with the vision of mother and child together, I closed my eyes, allowing the image of Rachel Mizrachi on that fateful day long ago to become the reality. Without a doubt, this life experience was the final straw in my decision to accept the offer. It was there, before my eyes — so fragile in a bed— the importance of life; the strength of the principal bond — son fed by suffering and identity. It was this — the flow of everything that had passed in a single breath — that brought me to the absolute decision.

"Let's start," I told myself.

8

Tel Aviv
September 20th, 2011

During the last three weeks since my meeting with Rachel, I had been playing hide-and-seek with the telephone, doing whatever I could to avoid it. I was dancing the dance of the demented - going around and around the room, creating asymmetric circles in my plight to stay away from the phone. Not even Jony could figure out what I was up to. Finally, exasperated, I grabbed the handset and ended my martyrdom. Rachel picked up the phone so fast, it seemed like she had been waiting with it in her hand.

"You can count on me," was all I could get out.

"You won't be sorry — I promise," she said.

"I hope that's the case. Listen, I need all the data you've got: the possible names of the children, who are now men; surnames of families; addresses that I can locate or places where they were."

"Leonel," she said softly, "we're going to work my way. I've been thinking for many years how things should proceed when the time came and I've put together many options. I've even grown a plan of action of sorts. First, I want to find the Muslim boy, who is the son of the Jewish woman. I know that at first I told you I was looking for two, but I want you to take care of that boy alone for now. All I want is that you bring him to me and I'll talk to him. Your job is to get him to meet me. If you need money or something else, just tell me. You need to find him and convince him to talk with me without saying the real reason."

"Do you at least know his name?"

"Ahmed Asad. He is 28 years old. The last time he was seen, based on the news that I have, was in Jordan, five years ago. Since then I've lost the track of him."

"Who gave you that information? Is it a reliable data?"

"I got it from a Palestinian from Qalqiliya who has good contacts. I don't know if he is very reliable — and he asked for a lot of money. Give me your email and I'll send you his number, so you can reach out to him. I'll also take the opportunity to send you any other notes that may help you."

When I was finished, and about to say goodbye, she said in a hoarse whisper:

"You can deposit the check now that I wrote you a few days ago."

After our conversation, I felt a heaviness lifted from my stomach; for more than a week, a huge lump had been forming in my esophagus. Doubts had not yet disappeared — indeed, the danger appeared to remain constant. Everything was still an enigma, and just as confusing as before. However, I was more than relieved to confirm my decision.

"With what reason," I thought, "do I bring him back?" Was it really worth communicating the truth of his birth now? Where to start? Money can do everything; with silver we can move Heaven and Earth.

Who knows of the life this young man now leads — or even whether he is still in Jordan? Or maybe he is in Iran or Iraq? How could I enter any of these countries? It was at that point that I realized I was talking to myself out loud.

Too many questions and too few answers. At that moment, I regretted not having completed the Mossad[6] exams. If I had, maybe I would have made more contacts and I would be better prepared. But it was time to "clean the slate." I had to change my college books for "books of life." I opened my laptop, checked my emails, and was surprised to see something from Rachel Mizrachi already waiting in my inbox.

Her email was flagged as important, so I opened it with great curiosity. The contents seemed to have been prepared well in advance; it appeared to be a copy of a very detailed document, including the names all Ahmed's close family members as well as some of his friends; directions to his house in Bethlehem; and the last place in which he had resi-

---

6 Mossad: is the national intelligence agency of Israel.

ded in Jordan. In the middle of the note, she had highlighted the name "Camel Harish," a possible contact residing in Qalqilya. It was a place you couldn't just enter; it was one of the places that had been occupied. The risk was such that the government had issued a statement which stated that any Jew who entered the occupied territories would be doing so at his own risk.

Qalqiliya was a small town very close to Kfar Saba. It had been occupied for over 30 years — ruled in totality by the Palestinian mandate, the Fatah[7] which was in power; but the Hamas[8] grew and eventually took command. The death of Fatah main leader had left nothing but confusion and doubt among leaderless Palestinians, who were like a flock without a shepherd.

I remembered the words of the old Moshe Cohen. I had promised myself that when I had the chance, I would provide data. He had a large number of contacts, and I was sure he knew many details. I also knew that before discarding a million shekels, Cohen would have learned much more about the matter. I thought again about Moshe's refusal to take on the mission, and again, questions raised themselves within me. *"Was he afraid of risk? What strange things or difficulties did he perceive? If it had been for his inability to travel, as he had explained, why not outsource someone to help him?"*

I decided to wait until the next day to contact him. I needed to sort out my ideas. I again opened the Brothers folder on my laptop and made my first file, which I named "Starting Point."

---

7 Fatah: A group from the Organization for the Liberation of Palestine.
8 Hamas: is a Palestinian Sunni-Islamic fundamentalist organization.

9

Tel Aviv
September 21st, 2011

I got up early — much earlier than usual. I had a shift at the hospital from 10 a.m. until five; after that, I would have to hurry to make it in time for my bank shift, from 5 p.m. to 12:30 a.m. I would make the most of the day, I thought.

It was seven in the morning and my stomach was spinning like a fish in a bowl. My mind was racing, thinking a thousand thoughts, but empty of ideas. I needed something to grab onto; something that would allow me to visualize where to start. The phone interrupted the silence like a thunderclap, startling Jony. It was Jacob Lachman. I immediately feared the worst.

"I have good news for you. I got them to reserve your space for one year."

"Wow!" My exclamation mingled surprise and immeasurable joy.

I was still a little delirious when Jacob said, "I'm happy for you; you deserve it. I want to keep in touch with you — you know that I think very highly of you. I hope you told me the whole truth."

"Thank you, thank you so much!" I whispered, and there wasn't time for anything else.

Lachman hung up.

The brightness of the news was overshadowed by his last two words. If I told the truth ... I would lose the spot — and if I didn't, our friendship, the most steadfast of all my friendships, would end!

I grabbed my wallet and tried to remain calm. I went to Bank Leumi, on Ben Yehuda Street, to deposit the check that Rachel had given me. I wanted to confirm the authenticity of the agreement and whether or not the funds were there. What's more, my account was in deficit. "Surely the bank would suspect something," I thought, laughing. There hadn't been so much money in my account since I opened it four years ago. Ten-thousand shekels wouldn't do any harm to my fragile infrastructure.

Once inside the bank, after enduring the exhausting path to the cashier, arguing with the troublemakers who weren't respecting the line and who were trying to creep forward, and putting up with the shouting and pushing human tide, I managed to finally get served. The employee's face registered her irritation. The last client, a toothless old woman who had difficulty speaking, had made her angry. I tried to smile. The cashier took the check into her hands and typed something on her computer and then she turned it over and looked at the screen again. She asked for my ID and my bank card. There was a moment when her gaze lingered on the computer for more than a minute and I froze in place, thinking that maybe the check had no funds.

Then, the silence was broken, as the printer awoke with a perplexed squeal and issued a receipt. I took a deep breath, and it all became clear in that moment: everything Rachel had said was real. While I had never really doubted the truth of the story, now it had been completely con-firmed.

The day had begun in the best possible way, with one less doubt.

10

Tel Aviv
End of September, 2011

A few days later, I called Moshe Cohen. I had five minutes to go before leaving for the hospital. I had decided to suspend my studies, and work at the hospital over the weekend; I knew that if I was late, nobody would say anything, but I wanted to finish on a good note. So I called Shoshi, the person responsible for resident students, to tell her I would be a little late. Then I called Moshe. The old man was very happy — happier than he could be to get considered himself normal — when I informed him that the deal with Rachel was already on. Perhaps he was expecting a commission. Or would there be another reason?

Camel Harish was our contact man. Moshe made it clear to me that Camel would need to be found outside of Qalqilya. His name wasn't that of a terrorist wanted by the army, but Moshe confessed to me that a year ago, he had passed false data to the Israeli troops, earning distrust from the IDF (Tzahal). So he was under scrutiny from the army; if he was found involved in any dirty or illegal business, it would not be good.

"What is the process and how much does he charge?" I needed more information before acting.

"Call him; tell him I sent you. He will explain the rest: the meeting place, how to dress, and how to transfer the money."

"But ... is he reliable? You just told me he lied to the army."

"Look, reliable or not, he's the only source we have at this time and only he can bring the data you need."

I appreciated the information. Everything was flying inside a huge cloud and the danger seemed imminent and difficult to avoid. As we said goodbye, I found it extremely strange that old Cohen hadn't mentioned anything about fees, given the time he had spent and his valuable contacts. That wasn't normal. I had the feeling that he was involved with the case, but how? And why?

I checked my watch. It showed 10 a.m. I dialed the number for Camel and a hoarse voice answered, speaking in Arabic. Without truly comprehending what was happening, I asked to speak with Camel, expressing myself in Hebrew. After receiving no response, it occurred to me to say, "Moshe Cohen of Jerusalem," and then, after a while, the hoarse voice gave me another number. I wrote it down quickly so as not to forget it. Then I looked and saw that their property was 08, the code for Qalqilya, and I called. After a few more minutes of me insisting, Camel answered the phone in near-perfect Hebrew. I'm quite certain that someone was answering his cell phone and gave the caller the number of a nearby public phone, and that was where the contact occurred. That explained the delay in answering. I had read this procedure in a fiction book from Ram Oren[9].

Camel didn't let me speak much. I asked if he had information about someone named Ahmed Asad and he said he might be able to get something for me. He emphasized that it was difficult, but he could investigate and then call me back. His voice was strange, somewhat thin, and I wondered whether he would go so far as to distort it to avoid being recognized. We quickly agreed on the conditions: 5,000 shekels for the initial information, with the option to continue afterwards.

I had to leave 2,000 shekels at an address in Jaffa, a very picturesque city connected to Tel Aviv, where the predominant inhabitants were mostly peaceful Israeli Arabs. The exact address was a warehouse. Immediately after receiving the money, he would start working and would contact me.

"From this point, don't call me anymore; if you try, the phone number you already have will not work. I will be the one who will communicate with you. Leave me your number." And with that, he hung up, without so much as a goodbye.

---

9 Ram Oren: An Israeli writer famous for his works of fiction.

The money didn't seem like a big deal; old Moshe had warned me that he would charge a lot and I felt that the amount was within reason. He hadn't given me much room to express myself, and I understood his position of mistrust.

The next day, I took the money and went to Jaffa, which, on days when there was little to no traffic, was about 15 minutes from my house. I looked up the address on a map: Hefetz Haim was a small street on the border between Bat Yam and Jaffa, south of Tel Aviv. I took Yafet street so that I could stop at the Abulafia, a place well-known for its tasty Arab pie, sambusak[10], which was a personal favorite of mine. Such was the temptation caused by the aromas surrounding this part of the city, that my car automatically slowed as it passed by. The smells were difficult to describe — not just from the pies, but from the fish, the hummuserias[11], the shawarma[12] and the falaferias[13].

Upon arrival, I stumbled across a very old, windowless warehouse. A heavy side door seemed to be all that held up the worn walls of the place. A Coca-Cola poster, which had seen better days, was the only sign that distinguished the place as a warehouse. I entered without knoc-king. An old, fat, mustachioed man sat behind the counter, showing no sign of any form of good manners.

"This is for Camel," I said to him.

He looked at me sourly, unsurprised. "Leave it on the counter and get out."

I left the envelope and walked out. I would have to get used to wor-king under this cloud of suspicion and mistrust, I thought. Nobody here would help me for nothing. Would the money get to Camel? No one offered any guarantees, but I also had nothing — only the name of a person to find. I had no choice but to trust; and so I clung to the sphinx Camel and his cronies.

---

10 Sambusak: A distinct type of filled empanada.
11 Hummuserias: A place where hummus is sold.
12 Shawarma: Seasoned meat, (normally goat), that is roasted on a vertical spit and served in slices, usually within a pita.
13 Falaferia: A place where Falafels are sold.

11

The weekend was entirely devoted to my family. After navigating around the subject for a while, I finally told my parents about my plans of dropping university for a bit. I knew very well that it was a dream of theirs to have their son be a doctor, and I felt really sorry telling them about my decision, but I promised I would finish whenever I could. My mother objected, worried that by leaving my studies, I would never get to finish; while at the same time, my old man was nodding along, crestfallen and meditative. I think he mumbled something like "don't do it," but I told him I needed a year of vacation, perhaps to see the world and decide what I really wanted to do with my life. They both stared at me with vacant eyes — both blatantly aware that they weren't being told the truth, but having no idea what the actual reason was.

My old man tried to ask me if I needed money, although I knew he didn't have much to give me. I said no, and that he didn't have to worry. I tried to reassure them, insisting that this would all be only a year. Lying to them wasn't easy, since my old man and I were so close. But I knew that if I achieved this task, I'd have a lot of money, and so I'd be able to help them instead.

On Monday morning I was a whole new person: no university, no hospital, and also no bank job. I was a man free from schedules — at least for a while. I got up later than usual, had a coffee at Ben Yehuda and Frishman's bar, and it was then that a text message came through: "You can go to Jaffa and get your package; pay the 3,000 missing. Camel." I was impressed; only three days had gone by and the information, just as I had requested, was already there.

I got to Jaffa and had the same ritual with the fat mustachioed man. This time, I spotted a bald man, medium-height, dark glasses, circling around. I saw he had a tattoo on his left forearm, very close to the shoulder, in the shape of butterfly or something like that. The fat man gave me the package, asked for the envelope, and once again, told me to get out of there immediately. Once I was in the car, I got the feeling that someone was watching me. I turned around and noticed that the guy was at the door of the warehouse, with one foot in and the other out. I was certain he was trying to memorize the license plate of my car. He went in right away. I started the car and left quickly.

At home, now in a calmer state, I opened the package. Inside, there was a rather neat brown folder. I sat on the couch, glass of Coke in my hand, and opened it. Right from the beginning, I was astounded at the level of detail before my eyes: it was a photo album, full of photocopied pictures and notes of Ahmed Asad's life.

I took the time to read the story of this young man. He was constantly moving; a nomad in different cities. Bethehem, Amman, Behlehem again, Ramallah, the Gaza Strip. A life in a suitcase, wandering without his parents since he was 12 years old. At that age, he had left his home, absorbed by the street and economic necessities, and he began to provide for himself. His first job was at a construction site in Amman, where he had moved with his 18-year-old cousin, Rafaq. They lived in a refugee camp. Rafaq became a father to Ahmed, and he protected and took care of him. After a long time in Jordan, the two of them came back to Bethlehem. In Amman, they had first-hand experience of hostility towards the Palestinians.

Rafaq managed to find a job with an Israeli contractor and worked in Kfar Saba. Ahmed, who admired his cousin for being brave and bold, couldn't find a job in Israel because he was a minor. Nevertheless, he was able to get a job at a service station in Bethlehem cleaning car windows, although the only money he made came from tips. Rafaq joined the Hamas and, in doing so, he transmitted his hatred to Ahmed by telling him about the atrocities concerning the Israeli army and convincing him that Zionists had usurped the Palestine lands. Rafaq engaged in his first dangerous activity at a violent demonstration in Bethlehem and three weeks later, was shot by Israeli troops while throwing a Molotov cocktail from the side of the road that joins Bethlehem and the Elazar settlement. He was just 26 years old.

Ahmed went to Rafaq's burial, which was planned as part of a boisterous demonstration from the Hamas group in the city of Nablus. The body, wrapped in a dark green flag with the symbol of the Hamas, was carried on a bier without a casket and on foot, as if it were a trophy. Ahmed followed the ritual and was impressed by it. There, he met Yasser Iben Dabul, one of the bosses of the guerrillas, and one the individuals most wanted by the Israeli army, responsible for the murder of the Ben Shimol family while they were traveling on the Jerusalem-Hebron route.

Yaser saw in Ahmed a rather bold young man, willing to do whatever it took after his cousin's death. Back then, he was only 20 years old. Ahmed was accepted as a member of the Hamas and, to get in, he had to go through a series of tests, which included participating in violent demonstrations, throwing rocks against the Israeli army, using slingshots, and training with guns.

He was seen by the group as one of the most brilliant young men. After some psychological tests, his intelligence was more valued than his boldness. When he turned 21, he received a computer from the organization, and with it he began to excel. He became a computer lover and designed the very first website for Hamas. The group valued his skills for this activity and decided to have him on the computer rather than on the streets. Ahmed dedicated himself to studying cryptography and decoding signals to help the group both in this sector and in their struggle with the Zionist enemy. He would also go on to train 10 young men in this field.

By just 25 years old, Ahmed had designed a sophisticated system that, through the Internet, would help the religious leaders of the group contact young, indecisive men who were yet to find their path on the streets of Palestine. This, along with a special coding system, which would allow the terrorists' networks to communicate with one another without using the Israeli telephone system, given that back then, the Israelis had almost completely intercepted all Palestinian communications. Those were his major accomplishments in those days.

Ahmed was promoted to be in charge of a group that would organize the entire IT section inside Hamas. His job involved communication across different parts of the organization. Without physically participating in the attacks and without going out to the streets, Ahmed became involved in each and every one of them and the Mossad, for the first time, included him on its blacklist, which motivated the Shabak to begin searching for him in the occupied Palestinian territories. By that point in time, he was only 26 years old.

The last page of the report had a current photo and a note that said, "Recently seen in the Gaza Strip; age: 28 years old".

It took me a while to digest the fact that I had been hired to follow a terrorist — and a member of the Hamas group. I was also shocked by the detailed, well-collected information about Ahmed Asad, although I felt sorry that there was no address, nor any exact data concerning his whereabouts. There was no reference to what had happened on the day of his birth, either, which made me think that nobody knew about it. I did not for one second doubt what the next step was. I called Rachel right away.

I wasn't willing to go on with this case. Me? Looking for a terrorist wanted by the Mossad and the Shabak? No way! Besides, how was I going to accomplish something that not even the Mossad had been able to do yet? I would be risking my entire life.

Rachel was relaxed and courteous, but I could not shake the feeling of nervousness that seemed to be taking over my entire being.

"I'm leaving the case right now. You lied to me — tricked me. I'm not willing to bring a terrorist before you so that you can tell him all about his life."

"Terrorist? Are you talking about Ahmed? Take it easy! I didn't lie; this is the first time I have heard about it! I had no clue about this young man. Five years ago I got non-validated information that he had been in a violent demonstration in Nablus, but as far as being a member of the Hamas group ... I had no idea. But think about it, maybe you can turn something complicated into something simple."

"What are you talking about?"

"I'm telling you that you need to think more carefully and calmly about how to get to this young man. Maybe the Mossad or the army, being the complex structures that they are, can't do what a single individual can."

"This is really insane!"

"Please, think about it. I'm willing to pay you more — sleep on it. Perhaps your medicine studies and your training in IT might help you."

"How?"

"Think it over; do not despair, you're a smart guy ..." and then she said goodbye.

It took some time, but I started to see my different options. I thought that perhaps Rachel was considering that I would volunteer for a hospital or Palestine entity to find my so-called booty, which seemed crazy and extremely dangerous. The situation in the territories was awfully chaotic; getting in would be a problem, and my stay would be a whole other dilemma. On top of that, my documents were Israeli. There were many stories about doctors from all over the world who had sacrificed themselves by treating people in refugee camps or at the overcrowded hospitals in the territories that couldn't cope with the demand.

Despite what I had told Rachel, I was very far from deserting or abandoning the case, although I disliked it more and more. Rachel had tricked me by not telling me the truth; her claims of knowing nothing seemed as absurd as her proposal.

Then I started to wonder about the truthfulness of the facts Rachel had told me. I realised I would have to corroborate the authenticity of everything she had represented and proposed. This whole thing could be a scam, or perhaps have a hidden agenda.

I decided to start with the hospital where the children had been born. I was familiar with the policies of hospitals, and knew that they saved the data of every person who had ever been there. I didn't hesitate, and since I had no other engagements, I drove my car straight to the hospital. At just past three in the afternoon, I was standing at its doors. All the way to Jerusalem, I kept thinking what my excuse would be for investigating an event that had happened more than 28 years ago — and at that, one with which I wasn't even involved. Suddenly, like a flash, it occurred to me to call old Moshe Cohen. I remembered he had his police badge and used it every time there was a door too difficult to open. This would be the second favor I had asked of him, and I had hoped it would provide a good picture of how Cohen was involved in all of this. If he was part of the clan, he would obviously not be willing to help me find out the truth about Rachel Mizrachi's story.

I called him while my Daihatsu contaminated the beautiful views of Jerusalem with its choking fumes, trying to climb the hills in second gear with the engine screeching.

Moshe picked up the phone, and we agreed to meet at the hospital entrance. Before hanging up, he told me that Rachel wasn't lying and that he would help me confirm her story and clear my doubts. He took me in hand and we went up to the fifth floor together. When the screechy doors of the elevator opened, the maternity ward appeared before my eyes. Rachel's story, in an instant, became very real. I never would have imagined the scenes that I saw there. The walls holding the roof and the floor stood there, filled with stories and moisture. The walls seemed to have been painted over and over, and were sick and tired of so many tones. The rooms were full, and just like on the day of the births from the story, the nurses were extremely busy. Moshe noticed that I was distracted, with my head in the clouds, but didn't wake me from my dream. An obese and cranky receptionist asked us what we wanted. Old Cohen went ahead and showed his badge almost like a trophy, while claiming to have come looking for information.

"What sort of information?" The nurse looked at us, expressionless.

"We need to check the birth of a baby born here 28 years ago."

"Twenty-eight years ago!" said the nurse, shocked and already telegraphing her inability to help us. "That's not here — you need to go to the seventh floor; when you step out of the elevator, you'll see a door on your left that says 'archives.' Look for Dana."

Dana opened the door. She was over 70 years old. I pictured her as that kind of antique you'd easily forget about in a place like this. Behind her, stood some huge cabinets that seemed to be from the time of the British Mandate, filled with dusty and yellowish folders. Dana sat down, and I noticed that she was using an almost new computer with an LCD screen.

"We need to check the birth of a baby born here 28 years ago," Moshe repeated.

"And who are you?"

Moshe showed his badge a second time.

"Ahmed Asad, October 22nd, 1982," informed Moshe, who had memorized the name and date.

The date struck me in the head like an arrow. It was the first time I had ever heard it in connection with this case, and Rachel certainly hadn't mentioned it. October 22nd, 1982, was the same as my own date of birth, and we just happened to be at the same hospital where I was born! A cold sweat ran across my forehead, while a warm spasm expanded through my body. Then, I thought of the mole. I had thought of my mole before — indeed, it seemed like a strange coincidence, one to which I hadn't paid much attention up until now — but the date, along with the whole scenario, suddenly took mere chance out of the entire equation. Moshe felt something was wrong and asked if everything was OK. I decided to try to sit down, so that I could analyze it all more calmly.

"Well, is everything OK?" I asked myself.

The woman typed slowly and then went to one of the cabinets; she went up a ladder and came down with a dusty and stained folder. Moshe verified the name and gave it to me. I opened it slowly.

    Name: Ahmed Asad
    Weight: 3.5 Kg
    Time of birth: 10:12 PM
    Name of the mother: Fatima Asad
    Name of the father: Gibril Asad
    Address: Ararat 30 Belen — Israel
    Doctor: David Levi
    Maternity Nurse in charge: Rachel Mizrachi

There was no more data, just the observation that it had been checked and that everything was all right. There was also a note saying that the mother had left of her own accord, before it was time.

Moshe let me digest it all. He was calm, gave me a pat on the shoulder, and said, "See? Rachel isn't lying."

I couldn't go on without satisfying my curiosity; I knew he was aware of all the details and was trying to convince me. I decided to confront him right there. His participation in this whole situation seemed too odd to me.

"Let me buy you a cup of coffee," I offered.

"OK, but not here — hospitals make me sick."

We descended from Mount Olivet and headed to the Grand Hyatt hotel, which was located on Mount Tzofim[14]. The hotel seemed to be embedded in the mountain, and from there, the views of the entire ancient city looked magnificent. The landscape relaxed me a bit; Moshe knew how to pick places and people. We sat outside and stared at the golden mosque behind the Wailing Wall. The spectacle before my eyes gave me the push to start talking.

"Tell me Moshe, how is it that you are involved in all this?"

Moshe didn't answer, but nodded as if he had taken a bullet. He snorted, adjusted his seat, took a sip of black coffee, and began:

"Leonel, I'm going to tell you something because I care about you. Rachel was always close to my heart; I've known her for 20 years now, and like I said, I have always loved her. You know, I'm not married. She always tried to avoid me. I always felt she was continuously disturbed and uneasy. Five years ago, she broke down in tears and told me her story — the same you know now. I was shocked and thought her rejection of me was a product of her bitterness, so I decided to help her. I made my first investigations and knew about the risks and all that this involved, but I couldn't bear seeing that woman suffering. Given my situation, I understood I couldn't help her, either, because this investigation would involve special energy, travels, roads, and time. It wasn't an appropriate adventure for me, which is why I thought of you. After making a list of all the people I knew, I decided you were the one — the best — and the most important thing is that you are the one who can get results. Anybody else could take the case and walk away with the money without actually getting concrete data. Being as desperate as she is, she's an easy target for scams. But you are honest; I trust you will be able to come back with Ahmed."

His words made me feel compassion. His eyes appeared to become watery. I could see that he truly loved Rachel. He was an old man, without a family of his own, a son he never saw — and he knew what he wanted. Everything concerning him became clearer to me, and perhaps I was wrong before for thinking he might have had ulterior motives. Fina-

---

14 Tzofim: lookout.

lly, with Rachel, the situation seemed real, absurd, sad, and silly — but intensely true.

"Do you have any idea what Rachel meant about using my medical background to deal with the case?"

"The Red Cross — think about it — it is everywhere and they always need volunteers with skills like yours."

While he was telling me this, he hugged me and left in a hurry. Obviously, he was too affected to pay for the coffee, and I was too immersed in my own thoughts.

12

Red Cross — two words. It all seemed so simple: you sign up, you get chosen, and then, you're working ... is that what Moshe thought? It was a lot more than that. The idea of hunting a terrorist formed an invisible furrow of concern across my brow. It wasn't easy to digest everything that had happened. I calmed down a little at the thought that he was a modern extremist, and not one of swords and stones.

Ahmed was a warrior of trojans, cookies, and spy software. His Hamas website, at first look, was a relatively well-designed Internet site. I decided to direct my focus toward him, though I was blatantly aware of my lack of experience in security.

I made the decision to contact my friend Daniel. He was a scholar in computing — one of the best students at the University of Tel Aviv. The Mossad had already approached him to bolster their ranks. Daniel knew his potential and was disciplined, but hadn't yet accepted the proposal. I had read that when the Mossad wanted someone, there were no barriers. When I told him I had chosen Ahmed's site for my work on websites because it contained innovative technologies for my security course at the university, Daniel sensed that I was onto something not particularly simple, and respected my silence. Daniel was smart and nodded his head, as if to ignore my lie. For more than an hour, he set to work — trying this and that; using different programs, until eventually, he conceded that the site was excellently designed and very well protected. Nearly all the relevant information, such as the web data, forms, and other details, were encoded with an almost indecipherable level of asymmetric encryption–256 bit. Daniel tried to sneak 'through the back door' (RAT), a term he used to refer to special access roads to a computer system, but was kicked out by the firewall. He tried to scan all ports, insert a cookie, and inject some special code, but again, found himself blocked. Likewise, the forms we had completed rejected us after detecting that the source IP address belonged to Israel. Daniel tried, albeit unsuccessfully, he was stunt to find a level of security sophistication that he had never seen before. Disappointed, even when he tried to sneak through the secure encrypted connection (HTTPS), nothing helped. My friend rested his forehead on his hands, with his face downcast. He continued to search, checking to see which code had been used to build the site; what he discovered was a combination of two highly complex, *open source*[15] languages.

"We're checking out someone who is very talented, who understands security systems very well," he said excitedly, "I really want to know who is behind these programs!"

That surprised me, because I had never heard Daniel speak like that about anyone. Naturally, prodigies don't give out compliments just like that, but it seemed to be a special case. Ahmed turned out to be a scholar in computer security. Daniel left the house crestfallen. Until then, he had penetrated any site he wanted. In the army, he had been part of Unit 8200 with me, but he was more focused on encrypted messages and confidential information. In reality, he was studying and working for an American company, analyzing and processing data related to biological issues, while in his agenda he still debated the possibility of joining Mossad.

I continued looking at the site. I tried to imagine Ahmed, his past life, and his current struggle. I thought how much cruelty there could be in a simple mistake. I tried to visualize how this person would react to knowing his true identity — a puzzle that I couldn't decipher in the hours that closed that day.

The next day, I called the International Red Cross. It was a 1-800 number. I had no idea who would attend me on the other end of the line. Would the person speak Hebrew or English?

---

15 Open Source: Software whose code has been made available to the masses.

A feminine but deep voice — one that appeared to be that of a mature woman — spoke in English. I explained to her that I was a student in medicine and that I was on a special project, part of a course which required me to volunteer with an international organization that had facilities in extremely needy locations. I explained that the course required me to prove my theoretical and practical knowledge in adverse situations and that, once finished, I would have to write a professional report on the experience.

To develop this idea/excuse, I had woken-up early that day, at almost 5 a.m. Upon hearing my story, Judy – for that was her name – grew more attentive. She asked about me, and seemed to like the idea of someone coming from a Hebrew University volunteering to work in conflict zones. She stressed that it could be a very good precedent for other students in the future. Judy asked me a few questions and exp- lained that she needed more information from me for the application and that she would send me some forms to complete. I would also have to submit all my certificates and my record of my work in the hospital.

I tried to avoid any possible intervention by Jacob in the question- naire or in the verification process. I asked at the university for a cer- tificate and in the hospital, the head guard, astonished, wrote me a recommendation, after having confirmed I was certain I wanted that from him.

Judy called me a few days later and told me that I had been invited to an interview. We set the day, the time and the place which would be the location of the Red Cross in the Talpiot neighborhood of Jerusalem.

Another forced climb for my little car. From first to second gear, it moved upwards and again the poor engine complained as if it had encountered an insurmountable castle wall. I arrived in Jerusalem early. The offices were in a four-story establishment, of which the architecture seemed vastly different from that of the surrounding buildings. It lacked the classic stone typical of Jerusalem structures. Judy was waiting in her office, somewhat harsh, almost barren of furniture. It was difficult to imagine her having been anything other than immensely beautiful in her youth. Her eyes — big and bright — flashed a shade of green not unlike the shiniest emerald; she was a woman of stature, held up by a pair of runway-style legs that no doubt would have caught the attention of many young men back in the day. She looked well preserved, though her face bore the passage of time. I figured she was about 55 years old. We talked for a while, as she obligingly gave a thorough explanation of the mission with all of its conditions and rules. After an hour of conversation, she informed me that I could choose from Nablus, Hebron, and Gaza, noting that Gaza was very troubled at the time, so it was the most dangerous option.

I gave my answer without hesitation, and Judy was not at all surprised when I opted for Gaza. We agreed to meet there in three days, and together we decided on the date, time, and place. Judy informed me that she would take care of the entry permit and all the procedures, and provided me with a list of things I should take for my stay. Having what I needed, I lowered my head, thanked her and left. As I looked back, I found myself contemplating the red cross displayed at the front of the room. I imagined that it was near the eye of the storm and that from here, there was no going back. The return to Tel Aviv was marred by an invisible blanket of uncertainty and fear.

13

LEONEL
Gaza Strip
Late September, 2011

The meeting was complicated by the location of the gathering place, which was a bit remote and at the time, quite dangerous. The Red Cross had opened its headquarters in the Gaza Strip, which had come about as a result of massive shortages, and because in Israeli territory there was another organization that fulfilled the same function: "Magen David Adom[16]". Judy told me that she would wait for me at the Erez[17] Crossing, which is the limit of a zone that separates the Gaza Strip from Israel. In calmer times, this was where Palestinian goods were transferred to Israel and vice versa. It was built in an industrial area, where Israeli factories operated with a workforce that was mostly Palestinian. Judy told me she would be easy to find, because she would be with a Red Cross ambulance, on the other side of the crossing.

Once there, she would be responsible for getting me into Palestinian territory. She asked me to bring my student card, clothes, and everything I would need to survive for at least two months. This was because you never knew for sure when the crossing would be open or closed. Any attempted or suspected violent action, and all territories would be closed indefinitely in the blink of an eye. This year the situation in the territories was very turbulent, and nobody was able to predict the future ahead.

---

16 Magen David Adom: Israeli Red Cross.
17 Erez: Border crossing between the Gaza Strip and Israel.

I prayed that everything would go well. I didn't much like the sound of two months, but did just as Judy had suggested. I considered it as time reserved for those who lived in the army. When you live in Tel Aviv, the facts are depersonalized and people are disconnected from events that happened in the frontline. Every so often, you hear that the territories are closed, but it's not given any importance because it's such a common occurrence. Daily life envelops us like a shroud, and human beings become accustomed to the worst atrocities, as they are known to do. In that period, the Katyusha (rockets) fell like summer rain, tormenting the city of Sderot, a relatively large city in the south, 10 kilometers from the Erez Crossing. The army routinely moved in and out of the Gaza Strip in search of terrorists. Gaza was a country within another, and a day without disturbance or problems was a distant utopia. And so it was precisely to this place that I went with an open mind, bag in hand, in search of my goal.

I left my car two kilometers from the Erez Crossing, hitching a ride the rest of the way in an army bus that was crowded with soldiers returning to their bases. I got to the crossing at 11 a.m. A kilometer-long line had formed at the entrance; almost all the people there were Palestinians who had found themselves stranded by the recent army blockades. Some had been there for days. They came to work in Israel and wanted to see their families, but, like everyone, they didn't know when they could enter and when they could leave. "Peace," in its loosest definition, existed from second to second, and was subject to abrupt interruptions. The whole scenario was delicate and extremely dangerous. Journalists, of whom there were few, used a special, differentiated pass to move quickly into Gaza. I also noticed that the Palestinians were stripped down completely and searched with technologically advanced devices used to control them; however, reporters only showed their cards and bags, and were allowed through.

Among the tumult, I heard a shout from the other side of the fence, and in the distance, I spotted a tall woman with dark hair. I recognized Judy. She called my name, waving her hands. She told me to go to the rank of correspondents and wait there. When it was my turn, a pretty female soldier with large breasts asked me for my identity card and my medical student card. Everything indicated that Judy had already spoken about me, because she knew about my student ID. She checked my bag thoroughly, asking about my belongings and my reasons for entering Gaza. I recounted the story exactly as I had told it to Judy, and she nodded. Beside me, a fence separated me from the row of patient Palestinians; I felt embarrassed at having been able to pass through so quickly while there were other people, who had been there waiting for days just to enter their own homes.

Judy greeted me warmly and we quickly got into the Red Cross ambulance. I was amazed at her demeanor and how she seemed to be coping; her determination and conviction were stronger than most. It was obvious that she was familiar with the movements in the Erez Crossing, and it wasn't long before I realized that she was also very well known by the army. The ambulance was driven by a man with a black turban and a moustache of enormous dimensions. Flying over the dirt roads with remarkable skill, Judy advised me to hold on tightly. We hardly got a chance to exchange words or to hold a conversation with so much bumping; the van slid swiftly on potholed and messy asphalt, constantly affecting our backsides, which could barely cushion the shock of so many sharp bumps. Judy finally introduced me to Ravi, our driver, an Indian Muslim volunteer who knew Gaza like the back of his hand.

Suddenly, an impact juddered the whole van, and I wondered how we had managed to remain upright. A crowd had piled up before us, causing Ravi to brake abruptly. Judy quickly asked me for my papers and put them in her underwear — just in time, as the rebel group aggressively dragged us out of the truck. They were seething with anger and brandishing green flags that I recognized as Hamas, as I had seen them on the news and remembered them from the website. Judy knew some of their leaders; Ravi was known to them, too. I understood that they wanted to know about me. Judy managed the situation quietly, without showing anxiety. I remained still, not quite sure how to react as I felt the unrelenting grip of one of the guerrillas as his hand made contact with my shoulder. Judy shook hands with the leader, and after exchanging a few words, we clambered back into the van and sped off.

Inside the van, the only sound that could be heard was the roaring of an overworked engine; it remained that way until we reached the Red Cross headquarters in the Shaati refugee camp, one of the most dangerous cities in the Gaza Strip. Most of the people there, were refugees but the most dangerous terrorists were also hiding amongst them; the place was a ticking time bomb because of its overcrowding and deteriorating infrastructure. I knew this from my time in the army. The army never had a good outcome when it went into that neighborhood.

The headquarters of the Red Cross was in an old building that had suffered the torment of shrapnel and bombs. It was strange to see how well these peeling walls were still standing. There was desolation all around: muddy streets; carelessly built, half-constructed houses; and a sharp, repugnant odor seeping from the sewers, which would accompany me throughout my stay in Gaza. Regular construction was non-existent. At the entrance to the offices, there was a family prostrated on a blanket: two babies, wearing nothing more than old cloth nappies that had clearly not been changed for some time, crawling on the ground; an unkempt little boy about four years old, imploring passing strangers to part with their money. The scene that confronted me seemed bizarre; outside of reality. The mother veiled her face with a black cloak, ignoring her children, as if her oblivion could somehow make their circumstance less desolate. Misery hit me and I forgot for a moment what I had come to do.

After the emotional impact caused by the surroundings, I sat with Judy in the windowless room from which she operated. A table, a computer, and a printer were the only equipment present. Two weak chairs were completing the furnishings. This time, Judy formally introduced herself. I discovered she was a German national. A doctor by profession, she had been with the International Red Cross for five years. For the last two, she had been living in Gaza. She took care of almost everything: human resources, health, and medicine. She told me that lately there were not many volunteers who wanted to work in the Gaza Strip. The team assigned to the place consisted of three doctors, four nurses, two ambulance drivers, two volunteer medical students, and from then on, me. She looked at me and smiled. I smiled as well. We shook hands and she took me to have a look around the facilities.

The day-to-day tasks were difficult and tiring. Not a day passed without something happening, and in the places where ambulances from the few local hospitals that were already overwhelmed couldn't go, the Red Cross went, since according to the laws of Geneva, they were supposed to be respected and protected. Judy told me that in many cases, the members of her "group," as she named her team, had risked their lives, acting under fire and shrapnel; and many times they had been involved in violent protests. Recently, the Israeli army had been blaming the Red Cross for infiltrating riots and special army missions with terrorists. Every time a Red Cross ambulance left, a doctor, a nurse, and a volunteer went with it. They only had two ambulances. Besides medical staff, there were five volunteers who helped with food and other social problems amongst the population. They too looked overwhelmed in the face of the people's great need.

The initial days were expressly for recognition and adaptation. I helped with routine tasks such as cooking, cleaning rooms, and stocking medical supplies, as well as some basic care of people with minor injuries.

After a few days, Judy called me to her office.

"I like your project; we have never had an Israeli volunteer here, in such a dangerous place. I have heard of one in the Nablus Red Cross. We will treat you as best we can. I don't want to scare you, but the situation is not easy and sometimes our mission is extremely dangerous. You will have to make the decision whether to stay or not. I suggest you try it for a month at least, then you can think about it and decide. What you do here, will help you a lot in your career — if you can stand it, of course. Remember that we are here to save lives and provide services to a population in need."

I have to admit that things didn't look rosy, but I liked Judy's attitude and sincerity. Once in a while, when my head cleared, I played with the idea of calculating her age. Each time I considered her to be younger, and even though she wasn't, she always looked neat, well made-up, and relatively pretty.

At one point when we were both quiet — something that did not happen often — I asked about the incident on the first day we entered the Strip, when the ambulance in which we were traveling was intercepted and almost flipped over. We hadn't spoken about this incident since it occurred, and I wanted to hear her explanation.

"Today, Hamas owns Palestinian streets, and tries to show that on every possible occasion," she said. "They have contacts at the border crossing and they probably saw someone new — you — and wanted to know who you were. I explained to them that you were an Australian volunteer. They asked me for your papers, but I told them that the army had kept them and they will return them when you leave the city. They know me, they trust me, and ... they believed me."

Australian? Me? How did that happen? Judy's imagination had turned me into an inhabitant of the land of kangaroos — and actually, when I thought about it a little, I didn't mind the idea.

"Will you at least let me keep the same name?" I asked.

"Yes, Leonel."

I smiled.

"You know what? I think you've convinced me. I'll do my best to complete a month here, and then I'll decide. I'm here to help, so you can count on me."

14

LEONEL
Gaza Strip
October 1, 2011

The days that followed were a combination of tension, emotion, and courage. The same day that I arrived, the Israeli army closed the borders indefinitely; that same night, three mortars hit Israeli territory. One fell in Kibbutz Ein AShlosha; the other two in Sderot. Two civilians were wounded and a child was killed. This sparked a terrible retaliation and the bombing was incessant, day and night. The planes seemed to touch the roofs. I don't think I have ever felt so anxious. I don't know if it was fear or a reaction to seeing the impact of so much disaster up close. We all shared the same feelings, although the others seemed used to it.

One night, the city infrastructure collapsed because of too much artillery. All services were cut. The entire city was left without electricity, incommunicado, without phone or Internet, and even the water stopped flowing from the faucets. Our headquarters was one of the few places that had generators. We huddled in a room that was considered safe, although it didn't look any different from the others. That night I met all of the members of the Red Cross, one by one, and I learned, not only their names but also their lives, their expectations, and why they were there? The noise of the bombs raining down and all kinds of strange detonations carried on nonstop for three hours. After that, the explosions became more sporadic. A battery-powered lamp and some candles kept us visible to each other. Everyone was sitting with legs bent forward, and it was very difficult to change position because there was not enough space. I didn't count, but as we were in full attendance there, I can say we were 16 in all. I paid particular attention to Mariana — a young, somewhat short Danish girl with dark Blonde hair. She was not one of those beauties who attract attention, but every time she smiled, her face became a light to those around her — something that was desperately needed in a place like this. Mariana was a nurse. That day we exchanged glances, smiles and perspectives on the Israeli-Palestinian issue. Everyone was convinced that I was Australian, according to Judy's introduction, who had recommended that I should maintain this idea to avoid problems that might arise even with my workmates.

After four days of being locked up, and doing nothing more than sharing our food and returning to hide ourselves away in the safe room, I became astutely aware of the ability of human beings to adapt to just about anything. With very little light, almost no water and very scarce health resources, we survived and lived in a five-by-five room. On the second day, I went with the ambulance for the first time. With radios that didn't work, we had to rely on the emissaries of the Hamas group to relay information such as telling us that a vehicle had been bombed by an Israeli helicopter. In the vehicle had been six green guerrilla leaders. Regular ambulances couldn't be sent, because there were still troops and Jewish helicopters in the area. As I prepared myself to respond, Judy passed me a bulletproof vest, which had a huge red cross on the front. We were all kitted out. It took us five minutes to leave with all the equipment.

The rescue team consisted of a doctor, Mariana, a volunteer, and me. Ravi drove us with enviable skill and great speed. The rumors had spoken of four dead and two seriously injured, but they were just rumors. We traveled to the Rafiach refugee camp, one of the largest in Gaza. The roar of heavy artillery explosions was a constant barrage in our ears, and yet we couldn't accurately detect where the shots were coming from or who the perpetrators were. Something hit the back of the ambulance, making it impossible to tell whether it had been a stone or a shot. Ravi remained calm and steady at the wheel, picking up speed. Inside the vehicle we rolled around on top of one another. A wild crowd greeted us near the site of the attack, signaling how to reach the exact location. People shouted angrily and beat themselves on the chest and head with their hands, in a sort of strange frenzy.

Upon arrival, what I saw there was terrible. The car was completely destroyed, as if a heavy steamroller had passed over it. A crater more than a meter deep had formed in the ground. From my experience in the army, I knew that the area was not safe for anyone. If a remote-control bomb had exploded there, other detonations could still follow. However, there were men and women around the large pit, ignorant of the latent risk. I tried to calm myself down, but to no avail. We ran to help the wounded, and as we did, I wondered who could have come out of such an event alive. The images I would always remember were heart-breaking and horrific: four incomplete bodies had been tossed to the side of the ditch, totally burned. Three of them were missing their limbs. There was no way to do a simple examination or determine a reason for it. Those who had come out alive lay on the shoulder of the road, surrounded by a crowd of people shouting and gesticulating. We pushed our way through; the two presumed survivors showed very few signs of life, and the prognosis looked grim. One was missing a hand, and the other, a leg. They had burns to much of their bodies. The doctor rapidly set to work, and the first thing he did was administer large doses of morphine to cut the pain. Mariana checked the vital signs of the dying men. It was decided that neither could bear up to an ambulance ride and indeed, one died after just five minutes. The other, who was missing a leg, miraculously recovered his vital signs, and we moved him to Gaza Hospital.

Back at Red Cross headquarters, there was a deep silence between us. It had become a kind of ritual. We hadn't spoken much at all during the operation — and then, upon returning, we all felt as if we'd just witnessed a death-penalty execution, and were relieved that the whole thing was over now. I didn't understand it very well, but the fact was that the incident had left me completely devastated. Mariana took my hand when she noticed my face betray my inner struggle. Ravi was examining the ambulance, which had suffered a gunshot wound. I watched him carefully. His black eyes evidenced terrible sorrow. It was clear that even two years in the Red Cross hadn't hardened him or made him indifferent. The next day, we had a similar experience — this time due to a point-blank firefight in the middle of Gaza city, between infantry from the PLO and Hamas, who were struggling for power over the city.

After four days, the army removed the curfew and opened the Erez Crossing. As soon as they did, I took my first shower and used my last pair of clean underwear, thinking that I'd need to purchase others urgently. Right then, I also made the decision to stay the entire month.

Judy was very happy with my decision and set up a permanent place for me with two other volunteers in a room. I started thinking about Ahmed Asad and how to find him. The important thing was to put together a strategy that would allow me to use the little free time I had to continue my mission. I had no contacts there and I was afraid to leave and journey across the city. Mariana and I started a closer and intimate relationship, which escaped the attention of my two colleagues. I enjoyed spending time with her; Mariana was an interesting person, passionate about what she used to do. She had strong and well-defined principles. But more than anything else, she was extremely sweet. I had to improvise a lot — with her incessant curiosity regarding my life in Australia, and as I had no idea how to respond. She also told me that she wanted to visit my country sometime — something I also wanted to do...

15

AHMED
Gaza Strip
Late September, 2011

Rafaq had left me the legacy of a fighter — and more importantly, of friendship, company, and all that I had received from him despite having been so young. For me, it had been very tough to find a person like my cousin in our society. When he was killed, defending what was for him a legitimate cause, his blood became sacred to me. Rafaq had raised me there, in Jordan, even while the local people had treated us like Class B citizens and had given us only the most demeaning jobs. Aware of this, he always had a melancholic view of Jerusalem and its territories. When I used to mention the Omani mosque or other holy places in Jerusalem, his dark eyes would become moist. I fed myself on those tears and they filled me with courage; it was through those dampened eyes that I got to know my town — and I gave myself over to the vital struggle, neither knowing where it began nor how it would finish.

While we were moving Rafaq's lifeless body — naked albeit for the Hamas flag, which had been carefully placed to cover his form but expose his face — I was pushed away by the gathering crowd as they fought to touch him. Unfamiliar with the ritual, I wondered why there was so much fanaticism. It was then that I met Dabul, a tall, thin, young man who was grabbing one end of the flag and who made a small space for me in the crowd. From there, I managed to touch the legs of Rafaq in my desire to feel part of the sacred rite. That day, we burned flags of both Israel and the United States and I got a chance to participate, standing alongside Dabul, whose actions belied his experience.

My admission into Hamas' ranks was the effect of a logical and natural outbreak of emotion. From the beginning, I was recognized as Rafaq's cousin, and for that reason alone, I was already part of the organization. But to really be accepted, I had to submit myself to routine testing and "softening" tactics, a term they used to refer to the hurdles which a rookie had to undertake to join the organization.

The first time I went on a test mission as a member of Hamas, it was with Dabul himself. I didn't really understand what he had seen in me, but he trusted me and in the short time since we had met, I came to realise he was one of the boldest young men in a small group that operated mainly in Judea and Samaria.

A week before the day set for my initiation, we moved to a small village near Nablus. For the next few days, we prowled the location where we were going to operate and we memorized the routines; we observed the traffic in the area, and we climbed up and down mountains until we found the most appropriate point for the execution of our plan.

On the day of my initiation, we climbed a steep hill which brought us within sight of a sharp curve in the roadway where a car would need to slow way down. The sun was hidden behind the clouds, almost as dark as night. We camped out all day and later that evening, Dabul taught me how to handle a Molotov cocktail, a type of homemade bomb. Speed was fundamental to using this bomb, he had informed me, igniting and throwing it quickly, because if you didn't do thay hurrily you could be burnt to a cinder as the bottle could explode in your hand. My initial test was to throw one of those bombs into a car owned by a local settler, a Jew from the city of Ariel, who used to pass by every night around eight according to our information.

On this night, the car took longer than normal. The road linking Nablus with the Tapuach intersection was extremely undulating and alternated steep climbs with subsequent descents. The terrain really complicated our calculations and I was afraid that the operation would not turn out as planned. As I waited behind a bush at the top of the ridge, my stomach churned and my hands dripped from the tension, shaking; the bottle slipped a little in my palms. The fuse of cloth and alcohol was ready to go and I had the matches at hand. I was waiting for the signal from Dabul, who was stationed about five meters away, watching the road with binoculars.

My eyes were fixed on Dabul's hand, which was raised in the air above his head. On the drop of his fist, I would be transformed into a terrorist, and be instantly blacklisted by the Israeli army. I thought for a moment about innocents and about Rafaq.

Finally, we could hear the sound of an engine and with that, Dabul dropped his hand — the signal. But I still couldn't see the car, so I waited. Twenty seconds after the signal, I saw the car's outline in the night — it was coming around the corner without headlights. When it was within range, I lit the bomb and leaped up like a catapult, then jumped from behind the bush and threw it towards the car. As the bottle arced through the air, I was frozen in place, dazzled, unable to move, fixated on its trajectory. With a crash, the bottle fell upon the hood of the car, bounced once and exploded as it hit the ground in front, igniting a massive fire under the car. The driver and his companion launched themselves out of the still-moving vehicle.

"Get down on the ground!" shouted Dabul.

My mind rapidly processed the images — which, to my eyes, were a slow-moving film. As the fire reached the gas tank, it erupted into an enormous fireball, incinerating the entire vehicle. The driver and passenger, meanwhile, had taken off back in the direction from which they had come. One was unharmed, and the other seemed to be slightly wounded, as he was limping. Dabul grabbed me by the collar and we slipped down the mountain together, the range above the way to Nablus. Already, police sirens and the noises of the army could be heard in the distance. Dabul was happy with his new foot soldier, but at the same time, he realized that I wouldn't be all that useful on the battlefield. Although he didn't say it, his lack of confidence in my usefulness was embedded in his eyes, leaving me feeling very much like a lost pet that had ventured into an unfamiliar yard.

I was rewarded for my courageousness in the operation and made an authentic member of the Hamas group. A little later, on my birthday, Dabul himself gave me a computer, because he knew I was a fan of technology. The speed at which I gained familiarity with the computer and programming was viewed well by the Hamas leadership. I was widening a path to the world of computing: reading books, downloading programs, and practising whenever possible. I spent days and nights in front of my screen, while my groupmates were risking their lives at the barricades, throwing stones and participating in maneuvers. Years passed as I watched the conflict from afar — a distant fable that reached me only through computer monitors and communications systems. I had realized early on that my knowledge and new-found skills could be of great use to the cause.

At first, I had been asked to design a database consisting of the infrastructure and members of the group, a task which I completed in no time at all. The speed with which I had built the program surprised me and, of course, my handlers as well. They realized my potential and asked what it would take to computerize all of Hamas' systems, including personnel training. I was somewhat star struck when they proposed that I study at a university in London, as I knew upfront that this would be a great responsibility. After some consideration, I made the decision to make a counter offer. I wouldn't feel comfortable studying in Europe while my colleagues were risking their lives on the battlefield, and I was also convinced that I could achieve my goals on my own. I replied to the organization immediately, without thinking twice.

"What we need is money to create a platform and a secure private network," I informed them. It was the first thing that occurred to me. All ventures need funds.

Money was not the problem, and it came fast and on time. The complication was in finding the right people — those who were fluent in systems and wouldn't require too much further training. I then asked for time; it was really what I needed the most. Regularly immersed in the colossal world of zeroes and ones, I understood first hand that we needed to focus on the security of our information. Upon presenting that concern to Hamas' leaders, they accepted, and across the next three years, I did everything I could to mold myself into an expert in programming, systems security, cryptography, and open source systems. I chose 10 young people who started to work and study with me, and at only 26 years old, I was effectively their teacher.

I began working on understanding the systematization of secret codes, something which I considered essential for guerrilla operations, as most of the operations that Hamas planned would then need to be scrapped because of an information leak before the actions could get off the ground. I was completely convinced that we urgently needed a system to encrypt messages and transmit secret positional information.

When the situation with the Israelis was relatively calm, we decided to act. Together with my "group of 10," as they called us in Hamas, I locked us into one of Hamas' secret quarters to work, and in mid-August 2011, we finalized a detailed program which would encrypt and encode messages, essentially securing the communications systems between our forces.

The day I presented my work to the Hamas leadership, I was seated in a place of honor at a long, old, wooden table. The meeting was held in "the basement" as they called it, which was the secret meeting room where important decisions were made. Simple party members were denied access, as were guerrillas and suicide bombers. I was led to the place with a hood so I couldn't see and I remember going down about two flights of stairs. Dabul had explained the precautions they took to enter the basement and I understood them perfectly. A murmur was audible when I entered. Dabul walked me to my chair, and after I was seated, he unveiled my eyes, taking off the black hood; if I hadn't known any better, I would have guessed I was a prisoner facing the gallows.

As I was running the program simulation, projected on a mobile screen via my laptop, I sensed that many of those present were unaware of the basic functionality of a computer. From some of the looks on their faces, it wouldn't have surprised me to hear they had never had a mouse or a keyboard in their hands. I guess that's why I had almost no interruptions or questions during my presentation; instead, the astonishment in the room created a deafening silence that had me wondering whether any of them had ever even heard of a computer. Dabul said, almost whispering, that it was very uncommon for all of the leadership to gather together in one place; the organization was typically quite dispersed, and communication between the different sections of the group was done through human messengers who went from one place to another running errands.

As I was giving my presentation, another man was brought into the room in the same manner as I had been — hood and all. Once he was seated, and his face had been uncovered, he was introduced as "the cryptographer"; there was no mention of either a first or last name. He had come from Pakistan and I had no idea how he had entered the Strip, nor did I dare to ask. The cryptographer sat passively and made no interruptions throughout the hour-long presentation. Instead, with a piercing gaze, he watched me, all the while stroking his bushy, black beard. At times it felt as if he was a little distracted and not focused on what was being said. At the end of my presentation, everyone in the room applauded. They were highly satisfied with the program and the results of the task which had been entrusted to me. As the applause petered out, I began to pack up my equipment.

But then, a thin voice spoke up.

"How will you secure your programs and systems, apart from using the firewalls you named?"

The cryptographer hadn't moved from his place, and I immediately recognised his demonstrated knowledge of the subject.

"The idea is to create our own encryption algorithm, and avoid using products from the market. I want to create an adequate defense system."

"How much do you know about encryption? You know that we are not dealing with a simple database."

I should have been offended, but I wasn't. I took it as a challenge, because I saw that this man had been invited to the site for some reason hitherto unknown to me.

"I don't have a lot of experience, but I am able to learn quickly and do everything that is required to achieve the goal."

The cryptographer rose from his place and surprised me by addressing the congregation: "I am leaving tomorrow for Pakistan. Prepare him to come with me."

An old man who was sitting at the other end of the table stood up and said, "Wait!"

He was one of the ones who I don't think understood much of the presentation, yet his words belied his obvious leadership status among the group.

"It may be that this system is not entirely complete," he said, "but what you have done seems impressive; to me, it is a huge advance that's going to bolster our communications and improve the capacity of our operations. However, I also want a program that can invade, disconnect, and destroy Israeli systems. We have to attack on all fronts. So far we haven't managed to assume computing superiority over the Zionists, but the time has come. I want a detailed project, an explanation of what the options are for doing it, the costs and other details. Money won't be a problem — we will provide whatever is necessary. I want us to be aggressive. By improving our position in this way, we will succeed; we have to use technology as much as our enemy uses it. The young man will go with you, he his precious to us. Take care of him and come back with results!"

I didn't know the old man's name, but he had spoken clearly and decisively. With his huge black robe, he appeared to be a religious or spiritual leader. It seemed to me that he had had an impact on everyone, so I figured he must have been one of the highest ranking in the organization. No one objected to or made any remark on what was said; not a murmur was heard. After he had spoken, the meeting was closed and everyone began to leave. The cryptographer rose, looked the old man in the eye, and said, "In a few days, I'll send you a list of our needs."

That experience and what would happen next were almost overwhelming. The meeting and the people ... it was all so special and so rare. I felt privileged! The next day, I was ready along with the cryptographer at the Rafah border crossing, the exit from Israel-Egypt. I had in hand a passport Dabul had given me that morning. He had coached me on my new identity as Ahmed El Asin, a Kuwaiti businessman. I didn't dislike it either; I had pictured businessmen in Kuwait, known for being millionaires and driving the best cars in the world, and I imagined that maybe this new identity would be my lucky break in winning the heart of a woman. But I caught myself quickly, because my head wasn't really in that space right now. Dabul had fitted me with an expensive black suit, patent leather shoes in the same color, a white shirt, and a red tie. When my reflection looked back at me in the mirror, it had taken on the image of what I thought, a French film actor might look like. The image reminded me of those

Egyptian films we used to watch on Friday afternoons at my house. The cryptographer didn't talk much. He wasn't dressed as a business-man and his passport recorded his true identity.

In Cairo, we boarded an Air Egypt flight to Pakistan. It was the first time I had flown, and everything was happening so fast that it seemed disconnected from real life. On the plane, the cryptographer broke his silence and introduced himself for the first time with his real name, Reza El Harish. Laconic and expressionless, he recounted some episo-des of his life. A designer and systems engineer, he had a doctorate in security systems from the University of Oxford in the UK, specializing in cryptography. His parents were born in Jericho, but he had been raised in Nablus with his brother, who had died in a protest at just 15, after being hit in the chest by a rubber bullet. At the time, Reza was only eight and he had been at his brother's side in that tragic moment. For two years, he was treated by psychiatrists and medicated as a result of the trauma. His parents had decided to leave the territories, and settled with relatives in Islamabad. He had the fortunate opportunity to work in the best British and German computing companies, and he was also employed for a time by the Pakistani Government. One year earlier, he had decided to dedicate himself to the Palestinian cause. It was his way of somehow avenging the death of his brother, whom he had never forgotten. His work with Hamas included the construction of a com-puter development lab in Peshawar, a Pakistani city on the border with Afghanistan.

To my surprise, he told me that he knew me already and that the database that he had tested was the exact database I had programmed. He said that Hamas had already begun to think about a computer project and that, for some time, the organization had been looking for someone like me to develop their projects. He said he wasn't surprised by what had been said in the meeting. He knew that sooner or later Hamas wanted to attack in different ways, and even he himself had proposed this for some time. Undoubtedly, in these times, given that a computer virus travels faster than a missile, the activity had to be included. Now, there was a real possibility of making their ideas concrete. The time had come to make the proposal, a reality; to program and develop an infras-tructure for carrying everything forward.

In Islamabad, we connected with a local flight to Peshawar. I asked why this city had been chosen to establish the Hamas IT base, and Reza told me that Peshawar was special. It was a city without order where no-one respected the laws; a no-man's land. It seemed as if the Pakistani government had forgotten this city. Most of the population was made up of Afghans who generally lived in refugee camps and were constantly trying to cross the border to escape the cruel Taliban regime. The Taliban themselves were also busy settling into the city so, taking advantage of such instability, they had guessed that no one would pay attention to a computer lab or question its legality. Luckily, they had found a very safe and suitable location.

Peshawar reminded me of Gaza, with its dirt streets, the refugee camp, the shuk[18], and a lot of mud houses with tin roofs and rickety structures. A cloud of hot sand, always present, welcomed us. A helpless police officer, in a narrow street, surrounded by dense and dangerous traffic was the only sign of security I could spot, amid a scrum of vehicles of all kinds.

I had read about the atrocities that the Taliban had inflicted on the Afghan population. Now I realised what was meant when people mentioned the denial of everything feminine. In these lands, women were excluded from everything, and were nothing more than mere objects; treated as worthless beings by the entire male population. Afghan female refugees in Peshawar moved like wraiths, passing through the streets in their black burkas[19] that covered them from head to toe, a custom very rarely seen even in the Gaza Strip itself. It is true that I was not expecting Paris, but neither had I expected this silent and heavy atmosphere that made me think I was trapped in a ghost town.

A taxi took us to a narrow street near the city center, which ran parallel to the central market and was really just a dead-end street with restaurants. We arrived at a wooden house that seemed no different than the rest. At the entrance was a tall man, much like a Lone Ranger from the seventies, carrying a bayonet in his belt. I smiled faintly at the sight of him. He had a black, cat-like mustache and so when he blocked the entrance with his body, a sneaky smile escaped my mouth. The

18 Shuk: market.
19 Burka: traditional clothing worn by women of Islamic religion, which almost completely covers the face and body.

cryptographer nodded his head and the man stepped aside reluctantly. We walked down a long corridor, which eventually ended in a steel door guarded by an excessively armed guard, who was watching from a glass booth. Reza punched a code into a control panel and the door opened; inside we could see steep stairs leading down to underground floors. We went down three flights before we came across a platform with white walls, giving the impression that we were not far from a hospital. At the end appeared a mysterious sliding door made of transparent glass. Reza ran his hand over a biometric detector and the door opened abruptly. I could not believe what my eyes were seeing: a huge laboratory with the most modern technological equipment I had ever seen. Some operators were going from one place to another. There weren't many — I managed to count just 12 in that area. I was ecstatic before that swirl of servers, routers, and optical cables, all neatly assembled in racks. I could be sure that the best hardware in the world was mounted there. As Reza showed me around the place, he told me, "You will work here from now on."

I was stunned. I seemed to be living a dream; a fantasy for a kid from the streets of Bethlehem. I felt like the luckiest person on Earth. It was a special moment and many images passed through my mind: my mother, my sisters... but especially Rafaq on his makeshift bier and the angry and bloodthirsty crowd, calling for death to Israel. Then I recovered and I understood what I was doing in this place: Allah had put me there with a mission, and I would answer it.

16

AHMED
Peshawar - Pakistan
Early October, 2011

From that moment on, I became fanatical about learning everything as quickly as possible; everything I read, saw, and touched was recorded in my mind like invaluable treasure. I demanded maximum effort from myself, working up to 18 hours a day in order to learn the systems thoroughly and specialize in cryptography. Reza, the cryptographer, imparted his wisdom to me, but the most important things I learned from him were his ideas, his way of thinking and analyzing problems, and how he unraveled different challenges. From the other technicians and engineers, I learned a lot about security and programming in languages that I had never heard of. The proposal was innovative, and creating a complex and indecipherable code seemed achievable for us. I had already designed and presented the mother algorithm, so we had a basis on which to work. The cryptographer improved it in a week and, as if by magic, everything began to take shape; after only a few days, we had an initial system up and running. Together we compiled a set of encrypted archives with the private key file attached to the program.

I was congratulated by the cryptographer for my efforts, and it was announced that the program was ready for testing. Afterwards, he mentioned that he had been surprised as well by the last request of the old man in the basement in Gaza. He was talking about the other project I would work on, which aimed to disrupt Israeli security systems. I still hadn't given it much thought, but I was aware that nobody in the lab knew anything about it; indeed, at least to begin with, only three people would know about this secret mission: the cryptographer, Samir, a talented Egyptian engineer, and me.

Samir was a brilliant person. He didn't seem Egyptian or Arab, let alone Palestinian. His skin was a very light pastel, to match his bald scalp; and he was rather short in stature. Samir had a resume as comprehensive as Reza himself. He had completed his computer studies at Yale University in the United States, where he also completed his PhD in cryptography and security systems. He used to follow orders well, not speak much, and he didn't mind sharing his wisdom. Everyone called him "the genius" and it didn't take me long to understand why.

There were 10 of us working in the laboratory and we took extreme security precautions. We always had two or three guards with us, and generally traveled in an escorted car. We lived in an ordinary house, similar to many others found in Peshawar; the only difference was that this one had a double-layered steel door. which added another level of safety. Several times I thought the door was holding up the entire building, which was quite precarious. The entrance led to a large courtyard, which in turn led to the kitchen via a long corridor. A huge patio was located in the center of the space. In the back was the room where we spent most of the day. That was where the television, which could just barely picked up the Pakistani national channel, was located. Two medium-sized bedrooms housed five people each, sleeping on mats. We ate in the living room, on the floor on a Persian-style carpet. Everyone spent their free time in their own world. I took advantage of the free time to read. We weren't allowed out without notice, because each of us posed a threat to the security of the organization. We had detailed instructions on what to say if we were arrested by the national police force or the Taliban. All of us had a speech memorized. Hamas had become stronger in Pakistan and even spoke about training camps that the organization had in the south of the country.

While Reza and Samir were designing a program to intercept Israeli infrastructure systems, I participated in discussions and contributed ideas, all behind closed doors. At the same time, Reza entrusted me with the task of creating an official Hamas website. I got to work on designs, features, and content that would appear on the site, as well as other specifications, all programmed by Reza. The new site would be a mix between the website that I had initially created and the current proposed design. Reza provided me with help in the form of Radek, a Jordanian–Palestinian who was good at everything to do with graphic design. I would be responsible for putting together the whole site, its content and security. Reza supervised me closely and approved both encryption and security, after he executed a very sophisticated attack against the website.

One day, as I was leaving the lab, I ran into the Cossack with the bayonet, who was always guarding the door. As I was the last to leave, he asked me if I wanted to go with him. It was the first time in more than a month I had seen him smile a little. I didn't even know his name.

"Where are we going?" I asked.

"Come on, let's go get something to eat. I'll take you to a good place."

"What's your name?"

"Asher," he replied.

We climbed into the rickshaw — a kind of scooter with three wheels, which was parked against the gate to the house. It wasn't the first time I had ridden in it, as it served as our daily transportation from the lab to the house.

Despite the instability of the vehicle, Asher drove it skillfully around sharp curves, narrow streets, and deep potholes. We stopped at a street near the market, where the tumult of people was overwhelming. On the way to the shuk, Asher called the house to let them know of our whereabouts. Then he started chatting. As we walked, he talked about a place that made delicious roast meats, with rice a la afganistana, in the heart of the market. I decided to ask him why he wore a bayonet like a separatist from the last century when we lived in an era of firearms. I was scared that he wouldn't like my question, but at the same time I felt like I was talking to a reliable person, he was just a little different. He gave a loud guffaw in response to my observations.

Asher, who was one of many Afghan refugees in Pakistan, told me that the bayonet had belonged to his grandfather, who used it to defend his family from a massacre by the Yahidim, a dominant ethnic group in Afghanistan representing more than 40 percent of the population. They were known for their violence and savagery against other races and groups. About 30 years ago, with that very bayonet, his grandfather had butchered four Yahidim robbers who wanted to burn down his house and take their women. Before he died, Asher promised his grandfather that he would always carry the bayonet, and he had done so until that very day not only for protection, but also because it gave him courage. To him, it was like a talisman that frightened away ghosts. He showed enormous pride as he recounted his story. He had been instructed not to ask about or try to find anything out about our work or private lives, and like any good security guard he was obedient, spoke little, and carried out his duties according to the orders he had received. It was clear that this connection of ours had a positive impact on him.

Aromas that were hard to identify drifted through the market. You could find everything there, from cheap electronics to goats and lambs for slaughter, to Western clothing and tailors who could turn out a bespoke suit on the same day. And, of course, take-away food was an elaborate affair, enveloped in all kinds of flavors and smells. There was some resemblance to the Gaza market, but this one was far more comprehensive. That day it was packed with passers-by who made navigating the narrow streets difficult.

At one point I was distracted and, after stopping to admire a business computer shop, I bumped into a woman of medium height. As I stumbled into her, her chador slipped from her head. We locked eyes, and I was astounded by the beauty that stood before me. She had big, brown eyes; her skin was white as milk; and her smile had the power to steal my thoughts for just a few seconds. We stood staring for a while — I couldn't tell how long; then she covered her head with her chador again and left. I stared after her, following her with my eyes. After about 100 meters, she stopped and turned to look at me, then continued on her way. Asher, who had noticed the situation, hurried me along. I was completely stunned — not only because of her beauty, but also because of her attitude: the way she had smiled back at me and paused in place for a few moments. It made me think that a typical Muslim would never have let this happen; even before the fabric fell, a Muslim woman would have covered her face. I was also surprised at the manner in which she had stared back as she was walking away. I had no idea exactly how I would do it, but I promised myself I would see that woman again. I saw sparks!

We sat at a small eatery that was inside a very old shopping gallery. A little crowded for my liking, it was a little intimidating to sit and eat there. Still, the place was packed and the food smelled great. Asher evidenced that he had noticed my reaction to the woman, because he asked me, "You want to meet her?"

"Who?" I asked, playing dumb.

"What do you mean who?" Asher replied. "The girl you ran into."

"Do you know her?" I asked. I wanted to know, but I was trying to hide my curiosity at the same time.

"No, but I know many people in this city and I have ways of putting you in touch with her."

I said yes without hesitating. I felt very comfortable with Asher, a feeling confirmed by the pleasantness of our dinner conversation. His confession that he had never really spoken to anyone else in the group struck a cord with me; out of anyone he could have chosen as a friend, he chose me — and that was all the persuasion I needed.

That night I swapped my dreams about HTML, C++, VBScript programs and cryptography, for that nameless girl with brown eyes and transparent skin, and I hoped desperately that Asher could get me her information.

Work was both hectic and trancelike at the same time. Two other programmers joined us. The website was almost finished and there were only a few details that needed to be added before it could go live on the Internet. When that happened, the old version would be withdrawn. All of the information we needed to enter into the database came from Gaza; papers with incoherent, sometimes meaningless data. We converted this mess of information into computerized text, files, and databases. We had designed a very meticulous encryption system for information and for the entire database site, which, when combined with the special program developed to isolate the site in a security bubble, was a powerful union.

The new Hamas site was well protected by a firewall system we had developed ourselves. We were missing only one crucial detail: the final approval of Reza, who was still busy with the main project. One week passed, during which I thought about postponing the site, but then I received an email encrypted with a basic code. It was one of the tests that Reza always subjected us to. I printed it and began to decipher it, made easier with pen in hand. The cipher text was:

Zooqnudc, dwbdkkdms vnqj, Qdyz

I started thinking what Reza would have used to encrypt this message. More than once, I had used different strategies and characters to encode communication within the group. It was not ASCII and bore no resemblance to any encryption language with a passkey. What confused me were the uppercase letters Z and Q. After carefully observing the text for five minutes, I realised that each letter had been replaced by the one that came before it, making the Z to be A, and the P —O. That was all it took to decrypt the message. I never would have thought that Reza would choose a code that had been at the very emergence of cryptography.

When decrypted, the message said:

"Approved, excellent work; Reza."

I raised my head and looked over at Reza's desk, one row ahead of me. He smiled. I replied with a wink. I was cheerful and happy; there was no better feeling than being appreciated for a job well done.

I hadn't been able to see Asher much over those last few days, because I had been too busy. Finally, one day as I was heading out, he tucked a folded piece of paper into my pocket and said, "This is what I promised, remember?"

Of course I remembered, but I didn't want to put any pressure on him, particularly because it was a favor.

"Yes, I remember. You don't know how much I appreciate this."

"You're welcome. A promise is a promise; my word is a word. If you need more information, you know where to find me."

We shook hands for the first time, and his firm grip acted as a sign that something good was developing between us. It was not friendship yet, but I felt trust between us, a very important bond. In the Muslim society in which we lived, it was not easy to find someone who could be trusted with a secret, or who could guard your privacy.

I unfolded the slip of paper. On it was written:

Name: Mariana Asirán
Nationality: Denmark
Profession: Nurse (voluntary)
Workplace: Red Cross Headquarters in Peshawar – Peshawar
the Harir 32
Length of stay in Pakistan: 6 months
Arrived only two days ago

Everything was so well detailed that it made me think that Asher was more than just a security guard with a bayonet. At the same time, though, I didn't want to ask too many questions, since he had delivered what I wanted. Suddenly, many things became clear: not a Muslim herself, she only kept up the practices of women in this country to respect Islam and remain inconspicuous. On second thought, maybe she had converted to Islam by conviction. Her last name sounded Arabic. All of this was a puzzle that I liked, and I struggled to hold back my intrigue.

The next day, I asked Asher if he could take me to the address indicated on the piece of paper, since I did not know the city well. This gesture was enough to consolidate our budding relationship. Asher was more than happy to be my "buddy"; he seemed to like the idea. I asked him to keep this secret. Asher's hand went to his heart and he bowed his head, a gesture far more than could have ever been expressed in words. And so I had secured the full commitment of the "Cossack" – both to my cause and to our friendship.

17

LEONEL
The Gaza Strip
October 6-7, 2011

The following days were spent drawing strategies in the air, and thinking about how to find Ahmed, although my head was out of focus; and the reason was Mariana. I had fallen for the sweet Danish girl in just a matter of weeks; our constant conversation had turned to gestures, which evolved from a glance to a kiss when people weren't looking. It didn't take me long to realize that this was an entirely new feeling to me. After a while, Mariana understood I wasn't a regular volunteer. Although we were trying to keep our relationship a secret, the rumor spread like wildfire throughout the hallways of the Red Cross.

One day, after dinner, we were alone in the kitchen doing the dishes.

"What are you looking for here?"

The question rung in my ears as its echo emerged from the surrounding pots.

"What do you mean?" I asked, a somewhat flimsy attempt to buy some time.

"Maybe it is good for your project, but ... why Gaza? Why does an Australian prefer Gaza to any other place?"

"Why are you here?" I asked her. Perhaps the answer to this question would offer me a way out of the awkwardness.

"I think I've already told you this. My father was Palestine and my mother Danish. He always dreamed of seeing his country free and I inherited that invisible legacy – the desire to do something he had always wanted to do: help his people, and, in general, Muslims in need."

"And that is it?"

"Yes. There are people who are born, grow, and live in a place where they just can't find any meaning in life; people who don't make a connection with anybody and need something to actually help them define themselves as living beings, to make them feel satisfied with their everyday life. Some people take a backpack and travel, looking to make it around the world. Others give up and follow the steps dictated by their parents: school, university, a good job, and marriage. But there also are people like me, who find meaning in life fighting for a cause, helping others. Maybe people like me are not that many, but you can still find some of us out there."

"I'm one of those, too."

She mumbled something, like 'blah, blah, blah' and left, laughing.

I felt as if I had tried to take a penalty shot without getting anywhere near the goal. It was obvious that Mariana could see straight through my lie, but had no idea about the truth. I knew I would lose her; the lack of honesty would deteriorate our relationship. I thought about my plans. Was a relationship between two people worth more than a million shekels? I don't consider myself too greedy; money isn't the only thing that pushes me forward. I remembered how difficult this decision had been, and so I decided to stick to my original plan for the following days.

One afternoon, I went out for a walk. I knew it was dangerous, but I needed to see if anything or anyone could lead me to Ahmed. I saw a huge crowd of people walking towards me from the south end of the city, and I grabbed onto my Red Cross identification badge just in case someone became interested in learning who I was. It was known that Hamas thoroughly looked for Israelis who had infiltrated into the territories, and when caught, they faced only one of two paths: being beaten and stoned to death by the crowd, or being taken hostage and used as an exchange for thousands of Palestinian people being held in Israeli prisons. Infiltrated civilians almost always faced the same fate, unlike soldiers who were generally taken as war trophies and were used as weapons of negotiation.

The crowd swarmed around me, making it easy to become lost. You could see green flags from Hamas, but also emblems from the PLO; it didn't seem like an organized demonstration, but the reaction to some special event. I stayed by the side of the road and followed the mass. Boys with Hamas badges were giving out pamphlets. I took one, and immediately read that they were announcing Hamas' new website, something that had already been announced in Israel about a month ago — the same website I had visited and analyzed with my friend Daniel. When I had first seen the Arabic script, I had no idea what it was. Arabic was a complex language, especially in its spelling. I had to study it for two years in high school and for six intensive months while I was in the military in Unit 8200.

Given it had been more than four years since I had had any exposure to Arabic, it was difficult to understand some of the words, but I was able to make out that they were talking about the new 'green' computing force (that's what the members of the organization were called); it was a new version, according to the release. Of course, there was propaganda against the Zionist enemy, which was something relatively normal during any pamphlet distribution from the organization.

After swarming along five or six desolated streets, the crowd of people finally arrived at its destination. Improvised perimeter fencing surrounded an area in which bulldozers had already destroyed two houses allegedly owned by terrorists. This was what had drawn everyone to march here. It really brought the crowd together. It didn't take long before it all turned into a battlefield, though. There were lots of stones, rubber bullets, some bottles/Molotov cocktails and plenty of gas. Ambulances were trying to make their way in to get to the place. I ended up with some boys, and together we climbed up to the roof of a house, from where I could see everything. One of the boys, pamphlet in his hand, asked me who I was and where I was from.

"I work at the Red Cross as a volunteer," I told him, showing him my badge.

"And what are you doing here? It's dangerous ..."

"Yes, it's dangerous for me, but also for you."

"I'm already used to it; it's part of our daily entertainment, but you..."

"I think I was curious; I saw people gathered and I followed them."

"What country do you come from? What's your name?"

"My name is Leonel and I am Australian."

"Australia … oh … is it true that kangaroos walk around the streets there?" he asked, naïvely.

The truth is that I wasn't sure, since I had never been to Oceania, but I replied anyhow, "No, that's not true."

"Have you heard about the new computer force?" a little boy asked.

"No, what is it about?"

"They're offering computers and free Internet to all the members. They also provide free courses, and the most important part is that a major computing attack is being prepared against Israel."

The boy was gullible and spoke more than he needed to — something I could use to my advantage. I figured he had to be nine or 10 years old; his eyes seemed to stand out from his face. He was wearing a green shirt and had a flag from Hamas on his shoulders. I found it rather cruel for him to be exposed to so much danger at such a young age. Based on what I knew about it, I imagined this kid could be of use, mainly as part of the anti-Israeli propaganda, since in demonstrations like these, there was always some kid who ended up injured or dead, and so the journalists would surround the place like crows to record the shocking scene and put it on the cover of their newspapers.

The boy finished his speech, waved, and took off with his friends, flying towards the demonstration, waving his flag all over the place. I thought about their computing force; it must have been related to my target, Ahmed Asad, since he had designed their website. Could he be in Gaza, or was he in another country? It was obvious that programming and development of any infrastructure inside the occupied territories was more than risky, given that they would always be within reach of the army, although they wouldn't be any safer outside Israel either — not with the Mossad lurking. It was also undeniable that the Hamas group wanted to let the Israelis know about their computing projects; if not, they wouldn't have distributed those pamphlets. I needed time to think. I had to analyze the pamphlet, go online, and do some research. Between the continuous hustle at the Red Cross, the wasted days under curfew and also Mariana, I just couldn't find the time to focus. I was going to have to ask for a few days off in order to go back to Tel Aviv, to continue searching and hopefully come up with some more ideas. Here in the Gaza Strip, it was too difficult to do so. I thought about following the computing lead. I also needed to talk to Mariana; I didn't want to leave things like the way they were. Telling her I wasn't an actual volunteer didn't seem like a good option, though, since it would hurt my search and my relationship with her — if there still was one.

I found myself unable to contact Judy to let her know about my plans, and the Red Cross had become chaos. After the demonstration finished, we took in more than 10 injured Palestinians. Some had inhaled riot gas, while others had been injured by rubber bullets. Since the hospitals were full, the ambulances were bringing them to us. Aside from the 10 patients, we also had all of their relatives to deal with, which caused a lot of noise, making our work even more difficult.

That very same night, for the first time, we set up an operation table. Mariana and I were in charge of sterilizing the room however we could. A 20-year-old man had been hit by a rubber bullet and was bleeding profusely from his stomach. The doctors said that if they didn't operate immediately, he would die in about half an hour. However, we lacked some basic equipment; we had neither the machine for doing a blood transfusion, nor the blood to be transfused. Judy called the local hospital and asked for O type blood and a mobile transfusion unit. Despite having doubts that help would arrive in time, we nevertheless continued sterilizing for lack of something better to do for this young man. While we worked, two doctors put pressure on the wound with their hands and, after 35 minutes, just as the man started to lose consciousness, an ambulance came with everything Judy had asked for, allowing for surgery to commence right away. I had already been in some surgeries, but never under these conditions. Despite the circumstance, the doctors' skill was notable and the whole procedure lasted around three hours. The only complication arose when they had to lift the liver up — a very risky procedure, especially under precarious conditions — but they were successful and the wounded man was transferred to the hospital in a critical but stable condition, far better than he had been just three hours before.

After the rush, we were all extremely exhausted. Cleaning the room to remove the blood and sterilizing it again took us nearly another three hours. By the time we finished, Mariana and I lay on the floor, completely beat. It was 3:30 a.m, and the doctors had left. There was no one else in the room. Suddenly, I felt her hand on my shoulder; and she said:

"It hurts me that you can't tell me the truth. I think ... I love you."

"Mariana ... I ... you're right, I haven't told the truth, but I need some time. I too have special feelings for you, and I want this relationship to work." After a few minutes of silence, I added, "I'm going to ask Judy for a few days off and I'm going to visit some people I know in Israel."

"I know you'll be back and I'll wait for you, but it's important to me that you come back with the truth."

And she gave herself to me without saying another word. A fragile bird, she rested her head on my chest and we hugged each other tight. I allowed my fingers to stroke her hair and face, indulging in passionate kisses as I became familiar with her paper-like, indelible lips. That night, for the first time, we locked the door and gave in to our carnal urges until exhaustion took over. Far in the distance, I could already hear the emissaries of dawn singing in the new day.

18

Tel Aviv - France - Pakistan
October 14-17, 2011

After having been locked up in Gaza for two weeks, the freedom — and the air — in Tel Aviv were the best things that could have ever happened to me. Suddenly, I remembered Jony, my cat, and congratulated myself for having taken him to my parents the day before I left. When I thought of them, I imagined they'd be worried. Nevertheless, I decided to have a day for myself without my parents or Jony; without anybody. It wasn't difficult to get Judy's permission, since she understood the emotional impact of what had happened on those days.

She asked if I'd be back, and I immediately said yes. The weird thing was that she had made no attempt to find out my motives, and when I told her I needed some peace and quiet, she nodded along as if she understood my request perfectly.

On the way into my apartment, I noticed the lock had been tampered with. It looked as if it had been hammered or whacked with plyers. The enormous anti-theft cylinder the owner had installed appeared to have worked though, and had withstood any attempt there had been to break in. But ... who could possibly have tried to break in? As I entered, a claustrophobic smell surrounded me, and I felt as if I had been locked in a dirty bathroom. I took a quick look around, noting that everything appeared to be as I had left it. Very soon, it occurred to me that the smell wasn't normal; indeed, it seemed toxic. As I had that realization, I started to feel as though I was suffocating. I opened the window and went for the door, but before I could get outside, a cramp wrung at my stomach, and I suddenly threw up. My mind was in overdrive, scrambling to process what was happening. I started shaking uncontrollably and lost my balance, falling to the floor. I had just managed to push open the door, when the world before my eyes cascaded into darkness.

As I regained consciousness, I was blinded by a ray of light. The place seemed familiar, but I was confused and my head was killing me. I heard my name twice. I closed my eyes and tried to open them again. Now I recognized the place with certainty — it was Ichilov Hospital in Tel Aviv. The nurse was also familiar — Martha, an Argentinian-Israeli; we had worked some shifts together not that long ago.

"What happened to me?"

"You inhaled a toxic substance. Do you remember anything? How do you feel?"

"My head's about to explode," I told her. "What did you do to me?"

"We performed a gastric lavage and we sucked the fumes from your lungs."

She checked my blood pressure and my pulse, changed my IV, and gave me two pills. One was Paracetamol[20] and the other I didn't know. I was groggy for a while, but after 20 minutes, as the pain diminished, I began to remember the scene at my house: the tampered door and the strange smell. I was baffled — who wanted to kill me and why? I was really scared, and sure these weren't normal people. Unmistakably, my search for Ahmed had something to do with what had happened to me. After all, I had never had any enemies — that I knew of, anyways.

After a while, I fell asleep. I awoke with a start, to the sensation of someone squeezing my hand. When I looked up, I saw that old Cohen was by my side, with a scowl and three huge wrinkles on his forehead that looked like snakes, all signs of his concern; even his typical smirk was gone.

"How are you doing?"

"Me? Great! I came to spend a weekend at the hospital." I replied with sarcasm.

"Listen to me," he instructed. His voice sounded as if he was about to give a speech. "The police are guarding the place, and I'm almost certain they're going to have many questions for you."

---

20 Paracetamol: Acetaminophen.

"Well, that's good! Maybe they can find whoever wanted to kill me!"

"Leonel, it's not that simple. You can't say anything about the story you're working on, because you'd be putting Rachel in danger and it'd all become public. That's highly dangerous considering that at the moment, Ahmed Asad is one of the Mossad's most wanted people."

"Really? Why? Is what he did that bad? Who did he kill?"

"No, he hasn't killed anyone, but he represents a victory in what they call the 'digital war.' "

"The digital war?" I was really surprised.

"Yes. Look, I can't give you many details; it's all highly confidential, almost a secret, but Hamas is announcing a project called 'the informatics bomb' with which they threaten to destroy Israeli infrastructure and IT systems."

This all sounded familiar, and then I remembered the pamphlet I'd picked up on the streets of Gaza and the kid I'd spoken to on the roof.

"Who tried to kill me?" I asked.

"I have no idea, but I've come up with a plan to cover for you and free you from the police. Their questioning and procedures are the last thing you need right now."

"How?" I asked. It all seemed like a story from some science-fiction book.

"Like I said, I have a plan. When they start asking you questions, you'll have to say you remember having left the gas on in the kitchen, that you had fumigated the place days before, and that you went in anyhow because of the gas issue, but since you didn't have the key when you got there, you had to break in. Then, the fumigation chemicals and the gas affected you immediately. Add that you remember having puked, and that's it."

"That's your plan? Seriously? You have nothing else?" Now, it did seem to me like everything was getting out of hand. How would the police believe something like this, such a crazy story?

"Don't worry, the police just want to close cases. They'll ask you a bunch of questions, get your statement, cross the t's and dot the i's. They'll drop it all in a file and before you know it, case closed."

"What if it gets complicated?"

"Look, I know the police like the back of my hand. I was there 30 years, remember?"

"And how did you get in here? You're saying the police is surrounding the place and that I'm under surveillance..."

"I said I was a relative of yours – and here, I am."

Moshe Cohen was sure of his plan. He knew the police and maybe he had already pulled some strings before he arrived. I was confused and dazed, but I was certain that I didn't want to be interrogated, and I certainly didn't want to be in the newspapers. I still wasn't sure whether I wanted to continue covering up my story about the search for Ahmed Asad, but in that moment, the other reasons were more powerful. I thanked Moshe, and he left satisfied. Before he closed the door, he turned around and said, "Take care. Call me when the time is right."

"Ok. Oh!" I said, "thanks for Camel's contact."

"You're welcome — but Camel no longer exists." And with that, he rushed out the door.

Camel no longer exists? Someone, apparently, had killed him — maybe the same people who wanted to get rid of me. I remembered the bald man dressed in black at the store in Jaffa when I took the money. Maybe he was involved; this was not what I needed ...

I asked the nurse when they would release me and she said that if I continued like this, probably tomorrow. She informed me that whenever I felt well enough, a detective from the police was waiting to talk to me. I told her I wasn't up for it yet.

"Alright, I'll tell them it won't be today. But you should know that they plan to come here and talk to you as soon as possible — and they usually get away with it."

I nodded, thanked her, and closed my eyes, drifting into an uneasy sleep. When I woke up, I could sense someone standing over me, even before I opened my eyes. It was one of the policemen. Without even asking, he had made himself comfortable in my room. He was a tall man, around 70 years of age with white hair. He introduced himself as "Yosi, first brigade officer with the Felonies section of the Tel Aviv police department," and didn't mention his last name.

"How do you feel?" he asked nicely.

"I'm afraid of getting better ..."

"Can you tell what you remember?"

By the look in his eyes, I understood that I was dealing with a very experienced person. Even so, I didn't have any options, so I ended up repeating Moshe's story — the fumigation, the gas, and the forced door — a sequence of inventions difficult to believe.

"You forced the door like that? How, if you don't mind my asking?" he queried suspiciously, while standing and heading towards the window. Instinctively, he looked at his cigarette package that was sticking out from his pocket, but quickly remembered he was at a hospital.

I was aware that my story hardly seemed plausible, and now I would have to improvise an answer.

"I found a piece of metal on the street and used it to break in."

"We didn't find any metal in the place. Are you sure, what you're saying?"

His gestures and face expressions made it blatantly clear he hadn't believed a word I had said. I tried to remain calm and stick to my story.

"Yes, I'm sure; at least that is what I remember."

"Do you have problems ... any enemies, perhaps? Did you acquire a loan recently?"

"No, I'm simply a student who works in security to make a living."

"Well, it's late." He had already lost his patience and besides, it was 10 p.m., and no visits were allowed after that time. "If you remember anything aside from a gas leak and the fumigation thing, call me on this number."

He tossed his card on the nightstand and left the room furiously, without even saying goodbye. I had, for sure, insulted his intelligence with my story, and I understood his reaction completely. Mr. Cohen's story was completely unrealistic.

The next day, I was already on my way home. I had contacted Daniel and asked him to ventilate my place, and if necessary, call a company to eliminate the poisonous gas. I told him the same story of the fumigation and the gas, but I knew that the story would soon get me in trouble. At noon, the time they usually release patients, he picked me up from the hospital in his father's car.

Daniel's dad was a big deal in neurosurgery — not only at the Ichilov hospital, but across the country — a fact that at times made Daniel feel uncomfortable. Old David Samuel would have loved for his son to have followed in his footsteps in medicine. He didn't appear to have any idea about his son's potential with numbers and computing. Since we were still students, most of us had no money to buy a car, and since old Samuel no longer drove, he had become well aware that his car had become ours to use at our disposal.

When we got to my place, it was as if nothing had happened. Daniel had hired some people to clean up the air, and they left no trace whatsoever of the toxic substance. The door had also been fixed.

Daniel told me the police had been wandering around the apartment for almost six hours. Then I thanked him for all that he had done, he looked straight at me and said:

"What is all this fumigation stuff about? Since when do you fumigate?"

"No, it wasn't me. The owner and the other tenants decided to fumigate the entire building. You know what old people are like; they spend their lives watching ants walk around."

It was just like Daniel to feel or know something and not say anything about it, so he changed the topic. He was too smart to start asking questions before the time was right. I was also sure he knew I was up to something strange — very strange.

"What happened with that website you made me check for you?" he asked me, casually.

"What do you mean?"

"The Hamas website."

"Oh! I haven't finished my paper yet."

Daniel looked me straight in the eye for the second time.

"What are you up to, Leonel?"

I understood that I couldn't lie anymore. Daniel was my faithful friend and I needed him by my side more than anyone — especially now, with everything that was going on. Besides, Ahmed was involved in IT, and Daniel could be of great help.

I told the story in detail, and asked for his discretion in keeping it confidential. It wasn't easy for me to talk about it, because I was violating one of the conditions I had promised Rachel. But I was sure my friend was absolutely reliable and able to keep a secret.

Daniel was impressed at my story — first with the part about the children, then with my decision to accept the case. He didn't interrupt; he just let me speak. Every so often, his eyes blinked rapidly, hinting at his astonishment. Just as I finished, he said, "I like it."

"What do you like?!" I exclaimed, casting him a puzzled look.

"This project ... it's challenging and more interesting than being on shift at the hospital or dismembering corpses at the university ..."

"Yes— it's so exciting, they want to poison me!"

Daniel was uneasy, and a nervous smile crept onto his face.

"I want to tell you something as well," he offered, his voice tense.

"What?"

"You remember what I told you about Mossad ... well, I couldn't get away from them."

"Congratulations," I said curtly. "Since when?"

"Since two months ago. I quit my job and they arranged a special program for me so I could finish university."

This was good news, I thought; a person like Daniel would be an important asset to an organization like that. Working elsewhere, he could make money, but would be wasting his time. He told me that he would remain on probation for six months and would deal with computer security — a special section that was growing within the organization.

"You've got to keep quiet about this — not even my parents know," he said.

"No problem; you keep my secret and I'll keep yours."

"And that's not all," he said with the face of someone who wants to unburden themselves of a heavy weight, "I'm working on the 'Computer Force.' "

"The Computer Force?" It took me a while to understand.

"Yes, we're investigating what Hamas is up to, and more precisely, your friend Ahmed Asad; that's why I decided to tell you about Mossad. If anyone knows I talked about this with you, I could go directly to jail."

"Don't worry; you know me. Ah, yes, of course, the Computer Force!" I once again remembered the pamphlet and the Palestinian boy, and I was afraid for a moment that the poisoning had affected my memory somehow. Daniel explained that Mossad knew about Hamas's plans to sabotage Israeli computer systems. They didn't know exactly what it was or when it would happen, but they were working hard on it and everyone was extremely alert at all times. Mossad was almost certain that Ahmed Asad no longer operated from Gaza, and so their agents were looking for him across Europe and in the Mediterranean countries.

"Do you know anything about it?" he asked me.

"No. As I told you, I joined the Red Cross in Gaza because that was the last known whereabouts of Ahmed, but now that you assure me he isn't there ..."

"Look, the information is not one-hundred percent reliable, but I think it would be very delicate and risky to operate a computer system from the Strip."

I had already thought about that, but how could I continue with the case when Mossad was trying to track Ahmed down too? They would have much more information and means of finding him, and if they found him before me, goodbye one million shekels. This mutual exchange of information with Daniel was risky, but at the moment, I had nothing else to go on. Zero! I had no alternative.

"What are you thinking of doing?" Daniel asked me.

"I have to go back to Gaza and sort out some issues. I want to finish at the Red Cross on good terms." I hadn't mentioned anything to him about Mariana.

"Don't you think it's a little risky, especially now that you know someone wanted to poison you?"

"Yes, but ..." I stammered. It was the first time I had felt afraid of returning to Gaza. "I'll have to give it more thought."

Daniel headed to the door and said his goodbyes, explaining that he had to go eat at his parents' house.

I was left thinking about the implications of my relationship with Daniel; an unspoken pact had formed between us. I thought about the people who were involved in this and who had information about my project: Moshe Cohen, Daniel, and obviously Rachel Mizrachi. No doubt there was another player I didn't yet know about, who was going after me, and who had already made an attempt to take my life.

Suddenly on my own, it occurred to me that it would be better to have some company over the following days, and to get out of my apartment. I called my mother and told her I was coming to stay for a few days. She was so happy at the news of my visit, that she didn't ask me the reasons for visiting. I packed enough clothes for a week, including dirty clothes that my mom could wash. Before leaving home, I called Moshe, like I had promised. His phone only rang twice before he answered.

"How's it going?" he asked when he heard my voice on the line.

"I'm fine now, thank you. I'm going to my parents' house for a couple of days."

"Good decision. How did it go with the police?"

"I don't think the agent believed my story, but he left me alone and told me to contact him if I remembered anything."

"What was the detective's name?"

"Yosi; he didn't mention his last name."

Suddenly the line went silent.

"Yosi, Department of Investigations, Tel Aviv ... a man in his sixties, with white hair, well-groomed?" he asked, to erase any doubt.

"Yes, why?"

"We're in trouble," he said, "Yosi would not have closed the case. He is persistent; he hates being lied to, and above all, he doesn't close cases without investigating them thoroughly. He also doesn't like being confused. He and I never got along well, even though that didn't stop us from working together.

"What should I do?" I needed Moshe's wise opinion.

"Give me a few days and we'll talk again. Meanwhile, it's a good idea to go and be with your parents. We'll keep in touch."

Moshe sounded worried and I began to feel the same. Having the police after me was not ideal. My parents' house wouldn't hide me from the police; it would be the first place they would look for me, but I didn't have too many options.

I took bus number 18n to Bat Yam. A one-hour trip lay ahead of me. I had decided to leave my Daihatsu in the garage, as I had no idea what the next day would bring. While on the bus, I thought about what I would do — spend some time with my parents, hardly leaving the house; wait for Cohen's call. I would travel back to the Gaza Strip and end my commitment with the Red Cross — and Judy, an agreement in word only, because there was no signed document. And I would talk to Mariana. What would I tell her? The truth? That was impossible, because if I told her the true story and my reasons, she would then become involved in this mess, which was quickly proving very dangerous. The only other option was to end the relationship by lying. But ... perhaps there was a possible future for our relationship? She in Gaza, and me... I don't know where. There were many questions without concrete answers. But one thing was clear: the main reason for my trip to Gaza was Mariana. I wanted to see her again; my feelings for her were deep, something I had never experienced before. At the same time, I recognized that if I held onto this bond, I would create obstacles in my search for Ahmed. Time, insight, and rest: that is what I wanted most right at that moment.

When I got to my parents' home, I got a shocking surprise. Yosi, the detective, was sitting comfortably on the couch. At his side, as if posing for a family photo, sat my dad and my mom. Yosi even had a lit cigarette in his hand — a forbidden sight in my house after my father had stopped smoking 10 years ago. The smoke formed shapes in the air and it was pointless trying to avoid inhaling it. I had barely said hello when Yosi beat my parents to it and said, "Let's take a walk; we need to talk."

My mother managed to breathe a "what are you mixed up in?" before Yosi guided me out the door. I reassured her and told her that nothing was wrong. It had been only four hours since I left the hospital and Yosi was once again standing before me.

On the street, I said, "What is this about?" I couldn't hide the anger in my voice.

"Leonel, if there is one thing that disgusts me, it's when people lie to my face, especially when their lies are childish and silly."

Then Yosi handed me a printed sheet of paper that read:

Police laboratories Tel Aviv

Attention: Yosi Rechter
Record: 34565 - Leonel Cohen - Intoxication

The substances found in the apartment at 1/32 Mapu, Tel Aviv
contain a mixture of methanol and methylene chloride.
By their very nature, these substances pose a serious risk of
poisoning if they come in contact with the human body.
Remainders of natural gas or other powders used in fumigation were not found.

Sincerely,
Alon Levi
Lab Director
Jurisdiction of Tel Aviv

"And now what?" It occurred to me to ask.

"Now it's time to tell me the truth."

"The truth is, I really don't know who put these substances in my apartment, or who forced the door open."

"Why did you lie to me before?"

"I didn't want to get involved with the police. As you already know, I'm a private investigator and I decided to take this case on myself."

Yosi shook his head.

"It seems to me that you do not understand that an attempt was made on your life. Make things easier for everyone and tell me everything you know."

"Listen, Detective Rechter, I don't know who tried to kill me, and I assure you I would like to know even more than you, wouldn't you agree? So if you can find those responsible, I would appreciate it. Understand that I'm not covering up for anyone; we're talking about my life here."

As my voice became louder and more aggressive, Yosi Rechter paused and muttered something to himself that I didn't understand. I began to think that he might have finally been listening.

"Do you want protection?" he offered, after lighting his third ciga-rette.

"I don't need it," I insisted. I didn't want the police following every move I made.

"Most people wouldn't refuse that offer ..."

"I'm not most people."

Yosi turned and walked toward his black Ford Sierra, which was parked in a space reserved for the disabled. "The police can get away with anything," I thought. Before leaving, he repeated the words he had said in the hospital, reminding me to call if I remembered anything.

"What a pain!" I thought. This detective wouldn't leave me alone. How would I explain to my parents what had just happened? How would I justify the presence of a police officer in their house? The last few weeks had been pure inventiveness and white lies. I just needed one more, though; I had to make one more effort to convince the old folks and make them believe that nothing had happened.

They didn't listen to reason, though. The story of a gas leak in my apartment hadn't convinced them in the slightest. Subtly, I made them understand that if they didn't leave me alone, I would go. Nevertheless, my dad had his reproach at the ready.

"First you quit university, and now you're involved in police investigations?"

It was obvious that my father was becoming worked up. Soon he went on a tearing rampage, screaming at the top of his lungs about my failings, and asking for answers.

I locked myself in my old room to shut out the noise. The threat to my life was greater than my father's scolding. Mom calmed him down, and the house became peaceful again. "What a mother will do for her child," I thought.

Early the next day, I took my clean clothes — ironed and folded as I liked — and packed them in my suitcase. My mom was the best. I bid her farewell and left quickly, avoiding seeing my father, to prevent any more confrontations. While riding the bus on my way to the Tel Aviv central station, my cell phone let out a trumpet-like blast. On the other end of the line was Daniel, and he whispered secretively.

"Hey Leonel, it's me. I'm going to send you an encrypted text message. Do you remember our secret codes from high school?"

He hung up before I could answer. Thirty seconds later, as promised, my phone got a message via WhatsApp that read:

1hm2d 2s 2n P2sh1w1r P1k3st1n.

At first, I couldn't decipher it. My head was already a balloon about to burst, so I forced myself to relax, calming the whirlwind that had developed in my brain. Eventually, the codes came to me.

The letters were regular consonants and the numbers were vowels, A = 1, E = 2, and so on until U. I transcribed it quickly:

Ahmed is in Peshawar, Pakistan.

I was perplexed; it was the first trace of Ahmed, and coming from Daniel there was no doubt as to its authenticity. The issue was what to do now. "Decisions," I thought, "decisions!" With my cell phone in my hand, the first thing that occurred to me was to call old Cohen to give the news of Ahmed's whereabouts and update him on my encounter with Yosi Rechter. He proposed that we meet in a coffee-shop in the industrial area of Talpiot, Jerusalem, suggesting that he could help me.

If Ahmed was in Pakistan, a rapid change of course was in order. I had to quickly decide what to do with Mariana and Judy. I had promised Judy, just a few minutes before speaking with Daniel on the phone, that I would return the next day. She said she would wait for me at the border crossing. I decided it wouldn't be difficult to cancel my return after all and explain to her that I wasn't yet ready to go back to Gaza.

But Mariana had become a problem. She had questioned my feelings and wanted to know the truth, knowing I was hiding something.

I called Judy immediately to resolve that issue. I told her I had received news that my father was in the hospital and that I had to stay in Israel for a few more weeks. I thanked her for her hospitality and explained that my stay at the Red Cross had been an excellent learning experience for me, but that I now needed to take care of my family. I crossed my fingers when I mentioned the old man, but it was the only convincing excuse I could come up with on such short notice. Judy was surprised — probably even shocked — by the quick turn of events, but she wished me good luck and thanked me for the work I had done.

I then called Mariana, but she wasn't there because she had left on a mission. I feared that Judy would announce my news to the whole group and that Mariana would find out that way. My female-scented fantasies and dreams would vanish if I didn't get to her first, so on the way to Jerusalem, I repeatedly tried to get a hold of her, but it was to no avail. When I arrived at the central station in Jerusalem, her angelic voice finally came through on the other side of the line. She sounded subdued and sad. I feared that Judy had already passed along the news.

"I knew it — you're not coming back."

"Mariana, you don't understand. I have things that I have to take care of here. I promise to fill you in on everything."

"Stop. What's done is done. You didn't come through today, and I'm not just here for you only when you want me to be. Obviously, you came to volunteer for a reason other than to help ... or to finish your supposed thesis. I want to know the truth. Do you think I'm asking too much?"

"Mariana, you don't understand ..."

"Yes, I understand — and you don't even know just how much."

The phone went silent in my ear, as if the line had been yanked out by an earthquake. I realized I had lost the signal and angrily threw the phone on the ground. I tried convincing myself that we didn't have a future anyway, that we had been doomed from the start, especially since the relationship had begun with a lie.

A huge storefront window, framed in bamboo, housed Sami's café. Almost all of the coffee-shop's customers were workers from nearby factories. Inside, the walls were covered with posters of Beitar Jerusalem, the most popular soccer team in the holy city. There was also an expert portrait of Sephardic singer Zohar Argov, painted in oil and signed "anonymous."

Old man Cohen was sitting at a table in the back, one step away from the bathroom. He was smoking a pipe that I hadn't seen before.

"When did you start smoking?" I asked.

"A friend let me try his pipe two weeks ago and I liked it. I've been a bit nervous lately and this helps me relax. Do you want coffee?"

"Yeah, a strong latte with sweetener. Now tell me, how can you help me?"

Moshe scratched at his beard, drawing attention to what I could tell had not been shaven for at least two weeks.

"Well, we've got a Yosi Rechter problem. I snooped around a bit and found out that his investigation is well under way. He even asked Shabak to collaborate, so I don't think I can help out there. The issue's too hot."

"I heard that Ahmed is in Pakistan." I went straight to the point.

"Is it true?"

"Yes," I said.

"Since you know of Ahmed's whereabouts, I would suggest you travel to Pakistan and try to find him."

"Travel to Pakistan ... but how would I get in with an Israeli passport? Besides, it's extremely risky and seems foolish to me."

"This is something that I can help you with. I'm going to take you to someone who will set you up with a foreign passport."

"No ... this isn't going anywhere. I'm tired of this scheme. It's too much. I can't go on. A fake passport? You're completely out of your mind! What if I get caught?"

I looked outside just as someone who I seemed to know unexpectedly appeared in the front window, peering inside. I scoured my memory. I knew that I knew him, but I couldn't remember from where. He was short, bald, and wearing dark glasses. Suddenly, I recognized him — he seemed to be the same guy who I had seen in Jaffa's store when I went to deliver Camel's money. Moshe noticed I was distracted. I looked again, but he was no longer there.

Within a few seconds, a motorcycle with two people on board streaked to a stop on the sidewalk, just outside the front window where the short man had been. The guy on the back stood up and, without removing his helmet, let loose a storm of bullets from a short-barreled machine gun, probably an Uzi or a Mac-10. The racket made me fall off the chair and I managed to drag Old Cohen with me. I covered my head to avoid the glass that was raining down everywhere and, once the shooting had stopped, I waited a few seconds, listening to the shouting and commotion around me. I slowly lifted my head and saw that Moshe still had his eyes closed. When I nudged him, he didn't respond and I thought maybe a bullet had struck him, but I didn't see any blood. I checked his pulse, which was regular, and he was also breathing normally. Clearly, he was in shock. I tried getting him to react by saying his name and slapping him in the face — a somewhat rudimentary tactic that I had learned in medical school. After a few minutes, he regained consciousness, delirious and bewildered.

The ambulances arrived unusually fast. As I stood up, I suddenly became aware of the bodies that were scattered all around me, not one of them showing any signs of life. A few people were moaning, and I tried helping one man who had a deep wound on the right side of his chest, but just as I was crouching down to help him, Moshe grabbed my arm and abruptly jerked me outside.

"What are you doing?" I asked.

"Let's get out of here, fast!"

"Why?" I asked, standing surprised outside the café, turning back and looking inside where people were still fighting for their lives.

"This attack was not like the others." Moshe was sure of his assessment. "I think they wanted to kill you."

"Kill me..."

And suddenly the bald, short man with dark glasses who I had seen just before hearing the gunshots flashed through my mind. Everything began to come together. Moshe knew it. There was a price on my head and I didn't understand why. We moved away from the place, leaving it in complete chaos. The police had surrounded the entire area, but we were able to escape through a narrow road that had not yet been blocked. We took a taxi to Ramot, a small locality east of the city. Moshe told the taxi driver which route to follow. From what I remember, Cohen lived in a neighborhood called Armon Anatzib.

"You moved?" I asked him inquisitively.

"No, we're not going to my house. Please stay quiet."

I looked at him, astonished. Moshe had taken control of the situation and it was obvious he knew what he was doing.

When we got out of the taxi he said to me, "You've got to leave the country, like we discussed — and you must do so as soon as possible."

"Leave the country as soon as possible ..." I repeated like a parrot.

"Yes, I will help you travel to Pakistan."

"How?" I thought that Moshe was still delirious after the attack in the coffee shop.

"A friend of mine will make you a Spanish passport. You will travel with that identity. Come with me now." Moshe had done his homework well. A Spanish identity fit me like a glove. I knew the Spanish language, having spoken it in my house as a child.

We entered an old four-story building that was part of a condominium complex in which all the buildings were the same. We climbed to the fourth floor, and as we walked up to an apartment door, it opened before we knocked. An old man with a white beard and glasses that covered most of his face was waiting for us. His prominent belly poked out from underneath his shirt. He beckoned us to follow him and walked back inside in a slow, stooping manner.

"Come in, come in. I've been waiting for you. Is this the boy, Moshe?"

"Yes." old Cohen said, as he headed to the kitchen.

It was obvious that Moshe knew the place. He came back with a jug of water and poured us both a glass. His face was still strained; the attack had really upset him. My time in Gaza and the terrible things I had witnessed there had desensitized me somewhat to these kinds of disasters. Despite all that, I still felt trapped by fear. I could feel the sweat forming on the palms of my hands and my whole body rattled with anxiety.

The old man with the beard took a picture of me with a camera that was at least 20 years old. He then went into a room, which I assumed was the "darkroom," where he would develop the photo. He took around 15 minutes, during which Cohen and I tried relaxing by settling into a loveseat couch and talking about the trip. Moshe made a call, and in what seemed like no time at all, we had the itinerary sorted out. Tel Aviv-Paris-Islamabad-Peshawar, all with Air France. The old man reappeared and handed me a Spanish passport with my picture and my new identity. My name was Carlos Torres. I tried making the name a part of me, without asking why he had chosen it. Although the camera was old, the picture was perfect, a testament to the old man's skill. Only my signature was missing. Moshe told me I had nothing to worry about, that even the police and the Mossad used this peculiar old man's services. I had never seen a passport forged so perfectly. Even the Spanish government's shield appeared to be completely real.

We said goodbye and left.

The next stop was a travel agency, a tiny shop located on a dead-end street that intersected Ben Yehuda. From the outside, it didn't look like a travel agency. Not on the inside, either. There were no posters of tourist sights, nor any of the images that usually adorn this type of business. As we walked in, a voluminous lady approached us. She introduced herself as the owner of the place and then went inside a small office and came out with the boarding passes. I looked them over. They had my new name and that day's date; in fact, the flight was leaving in just a few hours. Moshe and the woman hugged each other, indicating the age of their friendship. Moshe checked the tickets and asked if I had brought my check book or credit card. He had paid for the tickets, and wanted me to pay him back. This was my second expense, but I still had the five thousand shekels that I had deposited in the bank. Moshe's cunning and experience was most evident. He knew all the strategies and ruses. He had paid the tickets with his card so that my real name didn't appear on any list in the country. From that moment on, I was Carlos Torres. I would remain in France for one day and while there, I would meet up with a contact who would give me details about a bank account in my name, a French credit card, and a driver's license from that country. He'd also orient me a bit on my trip to Pakistan. As Moshe explained the details, I realised that this guy — this contact — would be essential for me, because in Pakistan I'd be left to my own devices, completely alone; I wouldn't have anyone there to turn to.

I asked Moshe to write down his bank-account number so I could transfer him the money for the tickets, and then I sent an email to Rachel asking her to deposit an additional 20,000 shekels, because I was almost out of money and I had to do some traveling.

Moshe gave me a guidebook about Pakistan and some leaflets with information about Peshawar, which had some addresses and the name of a hotel he recommended I stay at. Then, he hugged me and warmly said goodbye.

"You know my phone number," he said. "You know I'm here for you."

I then reminded him to write down the contact information for my guy in Paris.

"This is very important," he said, referring to another printed sheet, as he handed it to me. I tucked it away for safekeeping.

Before we parted ways, he shook my hand strongly.

From then on, everything happened so quickly. I would have liked to stop the whirlwind for a few moments and think about what I was doing. On the bus to Tel Aviv, the radio went on and on in its coverage of the attack in Jerusalem. The driver had the speakers blaring, and it was impossible not to listen in. Three dead and 14 wounded — the deadly toll from the tragedy that I had experienced in the flesh. They discussed motives for the attack, saying that it could have been due to a settling of scores of the Mafia, since the coffee shop belonged to one of the families who monopolized the drug trade from the Palestinian territories to Israel.

Maybe Moshe was wrong in attributing the attack to my presence in the café, I thought. Perhaps there was another reason why he wanted to get me out of the country. To me, it seemed that it was out of character for him to be so dedicated to this mission, given the bond that the old man had— or tried to have — with Rachel Mizrachi. Could it really be the love that he felt for that woman that made him crazy enough to get involved in this way? Does love cause these impulses? I was not one to judge, after what had happened with Mariana.

Ben Gurion Airport was crowded. It was common to find the terminal full, even though the country's statistics indicated a high level of poverty. The clock read 1:10 p.m. I had arrived on time, since the Air France flight was set to take off at 2:55 p.m. I hadn't slept much the night before, kept awake by what had happened during that day.

I followed the news about the attack in Jerusalem. The police had found the motorcycle lying on the side of the road that connects Ramle and Lod. The whereabouts of the terrorists were still unknown. A settling of scores had been ruled out, since Sami, the cafe owner, appeared all over the news denying this version of events, stating that his family hadn't been involved with drugs for a long time now.

I proceeded to check in with my new passport, and a shiver ran through every bone in my body while the young police officer looked it over. He finally stamped one of its pages and let me continue on my way. I thought about what would have occurred if someone I knew had been on the other side of the counter. Israel was a small country, so that could have easily happened.

I remembered that I needed to do two things while waiting. I needed to wire Moshe money for the ticket he had paid for, and call my parents to say hello and tell them that I would be outside the country for a while. I had an hour to come up with yet another reason why. I was getting used to being creative.

The plane touched down in France on time, as scheduled. A day in Paris would be a perfect opportunity to relax and charge my batteries. During the trip, I had prepared myself for my new identity. The new Carlos Torres was a computer systems engineer. It seemed like a good idea, since professionals in that field were incessantly moving about the world. I also needed a plan, and surely my contact would give me some ideas. I thought up a story of a Spanish man coming from Israel, visiting France on his way to Pakistan. It wasn't the most credible tale — and I suspected that the security checks at the airport wouldn't be easy — but to my surprise, they only asked me about my profession and the name of the company I worked for. My passport had a visa allowing me to enter Pakistan, courtesy of Old White Beard. As a Spanish citizen, I didn't need a visa to stay in France. As for the company that employed me, I told them I was working for IBM on a systems integration project for the Pakistani government. Fortunately, the security guard seemed to be finishing up his shift, because he was constantly looking behind him as if trying to see whether or not his replacement was on the way. Without much ado, he stamped my passport and I was free to roam in the Land of Gaul.

My only luggage consisted of a briefcase containing my laptop and a carry-on bag. I hailed a cab to take me into the city. The driver appeared to be Arab, so I addressed him in Spanish, and then in English, trying to find a way for him to understand me. I asked him if he knew of any three-star hotels and he nodded. Along the way, he tried to strike up a conversation, without much luck, because I wasn't eager to talk. I pretended to be asleep. On the way to the hotel, a Renault 12 car pulled alongside the taxi and then began following us, either trailing behind or to the side, depending on the other traffic. Noticing that two the men inside the car had their eyes covered with dark glasses, I immediately felt a lump in my throat, fearing that my persecutors had found me. Could it just be my paranoia? But the driver also saw that we were being followed and stepped on the gas without asking questions. We lost them as we entered the city's center. When he dropped me off at the Holiday

Inn hotel, the driver asked me whether I was in trouble and I told him no, that I didn't know anyone in Paris. I paid his fare and gave him a generous tip. When I entered the hotel to check in, I was informed that there were no rooms available and they recommended I go to the two-star motel located across the street.

La Jaque, as it was called, was a building that appeared to be on the verge of collapse. Its exterior had certainly seen better days; the logo L-J on the main sign was hanging down and ready to fall on an unsuspecting pedestrian. I walked in despite its unwelcoming appearance, and a fat, disheveled, grumpy woman assisted me with clear contempt. Without saying much, she assigned me a clean room with a view of the street.

As soon as I had settled into my room, I quickly took stock of the place: a double bed, a tiny TV, a small table, and a bathroom dating back to my grandmother's time. On the main wall, there was a cheap painting of a still life and, inevitably in places like this, a crucifix hung on the wall above the headboard. In the top drawer of the bedside table I found a Bible. "Perfect," I thought. I would need it.

When I went to the bathroom, I heard the main door and jumped around, but there was no-one there. I looked through the peephole and saw nothing outside either. I tried to relax and convince myself that I was hearing things — that maybe it was a sound from the motel itself, or a noise from another room. Suddenly, someone knocked on the door. Again, I looked through the peephole, but this time, I saw the maid with towels in her hand. I opened the door. She was young with full lips, broad hips, and an extra-voluptuous bust. For a moment, I was distracted by her figure. The top button of her uniform was open, as if it was demanding freedom for her breasts. My eyes were stuck on her body like a magnet. I not only liked her for her exuberant figure, but also because when she smiled, a different side of her emerged — alive, fulfilled, even pretty. She was the kind of woman I classified as perfect. She handed me the towels and asked if I needed anything else. I thanked her and responded that all was good for now.

I confess that during those moments, many ideas about that woman came to mind. I was surprised when she handed me a slip of paper. As I unfolded it and noticed her phone number, she added that her name was Silvia and she could show me around Paris if I wanted. I thanked her again, promising to think about it. At that moment, what I needed more than anything was rest.

When I entered the bathroom to put down the towels, I saw that there was already a set of towels lying on the bathtub.

"She must have made a mistake," I mumbled.

"Or maybe she had other intentions," I thought. I would be very pleased if her motives lined up with my imagination. But at the same time, I felt I should distrust everything at this point in my life. After all, it was rare for a beautiful woman to show up with unnecessary towels. On the other hand, "special attention" from the pretty woman who gives out her phone number to guests could be part of the hotel's side business. It occurred to me that after everything that had happened in the last week, this could easily be part of a chain of misfortunes. I threw myself on the bed and fell asleep for a while. When I woke up, the first thing I did was check the clock. It was 9 p.m. I had slept for an hour and a half.

On the bedside table, the piece of paper with Silvia's phone number was waiting for me. Silvia, the supposed hotel maid who had come knocking at my door. I remembered that before doing anything else, I should get in touch with Amnon, the contact Moshe had given me. I called, but no one answered. He didn't even have a voice mailbox where I could leave a message. I returned my gaze to the paper on the bed-side table. My male instinct got the best of me, and I lifted the phone's receiver to call her. She didn't seem surprised to hear my voice on the line. We hadn't even introduced ourselves, I thought, and yet she saved me the trouble of explaining that I was the man from the hotel, the one whom she had brought towels and offered to show Paris. She simply said, "I'll swing by to get you at 10 p.m.; wait for me in the hotel lobby."

I tried contacting Amnon again, but he didn't answer this time either. I found this strange, since Moshe had told me that he was aware of my arrival and my needs.

As promised, Silvia arrived at the hotel lobby on time. She was wearing a black skirt that didn't leave much to the imagination, along with a skin-tight turtleneck sweater. Her clothing accentuated her per-fect breasts. The outfit was topped off with black fishnet stockings that merged into high heels of the same color. Her soft makeup was just right for the moment. Just by looking at her, I knew I had made the right decision in accepting her invitation, and I soon realized that Silvia knew how to take care of everything. The hardest part of a first date is breaking the ice, getting closer to one another, and finding things to talk about. With her it was very easy. We went outside after our initial greeting and, without mentioning our names, she latched onto my arm and we started walking as if we were old friends. I observed that neither English, the language we were speaking, nor French, appeared to be her native language. She told me that she was Russian and had lived in France for five years. She worked at the hotel and studied art. She lived on the outskirts of Paris. To clear things up, I asked her if she frequently offered her services as a tour guide to hotel guests. She flashed a smile, showing that she took it well and wasn't offended by the question.

"No," she responded, "I just saw you at reception when you arrived; I liked you and, as you can see, I'm not shy at all. I don't have much time for good company ... or to play the seduction game. So here you have me."

"Where are you taking me?" I managed to blurt out.

"To San Celishe. There's a good strip of bars and pubs around there. Besides, that area makes me very happy. I guess that you, like all tourists, will want to see the Eiffel Tower."

"I'm willing," I said with a smile.

I liked her plans, her company, her everything.

We ate and drank plenty — maybe a little more than we should have. We went all over the city's center. The night was cold, but Paris looked elegant, as always, with its lights and its fabulous tower. We climbed up to the top floor and gazed upon the city while enjoying a good glass of Chardonnay. The day's events, along with the alcohol, gave us the urge to kiss and hold each other passionately. And so we did just that in a world high above the rest.

I was excited, and I could see clearly that Silvia was, too, so I invited her to spend the night at the hotel. She accepted my proposal without hesitation. By then, she was completely drunk and so was I. We hadn't spoken much; in fact, we'd pretty much spent the evening in silence with the odd joke here and there. Good humor was a highlight of my personality; I knew that if a man managed to make a woman laugh, no matter how ugly he was, he could seduce her. Just in case, as I didn't consider myself overly attractive, I put a little humor into play.

And so it was that night, that our sexual experiences outweighed anything I had ever experienced in my life. Silvia was an expert in stroking, and knew all the right moves. From the start, she took the initiative and directed the performance. Her tongue became an extension of her hands, and there wasn't a centimeter of skin we didn't mutually discover. I could feel her body quivering under my fingertips as I squeezed the nipples of her perky breasts between my lips. I grabbed her ass-cheeks in my hands and felt her clenching and unclenching them as she moved on top of me. I was going absolutely crazy. I remember it just as it was yesterday. We spent almost the entire night embroiled in passion, writhing together in lustful fantasy. What rest we had came solely between climaxes.

Drained and exhausted, I finally closed my eyes and fell asleep. I don't know why, but for some reason I woke with alarm, horrified to find Silvia about to pounce on me with a knife that looked as if it could cut metal. I jumped back just in time to avoid her first attack, which ripped through the air and barely grazed my neck. I remember screaming at her as I fell backwards off the bed, "What are you doing? Are you crazy?"

Despite my cries, the second attack came, but this time she had the upper hand. The knife hit my right leg, as I kicked at her with my left. She was about to go at me for the third time when, to both our surprise, the door burst inwards with a thundering crash and two men armed with pistols flew into the room. They shot at Silvia point-blank and, although the silencers muffled the shots, they had no effect on killing power — I saw four very big holes appear in her chest and she collapsed on the floor, dead. Her chest, which before had provoked love and excitement, had become a wreck of blood and torn flesh.

"Put something on. We're leaving!" the men said in Hebrew.

I slipped on my pants and took my bag. We ran down the stairs at full speed and went out through the back door, avoiding reception. As they holstered their guns, they put me in the back seat of a white Fiat and ordered me to lie on the seat and keep my head down. The car took off like a rocket and flew through the narrow streets of the city's downtown sector. We took one of the highways heading to the outskirts of Paris. No one spoke and I was too confused to say anything myself. Somewhere along the way, one of the men offered me water, suggesting that it would calm me. He made an effort to assure me that I was safe.

"Who are you?" I asked.

"We're agents of Mossad, your contacts in Paris."

"My contacts in Paris?" That made some sense. Moshe or Daniel, or both, had arranged this meeting with the Mossad people for me. I didn't know which or even why, but it was very clear that they had saved my life.

"When we get to our accommodations, we will talk. Try to relax. We have a journey of about an hour ahead of us," said the one behind the wheel, a young guy with blond hair and blue eyes. The other, who seemed more introverted, had a Mediterranean appearance and was probably younger than the driver. He was short and dark-skinned and his hair as shaved, army style. His muscles bulged under his green shirt. Both were wearing dark glasses when they entered the hotel room, but now they were gone and their faces were clearly visible.

Without realising it, I looked down and saw a pool of blood on the floor of the car. It seemed that the gash I had received on my leg from Sylvia's knife was quite deep. It was located just under my thigh. The younger man handed me a handkerchief as he said:

"I know you're studying medicine, so you'll know what to do."

I took the handkerchief, took off my shirt and asked the passenger to stretch my leg as far as possible. Quickly, I formed a tourniquet with the shirt, which I wound around my thigh just above the cut. I pressed the handkerchief into the wound itself, pushing really hard until I had to bite my tongue to withstand the pain. Although the bleeding began to ebb, I knew full well I couldn't be without medical care and medication for long. I risked infection and I had no idea how much blood I had already lost.

"How long before we get to where we're going?" I asked the driver.

"Almost half an hour," he said, annoyed.

"I need to stop at a pharmacy to buy gauze and alcohol."

"Is it urgent? Can it not wait?" he asked.

"No," I answered, "If I don't take care of this wound, it can lead to gangrene. I also need a suture needle and thread or I can bleed to death."

"I'm Yoni and my partner here is Ben." Surprisingly, he introduced himself and the passenger. "And we know your name from our report, so spare yourself the words."

That said, Yoni turned the wheel sharply and pulled the car off the highway into a suburb on the outskirts of Paris. I couldn't see the name on the sign at the off ramp, but after five minutes, we found a pharmacy. Yoni got out and brought back gauze, bandages, and alcohol, as I had asked.

"It's all right, the suture can wait," I said.

I untied the tourniquet, applied alcohol with gauze, and wrapped clean bandages around my leg. As I was cleaning the open wound with the alcohol, the pain was so intense that my body spasmed. I felt a cold sweat on my forehead and I felt myself fading. How different it was to be in the role of the patient!

When we arrived in Marseilles, I was fast asleep. Yoni patted my arm and told me we had reached our destination. We parked in front of a green gate that looked like the entrance to a winery. We went around the outside and entered through a back door. I could barely walk, so I leaned on Ben's shoulder. I was dragging my right leg, leaving a trail of red. The gauze pads I had applied were drenched with blood. I needed to urgently suture the wound. If I didn't, I would surely die.

When we entered, I could see we were in a warehouse. There were no interior walls or other doors; everything was wide open. I also didn't see any defined spaces like a kitchen or bedroom, and could only distinguish the different areas based on the furniture which I could see around us. I couldn't tell if it was a minimalist design or a lack of resources. There were two sofas, a mounted TV, two beds, a refrigerator, a microwave, and a dark curtain that hid the bathroom. The walls had been painted different dark shades.

I didn't question it; I only asked for the needle and thread I had requested.

"I have a needle, but no thread," Ben said, annoyed.

"How do you not have thread? What am I going to do with a needle and no thread? Do you understand that it is imperative that I suture my wound now?" Ben shrugged his shoulders in indifference.

I moved about the place a bit and saw a worn sheet on one of the beds. I started pulling it apart to draw out a thread.

"I need fire!" I told Yoni.

"Fire? What for?"

"I have to sterilize the needle."

While Yoni looked for a lighter, I passed the relatively thick thread through the eye of the needle. I was a little dizzy from blood loss, but I finally managed to get it through. Yoni came back with an old, rusty lighter, but it still worked, and as he held the flame out, I ran the needle through the fire to sterilize it. Then I asked Ben to hold down my leg, while Yoni held my body. I needed something to bite down on, so Ben brought me a rag that I stuffed into my mouth and held tightly between my teeth. I unwound the tourniquet from my leg and the blood began to bubble out. I asked for the alcohol and poured a stream over the wound. It felt like I was being stabbed by a hundred knives at once — I was certain at a time I was going to pass out, and I don't know where I got the strength to push the needle into the uppermost part of the gash. I pressed on, stitch by stitch, until the slit was closed, pulling the thread tightly between each suture. I poured alcohol over it again and covered the area with a bandage. I felt Yoni pressing on my chest and then everything went dark. I had collapsed once again.

When I came to, Yoni told me I had been asleep for three hours. I checked the wound and sighed in relief when I saw that the bandage was hardly soiled.

Ben told me that we needed to talk.

"I don't understand what's going on here," I said, stupefied.

"Leonel, we're from the Mossad and we've saved your life. In case you didn't notice, that woman was hired to kill you. If we hadn't reached you in time, she would have slit your throat. You were lucky we were following you. But that's not all: before her date with you that night, she had killed another man in his hotel room. All we know about him is that he was an Israeli living here in Paris."

"What was his name?" I inquired.

"Amnon or something."

"Amnon ... but ... that was supposed to be my contact here in Paris."

"Now you see?" said Ben.

"Nothing makes sense. The Mossad saved my life, but not Amnon's. Aren't we all equal?" I asked him ironically.

"No. You're smart enough to know that the Mossad has better things to do than bail out random Israelis who want to leave their country. We want the same thing as you do and we can help each other. Our man is Ahmed Asad and we know that you are also looking for him. We learned you have tickets to Pakistan to trace his footsteps. We're not interested in your reasons, but we want you to help us by working for us on this case."

"What if I don't accept?"

"Look, Leonel," scolded a much more serious Ben, "We won't threaten you or anything like that, but you know very well that with our help, you'll get further in less time. It'll be a mutually beneficial agreement. We'll provide you with information, support, and technology. Look at it as a way to serve your country."

That truly was the last thing going through my mind — serving the country. On the other hand, I understood what Ben was saying to me. There was obviously no way out of this. The Mossad knew I wanted to find Ahmed and wouldn't let me disrupt their own search. So, without having passed the intelligence tests, I was already part of the glorious Mossad, something I didn't much mind. The only question that tortured me was why the Mossad needed my help approaching someone, when they usually do that themselves. Surely there was another reason I wasn't aware of, and it was beginning to weigh on my mind.

I was still thinking about who might want to erase me from the map. "Coincidence" no longer played a role in this string of events. Everything that had happened was tangled up in the same pathetic web. Given the recent turn of events, the Mossad was my most convenient option. Even still, at this stage of the game, I couldn't get out even if I tried. It would disappoint my potential assassins, who would surely find me and kill me, along with Moshe, and especially Rachel Mizrachi.

"What's the plan?" I asked.

Yoni took charge of the conversation.

"Upon arriving at Peshawar, you will meet up with one of our kaza[21]. He will provide you with everything you need: housing, food, clothing,

---

21 Kaza: a field intelligence officer of the Mossad.

and what not. He will assist you with any arrangements you require. He also has some shaky information, but at least they're clues."

"Is this contact Israeli?"

"No. He's an Afghan refugee who we helped escape the Taliban regime with his family. In return, he provided us with the information that Ahmed Asad was in Pakistan. Now, he works for us."

"And you can trust him?" I asked warily.

"We have no choice but to trust him. The man is very grateful that we rescued him and his family from the Taliban pogrom, just as he was about to be executed in the main stadium, in front of his kin."

It occurred to me that I would be in the hands of an Afghan with pretty much no moral concern for my well-being. I was at the mercy of my luck. Even so, I thought the Mossad knew well what they were doing.

"We'll place a GPS device under your skin. It is a new 'made in Mossad' invention that the world doesn't know about yet. That way, we'll know where you are at all times; we'll constantly have your location. It also works in your favor, because if something were to go wrong — if you were to find yourself in danger — we'd always know where to find you."

Yoni explained the carefully-planned security precautions in detail. "The unit contains a small audio device that will live-stream your conversations and everything that happens around you. We'll also get you an apparatus that connects this device to the Internet." He continued talking while taking a key out of his pocket and handing it to me. He added that I should always keep it on me.

The key could connect to the Internet from any country. It was yet another innovation of the Mossad's research and development team. He didn't go into too much detail, only explaining that the key contained a Bluetooth device that automatically paired with the device inside my body. It would work within a distance of up to 20 meters.

"The key is only one option, since the device we'll insert in your body will have a direct connection."

And he went on: "Today, before your trip, we will install it. Don't make trouble; it's not painful and it won't bother you. Ben and I have had ours for over a year now."

I supposed the Mossad's product testing took into account the possible harmful effects of inserting an artificial device into the human body. I didn't know what that device was made of to give an accurate estimate as to how dangerous it could be. Plus, the fact that they'd constantly be watching over me did seem convenient, because they could save my life again. But the big downside was that, from here on out, I'd have someone at my side like a constant shadow, like a big brother who follows me wherever I go, stuck on me. Everything I do or say could be a test — pass or fail, but a test nonetheless.

Since they'd approached me just three hours before leaving for Pakistan, Yoni got right to the point by pulling out a kind of pistol that had a thick needle attached to one end.

"Eyyy!!" I yelled. "Wait a minute ... I want to know more about this device. I like to know what goes in and out of my body, and if it is reversible — that is, if I can remove it later. You know I'm a medical student ..."

Yoni looked at me in amazement. He lowered the gun, perhaps in a gesture of peace.

"Leonel, this kind of gadget falls under the umbrella of nanotechnology. 'Nano' means one billionth of a meter; some molecules and viruses move along a grander scale. Carbon is the principal element that drives this technology. This small module contains magnetic iron oxide nanoparticles that have been prepared with a special coating. In the US, this technology is used to detect diseases, like cancer, for example. In our case, we insert a special chip that links up to a satellite and enables audio reception. And this," he said, removing another gun-like device from a case, "this is a cool new device that uses ultrasound and a special chemical to heal small wounds."

I bowed my head in assent. I had read a little about nanotechnology as it applied to medicine, but didn't understand the technical details.

Ben disinfected my arm, and Yoni lowered the gun with the needle which, upon seeing it close-up, seemed huger still. He quickly injected me with the device, then grabbed the other gun and applied its healing effect to my skin, leaving me with no scar at all. The procedure was painful — and not just from the guns. I began to feel a warmth course through my body. Yoni told me it was normal and prompted me to lie down and be patient, assuring me the discomfort would soon pass. And that's just how it happened. I felt normal again after just five minutes. We tested the device. It was really extraordinary. Ben followed my steps throughout the house with a portable Wi-Fi monitor that streamed everything onto a small map where my avatar moved about. He asked me to speak to test the sound. I did, and when I said the first words, they echoed in the monitor's headset. I was shocked. This technology was extremely incredible, and I was experiencing it live in my own body. Yoni and Ben were pleased by the GPS' operation. We got into the car and they took me to the airport.

Along the way, Yoni told me that they would initiate contact with me, and that I shouldn't reach out to them. He gave me a green hat and a bracelet of the same color that would help my host in Peshawar to identify me. They dropped me off five minutes from the airport and told me to take a taxi for the rest of the way.

There were no special farewells, just a warm hand gesture.

I had the idea that the Mossad thoroughly trained their agents on trust and affection issues, so they could get accustomed to block their feelings and act with a straight head, a sort of "sentimental crudeness."

Once inside the Air France Boeing 747, I examined the cap and the green bracelet. The color reminded me of the high-waving flags of Hamas that I had discovered just a few weeks previously in Gaza. I questioned whether I should wear them or not. Did the Mossad have something up their sleeve? Was this a simple identification method or a symbol for something else? It was futile to try not to add doubts to the hurricane of my uncertainties. I wanted to avoid further upsetting myself by over-thinking a simple hat and bracelet. So much had happened, that my stress levels were starting to worry me. I centered my thoughts and made an effort to review the recent events calmly, without raising alarm: my stay in Gaza; Mariana; the gas in my house; the gunshots at the coffee-shop in Talpiot; my lustful night with Silvia in that simple hotel in Paris; the knife in her hand and the Mossad bursting in to save me and employ me at the same time. It was too much. I was exhausted, but anxious. I pulled out my pill box and popped a pink pill. I immersed myself in Xanax[22] Air.

---

22 Xanax: A pink-colored pill which helps alleviate anxiety.

19

AHMED
Peshawar - Pakistan
October 17, 2011

On October 10th, we entered the Red Cross through a back door that Asher had shown me. At that time, there was no surveillance, and the place seemed like a vacant lot. The Red Cross was housed in a building under construction — one of those works that was started but never finished, so someone decided to slap a fresh coat of paint on it, make a few small repairs, and call it a day. Outside the building, there was still DANGER: CONSTRUCTION signs hanging about.

There were many buildings like this in Peshawar. The Taliban's presence in the city was palpable.

After walking along a dark hallway, I came to an open space, a patio. I saw her there. Mariana was sitting on a bench beneath a dried-up fountain that didn't appear to have spurted water for many years. She had taken off her chador, and her blond hair glistened in the sunlight. The daylight accentuated her beauty. Her colleagues were alongside her, having lunch outdoors. Mariana looked back at me and our eyes locked together for what seemed like an eternity, as if we were old friends. If eyes could speak and act, ours would have come together in a kiss, I thought. When I snapped out of my moment of ecstasy, I heard a voice asking:

"Are you looking for someone? Do you need anything?"

The voice came from a man dressed in white, who looked like a nurse or doctor. His thick mustache revealed his Pakistani origin.

"I have to talk to Mariana Asirán."

"What do you want from her?"

"I have to pass along an important message."

The man pursed his white mustache and made an unfriendly face as he pointed me to Mariana, sitting a few meters from us. She got up and approached me. As she walked, she adjusted her chador to cover up her hair again. We looked at each other for a little longer, until she broke the silence.

"Who are you?"

She spoke fluently in Arabic. Her voice was coated with a relative smoothness. The smell of her skin reminded me of my childhood, one of those scents that you never forget. When we moved closer together, I recognized her aroma and associated it with the green eucalyptus trees that grew in the valleys of western Jerusalem. "What to say?" I thought; there was no time for hesitation.

"I know you don't know me, but I saw you and I thought we could be friends ... since I don't have many friends around here." I bit my tongue from the adrenaline of having mustered up the courage to talk to her. I had never been particularly awkward or shy, and I was usually at ease speaking with people, but at that moment a strange feeling had taken hold of my stomach and wouldn't let me think.

"I'm Mariana. What's your name?"

"Ahmed," I said, almost without thinking whether or not I should hide my original name. When I did, it was too late.

Mariana began extending her hand as a form of greeting, a very common gesture in the Western world, but she changed her mind and, as she brought her hand back to her side, she moved a step or two away from me, surely remembering that we were being watched.

"You aren't from here." The words were said with a tone that felt somewhere between question and assertion.

"No. How do you know? From what I can tell, you're not either," I said, although I obviously knew where she was from.

"I am a native of Denmark; I volunteer as a nurse here. My father is Palestinian and my mother is Danish. I was born and raised in Denmark, but my father always spoke to me in Arabic, so I would stay in touch with my roots, and that's how I learned."

Mariana smiled as she finished her sentence.

If I were a protagonist in one of those Arab films that the Israeli public TV channel broadcasts on Friday afternoons, I would say that I was in love. The situation had the right elements: the brazen young man from the countryside, the beautiful woman from the city — it was the perfect recipe to induce love at first sight. In an attempt to bring myself back to reality, I forced myself to pay more attention to her demeanor than her appearance. I hadn't had experience with women. In all honesty, I had never been with one, but everything about Mariana seemed refined and delicate — so much, that I feared I was looking at her too hard, as if my eyes could tear the delicate petals of that tender flower.

The following week, we saw each other every day after I got out of work. The place where we would meet was far away from the Red Cross, and sometimes she would get a ride from Asher to avoid having to walk all the way.

Mariana and I soon had a special bond, as if we had developed our own unique language; a catalyst that brought us together. I told her I was also Palestinian, but for security reasons, hid my real job and my involvement with Hamas, because our work should be kept a secret. I said I was working on a project for an international company that installed new computer systems for the government. She remained unconvinced, since I hid where I was living.

One day, we went to a park located near the Central Mosque. We didn't care about anything; we just held hands and ran like children. I had lost track of time and was more relaxed about my identity, my situation. Caught up in the joy of the moment, we sneaked behind a hill and snuggled close together under the branches of a huge poplar tree. The wind was blowing softly, rustling the top branches.

At one point, I slowly moved Mariana's chador aside, sealing her lips with a kiss. We pressed up against each other and became intertwined as if we were one. When we finally arose, it was nighttime and the shimmer of the moonlight illuminated our faces in the darkness. There were moments where we were afraid that someone would discover us — a fact that would cost me dearly, as it was forbidden to interact with the local population. We begrudgingly returned via the same path on which we had come, full of forbidden desires — the kind that take control of the body and lead to love.

We kept our love a secret. On one of those days, I asked Asher if he could find me a safe place to be alone with Mariana without fear of being discovered. By the following day, he had it all figured out. He led us to an aluminum house half-an-hour from the city, where he informed us that we only had one hour. I had never felt so grateful. During the time we had, I relished Mariana's caress, feeling exceptional as I touched her soft skin, white as milk, leading me to a level of ecstasy that was like no other. I was afraid of hurting her with my rough hands. My lips began to navigate her body, learning her by heart as I kissed every inch — from her small breasts to her tight belly. Again we came together, and when I was inside her, I felt a trembling deep in my body that put a Molotov cocktail to shame. We made love over and over, until Asher knocked on the door to take us back to the city. I knew that everything would be over as quickly as it had started if suspicion were raised, but all of those fears faded into insignificance whenever I was with her.

On various occasions, Mariana inquired about my work, and my blatant lies were no longer keeping her curiosity at bay.

"I know you're not telling me the truth," she said, "If you were working for the government, you wouldn't be living in hiding."

"The project involves computer network security, and I can't tell you where I live because the government has prohibited us from revealing any kind of information."

"If you want to be with me, you'll have to tell me the truth," she scolded.

A few days later, a new version of the website was launched, replacing my initial site design. When it was finished and published, the organization was proud and grateful for the work that had been done. I had started working with Reza on a special project that had yet to be named and was still under absolute secrecy. He had asked me to design a simple Trojan virus, which would be integrated within a program that he himself had created. I didn't ask what kind of program it was. Indeed, Trojan viruses are normally designed to allow an individual remote access to a system. Reza knew that I had no experience with Trojans, so he provided me with a comprehensive manual of over 200 pages.

"Read it. You have until next week," he instructed, his steady, high-pitched tone somewhat undermining his intention of authority.

Just the sight of the book made me want to die; delving into so many pages of computer theory just wasn't my idea of fun. Even so, I was being hurled into another world — a world that I liked, and one that lured me in. That week, I thought deeply about the course my life was taking and the changes I had been through, and I realized that I had never stopped to think about what I really wanted to do. I liked the idea of making a living from computer work, but I wasn't looking to become an informatics guerrilla. With her kindness and special nature, Mariana had changed something in me and I didn't even realize it. I was afraid of losing her forever for not telling the truth, and was playing around with the idea of confessing everything.

After a few days of intense study and work, I was about to start testing my Trojan spy program, when Reza called me into a room away from the others. I noticed that he was more serious than usual. "Let's sit," he said. Reza furrowed his brow as he fiddled with a pencil.

"I have to send you back to the Gaza Strip."

"Why's that?" I asked, shocked, although I sensed the reason why.

"We know that you're seeing a woman. That's highly dangerous for us, taking into account the fact that any recklessness on your part could get us discovered and dismantled in the blink of an eye. Remember that we are in a foreign land and our on-ground presence is extremely valuable to the organization. I don't need to tell you just how important this project is, and we can't risk the future of this informatics mission. Therefore, you will continue working with us from the Gaza Strip."

"But ..." I wasn't able to get the words out.

Reza handed me an Egypt Air ticket to Cairo with a layover in Islamabad. My flight was leaving at 3 p.m. that same day. There, I would find a contact who would take care of the logistics to get me through to Rafah and on my way to the Gaza Strip. As long as I live, I will never forget the date, October 17, with its double blow of losing Reza's trust and having to leave Mariana all in one day.

I was in shock. I felt a pang in my chest. I had missed my chance. My chance for what? Perhaps my chance to be free and happy. I checked my watch and saw that the time was already 12:30 p.m. Reza informed me that the bags with my belongings, including my clothes, were waiting for me downstairs in the car. The work had been done to perfection and without asking anything to me. In addition, I had been assigned a security officer to accompany me until my departure.

"Asher is waiting downstairs for you; he will take you to the airport. Please, go on without saying goodbye. I don't want to cause a scene. These protocols come from above and I have received precise orders. Ahmed, I respect you. I understand you're a man, and in part I get where you're coming from, but reality is harsh, very complex, and often difficult to understand. I'll be in touch shortly."

After saying this, Reza left the room. I was unable to open my mouth to respond. The look on his face portrayed just how hard it was for him to relay the bad news to me, but he knew that before everything else, he had a duty to uphold. I started thinking about who might have betrayed me. Asher was the only one involved — the only one who knew my secret. I regretted having trusted him and I felt stupidly naive.

Downstairs, Asher was waiting for me with the truck's engine running. I checked the trunk to make sure my luggage was in the vehicle, then promptly got in, carefully eyeballing him as he returned the favour. Asher wasn't one to express his emotions, but on this occasion, he looked upset. He was pale, as if someone had dropped a bag of cement on his back.

"Ahmed, I didn't rat you out — I swear it on my mother!" Asher turned his head to look at the road and put the vehicle into gear.

I believed him. There was nothing to hide in that agonized face. It was like transparent paper, making his words almost unnecessary.

"I believe you, Asher. Don't worry about it."

"Ahmed, they've been watching you for a week and half now. You drew suspicion because you didn't always get home at the same time and you made up several excuses that were hard to believe. I warned you that sooner or later they'd find out. It's a good thing you got off as you did; it means they appreciate you and consider you indispensable. Apparently, you're very good at what you do. You know, something similar happened with a young Iranian a few months before you got here, but they filled him with bullets. I know, because I dug the grave and buried his body with my own hands. The Iranian's problem wasn't girlfriends — he liked to go out at night and do drugs."

Great! I was spared from the same kind of death to which he had been sentenced, except my crime was loving a woman. The weight I felt in my chest was not caused by the missed opportunity, but to leave Mariana without saying goodbye. I considered sending Asher to explain to her what had happened, but decided against it, choosing instead to write her a quick letter for Asher to pass along. This way, I wouldn't have to send the message by word of mouth, which could confuse things. In the letter, I explained that I had been called back to Gaza for a family emergency, because my sick mother wanted me at her side.

In our conversations, I had already revealed some details of my life to her, something that I had never done with anyone before. I told her about the family I had in Palestine, and about the death of my father 10 years prior due to lung cancer caused by smoking cigarettes and construction dust from working on a bulldozer for more than 30 years. I also told her that my mother had always lived in the shadow of her husband and liked things that way. I described her as a very strong woman who took care of and gave her all to her family — to the extent that, in times of crisis when the territories were closed off and there wasn't much to eat, she went without food so we wouldn't go hungry. She had always given way to my dad. When he was in the house, it was like she wasn't there; she didn't make herself known. She was like a ghost that cooked, ironed, and took care of their children. That was her life and she didn't complain.

I also confessed to Mariana that I didn't remember my father having taught me anything. He always spent his days working and didn't speak much at all — even to his own family. However, Mom always had the sense to keep us together and united, especially after Dad's death. She raised five of us — four women and myself. I came in second in the sibling saga. My older sister married a young Jordanian and lived in Jordan. The other three, younger, were still living in the family home. Mom suffered heavily when they removed her ovaries due to a tumor after her youngest daughter was born. Just like that, she was rendered infertile, which, to her, seemed to define her worth against the other women. She had only five children, while all of her relatives and friends had at least between six and seven children. She was never the same again. Her appearance changed, even though her love for us remained same. I learned to take care of myself from an early age, because I didn't want to become a burden on her. She had too much to handle with my sisters and their sufferings.

After the death of my father, Mom moved to Jordan for a while to live with an aunt, and took my sisters with her. I divulged to Mariana that distance then grew between my mother and me, until one day she suddenly decided to return home to the same house she had left — where we had grown up, and where she would find a world of memories waiting for her. That's when she began to write to me; to look for me. Surprisingly enough, all distance between us instantly became non-existent. She wanted to know all about me. From there, our contact was never broken, and we vowed to never allow ourselves to grow apart again.

Since I had joined Hamas and begun receiving a salary, I had sent half to her, although she never asked for it. I remember that, in our nightly conversations, I also told Mariana about Rafaq, who was like a father and tutor at the most critical time of my life. The excuse I gave Mariana for my departure was inspired by these life stories that I shared with her during our calm, quiet conversations.

In the midst of these thoughts, I saw that Asher was parking the truck. He got out and unloaded the bags. His face betrayed him, displaying the utter despair of one friend saying a final goodbye to another. I patted him on the back, all the while becoming aware of the part he had played in my story; he had been the most discreet and sensible person whom I had known at that point in my life, a true friend. It was clear he reciprocated my feelings when he squeezed me into a bear hug — a most unusual thing for a Muslim to do. In addition, he said, "You may not believe me, but you're my only friend."

He quickly turned away, climbed into the truck, and was gone.

I thought about this Afghan a lot: he had been through so much to save his family. I thought about how difficult it must have been for him to feel affection for a person once again only to lose him. Perhaps he felt guilty for helping me meet Mariana — who knows? I won't ever find out.

The Peshawar airport was packed and, as I walked in the doors, I overheard an announcement on the loudspeakers announcing the arrival of a local flight from Islamabad. My plane was leaving in an hour and 15 minutes. I looked over my ticket. With time to kill, I began to observe the steady stream of people arriving. Almost all of them were merchants or peddlers, weighed down with bags and suitcases full of goods, as if they had disembarked from a bus.

Without knowing why, I fixed my eyes upon a slight young man — tall, with hair so short it was quite possibly just regrowth from having it shaved the week before. What caught my attention was that he was wearing a green cap and a bracelet of the same color, reminding me of the colors of Hamas. And he was limping, as though his right leg were in great pain. From the second I saw him, he seemed different from the other passengers, although I couldn't explain why. He only had one briefcase and a knapsack — not even a suitcase or duffel bag like nearly everyone else. I thought that perhaps my boredom caused me to imagine things by looking at someone whom I had never seen before, but I couldn't stop thinking that there was something familiar about him. I didn't know what to make of this mystery man.

20

LEONEL
Pakistan - Peshawar
October 17, 2011

Peshawar airport is tiny and archaic, even though its runways serve both domestic and international airspace. The city functions as a direct link to Afghanistan and other geographical sites in the region.

I had never suffered so much on a flight. The plane was like a bus; the aircraft was overflowing with luggage, and bags and suitcases occupied the most unlikely places in the cabin. From the moment when I boarded in Islamabad, until it finally took off, the plane rocked back and forth like a ship at sea, fighting an unseen battle against the tide and the wind. Vendors and dealers of goods they had bought in Islamabad could sell them for twice the price in Peshawar. Most of the people on board the plane had brought bags full of small boxes of cigarettes, alcoholic beverages, and other products for easy resale. Customs control must surely be "fixed," since none of these things were confiscated. I wondered if corruption had reached the Islamic world as well. I was impressed by the weight with which people had boarded the plane, and that wasn't even taking into account the baggage in the hold. I was afraid for a moment that the plane wouldn't be able to get off the ground due to the excess weight. But, after a fast lap around the runway and some whining from the engines, the airplane did take off normally.

Once in the air, traders began marching through the aisle as if they were still walking the city streets, and some even took the opportunity to sell their goods on board. My leg was still bothering me and, on the Paris–Islamabad flight, I had changed the bandages, more as a precaution than anything else. My Spanish passport allowed me to navigate unnoticed through passport control in Islamabad.

As the "troops" came down the plane, I put on the cap and wristband as agreed. My contact would identify me by these two green items. As I had carried on board nothing more than a carry-on bag and my brief-case, I had to wait for my luggage. As I passed the conveyor belt loaded with suitcases, I thought once again that these planes were generous and forgiving, as were the security agents.

I stood to one side and waited. Nobody approached me. The clock showed that 15 minutes had passed since my arrival. I was concerned that I had nowhere to turn, no name or address to go to if my contact fails to identify or see me. I began to worry, so I left the airport to see if my contact was waiting for me outside. Sweltering weather grabbed hold of me; a wet heat that could overpower anyone except the locals, who were already used to it. I remembered the Israeli hamsin[23], although that weather was a little drier and more intense. I went back into the terminal, back into the air-conditioning, and decided to wait another 15 minutes. A Gulf Air flight was announcing its departure to Cairo via Islamabad when someone touched my shoulder. I turned around to see a short man with curly, black hair and a large, purple birthmark on his neck. He offered his hand in greeting and said, "I'm Ali, your contact. Let's go, quick!"

His English was difficult to understand, but he searched carefully for words to make sure that I understood, and his urgency was clear by his tone. He wanted to take my bag, which I appreciated, and he brought me outside to the carpark. We climbed into an old Subaru from the eighties. The air-conditioning, if it had any, didn't work. We made our way through traffic to the city center with the windows open, so when we finally arrived at the Rose Hotel, located next to the central market, I was sweaty and nauseous. The hotel was somewhere between four and five stars in Pakistani style, which was far removed from the standards of the Western world. The floors looked pretty dirty, and dust-covered furniture told a tale of another time in history. I didn't know why Ali

---

23 Hamsin: A hot, dry wind that occurs in Northern Africa and the southern Mediterranean region.

had chosen that hotel; along the way I had seen others belonging to international chains such as the Holiday Inn, for example. I asked Ali to give me some time to freshen up and rest — perhaps even sleep a little.

The Rose was a five-story building that was close to everything; the center was about five blocks away and the market operated almost on its doorstep. Afterwards, I came to realize that this spot was one of the most popular and bustling intersections in Peshawar. The building had been remodeled and painted white, and the large windows gave it a very peculiar appearance. It took up a whole corner on the block; at the very top, it sported a red sign with the symbol of the hotel, its initials.

The staff were very attentive to the guests. I met Mr. Prince straightaway, who informed me of the most interesting places in Peshawar which I didn't even ask. I listened to him while he spoke excitedly about the city, which, even without having seen it, I seemed to know already. He was one of those people who are so passionate about what they do that they dedicate themselves to their job with pleasure. After it became obvious that he would never stop talking, I decided to explain to him that I needed rest and I would contact him later.

The best part of finally reaching my room was enjoying the air-conditioning, even though the equipment was stuttering and coughing, as if threatening to leave me without the basics — namely fresh air — in a place like this. I opened the mini bar, which, based on the Islamic status of the hotel, was completely devoid of alcoholic beverages. A large sign on the refrigerator informed me that this was the case. The Pepsi I took out was room temperature, as if the refrigerator wasn't even on. "Perfect," I thought, "this is all I need." I used a washcloth to bathe to avoid getting my bandages wet, then threw myself on the bed, but I couldn't sleep because of the noise from the street in the middle of the working day. It was awful.

Ali was waiting for me in the reception area. Mr. Prince tried again to bend my ear with stories of his walks through the city, but Ali said something in Arabic, and he walked away without saying another word. Once again, we climbed into the Subaru, which was smoking like a chimney. Given the noise and the smell, the tailpipe must have been full of holes. The heat was abominable and flies — the stupid things — relentlessly dive-bombed our faces as we tried to swat them away. In a nightmare of open windows, heat, and flies, we continued on our way.

I asked Ali where we were heading.

"I want to show you the place where I saw Ahmed for the last time," he said.

Ali was very skilled at the wheel, which turned out to be essential for navigating the narrow streets, where vendors, bicycles, and pedestrians were on par with cars in their road presence. The most striking thing I saw was the heartrending scene of children begging, while women in burqas walked the streets, eyes vacant and otherworldly like ghosts, their souls forever tormented and in limbo. Children and women — mostly Afghan — filled the area, each one a mere shell of hunger and misery.

Ali promised me that as soon as we had free time, he would take me to the Afghan refugee camps, which were located almost on the border. He also mentioned the strengthening Taliban control in Peshawar, to the point that they already had taken over the government offices in the center. From those offices, they were issuing visas to visit Afghanistan.

"They're cruel," Ali said to me. "I have seen people who have suffered their brutality and now live in the shadow of fear. It's terrible what's happening on the other side of the border, and the worst part is that the Pakistani government seems resigned to what is happening and is not doing anything. They feel paralyzed; they no longer know what to do, how to proceed. I think the Americans have suggested that they should stay quiet and do nothing so as to avoid getting involved in the conflict."

As he spoke, Ali added more than meaning to his words. When he mentioned the Taliban and their savagery towards women, his eyes reddened and quickly welled with tears. Afterwards, he told me that his wife was an Afghan refugee who had suffered the indignity and irrationality of that group — actions from which she would surely never recover, and which he would never forgive.

I must admit that the trip was emotional. When Ali stopped the car, I saw that he was having trouble regaining his composure. I patted his shoulder to show my concern and compassion.

"Look," he said pointing to the Red Cross offices, "I saw him there recently. He came to visit a girl with blonde hair. By the manner in which she was wearing her chador, I'm almost sure she was not Pakistani or Muslim. Plus, it is very rare to see blonde women here. Look around to see if you see any blondees," he said.

I froze when I saw the red symbol. What a twist of fate! The Red Cross once again appeared on the scene. Ahmed with a young volunteer? The story sounded very familiar to me.

Ali offered to take me back to the hotel, but I told him I would stay there. The market was open, so I would take advantage of the opportunity to visit it. We didn't plan anything, but he promised to contact me.

For the time being, I had no strategy for the moment when I found Ahmed. What would I do? What would I say if we met face to face? How would I convince him to come with me? How would I establish contact with Rachel? What role would the Mossad play? Would they help me or the other way around?

I had many questions and no answers. But, as Ahmed had still not come into my life in person, I had time to speculate. I got to thinking that maybe this time the truth was the best strategy. The story of the two young children switched at birth — surely it would intrigue him and awaken his interest in finding his true roots, his origin. As I could not reveal the details, I would maintain that I did not know them, and would explain that I had to take him to Rachel Mizrachi in Jerusalem, for only she could provide the evidence about what had happened.

Undoubtedly, the fact that Ahmed was a member of a terrorist group did not help these possibilities. Added to this, my Israeli identity decreased to zero my chances of getting him to come with me to Jerusalem. I thought again of the other young man, who, despite being Palestinian, became Jewish through the irrationality or error of a nurse. Or was it all planned? Where was this young man? Why did Rachel Mizrachi want to find Ahmed first and not the other? I realized that she had told me very little about the other boy; maybe she already knew a lot about him and didn't want to get involved. But these were all idle speculations. I had not had time to clear up my doubts since that day in the hospital; they were all too present in my head, even though acting now was necessary. Overwhelming myself with these thoughts would not help me now. I was in too deep deliberations, and decided to leave it alone for the moment, but each time it became increasingly difficult.

It was 5 p.m., but the sun stayed strong in a grayish sky and continued to harass the old city.

The Red Cross was set up in a building undergoing renovations, but I had the impression the work had been suspended for some time. A gate, a door on the side, and a scarlet cross were the only things visible from the street. Who would I ask for? The only information I had was just one name — Ahmed — and the hair color of the girl who appeared to be Muslim, of whom Ali had spoken. I stayed outside for a while, watching and trying to come up with some ideas. Vagrants came and went; a swarm of beggars swirled in front of me, begging for change. I told myself I could not stay here long. My tourist look was not suitable for walking these streets, so I chose to move and headed towards the shuk, the local market. As I expected, the market was crowded, my path hindered by people in every direction. It was different from Israeli markets, as in this one you could buy everything: goats, dogs, electronics, computers, groceries — everything was there at your fingertips. Afghan refugees sold what they could, but there was one group in particular that caught my attention: they specialized in bird cages. The smallest cost 25 rupees; the large ones, 60. The children were helping to make them.

A little cage took half a day of work; to build a large one, they worked all day. They were all engaged in the task. This was no place for the lazy. I even seemed to recognize people who had been on the same plane as me, who sold cigarettes and other prohibited goods.

Suddenly, the crowd began to open, split in two, as if a bulldozer were passing through it. Three men walked through the open space, dressed in white robes with color-matched turbans on their heads.

All three were very similar, as if they were brothers. Their thick moustaches seemed like copies. Frightened people parted before them. The three also carried baton-like sticks. In their wake, Afghan refugees gathered their things and fled in terror. Although I didn't quite understand what was happening, I took refuge in a sports shop that sold international clothing brands. Upon entering, I asked the shopkeeper, who looked nervous as well, what was happening.

"Taliban," he answered in strange English.

Agitated, he told me that they were trying to impose their power in the city. They charged rent from the market stalls, even though none belonged to them, and they acted as front men at other times, receiving bribes and all kinds of benefits.

"Look over there," he instructed as he pointed to a Pakistani police officer. "They become blind when the Taliban are around. It is said they receive money to ignore their presence. Those bastards also help to identify new businesses. The Taliban kick out anyone who doesn't pay, forcing them to close their businesses down."

The incidents he described were not entirely unfamiliar to me. I remembered a documentary that captured how the Taliban treated the Afghan people, but I had no idea that they had expanded so much, let alone that they were beginning to control Pakistani territory. But Peshawar was a city considered "no man's land" — something like a bridge between two sections of a divided territory; the meeting place of two opposing worlds.

I returned to the Red Cross an hour later with a strategy in mind. I knocked on the door, where I was met by a small man with a long chin. He had Western features; his pastel-white skin struggled to conceal the mole that had taken residence just below his mouth.

He immediately realized that I wasn't local, and adjusted his demeanour accordingly, becoming friendly. He even smiled.

"What can I do for you?" he asked.

"Good afternoon. I am from Spain, in the fourth year of my medical degree, and I'm doing work on common diseases in the Middle East. I thought I could help here. Perhaps I could talk to a doctor or nurse with experience in these matters. I think Red Cross people are the ones with the most knowledge of the subject."

"Indeed, we practice in these areas, and in other human health issues," he said.

He told me that the local population kept them completely snowed under; these people were often sick — especially beggars, although there were some who abused the help they were given, using it as an opportunity to steal.

"I am a medical student, too," he added. "My name is Heinrich; I'm German. I just finished my fifth year with the Faculty and I will remain here for one month. I can help you; come in and I will introduce you to the staff."

We walked down a long corridor that ended in a decent-sized yard with a very old fountain in the center. Suddenly, from a distance, I saw her. She was unmistakable: her long, dark-blonde hair cascaded down her shoulders, the sight of which sent a shiver through my entire body. Her chador was an extension of her beauty — and she was radiant. Her soft, white skin and luscious, red lips consumed my thoughts for a moment, yet I began to doubt if it was really her. If it was, what was she doing here? I was completely confused.

As I walked over to her, I saw that she was attending to a child who had a hand injury. When I got closer, I noticed the small boy biting down on his lips to counteract the pain; he had nasty burns, and my fleeting observation predicted they were of the first degree variety. As she sat there with her back to me, smearing ointment on the boy, a Spanish doctor stepped forward and very politely introduced himself to me.

"My name is Juan Hidalgo. I'm told you're from my country. Where exactly do you come from?"

I was about to respond, when Mariana turned to me. She had a jar of vaseline in her hands and, seeing me, the pot fell to the floor. Her hand went to her mouth in surprise.

"What part of Spain were you born in?" Hidalgo insisted. "I'm Valencian."

The last thing I needed right now was this nosy Spaniard interposing himself between Mariana and me. Clearly, I was as dumbfounded as she was. What was she doing here? Just a few days ago, we had shared a lustful night in Gaza.

"Hey, man, I'm from Madrid. Now, if you don't mind, I have to talk to the girl," I said to the doctor, scowling, to make sure he understood that his presence was unwanted. He got my message and left. As he was walking away, I heard him say that I didn't have an accent from Madrid.

"What are you doing here?" I asked Mariana.

"More like ... what are you doing here?" Mariana replied accusingly. "At the very least, you owe me an answer — a simple explanation ..."

The first answer that came into my head was that I had come for her. What else could I say? Love could conquer all. There was no better excuse and it was perfect for the situation. Watching her, I was certain that everything I had felt — and still felt in that moment —was love, real love. There was my blonde princess, with her fair hair and angelic face. I wanted to touch her, kiss her, make her mine — but that would be imprudent, a misstep. Her eyes showed no sign of love; her expression was not that of a girl who has just seen her boyfriend again after a few weeks. On the contrary, her face showed anger and disdain. Mariana had been taken by surprise, and perhaps the shock of the moment prevented her from expressing anything other than frustration and fury. When she heard my story, she didn't believe it at all. She lowered her head and sighed. When she saw Juan Hidalgo approaching a second time to take part in the conversation, she told me this was not the best place for explanations.

I promised the Valencian that we would return in 10 minutes and then we went outside. Mariana covered her head with the chador — a fact that seemed natural and strange at the same time, because she had not used it in Gaza. I imagined that covering her head, rather than being an act of respect toward Islam, was a way to conceal her true feelings.

"I know everything. Judy told me everything. You are Israeli. You have been lying to me from the very first moment. Why have you done that?"

It was like a bucket of cold water. I had no excuses, Judy had unmasked me. Or rather, she had revealed the truth.

"Look, Mariana, I'm a medical student, an Israeli. I genuinely came to work on a university project with the Red Cross. I didn't tell you because I thought that if anyone found out my Israeli identity, I would be at risk. I felt worried and afraid. Then Judy offered me a new identity and, as she had introduced me under that name to the whole group, I kept up that story with you, too. When our relationship became ... closer, I thought about confessing the truth. But then they called me urgently to Israel and I had to drop everything and leave."

At that moment, she took the chador off her head. She was upset, which was reflected in her usually white cheeks, reddened now by anger.

"Leonel, I know there's something else. What are you hiding from me? I really do not know who you are ..."

"And what are you doing here?" I asked.

"A few days after you left, I asked for a transfer. I was tired of Gaza, the constant danger ... I wanted to clear my head. I thought it would take time to find somewhere else, but after two days, Judy gave me the transfer letter. It was a miracle."

Suddenly, from behind us appeared the three Taliban men from the incident that had occurred just moments before in the marketplace. I recognized them easily. They came with two Pakistani policemen. All at once, shouting something in Arabic that I couldn't understand, they began to drag Mariana away. One of them immediately covered her head with the chador, while the other pulled her by the hands. In that moment, it occurred to me that she had violated the standard of women's clothing in public — rules of the Taliban world — even though we were in Pakistan. When I tried to stop them, one of the men hit me on the back with an object that I couldn't identify. The impact made me stumble and fall to the ground. I began shouting "Stop!" repeatedly in English and received another blow, this time from a policeman's baton, the impact of which left me splayed out. From the ground, I could see the commotion, the crowd, and Mariana being led to a white car that bore no police symbol.

I began to feel a cold sweat and my head felt heavier than usual. The second blow, which had struck me at the nape of my neck, had nearly knocked me out. I realized I was losing consciousness, and then...

***

I woke up in my hotel room. I dimly recognized Ali standing before me. My head still hurt and everything was spinning. Ali had been called urgently by the Mossad, who had been notified of the events via the GPS chip embedded in my skin, of which I had forgotten. It might have saved my life. Maybe being a human computer was not so bad. Ali told me that he had picked me up in the street as people in the crowd were trying to help me.

"I checked with the Red Cross and everything is OK. You have a bruise on your neck that apparently made you lose consciousness for a while. Juan Hidalgo, one of the doctors who treated you, wants to talk to you. I did not let him enter. He's waiting in the reception area."

I felt like I had a bag of rocks in my head and a plastic collar I found around my neck didn't allow me to move easily. It was all coming back to me slowly; I was remembering the last moments, up until the second blow, and then the name Juan Hidalgo popped into my head. Why would the Spaniard from the Red Cross want to see me? Ali also explained that while other doctors and nurses had wanted to take me to the hospital for observation, Juan had said it was nothing, that I would be more comfortable in the hotel and that he would take responsibility for going back to check on me. I didn't want to see him, especially now that I was so confused. I told Ali to explain that I didn't feel well and that I couldn't receive him right now. Ali went down and, after five minutes, there was a knock on the door. When it opened, there in front of me stood Juan Hidalgo himself. Ali came up behind, saying he couldn't stop him.

"Thank you very much for your help, Dr. Hidalgo; I very much appreciate what you did for me, but now I would prefer to rest and be alone," I said in an attempt to evade him.

"Leonel, I must speak with you briefly. It's really urgent." His face was a picture of worry. I didn't understand what the issue was, but I decided to listen, as I couldn't see a way to get rid of him. I told Ali I would be all right, and to come back to check on me later.

After Ali had closed the door behind him, I asked, "Well ... tell me what is so important that it can't wait."

"My real name is Gerard Loung. I'm American and I work for the CIA, the United States Central Intelligence Agency. I'm an expert in computer science and security. We've received a report from a very reliable source indicating that Hamas is planning a computer attack on Israeli intelligence services and, therefore, I'm here for information. The CIA and Mossad are working together on this. I know you're a Mossad agent."

These revelations caused me to momentarily forget about the drums that were pounding in my head. Juan, Gerard — or whatever his real name was — was speaking fluently without thinking or pausing; it seemed as though he was making a television announcement. I remembered the first time I saw him at the Red Cross; he had been speaking Spanish very well, with the accent of a Spaniard. Now he made his revelations in polished English, with an American lilt.

He was a tall man. He didn't seem particularly North American, especially because of his dark skin and bushy eyebrows, which met just above his nose. While observing his appearance, I was thinking about the credibility of his story. At the same time, I wondered why Ben and Yoni hadn't warned me about my alleged American partenaire[24].

"Where did you get your Spanish identity from? Why did you choose the Red Cross?" I asked, trying to get more information to validate his story.

"I have studied Spanish my whole life. My mother was Spanish and my father, American. I spoke Spanish with my mother at home, and then perfected it at university. I even carried out a few missions in South America. As for the Red Cross, it was the CIA's idea, as we have a contact on the inside here. In addition, I began my studies in medicine, which I broke off when I was in my fourth year and decided to move to computing. All this contributed to me being assigned to this mission. Look, I know that in the world in which we move, it is hard to believe anyone, but I can assure you I'm on your side. I know you come from France, you studied medicine, and you were a 'volunteer' like me in the Red Cross in the Gaza Strip. I also know that you live in Tel Aviv, more precisely on Mapu Street, and that your family is from Argentina. That's only a brief summary, of course."

My mouth was open, but I closed it quickly to hide my astonishment. This man knew a lot about me; he even spoke about my parents. I realized that I had been targeted by the Mossad this whole time, maybe since Rachel Mizrachi had contacted me. What did they know about this contact?

I tried to calculate the man's age. I figured he had spent four years in medicine, more on his computing degree, plus he worked with the CIA … he looked to be no more than 40, but that wasn't necessarily relevant. Whether I liked it or not, I now had a partner and I should get used to the idea. In fact, there were probably many more comrades of whom I still didn't know. This game was totally out of my control. I felt like a puppet being manipulated by strangers, in a scene where there were only three people, including an American.

As Gerard began telling the story of his life, I began to consider that perhaps creating compelling stories was part of CIA training. Why try to impress me now, in the situation that I was in? I thought maybe he wanted to gain credibility with what counted: medical studies at UCLA,

---

24 Partenaire: A French term for someone who accompanies you in the role of your significant other.

and then technology at university to complete his degree in computer science, specializing in computer security. Then he obtained a master's degree in systems security at Yale University a few years later, where he stood out for having the best grades, and was then invited to take tests to join the systems section of the CIA, where he began working in intelligence just one month after completing his studies. After that, he spent two years in Bolivia on an operation he couldn't reveal, and a year in Brazil helping the intelligence services of that country detect fraud in electronic accounts affecting senior leaders.

Then he headed back to North America to join the NSA, in its encryption department, which is one of the most secret and secure institutions in North America, and there he spent five challenging years working on special coding projects and the sterilization of systems. He said he had joined the team that built one of the largest and most powerful decoding systems so far. Finally, he explained that three months ago, his former boss had called to order him back to CIA headquarters in Colorado, because they needed him for a special mission in the Middle East.

"And here I am," he smiled. There was no doubt that he hadn't left out any details about his credentials.

If I could be sure of anything with Gerard, it was that we would not have computer problems.

Another important detail that I noticed was that he had declined to comment on his personal life. Was it forbidden by the CIA? I wondered, ironically. But I quickly stopped thinking about that. I already had enough going on in my own life. Another question that troubled me for a moment was that he appeared not to be aware of my relationship with Mariana. Or was he playing a role perhaps?

"And what's the plan?" it occurred to me to ask. "How are we going to work?"

"I'm here for two weeks. We're investigating the IT structure of Hamas and we've heard about Ahmed Asad, but the most important thing for us is knowing what their plan is — to anticipate and destroy it. We have information that technical specialists responsible for this objective operation in this city. Last week, I was intercepting emails, trying to unravel unknown codes that are slowly leading me to where they are hidden. You can help me with Mariana."

"Mariana? How can I help you with Mariana?" This man never ceased to amaze me with all the information that he possessed.

"I know she recently met a young man who we believe was Ahmed Asad himself."

I couldn't believe my ears, and, at the same time, I began to fear for what might happen to Mariana. If she was involved with Ahmed, perhaps her chador lapse was not the reason for her arrest.

"We have to find her," Gerard said. "She was the key until you came. I'm staying in a decrepit apartment I rented in the city center, where, with the help of my NSA colleagues in America, I established a mini-system to intercept emails. It's very similar to what we have at the NSA to monitor all outgoing and incoming emails in America. This is an exact copy, but in miniature. I intercept them using an algorithm that filters everything that comes in and out of Peshawar. It is based on two pieces of information: IP addresses assigned to this area and the defining domain names ".com.pk" and ".com," but we also process a lot of simultaneous online information. We have in our possession a huge database, which helped us to implement the system here. From the Red Cross, where I enrolled as a volunteer to create a cover, I go home once a day to check the information processed by the program. We had to modify the software to extend it so that it intercepts all domains and IP addresses, as we were not getting the results we were expecting. A few days ago I saw Mariana two or three times with a young man, a fact that I reported to our headquarters in America. They sent me pictures and I discovered that it was Ahmed Asad."

"And how was Mariana linked with this young man?" My question had more to do with my personal feelings than work.

"I don't know; I don't have any information on that. In the CIA, we don't know Mariana well. Mossad didn't tell us anything about her. In fact, just yesterday I confirmed that she's a nurse, the daughter of a Palestinian father and Danish mother. She worked as a volunteer at the Red Cross base in Gaza, from which she transferred to here."

She had told me about the transfer, but I suddenly realized that something strange was happening in the midst of this tangle of events. I sensed that someone wasn't telling me the whole truth, and I considered the possibility that everything — absolutely everything — was a big lie. At this point, I couldn't investigate; I was already in the game, so I had to move forward and play, without losing sight of my mission to take Ahmed to Rachel. Only then could I receive the million shekels. I had been presented with a great new mystery: first from Mossad, and then the CIA on these alleged plans to destroy some kind of information warfare program that Hamas had prepared, something that I didn't need to be involved in but in front of which I was now standing.

Gerard gave me his cell phone number and left, recommending that I get some rest. The next day he would make sure to ask the Red Cross to find out the whereabouts and status of Mariana.

Gerard had just left the room when Ali came in.

"Do you need anything else?" he said

"No, thank you, Ali. I just need to rest."

"If you need me for anything, contact the reception, ask for me, and I'll be here immediately."

I liked Ali's attitude. He hadn't asked me anything about Gerard, nor about the beating I had received. He was quiet and acted in a trustworthy manner. I started thinking that maybe he was aware of everything, after all.

The name Mariana was still hovering around in my head like a riddle that was difficult to solve. The woman I loved was now in danger, and it might be my fault — I didn't know. I had no choice but to wait for Gerard to exert his influence with the authorities at the Red Cross. Or would it be better if I went myself to the foreign affairs office that the Taliban had in the city center? I would have to think about it. By a trick of fate, Mariana had changed my direction. Instead of seeking Ahmed, doing everything possible to save her had become my immediate mission.

I tried to get out of bed, determined to act immediately, but as soon as my body separated from the mattress, the world began to spin; an unpleasant dizziness pulled me back, and I unwillingly spent some time staring at the ceiling — static, motionless. Once I could, I redoubled my efforts. I removed the plastic device they had put around my neck and, almost without realizing it, I was suddenly in the street suffering the stifling heat. Before leaving, I had inquired at reception as to the location of the Taliban offices and whether they worked at night — a question that stunned the receptionist.

"What do you want with the Taliban?"

I thought that telling the whole story would be complex and dangerous all at once, so I pretended that I wanted to visit Afghanistan, and I needed a Taliban visa to allow me to cross the border. The employee fidgeted before disappearing into the office, where he made a phone call and came out. "You're lucky — they work until 10 o'clock at night." Then he wrote the address in English on a piece of paper. I asked for it in Arabic as well, as I would be traveling by taxi.

The Taliban offices were located in one of the newest buildings in the center of Peshawar. When I arrived, two guards had taken posts at the door, armed to the teeth, as if they were expecting to engage in some sort of battle. They both had white turbans on their heads, and their appearance was that of twins. Actually, all of the Taliban members looked the same to me. They looked at me contemptuously and asked me what I wanted. I informed them of my intention to get a visa to visit Afghanistan, a request to which they nodded and let me pass. At the end of the corridor was a tall man wearing a white turban and tunic, with well–polished black boots that reached to his knees. The skin on his face had given way to coarse whiskers, and his green eyes possessed a penetrating, intimidating look, making him stand out from the others there. He said something in Arabic that I couldn't understand, so I asked him to speak in English. In heavily accented English, he asked what I was looking for. I knew it would not be easy to strike up a conversation with this man.

After exchanging words and mimicry for a while, he understood that a friend had been arrested by the Taliban and I was coming to get her. The Taliban took a black folder from a drawer. He asked the name of the woman I wanted and began leafing through the pages of the folder. He didn't make much effort, and after two or three minutes, said, "Not here."

I was losing patience, so somewhat exasperated, I rebuked him: "What do you mean, she is not here? I want to talk to your superior, someone who understands English."

He didn't like the tone of my voice at all. I knew that one false step could get me into trouble. The Taliban rose heavily from his chair, stared at me, put his face close to mine and shouted, "Not here!"

"I want to talk to your superior!" I insisted.

This got him angry — I could see it in the way he was acting. But suddenly, a man came out of another office, short and with the typical mustache but no turban, which seemed strange to me. He was also dressed like a Westerner, not wearing the white robe, but pants and a shirt. He motioned the other to leave. Then he told me in very polished English that there was no one there with the name of the person I was looking for.

"Why not? She was arrested about four or five hours ago near the market. I was there and saw everything. The woman was working at the Red Cross — she is a nurse." The words tumbled out of my mouth.

"Well, I have no information about it," he replied impassively.

Upset, I tackled him again. I tried to control myself, but I couldn't stand that he would lie like that to my face. Also, an old lesson I learned once in the army, came to mind: never accept "no" from a person who will not say "yes."

"And who are you?" he asked.

"I am a simple Spanish citizen, a friend of the kidnapped girl," I said, then tried to intimidate him. "Tomorrow you will have all of the international press here. Abducting someone from the Red Cross is a crime that the world condemns."

"Hey, Spaniard," he responded, "if you don't want to get into trouble, get out of here before those two (he pointed to the guards at the door) give you a similar lesson to the one you received a few hours ago. Maybe that one wasn't enough for you?"

His lie had been confirmed and my doubts were dispelled. The mention of the beating made it clear that this diabolical character knew who I was and where Mariana was. I turned around, thinking of the old proverb, "He who fights and runs lives to fight another day." I was unwilling to get another thrashing that would undoubtedly be more aggressive than the last. My body would not stand up to it.

Without another word, I left the office.

I returned to the hotel and asked the receptionist to call Ali. Twenty minutes later, he parked the Subaru in front of the door. I drank an ice-cold Pepsi in the bar downstairs. Ali was like my muhram[25], a name

---

25 Muhram: An escort or servant.

given to the guides in these lands. The muhram knows the routes and roads, and, most importantly, has contacts for accelerating bureaucratic processes. Ali was no exception. I told him my problems. He nodded; his expression hinted that he knew what was happening, but would never have gotten involved unless I asked. He mentioned a contact who could figure out where Mariana was, but he needed money.

"Money drives everything here," I was told. "We will need six thousand rupees to put my contact to work."

My quick calculations came to an equivalent of $100, a figure that was a fortune in the local currency, but I nodded. I asked when I could have the information and he told me it would be available in an hour. I deposited the money in his hands, and Ali left quickly. One hour was nothing, I thought. Perhaps his contact already had the details in his possession. I estimated that six thousand rupees would move mountains. The event had occurred in the middle of the street near the crowded market, in broad daylight — it would not be very difficult to find the information.

I went to my room. The receptionist gave me a strange look, like a visual slap, and I noticed that this was the second time he had done so. I didn't know what was up, but I didn't like it. It was as if he was keeping an eye on me, so I thought I would have to change hotels. Although Ali had recommended the place, I did not know who the good guys or the bad guys were in this movie of my life.

I had just sat down on the bed when the phone rang, shattering the tranquility. The receptionist transferred me the call: Yoni was on the other end of the line. We had already agreed in Paris that he would just give me a number that belonged to a payphone, and I would call back from another payphone. We would change phones each time we communicated.

I went downstairs and ventured outside. Next to the bar was a phone booth. I called from there.

"Listen to me, Leonel. Let go of everything to do with this girl."

Apparently the news spread very quickly.

"Abandon her? But she is our key to finding Ahmed. That's what Gerard, the CIA agent, said. By the way, why didn't you tell me that the CIA was also going after Hamas."

For a moment the line fell silent, but soon, nervous words rushed forth.

"What do you mean the CIA? And who's this Gerard? An intruder is trying to get in our way!"

I told the whole story of my encounter with Gerard after what happened with Mariana and explained that he had helped me. I tried to calm things down, explaining that I was unconscious in bed when Gerard barged into my hotel room.

"Leonel," he interrupted, "we had a lot of interference with your device, but I heard part of when you were talking to that guy. Do me a favor, for your sake, stay away from this Gerard at least until I do my research. Get away from the girl, too; she is extremely dangerous."

"But why? Give me at least one reason."

"Because if the Taliban are involved in this, this thing is serious, and we will double our problems."

"But Mariana is my clue, the only evidence that Ali showed me."

"Stop following that lead now. I need time to find out more. I'll send you a fax. At about 12 a.m., you must go to a kiosk located at number 20 Halal Street. Explain to the shopkeeper that you are expecting a fax, pay him 300 rupees, and he will deliver it to you. Bye."

I looked at my watch. It was 9 p.m. I was at the limits of my strength and didn't know if I could last for three more hours. As I was returning to the hotel, a honk roused me. I turned and saw Ali parking his vehicle. I was surprised how quickly the process had been. Either he had nothing, or he had it all.

"I have the information," he told me, though his voice did not show the normal satisfaction of someone who has done his duty.

"Tell me, man, tell me."

"They took her across the border."

"What do you mean?"

"They took her to Afghanistan; she is no longer here."

"Are you sure?" I asked angrily.

"One-hundred percent sure; there is no doubt."

I couldn't understand what had happened. What reason did the Taliban have to take Mariana out of the country? What benefit could she provide them? My stress was mounting and my interior dilemma, too.

Yoni had suggested I distance myself, but to me Mariana meant more than a million shekels and a game of espionage.

With the GPS installed in my body, I was like a human monitor. I could not lie to the Mossad. I had read stories recounting that when an agent did not follow instructions exactly, he was eliminated. They felt, it would endanger the integrity of the organization. I did not want that fate.

Ali left without asking questions. I needed advice, but my only guide had vanished quickly, as if sorry for the blow he had dealt me by delivering bad news. We agreed that he would take me to the kiosk at 11:40 to receive the fax; I would be waiting at the hotel reception.

I went to my room with the intention of taking a break. I was exhausted. To stay awake, I turned on the television, which was showing a very old American cowboy film, dubbed into Dari[26]. It was ridiculous to see John Wayne speaking in an Arabic dialect. I thought if he could come to life and see this situation, he would die again in disgust. Other channels aired in Pushtan[27], another local dialect. It seemed that television in this country had come to a standstill 20 years ago. Except for the color, I felt like I had gone back to a world of black-and-white interviews, spiritual speakers, and films from my grandmother's time. It was so boring that I fell asleep with the remote control in my hand.

Unable to find me downstairs by 11:50, Ali knocked loudly on my door. When I let him in, he confessed that he had been scared, thinking something had happened to me. I reassured him that it was only extreme exhaustion.

In order to arrive on time, we had to rush to the kiosk. It seemed to me that Ali was familiar with this strategy of receiving faxes in unknown locations. The kiosk was open 24 hours, so we didn't have any problems. Ali informed the owner of the place that we would receive a fax and I put the money on the counter while I stood next to the machine. It was 12 p.m. when heard a "beep" coming from the fax machine to signal a connection, but the pages were stuck and the delivery was interrupted. The owner of the machine removed the obstruction and adjusted the roller. There was a tense moment in which nothing happened.

---

26 Dari: A dialect spoken in Pakistan.
27 Pushtan: Another dialect spoken in Pakistan.

The machine remained silent and I thought I would lose the message. After a minute that lasted an eternity, the paper began printing. I took it without reading it and told Ali to take me back to the hotel.

I unfolded the fax in the solitude of my room.

And I read:

> Confirmed: Mossad is working with the CIA on the case, "Hamas Information Warfare." You can agree on strategies and actions with Gerard. Mariana seems to be the key, but we must avoid problems with the Taliban. Gerard will be easier to locate, since he is unknown to the Taliban. Meanwhile, we are working on a plan to rescue her and we have received news that she is in Afghanistan, where we also have a contact. Ali will give you our information on him. Until we have something definite, do nothing regarding her, await instructions, and continue with the search for Ahmed. We will contact you within 24 hours.

I was not impressed by the message. From the first moment, I had thought Gerard belonged to the CIA. What upset me was that everything was written in absolute terms, in a commanding manner. I was tired and it was already 12:30 a.m. — I had to make a decision. I had to take a chance on my instinct. Fate had reunited me again with Mariana for some reason.

I stared at the ceiling, hoping to find an answer. A spider was weaving a web to catch its prey. A huge, old-fashioned lamp hung over my head. One lightbulb was faltering, threatening to leave me in the dark. I moved closer to it, bothered by the flashing light. Standing on my bed, I started to unscrew the bulb and, in that precise moment, I saw the tiny camera beside it. I never thought they could make them so small. I left it where it was and hurriedly got down. I picked up my clothes and threw them all inside my bag, made sure that my computer was in my briefcase, then took all my luggage and left without looking back. I had already made my decision.

21

AHMED
Cairo, Egypt
October 18th, 2011

My trip was only supposed to take five-and-a-half hours, but it ended up lasting almost 16. The plane was unexpectedly grounded in Dubai due to a malfunction, so we had to wait for another flight from the same company to take us to Egypt.

I was planning to spend one day in Cairo. Late in the morning the following day, I would catch a bus from the central terminal to the Rafah crossing, and then take a taxi from there to the Gaza Strip. It was three in the afternoon and I had time to see a little of this unruly city, where intense traffic jams and disturbances were the norm. Reza had padded my pockets with $1,500 by way of Asher. I figured "one day of life spent idly is still living," and threw myself into the adventure. It had been a long time since I'd spent a day doing whatever I pleased, without thinking of serious matters, in charge of my own freedom and breathing in fresh air. Those days with Mariana had been amazing. To get to know and discover the woman she was had made me feel like a lucky man. Despite our cultural differences, I experienced a warm feeling of closeness between us, as if we had known each other forever and were destined to be together.

Cairo awed me with its climate, its people, its beggars. After more than an hour on the street I was left speechless by the enormousness of the city, impressed by its trade, its winding, narrow streets, its medieval buildings that housed oriental bazaars, and its Islamic architecture. At the same time, I was appalled by the pollution and the noise, the people constantly asking for handouts, and the prevalence of bakshish[28] in all types of businesses, as if there had been a call to action to beg on the streets. I quickly realized that it was a local custom and learned that it was better to give everyone a small amount than to give one person a lot and withhold money from the next hundred.

On foot, I toured throughout the beautiful city, lying forty kilometers along the Blue Nile, the city where the legends of literature frequently took place. Upon seeing it, I felt graced by the divine. I walked throughout the extensive museum and the cemetery upon which the city was built. I remembered reading that rich people with loved ones buried in the cemetery had built structures to monitor the crypts which eventually became guarded keeps on top of the graves. Gradually, a city was formed on top of the catacombs.

I went into an information center to see if they could recommend a relatively cheap hotel. They sent me to one that wasn't far from the city center. It had only three stars, but I was pleased upon entering the Hotel Pharaoh's Doki. Its white facade revealed seven floors, and my eyes took in the scope of its 102 rooms. Shortly afterwards, as I passed through Sheraton, I realized that I had been mistaken.

The receptionist assigned me to a budget room on the first floor that cost $100. It was not my idea of an affordable stay, but I didn't know what the going rate was in hotels anyway. Besides, the $1,500 in my pocket placed the room within my means — perhaps I could have even afforded to pay more.

The cozy room had a bathroom, a small TV, a mini bar, a safe, and a telephone with a direct line out — a real treat, I thought. But I had no time to lose, so I left my bag unpacked and went back outside to make my way toward the city center. I had to get to the bus terminal to buy my tickets for tomorrow to Rafah and find a taxi that would take me from there to the Gaza Strip. I knew which bus I would take; I just needed the tickets. When I reached the terminal, it was packed. I had never seen so many people so close together. They appeared to be moving about like ants — going from one place to another, weighed down by packages

---

28 Bakshish: Bribery

quite possibly meant to be lifted by two people together. The noise, the movement, and the commotion made me lightheaded. I sat on a bench next to a screaming baby, being held by a woman I presumed was its mother. I placed my head on my knees and closed my eyes for a moment to relieve the vertigo. When I opened them again, I no longer heard the baby's cries. The lady sitting next to me had been replaced by a tall, bearded man with a brown raincoat. Before I had a chance to suspect him, he pulled out a sharp object and placed it against my stomach while using his coat as a cover. I felt the steel pricking into my skin. Another man, bald, of average height, wearing dark glasses, stood next to me and whispered, "Don't move, if you want to keep your liver." The bearded man pressed his knife harder against my belly. "Come with us and don't say anything. Try to walk swiftly but as if nothing is out of order."

I nodded and obediently went with them. While the bearded man escorted me with his knife, the other walked on ahead, leading the way. I didn't know who they were, nor what they wanted from me. Perhaps it was all a plan from Hamas to get rid of me, or perhaps it was the Mossad. I couldn't organize my thoughts and I tried calming down, although the situation definitely didn't inspire serenity. We moved quickly towards a side street adjacent to the station, where an old, black Mercedes Benz appeared in front of us and stopped abruptly. The bald guy hopped into the front seat of the car, and the bearded man pushed me into the back. I tripped and banged my leg, and then got another strong push from the bearded man. In a second, I was lying in the back seat, helpless, as the man sat almost on top of me and slammed the door shut. As the car sped away, the bearded man urged me to lay my head on the seat and demanded that I stay down. His knife was now farther away from me, but still looked threatening. It was too risky to try for a heroic escape, so I resigned myself to wait and see how it all played out.

I didn't actually calculate travel time, but the whole process felt like an eternity. The situation was exacerbated by the traffic and the brutish manner in which our chauffeur drove. I was banged up from my chin to my legs from the constant braking, each time more abrupt than the last. When they finally pulled me out of the car, I felt like a cripple from all the blows. They took me to an extremely old three-story building. Again, the bald-headed man led the way. He opened the door and we followed him up to the top floor. Once inside an apartment, things began to change. I was allowed to sit in an armchair and they brought a jug with water and another with tea. The tension in the air faded. The bald man came over and said, "Ahmed, do not be afraid; we won't do you any harm."

"Who are you?" I questioned.

"We are part of the Islamic Revolution, a sect of the Iranian government. We need you to come with us."

"Go with you where?"

"To Iran."

"To Iran? What do you mean to Iran? I am Palestinian; I'm a militant of Hamas."

"Ahmed, we know you very well. We may know more about you than your mother. You will embark on an important, top-secret project. From now on, you will assume a different identity. We are aware that you have a Kuwaiti passport, and we will exchange it for an Iranian one. Tomorrow morning, we leave for Iran. Until then, we'll work on your personal traits."

"What do you mean?"

"We'll give you a beard and shave your head, and you'll wear dark glasses — at least until we get to Tehran."

It took me a while to get used to the idea that I had been kidnapped to be recruited for another project. I didn't understand what was happening. Had Hamas sold me? Was everything laid out for these guys? This turn of events added a new level of uncertainty to my situation. Iran was an extremely powerful country with a history of rebelling against all things Western, especially against the Israelis and Americans. Lately they had boasted of their nuclear progress, filling us Muslims with pride. Maybe all of this was part of the convoluted plan from the start. Perhaps my technical training with Hamas was all just to prepare me to help our Iranian brothers. Or it could be an alliance. So many hypotheses — I didn't know if any of them were true, and it didn't matter much at this point. I quickly understood that it was best to follow orders and do what my captors wanted. They were very nervous, anxious to finish their mission and drop me off in Persian lands. I deduced that any resistance on my part that they believed endangered their mission could make them fly off the handle.

They shaved my head, gave me a false beard, and took a picture for the passport. I was then given dark glasses. The driver immediately came back with my photo. I asked where he was going and the bald man replied that he was headed to the Iranian embassy to prepare my passport. When I heard that, I understood the magnitude of the mission. If the Iranian government was really involved in this project, then it had to be big — very important.

I must admit that that night I woke up and could have easily escaped. The bald man and the driver slept behind closed doors in different rooms. The bearded man, who served as my escort, snored like a bear. He wouldn't have budged if a tractor passed by. He had fallen asleep on the couch with a knife in his hand, but during his slumber had released his grip, causing the weapon to fall to the floor. I even had the pleasure of holding the knife in my own hands. The man was very close — so close that I could have easily cut his throat without him knowing. Although the door was locked, the windows offered an escape route. I thought about the possibility of taking one of the other men hostage and making him open the door for me to escape, but after a while I dismissed the idea. There was a reason that things were happening this way. Since my acts in Hamas had led Reza to deport me from Pakistan for violating the organization's rules, I couldn't hope for a rosy future or a warm welcome at the border with a red carpet and trumpets. I left the sharp object on the floor and tried to get some sleep.

The next morning, we were early to rise. Everyone was busy working and barely spoke to one another. I was instructed to get ready to get on a plane that day, which involved donning my disguise. With my beard and glasses, my 180–centimeter–tall frame added a special touch by making me look distinguished. We drove to the Iranian embassy in the black Mercedes, and the driver dropped us off at the door. Above us, the Iranian flag fluttered in the wind. As before, the bearded man escorted me and the bald man led the way. They were both known at the embassy. The building was one of the most modern I had seen in Cairo. The guards led us to a room at the end of the corridor, where we sat down to wait. The bald man told the other one that he should leave the room and wait outside. After five minutes, they brought a hearty breakfast of scrambled eggs, coffee, orange juice, a pita, hummus, and a slice of cheese. The bald man nodded his head in a gesture for me to eat. I was so hungry, that I think I started even before he gave me permission.

Ten minutes later, a well-groomed man in his sixties came in. He was dressed in an impeccable black suit and wore his silver hair slicked back, almost like a Sicilian mobster. He greeted me warmly and introduced himself as the Iranian ambassador in Cairo. I was dumbfounded. The bald guy hugged the ambassador as I looked on. The ambassador handed me a passport that displayed my picture and my real name, Ahmed Asad. As he did so, he said to me with a smile, "All right, you're Iranian now. Welcome to the Islamic Republic of Iran."

"But I am ..." I stammered.

"Now you are Iranian. Don't make trouble, this is all for your own good. It'll all make sense soon. Be patient. You will see things you've never seen in your life. You will work with the latest technology. You'll be surprised, I assure you."

I was speechless. I tried to say something, but the words didn't come out, so eventually I mumbled a "thank you" and shook his hand. The ambassador exchanged a few words with the bald man and left. I kept staring at my new passport; my new identity. I was no longer afraid. Two minutes earlier, I had been thanking my captors, and then received an official promise that this was all for my own good. Crazy!

I was literally ready for the next adventure. I was all for it because, apparently, despite the fact that my reputation had been tarnished a bit in Pakistan, the Iranians still showed interest in me and that was very auspicious.

The driver picked us up again and we traveled towards the airport, trying to avoid the heavy traffic. As we left, I looked back at the embassy and the Iranian tricolor flag waving above it in the wind. I guessed I would have to start warming up to the idea. Just like all other Palestinians, I felt like a true nomad — from Jerusalem to Bethlehem, from there to Jordan, to the Gaza Strip, Pakistan, and now ... Iran! What did my future hold? The driver dropped us off at the main terminal and went to return the rental car. The bald man told me to stay calm when they checked my passport. We would travel on a direct flight with Air Egypt to Tehran. The queue was endless. The bearded man was more friendly now, without the knife, of course, but always keeping me close by.

He smiled at me and said, "You'll see; the best Muslim women are in Tehran."

His smile revealed some unpleasant yellow teeth, covered in tartar. I smiled to try and reciprocate his friendliness, but a sudden image of Mariana and her magical smile came back to me, reminding me of that unknown dimension I had shared with her in such a short time. She would be difficult to replace. I wanted to know how she was doing — to tell her how I felt. I was dying to know if Asher had given her my note.

When our turn came, we were sent to another counter far away from the other passengers. An unfriendly-looking police officer was waiting for us. I showed him my passport. The officer reviewed and stamped it without thinking twice. That passport had no departure stamp, but he stamped it twice. That made me think that he was involved too. I supposed that the two embassies had made a deal. The mystery continued. The bald man cracked a smile as he saw the puzzled look on my face.

The flight went on without a hitch. I sat in the middle seat of a row of three. The bald man was in the window seat and the bearded man had the aisle; his snores kept me awake throughout the whole trip. The plane landed on time.

As soon as the aircraft touched ground, I noticed some vehicles with strange stickers driving next to the landing strip, staying alongside the plane. When we got out, everyone else proceeded towards the bus that would take them to the terminal, but we were transferred to a black car, which, accompanied by two other vehicles, sped us out of there before we could be seen. We left through an exit reserved for the army — I clearly recognized the signs. There was no passport control or baggage claim. It was nothing like a normal border crossing. A helicopter protected us from above. I looked up at the sky through the tinted car window and could see the Air Force Nuclear Unit insignia on the aircraft.

22

LEONEL
Pakistan - Afghanistan
October 18th, 2011

On my way to the street, all I was thinking about was how to get out of there as soon as possible. The idea of having been monitored the whole time by someone while I was in that room made me uneasy. The receptionist was surprised by my departure, and tried to get me to stay longer.

"Wait a moment, sir."

"No. Here's the money I owe. They are waiting for me."

"I have to prepare your bill ..."

"There's nothing to prepare. You asked me to pay 1,500 rupees per day for the room, I stayed one day and I paid for two, so we're all set. Goodbye!"

"No, wait!"

"No!" I retorted, and as he entered the office, I left the money on the counter and quickly hobbled toward the street. I turned the corner without reducing speed, but the pain in my leg was killing me. It was 2 a.m. and there was almost no one in the street. I kept up my pace while I had the energy, advancing in complete darkness. I reached a long corridor leading to a side street that seemed to be a dead end. I couldn't go on any longer. At the end, there was a white house, and although the street was pitch black, I saw small flashes of light, like reflections, that seemed to reveal an open steel gate leading up to the house. A closer look confirmed my suspicion. I opened the gate and saw tons of people sleeping on mats strewn all over the ground. I figured it was some sort of accommodation for refugees and tried not to make noise. I curled up along one side of the door and quickly succumbed to the fatigue and the pain.

When I woke up, two children were examining me as if I had come from another planet. I shuddered, still not knowing where I was. When they saw me getting up, they ran away and a man with a white turban, who had a long cut with stitches on his face, muttered something to me in Arabic I didn't understand.

"English, please."

I thought that would throw him off, but surprisingly, the man began to speak in very clear English, much clearer than others I had heard around here.

"Where are you from?"

"I'm Spanish. Forgive me for intruding, but I arrived in the city very late last night and didn't have anywhere to stay. I walked for hours until I found this open gate. When I saw so many people here, I thought I could get some sleep."

"Not a problem," he said. His response began to reassure me. "We're here to help one another. It doesn't matter where you're from; you have a place here in this house. That's why we leave the doors open."

We exchanged names. I preferred to keep my Spanish identity. His name was Muhammad and he said he was Afghani. He told me, he and two of his children had escaped three months of Taliban hell. His wife and other son weren't as lucky and the Taliban took them. He was able to escape with some of his family by jumping a fence that was almost two meters high, then digging a hole so the little ones could pass through. His face was filled with sadness, topped off by the gash that furrowed into his left cheek. He told me that barbed wire from the fence caught his cheek when he jumped over. Based on my medical training, what I saw on his face were some poorly done stitches that could become infected at any moment.

"Where did you learn English?" I asked.

"I studied electronics at the University of Kabul, and learned there."

I don't know why I felt I trusted him, but I didn't have many options, so I told him, "Muhammad, listen, I have to get to Afghanistan. I need to find a friend who was captured by the Taliban and don't know the way. I need someone to help me cross the border."

Muhammad smiled for the first time, completely altering the expression on his face.

"I also want to go back and find my people," he said. "I know the way, but I need the money. Here, money fixes everything."

"I've got the money, don't worry about that — but what will you do with your children? Who will take care of them?"

"I'll leave them with their aunt. In reality, she's already taking care of the children. She lost her husband; they killed him right before her eyes in the central square when they discovered he was against the Taliban. There she is." He pointed to a woman. "I have a cousin who remained in Kabul; he is living in hiding. He could help us at the border and take us to Kabul. When we get there, I'll look for my people and you do your thing. My big problem is getting in touch with my cousin, since he constantly moves from one place to another to avoid being caught."

"And will that take long? When do you think we could leave? I'm in a big hurry ..."

"I will try to have everything set by this afternoon."

"Good."

I decided the first thing to do was sort out the chip in my body that was constantly sending out information about my location. It definitely made me more vulnerable to being followed once again, and I couldn't leave Pakistan with that device functioning. Assuming that his studies in electronics would be of help, I asked Muhammad if he could disrupt GPS waves. I had to invent a story. I told him that I was part of a human experiment and, although I tried to make my story sound credible and natural, I realized that Muhammad was more interested in helping me than discovering why the device had really been implanted in my body.

"It's very simple," he informed me, "but I need some more money, because we have nothing here. To override the GPS signal I have to implant a device on you that produces a permanent noise — a constant sound around you. I'll do this by creating an electromagnetic circuit. I'll place the device in the belt that holds your pants up, so when you go through a metal detector you can remove it by taking off your belt. I'll need money to buy the circuits and a small tool."

"Are you sure you can do it? How will it work?" I was intrigued by this man's knowledge.

"The GPS receiver works by measuring its distance from the satellites and uses that information to calculate positioning. This distance is determined by calculating the time it takes for the signal to reach the receiver. Once that time is known, taking into account that the signal travels extremely fast, with the exception of some adjustments, you can calculate the distance between the receiver and the satellite. Each satellite indicates that the receiver is at a certain point on the surface of the sphere, with the center being the satellite itself, whose radius is the total distance to the receiver. With information from two satellites, we know that the receiver is on the circumference point at the intersection of the two spheres. If we get the same information from a third satellite, we see that the new sphere only intersects the previous circumference at two points. One of them can be ruled out because it offers an absurd position.

"This would give us 3-D positioning. However, since the clock that incorporates GPS receivers is not synchronized with the GPS satellites' atomic clocks, the two points in question are not entirely accurate. With information from a fourth satellite we can eliminate the distortion caused by this lack of synchronization of clocks. And that's when the GPS receiver determines an exact 3-D position, including latitude, longitude, and altitude. If the clocks between the receiver and satellites aren't synchronised, the intersection of four spheres centered on these satellites is a small sphere rather than a point. If that occurs, one has to adjust the receiver time until the sphere becomes a point. The electromagnetic field that I will place in your belt will block the signal between the satellites. The first and second satellites will be able communicate with each other, but the third and fourth will lose transmission and won't be able to triangulate to produce a valid signal. I'm going to prepare everything and, when I return, I'll bring the unit along with information about my cousin."

I was in shock. I didn't know how to thank him, even as I gave him the money to make his purchases. It was all too much. Before he left, he asked me not to move from here, as this place would surely not permit a GPS signal to escape — or rather, those on the outside wouldn't be able to access it.

The afternoon seemed like an eternity. I had sensed something special in those brown eyes that moved at full speed, and the colorful expressions of his eyebrows confirmed this. The Afghan seemed to be a man of principle, someone you could trust. Until then, the only person I could count on had been my muhram Ali, but after discovering the camera in the hotel, I also suspected that Ali was involved in my monitoring. In these lands, money was the boss, and he who paid the most bakshish received what he asked for. Maybe Ali had also had his price.

At 5:15 p.m., Muhammad was back in front of me. The smile on his face was a sign of good news. I had played with his children during the long hours I waited for him. It was impressive to see what a soccer ball made of rags could inspire in those who didn't have access to gaming consoles or computers.

"My cousin will be waiting at the border crossing early in the morning, around 7 a.m.," Muhammad said. Then he turned serious. "Now listen to me. It will be difficult — neither of us has a visa, although I think you can pass as a Spanish journalist and I could be your muhram. You will have to have money ready inside your passport."

"How much?" I asked, aware that I was already running low on funds.

"No less than a thousand dollars."

A thousand dollars! I had $1,500 and some coins.

In the meantime, I remembered that Rachel would have already deposited the 20,000 shekels at the Paris bank that I had asked for by email when it was decided that I would travel to Pakistan. Surely Moshe Cohen had already told her everything that had happened in the coffee shop in Talpiot.

"Now give me your belt," Muhammad commanded, showing me a round circuit with electrodes forming a field of mutual resonance. He cut the lining of the belt with a sharp blade and placed the circuit inside. He brought out a needle and thread and sewed the opening shut.

"And how will we know if it works?"

"If you want to test it, we can go to an electronics store. If your GPS is running, you will get another GPS signal. If you want to we can do it, but I assure you it works perfectly. My final thesis at the university was on satellites and triangulation systems."

Muhammad joined his kids in kicking the ball of rags, a smile lighting up his face. He surely felt the warmth of hope — a feeling so rare
in this place and at this time.

Neither he nor I knew what the following day would bring.

23

France
October 18th, 2011

The two screens were stained a dark blue color.

Yosi and Ben weren't too worried. Communication was often lost due to problems in the satellite's ability to capture the GPS signal. Meanwhile, the two continued with the task of deciphering the new data that had arrived from the Mossad offices in Israel. Since they had been in France, they'd already changed their address three times; moving hadn't been easy, as they had to move all the electronic equipment with them. This old house, located in one of the old quarters of Lyon, was a good refuge and had very good reception for the satellite system that the Mossad had installed in Europe. The two hoped that this was the last stage in the moving game. For safety, they mobilized every three months. If all went well with Leonel, they could return to Israel in two or three weeks. They would finish in Europe and would surely be replaced. This was how the rotation in the organization worked.

Suddenly, the signal returned to the monitors, but instead of the blue screen indicating the absence of reception, it had been replaced by a white screen with black lettering that read: " connection time-out, GPS signal lost." Ben checked the wireless connection and adjusted the position of the satellite transmitter, and everything appeared to be normal except for the screen. He disconnected, then reconnected and reinitiated the systems, but the white background and black lettering stayed on the monitors, something that very rarely occurred.

"Something's happened. We never lose the connection like this," worried Ben.

"What do you think it is?" Yoni demanded.

"Something's interfering. I think we're losing it."

"Call Roger," was Yoni's reply. Roger was the Mossad contact in Germany. Ben would ask him if he could detect Leonel's signal on their monitors. Ben picked up the secure landline and called Roger, a kaza[29] located in Frankfurt, who had a very similar setup to the one these agents had in France.

"It'll take him five minutes to connect; he'll call us back," said Ben.

After 10 minutes, the phone rang.

"Nothing? Are you sure?"

Yoni was sweating as he considered the implications of the absence of the signal on their monitors. As he hung up the phone, Ben shook his head and said, "Roger couldn't connect. He's getting the same signal as us."

"Call Israel immediately!" Yoni was about to explode, pacing from one end of the room to the other, forming invisible tracks in the carpet.

Ben stood with the phone in his hand for eight long minutes. Finally, he turned around and said, "Same result in Israel."

"No suggestions?" asked Yoni, nervously.

"None. They're going to connect with the CIA to see if they can locate him, with their equipment or through Gerard."

After half an hour, the phone rang in the small apartment in Lyon. This time, Yoni hurried and took the wireless with both hands, the same way he held his pistol in the firing position. Someone on the other side of the line said, "We've lost him!"

---

29 Kaza: An agent with the Mossad.

24

LEONEL
Afghanistan
October 19, 2011

I hadn't slept all night. A whirlwind of thoughts took its toll on my rest. I think I managed to fall asleep at around four, but my slumber was soon interrupted by a pat on the shoulder. I could barely open my eyes. When I managed to wake up, I was surprised to see Muhammad right in front of me, ready to go. In the absolute dark, he looked like a ghost in a dress, and he had a bag in his hand.

I wasn't worried; I was already used to surprises. I looked at my watch and saw that it was 5 a.m. The only light in the place came from my chronometer. I jumped up from the mattress, picked up my stuff and followed Muhammad. I gave myself a pat on the back for having gone to bed with my clothes on, as I had anticipated a quick getaway.

A taxi driver who knew Muhammad was waiting for us on the street, which made me feel calmer. The Afghan even made sure I fastened my seatbelt, something really unusual since I arrived here. We traveled over steep and mountainous terrain for half an hour. From time to time, the car would sputter and cough, threatening to leave us on foot. It was expelling lots of smoke, making it obvious that a vehicle had passed by. When we finally got to a high summit, the driver stopped his car and we got out. Muhammad paid the man and hugged him and the car drove off.

The sun hadn't risen yet, but it was starting to slide from its hiding place. Muhammad took out a flashlight, and we started walking downhill, navigating the rough, uneven surface.

"Where is the border?" The question came from my concern of walking there in the dark — and particularly on that terrain, which struck me as ominous and risky.

"We still have to walk for another half hour." It would have been very dangerous to continue by taxi, not only because of the characteristics of the road, but also because there were many thieves and vandals around there.

That walk seemed to go on forever. I couldn't see a border anywhere and the terrain had become steeper, making the climb even more difficult. Also, my injured leg hurt. Every now and then, Muhammad would stop and look at a map and a compass. It seemed to me that although he was an expert at electronics and satellite systems, in practice, he appeared to be more comfortable turning to devices used in the olden days. He stopped several times to look around, which made me suspect he was lost. Because I couldn't help much, I just kept silent and followed him. After about 40 minutes, we saw a light in the distance. The terrain had become much flatter. "Look, there it is," Muhammad whispered eagerly.

I was able to see the crossing point as we approached the border. On the other side of the road, the traffic was heavier. There were at least 10 tractor trailers, all attempting to enter Pakistan, and the line they had formed seemed to go on for several kilometers. On our side, there were just two cars and a family on foot who looked as though they had spent the night there. Nothing was moving on either side. I didn't know if the quiet was because the Taliban only started working after 9 a.m. — or because they were lazy.

Muhammad was nervous; he repeated and confirmed the plan to me in detail: the money in the passport, my fake ID of a Spanish journalist, his role as my muhram. I had to pretend I didn't know I needed a visa to enter Afghanistan. I knew everything I had to say like the back of my hand, but Muhammad kept repeating it like a formula, perhaps to calm himself down. We waited for an hour and a half in front of the post. When it was finally our turn, two Taliban soldiers took us to an old, white room where an exhausted-looking soldier waited behind a counter, under a fan spinning at full speed. These men were exactly what I had imagined a Taliban would look like. They even had swords hanging from their waists in a nod to the past. Although I doubted he spoke English, the first thing the waiting soldier shouted was a shrill, "*Passports!*"

I had fit the money between the pages of the document to keep it from falling down, and when I handed it to him, he looked at my passport, and, expressionless, stood up and told us to wait. Muhammad was sweating more than usual, the drops sliding down from his temple all the way to his curly beard. I wasn't calm, either, but from my experience on these lands, I knew that money could buy anything, from a man's freedom to his death, and so I figured that a visa to enter a country in a state of crisis would also be for sale. Besides ... who in their right mind would want to visit Afghanistan these days?

Minutes stretched on like an eternity, until a man dressed in black, without a tie, and with a folder in hand, asked us to follow him. He was of unusual appearance, and some of his features were Western. If my memory was correct, he was the first man I had seen there who didn't have a mustache. Muhammad kept sweating and it was obvious he was nervous. I gave him a handkerchief to wipe up the evidence. We went into an almost empty office with just three chairs, a table, and a picture of a man I didn't recognise wearing a turban and a handlebar mustache. I found it weird that there were no computers. How do they register people? I wondered.

The Taliban official took out my passport. Then, in plain English he asked me, "Don't you know that you need a visa to enter Afghanistan?" The Taliban stressed each word as he looked through the passport. The money was no longer there.

"Visa? No, I didn't know..."

"Well, now you do," he added, "What's the purpose of your visit?"

"I came to make a documentary about the sacred sites in Afghanistan."

"What TV network do you work for?"

"I usually sell my videos to the Spanish National network, TVE, but I'm a freelancer. I'm independent." I was afraid he was going to ask for an identification badge from some TV channel.

"Who is your partner?"

"My muhram, my guide." Muhrams didn't need passports or visas.

"What's your name?" This time he addressed Muhammad.

Muhammad stuttered when he said his name. We had agreed he would say he was Palestinian and that he had no papers. The Palestinians were welcomed by the Taliban.

When the interrogation finished, the Taliban man told us to wait. Muhammad had already gotten the square of cloth soaked in sweat and I explained to him that in the worst-case scenario, we would be deported to Pakistan.

"You never know what these men can do," Muhammad mumbled.

I felt so weird. I had come so far. Just a few short weeks ago I was in Tel Aviv, peacefully studying for my exams at the School of Medicine. Now, in such a short time later, I was risking my life at the hands of a second-class officer to whom I had given a rather good bribe.

The Taliban man came back after 15 minutes with my passport and a temporary visa in his hands. He showed me the stamp and told me that this would be the last time he would ever let me pass without a visa. He pointed out that I had to register at the Taliban office of Foreign Affairs in Kabul in 48 hours. He gave me a paper with the address written in Arabic.

"If you don't register, we'll search for you all around the country, and you'll be convicted according to the laws of the state."

That did not sound good at all. I wondered what country he was talking about when he said "laws of the state." To be more precise, he should have said Taliban laws. When we got outside and finally stood on Afghan soil, I turned to Muhammad and said with a smile, "Hey, they forgot to give me a receipt for the thousand dollars ..."

Muhammad laughed heartily, knowing I was joking. His nervousness evaporated. He knew the area and the route well, so he took over and led the way.

"Where is your cousin?" I asked.

"We need to walk about 20 minutes more to find him. It's too dangerous to park close the border."

We walked on the shoulder at the side of the road. The scene was desolate and there was no traffic, just a few taxis going in the opposite direction, towards Pakistan. The family that had been in front of us in the line was nowhere to be seen. Muhammed assumed they had been sent back to Peshawar.

When we arrived at the agreed-upon place, an intersection, Muhammad's cousin was waiting for us on the right side of the road. Only the two of them could have found that place. They hugged intensely and exchanged a few words I didn't understand. His cousin came to me and shook my hand politely. He was wearing dark glasses and the traditional white gown, which covered his entire body. His radiant smile was gleaming.

His car was a Peugeot 404 wagon. When we took off, I doubted it could take us all the way to Kabul, even without knowing the distance. I never imagined that a car could make such sounds. The heat was overwhelming, and the air conditioning quite obviously didn't work. I never ceased to be amazed by the ability these people had to drive on these highways, riddled with unforgiving weather and transported by substandard vehicles that could quite easily be called death traps.

Muhammad's cousin had booked us into a hotel, because with the whole journalist plan, it was the most convenient thing to do. After about four hours of driving, we arrived at an especially modern and clean hotel in the center of the city called the Spinzar. Surprisingly, the building was in perfect condition — which was very unusual, especially in that place. What's more, the staff were very helpful; they registered my passport and temporary visa and they also reminded me that I had to go to the Taliban office either that day or the next. I was literally melting in the heat of the day; a thermometer in the wall showed 39 degrees in the shade, and delirium was beginning to set in. I was saying yes to everything. That journey had been an exhausting odyssey. Muhammad, on the other hand, wasn't suffering at all; he was thoroughly used to the heat. The air-conditioning in reception was exactly what my body had been craving. It came just in time, too — I was about to collapse.

The room they gave me was climate controlled, which helped me recover. I threw myself on the bed, a tired victim of dehydration. I needed to keep my body cool and drink as much water as possible, although I knew well that the only thing that could actually help was a bag of saline. Seeing how bad I was, Muhammad asked me if I wanted him to go get medical help. I don't remember what I replied, but I know I passed out, asleep.

When I regained consciousness, five hours had passed and Muhammad was sitting by the side of the bed. I searched for some sign of a needle indicating I had been given saline, but I didn't find any. Muhammad explained to me that I had fallen asleep and so he left me alone. The exhaustion could have been fatal, but fortunately, thanks to my sleep, my body found the strength to function again. I was still weak, but I felt much better.

We went down to the restaurant and had some appetizing local delicacies, which I found too spicy, but if I wanted to get better, I needed enough food. It was already 6 p.m.

Muhammad asked me what my plan was.

"To tell you the truth, I don't know where to begin. I think I'll start by going to the Taliban office to register. There, I'll try to find out about Marianna, my friend. What do you think?"

"You know that money is everything around here; if you want to find that girl, you'll need it."

I knew I needed to make a transfer, and one thing I was sure of was that anything I decided to do — no matter what — I would have to do it quickly and efficiently; there was no room for mistakes.

"What about you? What are you going to do? From now on, you can get on your way and look for your family. I appreciate everything you've done for me, but your family is more important than anything."

"My cousin has a plan. Anyways, I'll try to stay in touch with you and help you with anything I can. I'll be back by nine — with my family, I hope. You had better stay at the hotel to rest and recover."

After that, he left, wrapping his head in a white turban he had taken off during the trip. After he had gone, I thought about his missing wife and son. The man stayed optimistic in spite of so much adversity. From what I had seen, the phenomenon seemed common amongst the Afghans.

I went to my room and lay down on the bed to rest my eyes, but in no time at all, with my energy sapped, I passed out, asleep. When I saw the light again, I looked at my watch and was surprised to learn that I had been sleeping for almost 12 hours. After using the bathroom and checking my leg wound, I went to the next room to talk to Muhammad, but he wasn't there. His bed was made and it seemed as though nobody had slept in it. Worry began to creep over me, but I understood that worrying would not help.

I got dressed, took my bag, and headed for the foreign affairs office. The Taliban receptionist informed me that although it was close by, it was best to take a taxi. He wrote the address in Arabic and called a taxi, which arrived almost immediately. I didn't even have to give the note to the driver, because he already knew where to go. The trip lasted exactly three-and-a-half minutes; only four blocks separated the hotel from the Taliban offices. The heat was unbearable, too, the stickiness and moisture in the air making it almost impossible to breathe. The inside of the building was worse, as there was no air-conditioning at all. The security officers at the door treated me with relative calm. "Taliban don't smile," I thought. I showed them my passport and tried to make them understand why I needed the stamp. The place was empty, and I assumed this was because of the time. It was barely eight in the morning.

I had to wait on a chair in a long hallway. The time spent waiting allowed me to see there were no pictures or symbols on the walls; they were empty and carelessly painted.

After an hour, a man approached. He was of medium height, with perfectly combed, jet-black hair. He was wearing a white-and-blue uniform I didn't recognize. He took me to a room without windows. When I was about to talk, he asked for my passport. He checked it and asked me the same questions: what I was doing there, where I was staying, how long I was going to be there. Without paying too much attention to my answers, he stamped my passport. Then, I started to ask some questions. I went straight to the point and asked about Marianna, explaining she was a Danish friend of mine.

"I have never heard that name. She isn't here," he answered without much enthusiasm.

"How can I find her?"

"I have no idea; it's not our job to find missing people," he snapped.

The phone rang and his face changed. He spoke quickly for a short time, took my passport in his hands, and told me to wait. When he left the office, I suspected his phone conversation had had something to do with me. Why had he taken my passport with him? Why hadn't he let me go? Time was passing and my uncertainty kept growing. I tried to open the door, only to discover that it was, in fact, locked.

After nearly two hours, the Taliban man came back. He pushed the door open. I saw that my passport was in his hands and that behind him were two security officers armed with swords.

When I saw what they were dragging behind them, my jaw dropped open.

25

AHMED
Tehran, Iran
October 19th, 2011

After getting out of the black and polarized world of the car, I saw that the helicopter was still hovering nearby, and as it passed overhead, it sent up a cloud of hot air and dust, blowing a swirl of particles from the burning ground straight into my eyes.

I had no idea where we were. I estimated that we must have traveled for about four hours or more, with the helicopter guarding us always. I didn't really understand why we hadn't made the trip on that aircraft; it would have been much nicer and a lot shorter.

The bearded man had been snoring in my face for half of the way, while the bald guy slept intermittently. Eventually, a building that was obviously new appeared before us, seemingly situated in the middle of nowhere. A sign that was nearly too small read, "Bushehr Power Plant." My knowledge of history was not particularly large or solid, but the topic of nuclear energy had always interested me, and I had once read that the Bushehr nuclear reactor was built in the seventies with American aid. I remembered having heard that the reactor had been damaged in the war with Iraq, and that in the nineties, Iran had signed a contract with Russia to resume construction of the Bushehr plant, using the same building. I knew that if my memory served me right, Bushehr had a pressurized water reactor that should have been up and running by the end of 2007. As there was no sign of construction, I assumed it must have been finished on time.

Bushehr was the name of an Iranian city about four hundred kilometers from Tehran, noted for its large port. I had read an article explaining how the reactor supplied energy to cities like Shiraz; and the same article noted there was no enriched uranium, as that process was carried out at another plant, Natanz, which had been put on the Israeli and American blacklist in recent years.

The bald man led the way as the helicopter slowly moved away from us. We entered a white building next to a huge electric generator. I had no idea why the Iranians had brought me here, as I was neither a physicist nor an engineer. At the entrance, we were greeted by an old man wearing a white apron. He didn't introduce himself, choosing instead to only exchange one or two words with the bald guy. All equipment and points of access appeared to have security measures based on the retina, an extremely safe and common system that uses a small camera to read the membrane of the human eye. As we walked down a long corridor, the old man opened three doors in succession, in each case exposing his eye to the cameras. My Iranian companions showed astonishment at such technology, so I assumed they had never been there before. The old man dropped us off at a small room with a large window, through which you could see an industrial control room with endless rows of booths equipped with servers and communication devices. On this side of the glass, the room was barren with just a few tables and swivel chairs. I was intrigued by the amount of technology installed beyond the glass, and I was very curious to know why I had been brought to this place. Five minutes later, a door opened at the other end of the facility, on the other side of the servers. In an instant, my doubts vanished as I was pleasantly surprised.

26

LEONEL
Afghanistan
October 26th, 2011

For some reason, we don't believe extreme cruelty exists until we witness it ourselves. And we don't believe those who say they have suffered atrocities, as though we need those horrific images before our own eyes to find out the truth. Mariana's body hung from the hands of two Taliban officers, as if she were an object escaping gravity, with neither stability nor weight. Her face had been completely disfigured, and the way she was opening and closing her eyes reminded me of a person who had been heavily drugged. Her body was shrouded in a white sheet. I tried taking a deep breath to recover from the shock that had me shivering, but in reality, I fell to my knees, then began retching uncontrollably. It took me a few minutes to pull myself together and when I did, I asked the uniformed Taliban what they had done to her.

"Nothing. We rescued her from some hooligans. Does she belong to you?"

"Some hooligans? You took her to Afghanistan after kidnapping her!" I felt a vein in my forehead about to explode.

"I don't know what you're talking about, Spaniard. If she belongs to you, take her. But before you do, hand over a thousand dollars to cover the attention and care she's gotten until now."

"What? What care? Look at her! You've disfigured and mutilated her! You want to charge me for that?!" I shouted hysterically.

In that moment, the two agents dropped Mariana and approached me menacingly. I instantly realized that I was standing on thin ice; an entire nation was already suffering this cruelty and nothing had stopped them so far. If I wanted to get out of it unharmed and save Mariana, I'd have to just pay and go. The problem was, that I didn't have that kind of money with me; in my pocket I just had $300. I explained the situation and asked them to go to a bank with me to complete the payment. While I was making that suggestion, the Taliban had been playing with my passport in his hands. When I finished, he pocketed it and told me I had an hour to get the money. Until then, the passport and Mariana would stay with him.

"But I need my passport to make the transfer," I argued.

"You're right, Spaniard." He tossed my passport on the table. "If you don't come back in an hour, the girl will die."

I thought about how cruel and ignorant these people could be. First, they blamed hooligans for Mariana's condition and now they were threatening to kill her if I didn't pay them. Without saying anything, I left the place as quickly as I could. I had to get to the bank to make an urgent bank transfer — something I knew was easier said than done. Making a transfer from an Israeli bank to an Afghan bank was almost unheard of, as these countries didn't get along at all. I was also scared that someone would recognize me as an Israeli. If that happened, the Taliban would kill me in an instant.

In the end, I decided to chance fate and went to a bank in downtown Kabul. On my way out, I sneaked a look back at Mariana. She couldn't fix her eyes on anything; they seemed lost and without direction. Her body was shivering.

It took 10 minutes to get to Azizi Bank by taxi. Just like almost every other building in Kabul, the walls were bullet-ridden and deteriorated. Surprisingly, the bank appeared to be completely empty. Had it not been for a nice employee who quickly offered to help me, I would have thought it was closed. I explained to him that I urgently needed to transfer money from a bank in France to their office, and that it was a life-or-death situation, which indeed it was. I wasn't even sure whether my contact in France had opened the account or not, and if he had, in what bank.

The man was dressed in a very neat, blue suit with the bank logo. He asked for my passport and for the information about my bank in France. I remembered that we had passed by the Central Bank of France on the way to Paris from the airport, and since it was all or nothing, I took the chance and gave him the name of that bank, however I told him that I lost all my belongings and I don't have my account details, I suggested to call the bank and to explain the situation and try my passport and name.

He picked up a phone and placed the call to the bank in France. His English was worthy of admiration. While waiting, I closed my eyes and offered a prayer to God.

"Sir, the French bank reported that the transaction will take an hour."

"One hour! I don't have that time! I urgently need that money right now." Exasperated, I raised my voice. "Do you understand me?"

"Sir, it doesn't depend on us."

I reached over and took the phone from his hands, explaining the situation and urgency to the person on the other end of the line. For a moment, there was silence.

"Sir, we have a process," the French bank employee attempted to assuage me.

"Give me your manager immediately!" I shouted with obvious anger. "Give me your manager, his manager, the chairman of the bank ... I don't care! Get me whoever can solve this situation now!"

There was more silence on the other end of the line. I once took a course in meditation and reflexology in Israel, where I learned from a guru how to cope with stressful situations such as this one. Unfortunately, I had stepped beyond that threshold and couldn't contain my frustration. Luckily, someone with a placating voice came on the line.

"Sir, I am the manager of this branch. We will attempt to transfer the money now and it will go through in half an hour. That is as fast as the system will allow. Now, please hand the phone back to the bank employee."

Feeling somewhat calmer, I gave the phone back and waited as the clerk and the Frenchman exchanged information on the figure and the necessary codes. When he finished, the clerk invited me to sit down and offered me some traditional Arab coffee — very muddy and strong, in a golden finjan[30].

The time limit was closing in fast and my nerves were starting to show in my breathing; I was feeling suffocated when, at last, the clerk got up from his chair and confirmed that everything was ready. He immediately put the American dollars in my hand, gave me a sign to wait, and started dialing on the phone.

"What are you doing?" I asked him.

"I'm calling a taxi and a security guard to escort you. It's far too dangerous for you to go outside with this amount of money. It's part of our service."

I thanked him. As I was about to leave, a man about 6-foot-6 in height escorted me to a taxi already parked on the street. He opened the door for me, then warned, "Be careful; you're in danger ..."

I entered the Taliban offices in a rush. The man in the uniform didn't take long to show up, so I gave him the money, which he counted, and then said, "Wait here, Spaniard."

After a few minutes, he came back with Mariana; the two agents threw her violently on the floor.

"Spaniard, take her fast, before I regret it."

"Ok," I replied.

I took Mariana in my arms as quickly and gently as I could; noticeably, her body was almost weightless and she was shivering as if frozen. I could feel her heart beating weakly and I knew at once that she was suffering the symptoms of convulsive shock. I knew I had to get her to a hospital and I was afraid she wouldn't make it if we didn't get there soon. Since I couldn't find a taxi, I started to shout desperately, "Help! Help!"

A white Peugeot screeched to a halt in front of us and a young Afghan man jumped out. I shouted, "Hospital! Hospital!" with Mariana still in my arms, dying. He helped me put her in his car and we sped off to the hospital — which, luckily, was just two streets away. As we ran into the emergency room, the staff took over immediately, placing her on a gurney and rolling her through a set of doors and out of sight. I tried to follow, but they shut the door in my face.

---

30 Finjan: a cup

27

AHMED
Iran
October 19th, 2011

Reza stood in front of me like a ghost. If there was one person I wasn't expecting to see there, it was him. He seemed strange, absent — almost as if he were there out of obligation and not because he wanted to be. He was also being escorted by a soldier.

The bald guy gave an order with a shake of his head and everyone left the room, leaving Reza and me alone. In the silence, Reza paced nervously around the room.

"Don't think I'm here because I want to be; we're in a similar situation, you and I. I was also kidnapped just three hours after you were, though I don't know if it can be called 'kidnapping' exactly, because it seems like Hamas has joined the Iranians in this project."

"What project are you talking about? Look where we are. Are we going to build bombs?"

"No, we'll continue doing our thing."

"What do you mean? What thing? Tell me at once!" I demanded, impatiently.

"Since more than a year ago, the Iranians have been preparing a technological program like the one we were starting to design in Hamas, but they're already very advanced. In fact, they've almost finished it. They want us to test it and add in the encryption, so they can start using it against Israel."

"What?"

"Look. I arrived here two hours ago, and I know no more than what I just told you. What I understand is that this whole campaign is to make the world believe that Iran is developing a nuclear bomb — a ploy to conceal the real 'bomb'."

"What 'bomb' are you referring to?"

"It's called 'The Hiat.' It's a viral bomb, an extremely powerful computer virus. The goal is that this virus will penetrate Zionist computer systems and destroy them. I still don't know all the details or the actual physical places where they plan to inject it, but from what I understand, it's all very advanced already."

"And do you know how are they planning to introduce it? It's well known that Israel has the best security systems."

"Manually."

"Manually? What? How?"

As I was trying to wrap my head around this new revelation, a man appeared wearing an impeccably ironed white apron, like those you might see in a laboratory. He was of medium height and was quite bald. After introducing himself as a lead engineer, he brought us to a massive control room packed with PLC (Programmable Logic Controller) systems and, on the wall, a giant screen displaying a graphical representation of what appeared to be a heavily damaged nuclear centrifuge. I immediately noticed the logo for the Siemens company in the image projection program.

"Surely, you're wondering why you're here. This is a typical centrifuge control room. The centrifuge you see on the monitor is just like every other, except that this one was damaged by the virus Stuxnet six months ago."

Reza looked at me with his mouth open, and I realized that I, too, hadn't yet closed mine. I remembered having spoken with him about this issue during our stay in Pakistan, but we didn't give it much thought. We'd read a bit on the topic, but now we were up close to the digital beast that had destroyed thousands of centrifuges.

Just then, the door opened and two white-jacketed waiters entered with trays of food.

"Ah, here we go," the engineer said. "We thought you might be hungry. We don't have much time, so I'm afraid I'll have to talk while you eat."

I looked at Reza, who shook his head in amazement. Although I'd never had a meal in a nuclear control room, it was delicious nonetheless. It had rice, mushrooms, chicken, and a thick pea soup, and was accompanied by a very sweet tea to aid with digestion.

The next four hours were as intense as they were interesting. At first, the engineer walked us through the different ways of powering PLC systems, and he showed us how the virus confused the systems by masquerading as false commands. Next, he gave us a live demonstration of the functioning of the virus and of the infection process of a simple computer. After that, he demonstrated the vulnerability the virus targeted, the two "zero days" it used, and the fake certificates of the drivers that had been acquired somewhere in Taiwan. Everything was so advanced. It struck me as nothing that had ever been done before. I lost complete track of time. That evil mutation was truly a work of art, an impeccable job. I realized this couldn't have been the product of just one programmer; it had to have been a team job — one with powerful infrastructure, such as that available to a whole country.

My thoughts were disrupted as the first bald guy burst into the room.

"OK, guys, we gotta leave," he said. "Let's go; we have a long journey to Tehran." The black car with the tinted windows was in the same position as we had left it just hours earlier. Besides Reza and me, the driver, the bald guy, and the bearded man were traveling, too. Any questions I had as to why I had been brought to this place now had answers; now I could understand everything. As the car began moving along the road, I could hear the rotors of the helicopter once again, a ghostly presence tracking behind us in the eerie night sky.

Reza was overwhelmed; the situation wasn't good for him. I, on the other hand, struggled to contain my excitement with the idea of working on a project like this, having direct contact with this virus. Reza explained to me that the project was well under way, almost finished. He said that a lot of people were working on it and the Iranian government had classified it as ultra-secret.

But why Reza and me? I had time to consider that question while the car flew down the highway. In my opinion, Reza was a genius in everything related to security, so his presence was clearly understandable, but what was I doing there? Did they think I was a wunderkind, without having demonstrated it yet — or was there something else I didn't know? I wondered whether Reza knew something that he wasn't telling me.

I tried to be optimistic by not overthinking the situation, because I knew that destabilizing myself wouldn't solve anything.

"We have a long journey ahead," the bald guy said, showing a smile. "Get comfortable, guys."

This time, I had made an extra effort to get in last and be next to the window. Reza hadn't understood what the big deal was about traveling in the middle next to the bearded guy, but before long, he learned well enough. The snoring commenced the moment the guy fell asleep and the sound was reminiscent of a freight train.

The trip lasted four hours. Since the windows were heavily tinted and the front and back cabins were separated by a manually operated black curtain, it was almost impossible to see where we were; but by calculating the time, I concluded two possibilities: either we had traveled 400 kilometers outside Iran, or we were now in Tehran (even when the bald guy said that we were heading to Tehran, I didn't quite believe it). When the car slowed down and began to stop periodically, I assumed we were hitting traffic lights, and I realized we must be close to our destination. The bald guy drew the curtain aside and woke up the bearded locomotive, giving him orders to get ready, because we were about to arrive. We exited the car on a dirt road and quickly entered a mud-colored building. I didn't have enough time to capture any more details of the place. We went into an elevator, and I noticed that the bald guy pressed a button that said -5. The elevator lurched and we began to descend at an incredible speed. Then, just as quickly as it had taken off, the elevator ground to a halt. The doors opened to reveal an automatic gate with another retina security system. A skinny man with a thick moustache greeted us and introduced himself as Raji. At that moment, our bald and bearded companions bid goodbye, and I sensed their flood of relief, not unlike that felt upon the completion of a mission. Raji placed his eye in front of the camera and the door opened. Beyond it was another similar door, but this one required a fingerprint; a biometric scanner. Once again, Raji did his thing and the door swung open. When we entered, I was stunned by the technology surrounding us — equipment which was completely unknown to me. A gust of cooled air numbed my lungs, but I recovered quickly. Before my eyes, row upon row of super-modern machines filled the room.

My mind still harbored the image of our laboratory in Pakistan — the one which until now I had considered the latest and most modern in computing. Clearly, I was mistaken. Here, every desk had a 32-inch LCD screen and each operator handled a computer and a server with 16 CPUs and what I assumed had to be at least 128 gigabytes of memory. What impressed me most was what I saw behind the clear glass in the data center. When we entered, the air was frigid — even colder than the last room. In the center of the space, there was a large steel box, approximately two meters high, letting out a deafening drone, likely caused by the rows of fans I could see encased on its sides. A huge LCD monitor was installed on the front of the box and there was a keyboard and mouse below it. All around were enormous racks brimming with servers and high-tech communication systems.

Before Raji could explain, my curiosity bubbled over and I asked him what the box was for.

"That, my friend, is the big secret," he said with a smile.

"Big secret? What secret?"

"You have in front of your eyes one of the most powerful servers in the world," Raji said. "The design was perfected by Russian and Chinese engineers, who finished it just six months ago. It has 3,000 physical CPUs and 16 terabytes of memory, with eight communication cards holding 100 gigabytes each. This baby can process any program format within milliseconds. The improbable is possible. Anything you can imagine and even more can be accomplished with this computer."

Raji looked proudly at the magic box, then went on: "This device can decrypt a 12-digit password in four minutes, generating 300 million combinations and establishing which one is right — something that would take a normal computer 25 years. It compiles programs in seconds, and we've tested entire platforms in minutes. It's extraordinary. What's more, there's no secret data here; we use it as a weapons processor. It helped us to build in just six months something that would have taken more than five years."

If everything Raji had said was true, indeed we were facing a machine very rarely seen by anyone in the whole world.

The days that followed were occupied by intensive study, learning, and reading of documentation. Nobody had given us the foggiest idea of what we were there to accomplish. We didn't ask, either, since the air was tinged with secrets and we figured we'd eventually be let in on our role. Our curiosity was getting bigger and bigger. By saying "our," I was including Reza, who had begun to lower his shield of mystery and open up a little more. We also discussed the project we had had in Pakistan — which was still his dream — and he confessed that he believed in me and in my ability to become the best in the land. He apologized for kicking me out of Peshawar; the only explanation he gave was that it wasn't his decision.

We lived and slept on floor -7, two floors below the laboratories. Everything we needed was provided, so there was no need for us to venture outside into the light of day. We shared work and rooms with three Russians, two Syrians, and four Iranians. Raji, our tutor, was one of those four. The Russians didn't say a word in front of us, and we hardly spoke at all with them. In fact, the Russians used their own language. The rest of us made efforts to understand each other and live as pleasantly as possible. We began to shape an interesting core, but still didn't understand anything of what was happening around us. No one spoke about the job; it was as if it were a secret code.

After a week of reading and documenting material about encryption and general security computing, Raji called us to his office. He had finished the adaptation and observation phase. We all knew that we were being watched; our attitudes and behaviors had surely already been put together in a personal profile on each of us. I still hadn't quite understood what Raji's position was in it all; was he the project manager? Everything related to logistics was in his hands and, when he began to communicate with us more, we realized he had been watching us the whole time to learn if he could trust us. I figured we had passed that challenge without a problem.

"Guys, I have to say I am very pleased with your progress so far. As you've probably surmised, you've been brought here to help us work on a very special project of huge magnitude — a 'viral bomb.' For the past six months, along with Russian engineers, we've been preparing a special program which, when introduced into a system, will infect and destroy it by violating its laws of operation. It's not yet completely finished, but we have already passed into the second phase of testing. The most important thing is that it recreates itself, and deletion will be immensely difficult for the Zionists; they simply won't succeed, because it spreads and regenerates too quickly. We are now in the third phase, and we are about to inject it into a computer in our local network that is connected to a PLC system, to see if it will generate a simulated attack on one of our own systems. Our work is based on a copycat of Stuxnet, of which I know you saw the results not so long ago. That means that our first objective would be a platform for industrial control. But not only that, the program has the ability to attack any system. We want to put Israel on its backside."

As Raji spoke these words, you could see the hate written on his face.

"We've tested all the processes with an electric turbine located on the second floor, and we're still analyzing and solving problems in the main program," he went on. "Something I didn't tell you is that 'The Hiat' — what we call the viral bomb — can execute on any platform, whether it's Windows, Unix, or Mac. The virus can easily detect the system, whatever the platform is, without a problem. The files were created for the three operating systems — something that is very difficult to see in just one code, because programmers only choose one operating system.

"Our goal is to introduce it into private networks in Israel without injecting it through the public web. That will help us overcome the Zionists. Since going through the public Internet is impossible, because antivirus and firewall systems would quickly detect and block any anomaly, we need to do it physically, manually. It'll be enough to simply insert a USB key with the virus into any computer in any of the places chosen. From there, it will quickly spread throughout the entire system, and in no time at all, it will finally explode in the central database. You two will be part of the final execution of the project, the decisive stage. You'll be accountable for building in the encryption and incorporating the certificates and private keys, so that we can compile everything in a USB key."

Raji paused to let us digest this information.

"What's more," he continued, "the virus isn't going to auto-run in the system. Instead, it'll ride on a DLL process in the operating system itself, violating any protection of the personal computer. This is the beauty of the whole thing: as a DLL, there won't be any need to log in and we'll be able to completely skip the password process. Ah ... I almost forgot: one of you will be involve in the execution process of the viral bomb."

"How?!" Reza and I both cried in unison.

"As you heard it. But don't worry about that — you'll receive more information and all the necessary training; no big deal."

Raji left no room for any objections. He simply got up, took a deep breath, and said, "Let's get to work."

Throughout his explanation, Raji's swarthy face had been immovable, except when he mentioned the words "Israel" or "Zionists," in which case his features become a scowl.

"From tomorrow, you'll begin working on 'Hiat' and you'll get some practice running the main program of our 'viral bomb.' "

In his speech, Raji had been extremely circumspect, being careful not to mention the name of the actual place we would be attacking; nor did he explain the objective of this operation. We knew PLC systems were involved, so we assumed it was about destroying infrastructure of some sort, but there were also rumors about an attack on a base of valuable data. What exactly were the Iranians planning to perpetrate?

28

Herzliya
October 21st, 2011

In Mossad's offices, the loss of communication with Leonel had gone down like a bucket of cement in a fishpond. The kaza of the organization in Pakistan, who could regularly be found in Islamabad, had already been notified of the urgent situation and was preparing the last of the formalities to step on Afghan soil. Yoni was also asked to provide all the information that they had in their possession.

Like a wrecking ball destroying everything in its wake, news of the "viral bomb" had already passed through one of the secret meetings in the Knesset, the Israeli parliament. The case of Leonel lost in Afghanistan wasn't something that should bother the politicians, but the senior officials of Mossad instead, and the latest news presented at the session was that the project had been moved to Iran, possibly together with Ahmed and another unidentified person.

In another emergency meeting, the government asked the Mossad to clarify the latest events, to which the leader of the organization requested a few days to deepen his understanding of the situation by reaching out to his agents in the field.

At the same time, rumors began filtering throughout the cabinet about the switch of the two children at birth. News of Leonel's and Ahmed's true identities circulated up and down Knesset's corridors. The prime minister felt he needed to resolve this issue, but at the same time, decided to assign someone to observe the Mossad's handling of the viral bomb hot potato. Two days later, the government appointed Eli Regev, the commander in chief of Army Intelligence, to front up the situation and specially to establish the validity of the identity swap. The appointment took place during a secret meeting of the security headquarters at HaKirya in Tel Aviv. In Mossad, this appointment was totally unexpected, and for many was like an electric shock. The head of the Mossad submitted his resignation, but it wasn't accepted. Instead, they explained that what they needed was a powerful leadership who could get in front of everything and, as it happened, Regev met these conditions and was the right person for the mission. Nothing that was discussed ever reached the press and everything returned to relative calm.

Mossad would continue its investigations into "The Hiat," while Regev would focus on the problem of the two men's identities. Plus, he'd check into the activities of the secret organization.

Regev's first interview with the head of Mossad was rough. The information the government had asked for wasn't ready yet — at least, that was what Mossad said. Regev, furious, left the office, banging the door with his fist, and almost shouting, "Nobody here understands the size of this issue. Obviously, I'll have to take the helm of this ship myself."

Regev requested an interview with Yoni, who had recently gotten back from Paris, and who had had the last contact with Leonel. He wanted more details about the young man's disappearance and he needed the data regarding his contact in Pakistan. Yoni went directly from the airport to his meeting with Regev, where he explained in detail all he knew about the GPS implant malfunction, the girl from the Red Cross, the CIA, and everything else relating to Leonel.

"How could a GPS signal be blocked?" Regev asked.

"We don't know; it's never happened to us before. Blocking that particular signal would require the participation of someone very highly skilled in electronics."

"Do you know anything about Ahmed?"

"From our contacts, we know that Ahmed was deported from Pakistan and was seen in Egypt near the Iranian embassy. It seems that Iranian intelligence agents kidnapped him and took him to Tehran, although this information hasn't been verified yet."

"Why was he deported from Pakistan? Why would they have wanted to do that?" Regev wanted to know.

"He was seeing a young woman from the Red Cross in Peshawar, which is prohibited due to the secrecy of the project they were working on. We don't understand why the Iranians kidnapped him. We're not entirely sure, but we have clues that Ahmed is an expert in computing and computer security, and it's believed that the Iranians are cooking something up in that area. That might be the reason."

"I've heard something about another man, someone called Reza ..."

"Yes, he worked on the same project as Ahmed in Pakistan. In fact, he was the technical leader of the project. Ahmed and Reza both belonged to a program initiated by Hamas. We know Reza's capture occurred in Pakistan three hours after Ahmed was deported. They apparently took him directly to Iran. Anytime soon, we expect to have the information on whether both are in Iran; our agents are working on that."

"It means that something big is being put together in Tehran, and I wonder ... What is Mossad doing about it?" Regev asked.

"Well ... we were working hard on the project that Hamas had in Peshawar ..."

Regev raised his hand and stroked his bald head. It hadn't occurred to anyone that this other project may have been a way to throw them off the real project.

"How long have you been working on this?"

Yoni took a moment to respond.

"It all started in the Gaza Strip, when we discovered the existence of a cell that was planning to develop some sort of computer-based offensive. But then these guys appeared on the scene. Ahmed was quickly identified as a prodigy, as he had been singlehandedly responsible for building the first computing system for Hamas. Next came the trip to Pakistan. In total, all of this took around three months."

Regev rested his hands on the desk, then clenched his fists.

"Shit!" he said. "You mean to tell me that for three months all we've done is eat the bait that the Iranians put out for us? I can't believe it! The whole world assumed they were creating an atomic bomb, with the uranium enrichment, the hard water plants ... and here they were quietly developing a cyberattack to destroy us. Surely, in the knowledge that we are always one step behind Hamas, they agreed to help Iran. And we fell into the great trap! Who the hell knows what step of the process they're at?"

Regev was fuming. Yoni sat rooted to his chair — not because it was comfortable, but because everything Regev said had rung true with his own thoughts.

"Look, I know this issue isn't your fault, but instead of starting this case from scratch, I'm going to have to run with all the info I can. I hope you told me all that you know — in this case, we have everything to lose. Thanks for your help. You can leave now."

Regev tried to remain calm, but he had to act quickly. His career as head of the Army Intelligence Department had taught him similar tricks to distract an enemy, but this was of a different magnitude, a much higher level of danger. The whole nation was at risk. The government would soon be requesting a report, and were likely to blame Mossad for inefficiency — but what would be the good of that if the whole house of cards came tumbling down? So what if they found a scapegoat within the organization? It wouldn't forestall the impending disaster, he thought.

So without further ado, he grabbed his phone and dialed the number of an old friend.

29

LEONEL
Afghanistan
October 26th, 2011

After six days in the hospital, Mariana began to show signs of improvement. In a normal hospital, she would have recovered in half that time — it's not that the doctors or nurses were bad; rather, the problem was that they lacked even the basics, from instruments to drugs. When she was admitted, she had clinical signs of acute dehydration, several bruises, and, above all, a state of emotional shock, all of which had everyone thoroughly worried. After the first two days of care, the hospital informed me that antibiotics were scarce and they didn't have any more for her; her situation was no longer considered critical in relation to other patients, and therefore Mariana was no longer a high priority. I had to get antibiotics on the black market.

In those moments, I had no thought of Ahmed, nor my mission, nor of Mossad. I just wanted to return to Israel and, if possible, take Mariana with me. I'd gotten accustomed to sleeping on the floor, and if it was a lucky day, maybe I could sleep on a bench. I could have written during those days about the victims of the Taliban — women, most of them — for whom the hospital had become a second home; who we saw each day in the hospital — wounded, bleeding. There was even one time when I helped in the hallway, doing what I could with the little I had to offer.

On the sixth day, Mariana finally opened her eyes, and I was pleased to know that she recognized me, although her reaction was far from the hug or warmth I had been expecting from her. But her mind had taken her far away, and I understood why. Two days earlier, Muhammad had made contact through the hotel where we had stayed the first time. I had left a message there of my whereabouts. I found him later the same day, distraught because he hadn't yet found his wife or son, and there had been no sign of either of them. He asked me whether I had been lucky and I told him what had happened with Mariana. He informed me that in three days, his cousin would be close to the border of Peshawar and, from there, there was a way through which we could slip away to the other side. He said we'd have to walk at least three hours and asked if I wanted to go with him; he had space for two.

I didn't think Mariana could survive the trip. I wasn't even sure I could survive, so I dismissed the idea altogether. We shook hands, hugged quickly, and I tried to encourage him regarding his family before we parted. This was a man of great kindness and affection. He had an enviable spirit, unwavering in the face of adversity; he was the image of his people.

Finally, I decided to go to the Denmark consulate, located in the ambassador's area near the city center. With the exception of Pakistan, any true embassies that had once been there had ceased to exist. However, most countries still maintained a consulate with a trade commissioner in charge. When I arrived, a tall, blond man was exiting the gate. I stopped, thinking he was the consul. He saw me, and in his sudden panic, pulled a gun.

"Wait! Don't panic! I'm not Taliban," I assured him, raising my hands above my head.

Obviously, my appearance didn't help to convince him — I had gone several days without washing, sleeping, or changing clothes.

"Then let me go on my way!" he demanded, rather gruffly.

"I need help ..." I tried to convince him, and I think my English calmed him down a little bit.

"But we can only help Danish citizens," came his explanation.

"I'm a friend of a Danish citizen who is in the central hospital." I told him the whole story, mentioning her capture and the events in Afghanistan, always trying to exclude myself.

"Let's go to the hospital," he suggested.

I liked his taking this initiative, and he looked like a person I could trust.

"If the story you're telling me is real, your friend probably doesn't have any documents with her. What about you?"

"I do. I'm a Spanish citizen. Here you go." I showed him my passport and he carefully examined the document.

"It must be your lucky day. Tomorrow, I am traveling to Copenhagen on a private flight from the Danish army. If they let her leave the hospital, it might be possible to include you both on that flight, although I understand that you're also in trouble."

"What do you mean?" I ask him, feigning surprise. "I just want her to return safely."

"Your passport has the Taliban visa, so you can't leave this country. If you do, it'll be very difficult. I should ask you how you came in, but I can imagine."

"I would appreciate everything you can do for us; as I told you, things haven't been easy for this girl and now she's in a very delicate situation."

"I'll have to verify her Danish citizenship; I'll pass you off as her partner. Tell me her last name."

"Look, I only know her first name: Mariana. I hope she's able to give you all the information you need. She's been affected emotionally; she's in a state of shock."

When we got to the hospital, Mariana was sitting in the room she had been sharing with six other people. We tried to get her attention by talking to her, but she appeared to be in another world, a typical manifestation of her delicate situation.

After more than half an hour, the Danish man said, "Look, it may be that she has all the physical traits of a Dane, but without her full name and without verifying her identity, I can't take her with me. I'll be in my office tomorrow until noon; the plane leaves at about three in the afternoon. These flights are never on time, but I need the data anyway before noon, to prepare the documents. Understand that I have to send a temporary passport."

Yes, I understood ... but how would I get through to Mariana? Never before had I thought of asking her last name. I tried looking into her eyes and speaking to her heart. I thought the only way to jerk her back into reality was to say something that would move her intimately.

"I love you," I told her. Then I paused and said, "Look, we're in terrible danger here. I just need your last name so I can get you out of here, so we can leave together. Please, please — tell me your last name!"

The silence set us apart from the bustle of the room. I thought I saw her lips flutter, but then quickly put it down to my imagination and anxiety in the situation. More silence and stillness. In a trance-like state, Mariana continued her lost stare into nothingness.

I didn't have a Plan B, and the truth is that I wanted to leave this country — leave everything, get out and rebuild my life. I wished I could do it with Mariana. Something inside me was telling me that I couldn't leave her. Do I love her? I asked myself. Yes! Yes, I love her. It was that simple. I went out for air. The few city lights brightly lit the space. A truck with Taliban passed by, patrolling the streets, and two young men who saw it ran away, scared. I went back into the hospital, taking the opportunity to talk to the doctors to see if they would let Mariana leave. They were satisfied with the idea of her going; for them, it was one more bed available and one less sick person to care for.

I lay down on the floor beside Mariana's bed, as usual, trying to sleep. As I was closing my eyes, I heard a soft, feeble murmur, like a quiet hum: "Asirán, Asirán ..."

I got up and went closer, but Mariana had already closed her eyes. Something was very much alive in there. She had told me her name, and that was worth more than any expression of love. If all went well, soon we would exchange the heat of Kabul for the cold of Copenhagen — or so I thought.

30

ISRAEL
Jerusalem
End of October, 2011

Moshe Cohen knew his day had come. After waiting so patiently for so long, he'd finally be getting his trophy — the woman he had always wanted, the one to whom he had devoted so much of his life. He had drawn that moment many times in his imagination; dreamt about his hands touching her skin, caressing her breasts, while his lips seized her mouth ... it saddened him a bit that the moment hadn't happened before, when they were younger.

All his life, he had settled for loveless stories, watching her live her life and having her only as a friend but nothing more. Now, he knew his wish would soon come true — a little late, perhaps, but true nonetheless. He had gotten Leonel for her, and she would pay for the favor. That's why, after avoiding him for more than a month, she had invited him to come over for dinner. She didn't make anything special; she just bought chicken at the supermarket, heated some potatoes, and made a salad. She remembered she had some dietary ice cream in the freezer that she could serve for dessert. She also assumed that Moshe would bring a bottle of wine, since alcohol was his specialty.

She dressed in a slinky black dress, complemented with stockings of the same color, covering her legs up to her thighs. She put on the sexiest panties she could find — although without a second opinion, it was very difficult for her to know if they really were sexy — and she looked for a bra that matched. She felt strange — something which shouldn't be happening to her. She didn't have a clear idea on how to act when the moment came. In front of the mirror, she put her hands on her breasts, breathing in slowly as she felt her nipples become erect beneath her fingers. Her sensuality was strong; she had just forgotten how it felt being attractive.

Moshe appeared at her apartment five minutes before their agreed time. As she opened the door and invited him in, he cajoled her as he usually did, sneaking a look, feasting his eyes from head to toe, while he placed in her hands a bottle of exquisite Carmel Chardonnay.

"You're beautiful, as usual. Black looks really great on you." The smoothness dripped from his lips as he spoke. "You're going to like this wine; it's from a great harvest."

Rachel was accustomed to hearing compliments from Moshe's mouth. She knew she was no longer that pretty, slim girl from 25 years ago; age and life had given her a bulky abdomen and her legs were a patchwork of varicose veins. More than anything, the bags under her eyes had become more and more pronounced. But that obviously didn't matter, she thought; many times, including tonight, she had felt the way he undressed her with his eyes.

During dinner, their trivial conversation accompanied the consumption of glass upon glass of wine. Moshe drank more than he should have, and she accompanied him, to prepare herself for what was surely ahead for her that night. When they finished the first bottle, she brought out another that she had been keeping for a special occasion. Sleeping with old Cohen wasn't something she fancied doing, and when she saw how much he was drinking, she had a faint glimmer of hope that maybe he'd fall asleep, but she quickly realized that wasn't to be her destiny. The alcohol had no effect on Moshe, and he very clearly still wanted her.

When they finished the ice cream, she went to her bedroom, took the dress off, and came back out to the living room. He was waiting for her, sitting on the couch, his eyes entranced — completely consumed by the desire he felt. She had left only her stockings on, and as she entered the living room, Moshe lost control of his inhibitions, his anticipation proving too much and causing him to jump from the sofa with the excitement of a 12-year-old boy. His hands flew toward her body, eagerly groping her flesh; his mouth suckling her breast in a frenzy of passion. He could have taken her right there on the floor, but Rachel was in no hurry. She took him by the hand to the bedroom, where she lay face down on the bed, waiting for Moshe to take off his clothes, which he did surprisingly fast. He immediately climbed on top of her and began kissing her whole body, rubbing her back with his beard. Hoping to end it quickly, Rachel rolled over on the bed and took him with her hand, guiding him in. He penetrated her with an erection he had forgotten he could have.

She felt it slide into her — not with the pleasure she would have expected, but in more or less the same way as if he had entered her with some foreign object. Still, as Moshe went through his motions, Rachel began to feel like a woman again, as if something were waking up within her, perhaps reminiscent of her youth. Moshe's moans came faster and shorter, then with one final bellow, he collapsed on her body, sliding down between her legs, a smile drawn on his face.

In seconds, he fell asleep. She pulled herself out from under him, making a quick dash to the shower, where she allowed the scalding water to wash over her, scrubbing herself almost raw, as if her attempts to cleanse herself would somehow rid her body of the inner filth she now felt. The next morning, Moshe rose and dressed while she pretended to be sleeping, although she actually hadn't slept a wink all night.

Moshe left the apartment at 9:30 a.m., swearing to himself because he had just realized that he had to go to the local police headquarters in Rishon Lezion to renew his private investigator license. He would have preferred to stay, though; his dream of so many years was finally coming true.

At 9:40 a.m., Rachel's apartment bell rang. She thought that maybe Moshe had forgotten something and for a while she ignored the sound, hoping he'd just go away, not relishing the thought of surrendering to him again. The bell continued to ring, though, so she figured that perhaps it was urgent. She dressed in her black lingerie, and resigned, went to open the door. Through the viewfinder, she saw a tall man with dark glasses she didn't know.

"Who are you and what do you want?" she asked through the door. She knew better than to open the door to strangers. She had heard all kinds of terrible stories.

"I came here to talk to you about Leonel. I have information that might be useful to you."

Desperation to know about Leonel was stronger than prudence, so she opened the door. Just as she did, the door burst inwards, sending her sprawling on the floor. As she lay there, her mind spinning too fast to think, the attacker pulled a 22-caliber Beretta with a long silencer attached, and without pausing, put three shots into her head — sending flesh, hair, and brain matter across the floor. A consummate professional, he checked that she was dead and then shot her again, this time in the stomach. He lingered for an instant, contemplating the expanding pool of blood, and then left.

31

Paris – France
October 28th, 2011

On a day of torrential rain, Ben slept in the old apartment located on the outskirts of Paris. He was alone because Yoni was in Israel, having been summoned for urgent consultations, which never meant good news. Hectic days had passed for the Mossad, especially for agents who were located in Europe. Everyone was on high alert, and many had been diverted to concentrate on finding Leonel — not to mention the scandal of the Iranian case.

Due to all the infighting in Mossad, the organization wasn't able to work in peace. Too many limits were violated when the government decided to allocate someone of its own to monitor a case that completely belonged to the Mossad. Sacred codes of the organization had been uncovered, both shocking and demoralizing senior members of the leadership organiztion. The structure was on the verge of total collapse.

In an attempt to calm things down, the prime minister went out on a limb, making it clear that the Iranian issue required direct government involvement, and in this case, had no relationship with the operation of Mossad. He emphasized that he had never questioned the actions of the Mossad, repeating several times that these ideas were simply lies by the press.

From the dining room, a loud buzz began to emanate. Ben leapt out of the bed, as if launched by a catapult. He knew the noise was coming from the GPS monitor that for the last few days had disappeared without a trace. When he saw the sign, he recognized it immediately. He pulled up a map and quickly pinpointed the location of the signal, surprised to find that it wasn't in either Pakistan or Afghanistan. He looked at the monitor, rubbed his eyes, and looked again, but there was no doubt — it was pointing at Copenhagen, Denmark.

"Son of a bitch!" he exclaimed. "What are you doing there?"

Excited, he immediately called Yoni's mobile in Israel, but there was no answer. Under pressure, Ben could feel his nerves buzzing. Nervously, he called the "'red phone," the number Mossad intended only for emergency communications with the operations unit. Surely they would be able to connect him with Yoni. Indeed, just five minutes later, the phone buzzed and Yoni was on the line.

"Ben, what's wrong? What's so urgent?"

"Leonel's signal just came back online."

"At last! Where is it?"

"You won't believe this — it's coming from Denmark."

The line went silent.

"He's in Copenhagen, Denmark," repeated Ben.

"What is the exact place?"

"A hotel called The Ramada in the western center. What do you want me to do?"

"Did you call the hotel?"

"Yes, and I left a message, because no one answered in his room."

"Do we have an agent there?"

"No, no one. The nearest is in Germany."

"Call the Israeli embassy in Copenhagen immediately and ask to speak with the chief of security, and then tell him to send his agents to follow Leonel. Make it very clear that we're only interested in watching. I don't want him apprehended. If they need confirmation, tell them to contact Eli Regev. I will leave for Copenhagen as soon as possible. Set up a flight for yourself as well."

"Okay. See you there."

"Do you still have the signal?"

"Shit! Wait, it just cut off and the same static screen is back again."

"What do you think it is?"

"He must have a GPS signal blocker device."

"Yes, it may be that."

Ben hung up and hastily began packing for his trip to Copenhagen.

32

LEONEL
Afghanistan - Copenhagen, Denmark
27th and 28th of October, 2011

I hated the cold, but even so, I felt calm after so many days of tension. Upon landing in Copenhagen, an ambulance was waiting on the runway. Mariana remained silent throughout the flight, completely cut off from the outside the world, as if shell–shocked. The Danish business mana- ger left me the name of the hospital to which she would be sent, along with a list of officials to whom I could reach out for assistance. I told him to contact my country's — Spain's — embassy. He nodded and passed me a $100 bill.

Communicating on my own with the Israeli embassy would put me in direct contact with the Mossad, the last thing I needed right now. Perhaps after a night in a hotel with a shower — and a real bed — I could finally sleep well. Then again, my body was already accustomed to resting on the floor.

I had my handbag and I was dressed in ragged and dirty clothes. I had to find a place to sleep and, more than anything, I needed shelter for a few days. I waited inside the terminal until the first taxi appeared.

Everywhere in the world, taxi drivers know all or at least most of the hotels in their city; you just have to specify what kind of hotel you prefer. If you don't say, you risk being taken to one of the most expensive, which are the ones that give them a commission. He took me to a hotel called The Ramada, located just east of Copenhagen, 10 minutes from the city center. The facade was Tuscan and the service seemed pretty good. I checked my pockets and saw that I had $200 total, including the hundred the Dane had passed me. I figured that would be enough to pay for the night. I needed to sort out my ideas, get back to my normal life, get some sleep — just close my eyes and forget.

I don't remember how, but as soon as I hit the bed, I passed out. I was awakened from my deep slumber by a thread of light that filtered through the curtains and pointed directly at the space between my eyes. At first, my mind registered it as the little red dot of a sniper's rifle, and I felt a jolt in my heart, but quickly realized that it was just a reflection from a street light. My stomach was growling, writhing in need of food. Part of me wanted to stay wrapped up in the sheets like a mummy, but my craving for food won the battle in the end. I went down to reception like a zombie in search of breakfast. When I asked where I could find breakfast, the receptionist laughed and pointed at the clock behind him, in which the hands clearly showed 1 p.m. He also said he had a message for me, which, as you can imagine, threw me for quite a loop. How could anyone have found me so fast? As I took the curled slip of paper from his hands, my head began to throb. I instinctively reached down to my waist and realized I wasn't wearing the belt, and therefore I wasn't using the device created by Muhammad that interfered with Mossad's GPS. Across the last 10 days, I had been constantly wearing that belt. To the receptionist's surprise, I bolted from the office and ran to my room, where I found it caught between the sheets. When I opened the slip of paper, it confirmed what I had feared: Mossad was once again connected with me. The note read, "Get in touch as soon as possible, or the consequences will be severe."

33

Copenhagen, Denmark
October 28th, 2011

I quickly put the belt back on. As I thought of the ramifications of what I had done, a cold sweat fell across my face and my chin. The Mossad knew my whereabouts and I had no doubt that they were already on my trail; if they had agents in Copenhagen, they would certainly already be looking for me.

I had to escape and run away. Something about all of this smelled foul, and I didn't want to be involved any more than I had to. Neither a million shekels nor even Ahmed could make me interested anymore. Vague sequences of a normal life ran through my head as I thought of going back to school and someday becoming a doctor. Mariana appeared in all of those beautiful images.

Again, haunting thoughts began to take over my mind as I considered the other half of the equation. Everyone was looking for Ahmed, but … where was the child born on the same day and raised Jewish who was, unwittingly, Muslim? I had begun to think more frequently about why Rachel started the search for Ahmed without giving me any information about the other boy. I didn't really understand why. Undoubtedly, it was easier to find an Israeli than a Palestinian. I had less and less doubt; but what would happen if I were right?

I had the paper with the name of the hospital where Mariana had been sent; so, given the urgency of the case and despite the hunger I felt, I dismissed the idea of breakfast, especially considering the danger I would be in if I stayed at the hotel. I went outside, found a taxi. and took it to the hospital. At reception, they guided me to Traumatology, located on the second floor. I climbed the stairs, and as I approached the door, I could see from one angle and through a mirror, two men in black suits standing around, looking for something, or someone. Unfortunately, I had lost this hand; the Mossad was already there, I thought. I felt a great sorrow for Mariana, and I wanted to see her, because I really cared. If I left her, what would become of her? Could we meet again? Would I forgive myself for having left her helpless and alone? In the end, I didn't see that I had a choice. I decided to leave.

I didn't know what to do. With only $60 remaining in my pocket, I wouldn't get very far. As I stood outside the hospital, a cold mist enveloped my body. I heard the siren of an ambulance that had surely come with a patient for the emergency room, and had I been a few inches further on the road, it would have hit me. The fog hid everything. I used the time to think about my options. Using the airport would be impossible, because the Mossad would have already contacted their Danish peers alerting them about me. I needed a way to escape from this country, and the only way I could think of was by the sea. Denmark is a country with generous peninsular coasts. I asked a passerby where the port was, and he kindly gave me the directions.

"On foot, it's about two kilometers that way," he said.

I had intended to save the last money I had, but the cold was ferocious and I had come wearing light clothes, so when I saw a billboard advertising a shopping center, I thought that a coat would be my best investment before I died of pneumonia.

In the shopping mall, coats cost much more than I had expected — much higher than I could afford. Fortunately, I still had my credit card, but I knew if I used it, the Mossad would be able to trace it, and perhaps even intercept me. Using the card was not a good idea, so in the end, I made do with two thick wool sweaters that I found for only $20 in a bargain store. When I put them on, my body heat increased immediately, and I was ready to walk. In half an hour, I reached the port, although the fog by that point had become extremely thick and I had to watch where I was walking to keep from tripping and falling into the sea.

"So, what now? And then ... where?" I thought to myself.

I spent 30 minutes exploring the area. I began to make out some of the boats through the fog — boats that seemed to be privately owned, stationed on the pier. A passenger ship was also waiting out in the bay. I asked around and found out that the ship's destination was Germany and that a ticket for the passage cost $350; I would also need to acquire a visa in my passport. I was beginning to lose hope, when I suddenly heard a voice a few meters behind me. An old man with a gray beard and a brown beret — exactly what you would expect to see in a copy of the magazine, Asterix — was babbling something in what I assumed to be Danish. He was accompanied by a huge, white dog.

"English, please," I said.

"Work ... work ..."

"No," I said. I didn't need to work just then; however, I did need money.

"Work ... boat," he insisted

I understood that he was speaking of working on a boat. I thought to myself, "Maybe he could take me to another port in another country, clandestinely."

"Okay," I answered him, without really thinking about it, "Where are you going?

"What ..."

"Where?" I repeated again, "Where?" making the motions with my hands in the air.

"Oh ... Faroe Islands," he said at last.

For me, it seemed to be a good place to escape. Besides, there really wasn't any time to think.

"Let's go!" I replied.

34

Israel
Late October, 2011

Yosi examined himself in the mirror once more. He thought he would have to dye his hair again, for a few silver-gray strands had appeared in his almost perfect coif. He was careful to use only the right amount of gel, because the product he preferred was no longer for sale, and the chances of the brand appearing on the market again were slim. He had just begun massaging it through his hair when his cell phone rang. The vibrations made it slide off the table and hit the floor, and by the time he'd cleaned his hands and picked it up, the ringing had stopped. Instead, the screen displayed a voice message from "Randolph." In the past, Randolph had been a Mossad kaza, operating from the base in Frankfurt. Born in Germany to a Polish mother and a Turkish father, he was now Yosi's new assistant at the Tel Aviv investigations unit, as he had decided to make Aliyah[31] with his family. A few weeks ago, he had begun an advanced course in data decoding and email security and encryption. He had joined the secret police just a short time ago, and he was highly efficient.

Now, he was urgently trying to reach Yosi. In the short time he had been working alongside the German, Yosi had never seen him so insistent, and he had never left a message asking him to contact him urgently. Randolph was in his car on his way to Jerusalem when Yosi finally managed to locate him.

"Hey, what's up?"

"I think I have some information about the case of our Tel Aviv boy."

---

31 Aliyah: The Jewish immigration back to Israel.

"Who do you mean?"

"Leonel."

"Ah! What do you have?"

"Do you remember the footprints we found in his house, those belonging to that woman ... Rachel Mizrachi?"

"Yes."

"She was found dead today in her apartment in Jerusalem."

"How did you find out?"

"I talked with Gonen, our contact in Jerusalem. They shot her three times in the head and once in the abdomen."

"I suppose you are already on your way to Jerusalem."

"Correct. I will wait for you there. I will send you the address right now in a text message."

Yosi had known for some time that Leonel's case had nothing to do with a simple gas leak, but had actually been a botched assassination attempt. He had had his eye on Rachel for some time, as she was the prime suspect. Although he didn't understand why this woman would want to kill the young man, the only footprints found in Leonel's house were hers. Now, he was certain that Rachel Mizrachi was not responsible. What's more, the gas found in Leonel's house was very difficult to buy; recent information indicated that it was used exclusively by Mossad agents and perhaps some other Mafioso who managed to get hold of it clandestinely. Apparently, the Palestinians were unaware of it — but, then again, one never knew.

When he received the SMS with the address, he put on his jacket, took his blue notebook, and went to his black Ford Sierra. On the way, he thought about how to convince the Jerusalem police to let him intervene in the case of Rachel Mizrachi, or at least to enter the apartment of the deceased and observe the scene. He knew well enough of the typical competition within the police force between departments and districts — the raw and dirty kind. But he still thought that Gonen could probably help him get in. Gonen, an agent pushing 60 years old, like himself, always flaunted his shiny, bald head. Yosi knew very well that good contacts were necessary to solve any case, and Gonen had them in Mossad and Shabak; plus, he frequently dined with the chief of police. Without a doubt, this was his man.

When Yosi arrived, the scene was in chaos, out of control. Police had closed the area surrounding the crime scene with barricades. He saw Gonen standing with Randolph near the stairs, and as he approached the scene, Yosi showed his agent ID, but they wouldn't let him through. When Gonen saw him, he came and let him in. Gratefully, Yosi shook his hand.

"What happened here?" he asked.

"She was killed with four bullets fired at close range."

"Any indication of who it might have been?"

"No, not yet, but we have a clue — or perhaps more than just a clue."

"What clue?" Yosi asked, surprised."

"We found traces of a man in the house, throughout the whole house — especially in the bedroom."

"Do you know who he is?"

"Yeah, you're not gonna believe this."

"Come on, spit it out."

"Moshe Cohen."

"Moshe Cohen?" he asked, as if he did not recognize the name.

"Yes, from the Research Department of the Jerusalem District."

"Ah, yes, Moshe Cohen, he retired a while ago ..."

"Right."

Yosi scoured the house and found nothing significant. He hadn't had much hope of finding anything. This seemed like the work of a professional, a paid killer. Even though Cohen was the only one who had been there, at no point did it occur to him that the old man had committed the crime. The question was, who had sent the murderer and why? What was it that Rachel was hiding, that someone had murdered her for? For a moment, he felt the circle tightening.

He lit a short cigarette and wrote something in his famous blue notebook. Then, he addressed Randolph with a decisive and affirmative tone.

"Get me the old man as soon as possible."

35

Israel
Rehovot
October 21st, 2011

Shmulik Sade rubbed his head with his left hand, looking for an answer to this new enigma. In recent years, he had been studying the adaptation of immigrants from different backgrounds. His research had produced mixed results. Of the million or so Russians who, according to their data, had settled in the country, more than 50 percent showed an unusual level of discontent and were potential deserters in the army and candidates for yerida[32].

Shmulik would present the results to the government in three days, and had to attach recommendations and comparisons between different groups of immigrants. He was one of the most recognized sociology scientists in the country. He had obtained a doctorate at Harvard in Contemporary Philosophy and Social Sciences. His empire, not small by any stretch of the imagination, was located in the Machon Weizmann Institute[33] in Rehovot, and his office was two floors underground. Security in the building was high — exaggerated even, as per his demands. His department worked on large projects, often initiated by the government or any of the intelligence services. His telephone line was permanently blocked, and only a privileged few had his direct number. So when the phone rang, he started, as he almost never received calls. His ex-wife

---

32 Yerida: The emigration of Jews from Israel.
33 Machon Weizmann Institute: Center of scientific research in Israel.

communicated by phone to arrange routine visits with his daughters, and this was only in accordance with strictly agreed-upon schedules.

"Shmulik Sade. Who's speaking?"

"Shmulik! How are you, you bastard?"

Shmulik was struck by the expression, and he didn't recognize the voice.

"Who is this?"

"What do you mean, 'Who is this?' Don't you recognize me? See if you can remember when you lost your virginity ... who was next to you? Or when you got married ... who took you back to the hotel, drunk?"

"Oh, noooo! I can't believe it! Eli Regev. How are you, you old bastard? It's been so long."

"Good, very good — and you?"

"Oh, you know. I, as always, am examining monkeys, molecules, and immigrants. But you have risen so far ... you don't remember the poor folk."

"How so? Wasn't it me who called you now? I propose that we get a coffee. What do you say?"

"I'm very busy. It would have to be next week."

"No, no. I need to talk with you briefly. I will come to get you in half an hour." The seriousness in his voice could not be mistaken as he uttered those words.

"Are you crazy?"

"I'll come and get you — it's urgent. I'm guessing you are where you always are, in your hideaway."

"That's right. But can't this wait?"

"No, it can't. I'll be there in half an hour."

Shmulik was stunned by the hurried nature of the meeting. He hadn't seen Eli Regev for more than five years. The last time they'd met was at a seminar in the Ramat Aviv exhibition center, the theme of which had been "Digital Terrorism before the Advent of Internet: Opportunities and Risks." The event was sponsored by the Ministry of Intelligence. Shmulik and Eli were among the select few who had attended. There, in the second row, they had embraced after years without seeing each other. Shmulik remembered as well that many of the predictions made in that seminar had come true, especially those about digital terrorism, which had grown substantially. Now this "emergency" meeting had cropped up out of nowhere; who knew why?

Shmulik tidied up his desk and put his things away. It was 3:45 p.m. and it would not be worth going back to the office afterwards, he thought. He told his secretary he had to go get his daughters, that they had called from school with an emergency. This week, though, was not his turn to take care of the girls. The agreement with his former wife stated that they stayed with their mother for two weeks and one under his care, "the two for one," as he called it.

He waited for five minutes seated on a bench outside the Machon Weizmann. Eli Regev soon appeared in his black Volkswagen. Shmulik quickly got into the car and they set off for Tel Aviv via the old route. They took off at such speed that Shmulik didn't even have the opportunity to shake hands with his old friend; they only managed to exchange a quick glance and a smile.

Shmulik settled into his seat and leaned back. Then he moved forward again with a nervous grin. He broke the eerie silence and started the conversation between them.

"Where are we going, old friend?"

"To the center of Tel Aviv."

"What's there?"

"My office."

Shmulik knew what that meant. They were heading to the HaKirya in Tel Aviv. The Ministry of Defense and Eli Regev's office were located there. Trying to get some more information, he asked, "Where is your office?"

"In the HaKirya ... you know it, right?"

"Ah, yes. Do you have a security pass for me?"

"Don't play dumb ..."

"Why so much mystery and urgency?"

"I'll explain soon. Just relax. When the guard asks you who you are, say your full name, as you always do when you come here."

It was not the first time Shmulik had been to that place. The Machon Weizmann always had projects related to state security. The scent of trees was familiar to him and reminded him of old and better times. The HaKirya was home to Israeli security. Its walls were heavily guarded. In the basement of the building the "war headquarters" were found, where all the crucial decisions in times of crisis were made. He knew it; he had been there in '82, when war raged in the north, and again in '91, when Saddam Hussein tried to show his strength against Western forces.

When the guard asked for his name and identification, Regev was surprised, because Shmulik didn't have to provide any information; he had a special card which allowed him access to anywhere in the HaKirya. They looked at each other and smiled.

"I know this place," Shmulik said with a sly smile.

"I see ..."

In his office, before Shmulik could even take a seat and make himself comfortable, Regev got straight to the point.

"I need your help."

As Shmulik seated himself, he said, "Yes, I already figured that. What is it about?"

"Roughly 28 years ago, I heard that you were involved in a special project ..."

"I need more information than that; I have worked on a million projects, Eli."

"I came across some information that the Mossad required a special study relating to the situation of a Palestinian child and Israeli child, something about them being switched at birth. You were in charge of that investigation, right?"

Eli had used his ingenuity to coax information from Shmulik, making him feel like he was his friend, alleging that it was really the Mossad which was behind all of it. In fact, they actually still didn't have a clue.

His words fell like bombs to Shmulik, shattering the past and bringing back memories of those distant times. That project had changed him as a human being, as a person. Back then he had been new in the Machon Weizmann Institute; he had had lofty ambitions, and taking on that task had been promising for his career. After the project was launched, because of its secrecy and delicacy, Shmulik had been offline for more than six months.

He followed the two children and their development, recording and analyzing their behavior. He didn't understand why Eli had mentioned the Mossad so confidently, as he hadn't reported directly to anyone in that organization. He sent his reports to some unknown person who allegedly came from the very top. It was never revealed to him who received these reports; everything was conducted under a cloak of secrecy. For his work he was paid in cash, wads of which were left in his mailbox every two weeks — an exchange which required a high degree of trust. Within the Machon, the only one who knew about his work was his manager, and he didn't ask any questions.

He closed his eyes for a second; he thought he must be dreaming. His thoughts skipped back in time to nearly 30 years ago. He recalled that at that time he had been young and ambitious, and that the project was his "baby," something he really wanted and believed in. Many things had happened back then. When he opened his eyes, he didn't want to be there, opposite Regev.

"I can't talk about this subject." He barely managed to get the words out.

"Yes, you can." Eli Regev shifted back in his chair, reached into his briefcase, and pulled out a sealed paper that he shoved before Shmulik's eyes.

"Read it. Take your time. You see, I came prepared."

It was a letter from the Minister of Defense, bearing the government seal and signature of the minister himself. It specified that Shmulik had to cooperate in the "Achim" brothers case, volume 72, module 48, bar 37. There was no doubt about the authenticity of the document. Shmulik contemplated it for a while. He had seen this kind of writing in the not-too-distant past. He called them "certificates of extortion." Regev sat comfortably in his chair; he felt more relaxed now than at other times. He was preparing to listen. He understood the pressure Shmulik was experiencing; he knew his old friend was not happy with this situation, but he had a mission and it had to be fulfilled.

"I'm all ears, Shmulik."

"What do you want to know?"

"I want the whole story, and I need to know if there was any involvement from Mossad or any other organization."

Shmulik told his old friend everything he knew. When he had finished his story, he was relieved. The secret that had been trapped inside for so long was now a burden lifted. Regev finished writing something in his notebook and, internally amazed, stood up, put his hand on his friend's shoulder, and walked him to the door of his office. He was truly shocked by what he had just heard, although he had not obtained all the information he wanted. He still did not understand who was behind all of this — who had paid and why they did it. Someone had to know. A great sociological study had been carried out, with remarkable results. Shmulik confided in him that for a long time he had felt hounded, but when they were sure that they could trust him, things went back to normal.

At the end of the meeting, Eli asked if he needed a ride to his house. Shmulik thought about it and decided he'd rather walk to his home, located in northern Tel Aviv. The fresh, mid-autumn air would calm him and help him to realign his thoughts. When he left the army compound, he glanced at his watch in disbelief — he had been with Regev for more than two hours. The night enveloped him as he set out. He was troubled. After five minutes, he reached the intersection of Zabotinski and Iven Gevirol, a place full of lights and nightlife. When the pedestrian signal light turned green, Shmulik began to cross, slowly. Out of nowhere, a black Ford Sierra struck him, launching him high into the air. It had been traveling at full speed. He didn't stand a chance. His body flew more than two meters, crashed onto the sidewalk, and lay there, unmoving. The vehicle didn't even slow down; on the contrary, it sped off faster than it had come and disappear.

36

AHMED
Tehran - Iran
November 1st, 2011

"The Hiat" had been reverberating for several days inside my head. And the idea of being part of its implementation, of being involved somehow in trying to liberate my homeland, Palestine. But ... How? When? Why? It would also be a way of going back to where I was born and raised; or at least that was what my Iranian counterparts claimed in their attempts to convince me.

A few days ago, they met with Reza and me in a room where they very excitedly told us we had been chosen to implement the virus in Zionist territory. For over two hours, they drilled into us hate and loathing for Israel, essentially attempting to brainwash us. Then they went on to the practical side of things, explaining how the operation would be carried out, and what to do in different situations that could arise, although many details were unclear and most of our questions remained unanswered.

After that meeting, I abandoned logic in favor of my feelings: a heady cocktail of confusion, anxiety, fear, and uncertainty. In a technical sense, the project was advanced, almost ready, and our departure depended solely on a decision from the high command. Our technical task — the encryption part of the program — had been completed, the falsification of public and private keys had been finalized, and its functionality had been tested. From the moment we knew of the plan, our guards became our shadows.

The plan was to load the explosive worm onto a small USB memory stick. Upon entry to a USB port, the stick had software on it to neutralize security systems and, even in the case that those ports were disabled by the operating system, or something similar, the key would download a signal to the computer registry by opening the port temporarily and without a trace. Once in the network, the worm would multiply rapidly, spreading via lines of communication, blocking and flooding the network using the TCP, UDP and HTTP protocols and infecting other computers by way of local network or "peer to peer" propagation systems. The content consisted of a string of DDoS attacks; the effect, put simply, would be that the network would instantly collapse from receiving so many requests after activation. After propagation each computer would become a botnet, or what we called it in our slang, "a robot".

We hadn't yet obtained information on our objectives. We were told that we could expect more details when we were in Israel. Another important detail was that, to avoid risks, we wouldn't carry the entire program with us during the trip. Nor were we aware of the entire contents of the worm; we only knew some features and parts of it. According to the rumors, army networks and Mossad would collapse first, and then the whole country would freeze for a while, which would generate enough time to allow ground and air attacks to be undertaken by Iran and its terrorist associates. This plan was not based on any real information; however, it was all based on things that were said in the corridors.

The entire program had been designed by a genius, a Palestinian–Egyptian named Rohan. He had begun working in mid–February 2011, after Stuxnet had already been revealed to the world. His plan was based on the intelligent code that Americans and Israelis had supposedly implemented in Iran to halt the advance of Iran's nuclear program. That program had infected computers by manual means, and only launched its malignant offensive once it had located the Siemens PLC systems. From there, the worm caused the destruction of thousands of centrifuges at Natanz and Bushier, and its activation was stopped only after it was discovered by three Germans who specialized in PLC system security, together with the companies Symantec and Kaspersky.

On this basis, for six months, Rohan tried creating a mutation that would go unnoticed by antivirus systems and firewalls. Eventually, he found a worm that could do everything he needed. I had watched him work with admiration, but also some compassion. Rohan looked like a human robot. He spent 14 or 15 hours a day in front of his computer and refused to be entertained or distracted by anything. He only he cared about his program. Rohan's personal history was similar to that of many Palestinians who had fled to Egypt and become refugees there. His father and brother had been killed by an Israeli mortar that had destroyed his small house. Since then, he had vowed revenge, and every line of code added to the program elicited the same feeling for him as throwing a stone at a roadblock or launching a Molotov cocktail.

A group of six programmers tested each step of Rohan's program code. Often, they would stay for whole nights in order to reach the final phase: the compilation of the entire program. One of the parts of the program consisted of a combination of different methods of DDoS (denial of service) attacks. This part contained four sections. Part 1 was for intervention by TCP/IP connection: the first code sent requests for TCP/IP connection from ghosts, or non-existent addresses. The server would accept the connection and wait for a reply, but as the IP address didn't exist, the source server would never receive any response. When making thousands of requests at once, from different computers all resources will be consumed and thus the entire service will be blocked. Part 2 would consist of a volumetric attack or ICMP flood. When running the second code, massive data packages would be sent, requiring the return of millions of response packages, consuming all the bandwidth on private networks. Part 3 used a UDP flood attack on the network, hindering the reassembly, causing a slowdown or crash. Part 4 of the attack would be directed at applications, with the last code in the series to be executed a specific breach of known programs, all to create additional traffic.

Reza and I had worked on this part of the program together, and as if all this were not enough, Reza had added two other codes that were automatically interconnected — one called "Smurf attack" and the other "attack reflex DNS," which amplified the power of the mother attack even further.

Designing this system and creating and applying fake certificates and key encryption was our task in the program. I later learned that

Reza had already started this in Pakistan as part of a special project, and much like everything else at that time, it did not take long to implement. He told me that he didn't know who was the recipient of this program. We worked with three other programmers on a mini-project that lasted for 12 intense days, with shifts of up to 18 hours. I didn't know the other components of the code, and everything would be put together when I was in Israel. I had no idea how to work the entire program, but I was aware that a group of more than 15 programmers — nearly all of them testers — were aware of the different parts of this puzzle.

Once he realized the scope of the project, Reza had begun to behave strangely. One night in his room, he told me that he wasn't prepared for the mission, and dared not inform anyone. He was afraid the Iranians were just like Mossad. He had always liked working in the background, transforming initiatives into programs that were worth more than bullets and weapons, according to him. He didn't like the idea of being on the front lines, in physical contact with the enemy. I agreed with him that it was a waste to send someone with Reza's potential on this operation. After that conversation, I didn't see him again. He vanished like a ghost along with all of his belongings. The next day, we were informed that he had been referred to another project. Nothing more was said and the matter remained a mystery. I couldn't ask anyone, and no one offered any information.

I quickly realized that the Iranian intelligence department was monitoring us with micro-cameras. One day, lying in bed, staring at the ceiling, I noticed one in our room: it was embedded in the light fixture, very well hidden. Given the importance of the mission, our superiors wanted to be sure that the group members were confident of what they needed to do and were well-prepared. I never said anything, but I greatly resented what had happened to Reza. I wanted to believe that he had actually been commissioned for another mission, but the reality was different; soon rumors began to circulate, saying that he had been hanged that night in the central square.

During that time, a kind of metamorphosis began to occur in my head. I was no longer sure of my feelings, but I was certain that I was tired of escaping, of hiding. I was tired of living this way. The last month had seemed like a year. I didn't know if the fight in which I was involved was worth the lives of so many people, and I was frightened at the thought of losing my own. I thought a lot about my family, my cousin, and the many strange events that had occurred around me, but I didn't let my feelings show, not wanting to suffer the same fate as Reza.

It was 5 a.m. on a Monday when I was awakened by a knock on my door. I hadn't quite managed to get out of bed when two men in green jackets burst into my room. Behind them came another man of medium height, with big glasses and a large bag in his hands. I tried to get up, but one of the men in green squeezed my shoulder and ordered me to sit down. The man with the bag, wearing a crisp white shirt, had a scary look about him that could have made Goliath shiver in fright. Some of his front teeth were missing, revealing a gnarly smile that was in no way a display of pleasantness. He sat at the small desk, took the bag in his hand, and pulled out a head still dripping with blood. I looked away at the same time as my vision clouded over. Then I blinked several times, forcing myself to turn my gaze back to the table where the head lay. My stomach heaved and I started retching, then my body shook as I vomited violently. It was Reza's head. The man in the white shirt smiled.

"We don't like to do these things, but he tried to betray us," he said.

I didn't understand what kind of betrayal Reza had committed; to tell the truth, I wasn't aware of anything.

"What did he do?" I asked in a low, strained voice.

"We found him transmitting messages with a homemade, makeshift radio."

I was stunned, speechless. I thought that anything I said at that moment could be used against me, regardless of what I expressed. So I preferred to keep silent, but I couldn't believe what I was hearing.

"We have only come to inform you that tomorrow morning, you will leave on your mission. In the afternoon, you will receive precise instructions and — always remember Reza. We have confidence in you." He smiled again, this time with a forced grin that betrayed annoyance. He grabbed Reza's head by the hair and shoved it back into the bag. A few drops of fresh blood still leaked onto the table, indicating that Reza had been beheaded just a short time ago. Then they grabbed me by the arm and we left the room.

37

Tehran - Paris
November 2, 2011

The plane moved slowly on the runway — so slowly, that I didn't feel the nerves that usually appear when I arrive in an unknown place, which was strange, given the importance of my mission. I would have liked to have been a tourist and had a chance to discover Paris properly. My tie choked me and my face still burned — especially my chin, after being shaved professionally. It had been at least five years since my face had felt such a sharp razor. As the aircraft glided smoothly, the events of the day before came back to me. After bullying me and showing me Reza's bloodied head, the men had taken me to the headquarters located on the third floor underground. It was the final floor. I had been there only once. The man who had held the head in his hands and had been forcing me to look at it just minutes before, now took me by the arm and made me face a steel door. He left without saying anything. The door opened, and a familiar voice sternly ordered me inside.

He sat at the head of a long table, on which there was a map spread out before him. I recognized him right away — he had been in Bushier when we arrived. On that occasion, he had taken us on a little tour of the base and we had said goodbye cordially, but I could not remember his name or his rank, which was strange, because if there was anything I was proud of, it was my memory. This time, his dark face showed concern, intrigue. Beside him were seated two other men, neither of whom I had ever seen before.

"Sit down," he said.

When I settled into the chair, I could see that the gigantic map represented Israeli territory. Cities and neighborhoods were clearly depicted. The man who had spoken took out a box with plastic figures representing buildings, houses, shopping centers, and military bases, among other structures. One of the others began to place the figures on the map, while the third took out a mini-laptop and a miniature USB memory stick. No one spoke; they were all preparing for the presentation. I chose not to try and get ahead of things; I was anxious, but not afraid. The man with the laptop was introduced as Asher. He hit a button on a tiny projector and an image spread like lightning on a white wall. Then, the man from Bushier broke the silence.

"Tomorrow, you will leave on your mission. It will not be easy, but we've observed you for a long time, and we believe that you will carry it out effectively."

Then, he pulled a white envelope from a drawer and took out a red passport that was stamped "Belgium."

"Your new name is Enzo Shiles — remember that. As of today, you are Enzo, and that is how we will address you. In this envelope, you have a ticket to France. The flight leaves tomorrow at 8 a.m.; it is Air France 545. There will be a car waiting for you at 6:30 a.m. Do not worry; you'll pass all airport controls and security easily. There is also money here, but not too much — we do not want to arouse suspicion. It will be enough until you reach your final destination."

"Final destination?" I repeated.

"Yes, your final destination is Israel — Tel Aviv."

Once the jet bridge was positioned at the airplane's door, I opened my eyes. My head was a whirlwind of images of the last day on Persian soil: the program, the locations, the word "Israel." Reza and I had been confident that we would go to the occupied territories. Now I was nervous, and with poor instructions and many unanswered questions, everything was mixed up in my head. I checked my passport to make sure it was real; indeed, there was my new name and my new identity looking up at me.

In actual fact, the name Enzo didn't displease me. It seemed original, genuine, and I felt that it suited me well. Now it was time to trust the Iranians and see if their passport forgery was indeed perfect. I was in the hands of people I didn't know, who had killed my friend for simply having had different thoughts. I never believed the story about the radio and broadcasting. I just wouldn't accept that Reza was a traitor.

The immigrations officer looked at my passport, then at my face, turned, made a signal to his boss, turned again, stamped the visa quickly and returned the document. Everything happened very fast, as if it were a scene that had been practiced beforehand. The big arrivals lounge was full and people were pushing their way through to their bags, which were dancing around the luggage carousel. I had only a carry-on bag, so I made my way to the exit. My instructions were clear: wherever possible, I should avoid places where there were police, so I hurried away. In the blink of an eye, I was outside, breathing the cold air of Paris. I thought about how I would recognize my contact in this sea of human faces. I didn't know him, so I decided to wait and see what happened. Suddenly, I felt a tap on my shoulder and, as I turned around, a short, bald man with a pointy, bushy beard greeted me warmly.

"I am Omar Nahaf, cultural manager of the Iranian embassy in Paris, at your service."

I extended my hand in greeting, a little impressed by his position; the cultural manager of the Islamic Republic himself was in front of me.

Omar did nothing but smile. I had already learned not to ask questions, so I let him lead me away. He directed me to a black limousine with tinted windows. The driver already had the engine running, so when Omar and I got into the back seat, the limousine quickly pulled out from the carpark.

Looking out the windows, knowing that others couldn't see in, gave me a strange feeling. The images of poor suburbs, whose names I didn't know, reminded me of where I had lived. When we passed through an Arab neighborhood, a memory came to mind of my childhood with my parents in Bethlehem — of dust-covered streets where the universal children's sport was throwing stones at Zionist cars passing through the area. Each kid had his own slingshot; we weren't lacking in stones, and even though it was almost nothing, it was enough to make us happy. When we left school, we would risk approaching the border posts and practice to see how far we could fire the stones from our slingshots. As if it were yesterday, I remembered the first slingshot I owned: my father had made it himself with his own hands. He hadn't done it out of hatred towards Jews, but because he knew I really wanted it. He always wanted to make me happy. Ours was not a normal Palestinian family. My father was never part of any political party or warlike activities; my mother didn't care about revolutions, either — she was an old-fashioned woman who believed that her place as a woman was in the house, caring for her family. In addition, she suffered her own torment for having brought only one male child into the world, a real trauma in Muslim society.

My father always stayed faithfully by her side, without blaming her for anything. He was a good Muslim: he prayed five times a day; he went to the mosque and tried to teach me the verses of our holy book. But when things got heated in the mosque, he would quietly withdraw. For him, the most important thing was keeping his job, as well as supporting his family. That was why he put up with the routine of getting up at 4 a.m. and waiting at the border to meet the contractor he trusted so blindly. Often, in critical times, when the borders were closed, the Israeli would manage things by disguising him and even sheltering him at his home until things returned to normal.

I will never forget when I was nine, my father giving me a dark-colored kite. I loved to fly it. He taught me so many techniques, like how to make it go as high as a comet, which I hadn't known how to do, and we would run together watching the flimsy fabric and wood construction flutter through the sky. How I loved those moments. That year, the Intifada[34] erupted with force across all the occupied territories and life changed. From then on, my father hardly ever went to work, and when he did, he did so in hiding. I will never forget those days. The streets became violent and my father wouldn't let me outside. We spent weeks under curfew. Because of the Israeli army patrols, the streets remained empty. Every day, barricades would be thrown together and violent demonstrations ending with the deaths of people we knew. I remember ambulances constantly going back and forth with their sirens wailing, making their way through to the wounded and dying.

I wondered if maybe everything I had experienced in my childhood had marked me somehow, had led me to the situation I was in now. I guessed I would never fully know the answer.

---

34 Intifada: the Palestinian uprising against Israeli occupation of the West Bank and Gaza Strip.

Although my father was always very religious, I never felt any attachment to religion. I usually only practiced it out of duty and respect for my elders. When we threw stones, it was more like a children's game than out of hatred towards Jews.

I was unsympathetic, but neither did I detest them. And yes, I loved my cousin. He was like a talisman for me. He was eight years older than me, and I'd seen him handling a Kalashnikov[35]. If my father had known, he would have separated us, but luckily, no one knew. Rafaq was one of the best slingshot shooters I had ever seen. At 18, he was a hero for having hit a soldier in the eye. I admired his daring, his bravery, his courage, but I didn't understand the blind hatred he had towards Jews. He wanted me to follow his lead and I followed him everywhere. That's why when he offered me the chance to escape with him to Jordan via the Allenby Bridge, I accepted right away, and I threw myself into the adventure. I was only 10 years old. I begged my father to let me go, saying that the Intifada would overwhelm us. My cousin spoke with him as well and promised him that he would take care of me. My mother wept inconsolably for weeks before I left, and it was the weeping of someone who has no more tears left. Although I understood her pain, I wanted to go with my cousin. I was tired of so much violence. A few days before leaving, I lost my kite — one of the most valuable objects I had, as my father had made it with his own hands. A wild wind swept it away and sent it to Jerusalem. I ran after it until the soldiers in green obstructed my path. Finally, at that moment, I decided to change my course and leave. I was a kid, but strangely enough, I knew what I wanted. I wanted freedom. I wanted something better for myself, and I trusted my cousin implicitly.

Even then, I knew that Jordan was no paradise for Palestinians, but I thought it couldn't be worse than Bethlehem, with the Intifada in full swing.

I remember dreaming many times about the old city of Jerusalem. I loved its colossal walls, its scents, its green eucalyptus trees, the mountains that seemed to hug and protect the city. When I was five years old, my father took me to the shuk, the central market in West Jerusalem, where I feasted my eyes upon all of the things in each store. I had never

---

35 Kalashnikov: a series of automatic rifles based on the original design of Mikhail Kalashnikov.

seen so many goods and so many tourists. Many of them greeted us in passing. We ate a delicious, sweet knafe[36] and exquisite shwarma. On one of the streets I saw the Wailing Wall, and I was struck by its height and the beauty of its stones. Looming behind it was the Mosque of Omar, with its gilded cap, which stood tall as if asking permission to exist. Those images would stay in my head forever.

One cloudy day, during the Intifada, my cousin Rafaq and I fled through a hole in the wire that he had prepared in advance. The hole was so small, I remember hurting my leg as I climbed through. Rafaq scurried through like a lizard, without any problems. We walked through the bushes for a whole day. Rafaq was equipped with a map and a compass. The army had spread throughout the West Bank without leaving any areas out of their control, yet my cousin managed to find the way to the Allenby Bridge — the only land crossing between Jordan and Israel. I was totally stunned, amazed that Rafaq had everything fully prepared. We climbed into a Jordanian truck, wriggling like rats under the rear seats. Just moments before, Rafaq had given an envelope to the driver. We passed the two border posts without problems. Later, I learned that Rafaq had been planning this for over a year with great care and attention to detail. I also learned that he had paid dearly for the Jordanian guide, with money earned at work in one of the few gas stations in Bethlehem, where he washed windows and windshields.

After a while, we found out that Rafaq's house had been demolished by the army; an antitank mine had exploded out front, destroying his home and two others. His older brother had been there with an arsenal of weapons and, by then, his family was gone. I never saw his mother. It was as if the earth had swallowed her whole. Mysteriously, his father was killed just two weeks later after being accused of collaborating with the Israelis. He was stoned to death at the hands of PLO members. I later learned that some of Rafaq's supposed friends had participated in it. My cousin was very sad; the grief was evident on his face; but with his goals in mind, he managed to overcome it and move on. After that, I clung to Rafaq like never before. At first, we took residence in a Palestinian refugee camp near the port of Aqaba in the south end of Jordan. It was a tourist area, and I enjoyed running along the beaches. We both did wha-

---

36 Knafe: A sweet, Arabic dessert.

tever jobs were available: carrying bags of potatoes in the market and even packing goods on ships leaving the port. Those were the happiest moments of my childhood. I had forgotten about school, but as I could read and write, Rafaq treated me like I was super-gifted; I helped him whenever I could.

When work became scarce, we moved into a Palestinian refugee village near Amman, close to the city entrance. There, it became clear to me exactly how much the Jordanians hated us. I had heard stories about the "Black September," in which many Palestinians were slaughtered in their own homes and villages, but now I felt it for myself. It was almost impossible to get a job. Not even other Palestinians would give us work for fear of losing the trust of the local community. The frustration was obvious; our own Muslim brothers despised us. I didn't understand at the time why these attitudes existed. Everything erupted one summer night in a nearby village, when local citizens had gone into their neighbors' houses with shotguns and carried out a brutal massacre, riddling children, women, and men with bullets and butchering them without pity for anyone or anything. I remember that night in detail. Rafaq had covered my face so I wouldn't see the horrific images when we went to try to help the few who had survived. That night, he grabbed me by the arm, took a bag with our things, and we left; I wasn't able to ask him anything. His face was contorted, his eyes moist. By that point, I had blind faith in him.

We headed south; we walked a lot, ate little, and slept less. Finally, we reached the place where we had lived: Akaba. I was very happy to find myself by the sea again, but soon I realized that Rafaq didn't want to stay in Jordan. His words didn't express his hatred, but his eyes radiated it. One day, he told me that we would have to return to Palestine, our land. By then, the Intifada was over. He expected me to say something, but I remained silent. I knew if Rafaq thought it would be best, it would be. I began to feel the abuse as well and to realize that we were not welcome in this "land of kings," as Rafaq called it. We tried to raise some money by keeping ourselves busy with odd jobs, and one night we headed to the port holding the same bag with which we had arrived. Rafaq had brought an envelope in his hand. A fat man with his arms covered in tattoos greeted us with a sour face. While examining the envelope, he asked, "How old is the boy?"

"Sixteen," Rafaq said, although I had not yet turned 14.

"He's very small; only you can travel," announced the man.

Rafaq started arguing and, for the first time, I felt afraid of being separated from him. But Rafaq gave more money to the fat man and convinced him to let me go. After taking everything we had, he agreed. Upon reaching the barge, I realized that the ship was extremely precarious, even for an adult.

"We will journey out in the open," the man informed us. And he added, "You are responsible for the boy, understand?"

Rafaq nodded. He told me we were headed to Sharm el-Sheikh, and mentioned the beautiful beaches there, nothing else. I nodded, although no one had asked me anything; in fact, nothing mattered to me at that point — my sole focus was just continuing along with my cousin.

I don't remember much from that trip. Fatigue overcame me quickly, and I slept curled up next to Rafaq. I can only recall the beautiful beaches of Sharm that I saw upon waking, when, completely soaked, we finally came ashore.

From then on, everything happened very quickly — almost without time to remember the events, or perhaps, those that came up were blocked from my memory. In Sharm, a paradise island that belongs to Egypt, we were rejected just as we had been in Jordan, so Rafaq decided we should cross the border and return to our homeland. We climbed to the Rafah Crossing and hurried across to the Gaza Strip. Rafaq seemed quieter there and we found ourselves odd jobs in the blink of an eye. More and more, we began to frequent the same street that had been burned again and again by different militant groups and organizations, most of whom tried to recruit us for their causes.

Any youth, no matter his age, was a potential soldier. Every other day, there were violent demonstrations and marches, and there were often funerals where the dead body was wrapped in flags of the PLO or Hamas. Soon, other organizations began to challenge the power and representation of the Palestinian people, and not only that, but also for the money that came from the wealthy Gulf countries. Rafaq quickly joined Hamas, the most popular group in Gaza, and so, of course, I did, too, but not on the army forces, just as a supporter. I remember my youth ID card, green with a huge picture. We were promised we wouldn't be involved in any violence, but shortly after joining, they offered Rafaq his first mission. From then on, he wore the green uniform and carried a Kalashnikov to every protest or event. We didn't talk much after that, and we lost the connection we had had between us that had kept us so close. I returned to school, a small facility which had been set up in a mosque[37] by the organization.

From the beginning, I was the most advanced, simply because I could read and write, which was not common at all. It was quite sad to see 11- and 12-year-old children taking a book or a pen in their hands for the first time. Classes were repeated day after day: one hour dedicated to reading and writing, a half hour for mathematics, three hours devoted to religion, and one hour set aside exclusively for discussing the organization and exploring its foundations and ideals. It was a very routine system, the goal of which was to instill hatred for Israel and the United States.

One day, in my last year of high school, Rafaq didn't come back, and that night, I finally understood what it was to be truly fearful. The next morning, I found myself before a crowd carrying his body through the main streets of Gaza. I was his family; his only relation. So they made me sit almost on top of his bier — which, for the time being, was covered with nothing more than a simple flag; all that separated my body from his was a thin piece of green fabric. What comes to my mind is that I didn't have the slightest chance to mourn or say goodbye to him as I wanted to. I just remember the screaming, the gunshots, the contorted faces, rage, and his gaunt face with half-closed eyes. I glimpsed some signs of harmony in his last expression. Perhaps he had found peace after so much time spent looking for it; perhaps death was his much-desired peace.

As my memories shifted and changed, so did the Parisian views and landscapes outside the limousine. We were leaving the suburbs behind and getting closer to neighborhoods. In the distance, I saw the famous Eiffel Tower. Inside the car was total silence; no one spoke, and Omar was still smiling as if that were part of his mission. When the car pulled up outside the luxurious Sheraton Hotel, Omar gave me an envelope and bid me farewell, telling me to have a good rest. When I opened the

---

37 Mosque: A place of worship for followers of Islam.

door to room 214 on the 14th floor, I inspected the envelope and anxiety consumed me anew. Inside was a ticket for Air France flight 866, bound for Tel Aviv.

Back to Palestine.

38

LEONEL
Denmark, Faroe Islands
October 29th, 2011

Waves crashed against the sides of the boat, drawn higher by the rough winds that tormented us, its passengers, threatening to snap the vessel in half as if it were no more than a small child's toy. When I first saw how small it was, I had a moment of apprehension, as I thought it could handle no more than just a few buckets of water, but to my surprise, it easily withstood the fierceness of the sea.

Me and the old man, the only crew, were soaked to our souls, frozen in the cold weather that registered at 12 degrees below zero. We raised and lowered the sail to the rhythm of the fierce winds and even allowed ourselves to enjoy the fishing. At last, we reached the Faroes, having completed the task at hand: our nets were packed with an enormous haul of fish.

When we arrived on land, old Asterix (I never did learn his name) anchored the barge, thanked me with a nod while mumbling something unintelligible in his language, and extended his hand to give me a woolen bag of colorful coins. I immediately lowered my head in gratitude. Undoubtedly, he knew I was in trouble and had thus decided to take me along with him. We had spent 20 interminable hours at sea, immersed in salt, vodka, and smelly fish. Along the way, the old Dane had tried to convince me that alcohol warmed the bones. I wasn't sure myself, but I drank it anyway, hoping at least to forget.

The old man left quickly and headed to the market to sell his merchandise while it was still fresh. I stayed, wandering around the port. I needed time to think, to decide in which direction to take my life. I completely ruled out the idea of surrender, but how much longer could I stay in hiding, away from the Mossad's tentacles? While I was still meandering around the port, I looked at my right hand. Somehow, I should get rid of the GPS implanted under my skin. I thought of cutting myself open to remove the device, but at the same time I knew that in these low temperatures and high humidity, an open wound without proper disinfectant could be lethal.

I was uncertain how much money the old man had paid me. I didn't recognize these coins, but they didn't seem to be normal currency. Some of the golden ones did in fact seem like gold. I fingered them and bit one, arriving at the conclusion that they were real.

After walking down a seemingly endless hill, I came across an old tavern on the side of the road. The scenery was beautiful — accumulated snow adorned the tops of the trees, although my cold and wet clothing didn't let me enjoy the setting. I went inside. Some old men were sharing a pitcher of beer at the bar. Using more gestures than words, I asked one of them where the bathroom was. They laughed at my appearance and pointed to a door beneath a wooden staircase. When I stepped inside the door, suddenly I felt a sharp blow to my neck, followed by a hollow sound like broken glass; then, nothing more.

Like a gentle caress, as I regained consciousness, I began hearing voices and tried to recognize the language. I opened my eyes, raised my head, and was momentarily paralyzed by a sharp pain in my skull. I lifted my hand to check my neck and was surprised to see that my hands had been bound together with a plastic tie — the kind they use on protesters in a riot. With some difficulty, I managed to touch the nape of my neck and didn't find any blood. I'd received a strategic blow that had left no traces, possibly executed by a professional. I looked around the room; aside from the bed and a coffee table, there was nothing — no windows, no other furniture. I soon became aware that the voices were speaking in Arabic. It was clearly Arabic. What did they want from me? The first thing that crossed my mind was that the Mossad had found me. The voices came closer and the door opened abruptly. Two men of average height entered the room in silence. The one that seemed to be the boss had a shaved head, and the other had a beard that almost reached the middle of his chest. The man with the shaved head ordered the bearded one to take off my clothes and frisk me, and when he did, my body started shaking uncontrollably. The man with the shaved head shouted something in Arabic and the other hit me hard in the stomach as he continued searching my body. As his fingers came upon my arm, he felt the magnetic GPS device under the skin and said something to his friend, who came over to confirm what he had found. Then they shared a knowing look and suddenly left the room.

With great difficulty, I tried my best to reach an old blanket that was lying on the floor, but as I did so, the two men came back into the room shouting. The man with the shaved head had a sharp knife in his hand and a kind of bandage. I wasn't sure what they were going to do. When I saw the objects they carried, I began screaming and shaking like a crazy man. The bearded one put his knees upon my chest to keep me from moving. Then the man with the shaved head came towards me with the knife. I thought he was going to stab me in the chest, but suddenly he drove it towards my arm. I felt the metal piercing my flesh, saw a stream of blood, and then silence again; nothing.

When I opened my eyes, I found my arm crudely bandaged; a bloodstain pierced the white cloth that seemed to contain the bleeding, but I knew that if they hadn't disinfected the wound and the bandage, an infection could lead to gangrene. I had no notion of how much time had passed, which worried me. I needed to be treated by a doctor quickly. I still had my hands tied and couldn't do anything. I realized, though, that they had removed the GPS device. I started to scream with all the strength I could until the man with the shaved head entered the room.

"Listen to me, I don't know what you want from me, but you should take me to a hospital," I said. "If not, I will die."

"Not so fast," he said, shaking his head negatively.

"Why me? Who are you?"

"We are your cousins," he laughed, "we are from Hamas. Very soon you will be close to home."

"What do you mean? I need a doctor now."

"Quiet, quiet, I'll change your dressing in a moment. Now relax, it is nighttime. Tomorrow we have a big day ahead of us."

I couldn't think straight because of the pain. My head hurt and I didn't dare to look at the wound. I couldn't even consider sleeping. Five minutes later, the bald man entered with a syringe and stuck it in my arm without preamble. Just as I began to wonder what it was, I fell asleep.

39

AHMED
France - Tel Aviv
November 3rd, 2011

As the captain announced the last door check before landing, Air France 866 gave two turns and nosed toward the empty landing strip. I curled up in my aisle seat in the twenty-sixth row and pulled my passport out of my jacket pocket. I saw the name Enzo Shiles. I still wasn't used to my new identity. In the same pocket, I had the USB memory drive that would destroy targets unknown to me, along with my reservation at the Plaza Hotel in Tel Aviv. I was nervous and my hands were sweating. "You have to stay calm," I repeated to myself over and over. I had to complete this mission. If not, I would be easy prey to catch.

When the aircraft hit pavement, a group of religious folk with their black outfits and kipas[38] fervently applauded, and the rest of the crew joined them in a kind of ritual that I had never seen before. I grabbed my satchel and, after disembarking, headed towards passport control. At that moment, I felt like all eyes were on me. Behind the counters, young Jewish women dressed in shirts colored the same light blue as the police uniforms were deeply fixated on their computers, checking passports. When it was my turn, I handed my document over to a dark-skinned woman with jet black hair. She looked into my eyes for 10 suspenseful seconds, then lowered her head to focus on her LCD monitor. She began typing and got started on her laundry list of questions.

---

38 Kipa: a small ritual cap traditionally worn by Jewish men.

"What is the purpose of your visit?"

"Business."

"Where will you stay?"

"The Plaza Hotel." I showed her my reservation, thinking that having it in writing was more convincing than my word.

"Enzo?" she asked.

I nodded my head while she prepared to stamp the visa in my passport. When she handed it back, my hands were sweaty. I rubbed the passport between my fingers and took a last look at the stamp. Without any checked baggage to pick up, I quickly went outside to take in the fresh air and enjoy my limited freedom. It occurred to me that I was living the dream of a terrorist: in the heart of Israel itself! Yet I didn't feel that there was anything special about it; I didn't harbor a strong hatred. I was there to fulfill a mission, nothing more. Those feelings would haunt me over the next few days.

The room on the 18th floor of the Plaza Hotel had a view of the Mediterranean Sea. Although we were in the last days of autumn, the coast was full of young people. A strong breeze from the east made the waves choppy and red flags set the areas where people could swim.

The clock showed 2 p.m. and I thought about how enticing the double bed looked. I placed the USB memory drive under the pillow and lay down for a nap. When I awoke, the sun was still beating on the windows and gently trickling in through the heavy curtains. I immediately felt a presence in the room. My heart thumped in my chest, and I shot my hand under the pillow to make sure the USB key was still there. It was. I relaxed a little, but then as I turned around, I saw that there was a man sitting in the armchair next to my bed. I withdrew my legs in fright and blurted, in English, "Who are you? What do you want?"

"Do not worry," he replied in Arabic. "I'm your contact, so ... relax."

"How did you get inside?"

"It's a long story that doesn't matter now," he said, stroking his bushy mustache.

"OK. Where do we start?"

"Get dressed. We're going out."

I still wondered how he had entered my room, a question I knew would remain unanswered. As I dressed, he inspected our surroundings.

Outside, a pleasant freshness came from the sea as we walked along the coast in Tel Aviv. The sun was like a huge, dark-yellow egg that left its shimmer in the sky. There was something about those people that made the sea a part of them — those youngsters building their castles on the beach, braving the cold of early November — something I couldn't define. My contact walked in silence beside me and seemed somewhat fixated on what was behind us. He hadn't told me his name and I didn't want to ruin his clandestine act.

"Do you have the USB flash drive with you?"

"Yes, here it is," and I took it out of my pocket so he could see.

"Listen to me well: when we're done here, immediately return to the hotel, pay the bill, and leave. Today you'll move to an apartment on Arlozorov Street. The place you're at now is fenced in and there's too much security — we made a mistake by putting you up there. Here's the address to the new place and the key to get in." He handed me a piece of paper with writing on it and a key on a small ring. "Give me the USB drive. Now, listen to me well ..." he repeated. "At the apartment, you'll find a laptop. These are the credentials and instructions to operate and run the program. Here is the mother program with the login code." He pulled a CD out of his bag and handed it to me. "You have to stay alert, very attentive. Don't go out into the street. The refrigerator is stocked up with a week's worth of food. The phone is disconnected. Here you have a cell phone, but don't use it. Listen to me well." He repeated the phrase a third time, which made me a little nervous.

"I'll call you in the next few days to give you an IP number," he said. "You'll run the program by inputting that number."

"I need to know the full plan," I managed to say.

"You already know your part in the plan, and that's enough."

"I need to know more; I can't continue on like this."

"Shut up. You'll know when the time comes. Meanwhile, wait; study the instructions that you have received and get to know the program, but don't run it yet."

And just like that, without telling me his name or saying goodbye, he scuttled into an alleyway that intersected with Hayarkon Street. I was left with the CD, a small slip of rolled-up paper with instructions, a key, and the directions to my new home, plus a terrible uncertainty: how could I survive the next few days, locked in an apartment waiting for a phone call, knowing nothing, without communicating with anyone? I became more impatient and nervous with each passing moment. My morale was not at a high point. It had all started with Reza's disappearance in Iran — and later when I saw his head, with everything worsening over time. The idea of carrying out a plan like this without knowing fully what or why turned my stomach. But I sighed and resolved to follow the instructions. I had pledged revenge so that my cousin's death at the hands of the Zionist enemy wouldn't be in vain, and I was going to keep that promise.

40

Tel Aviv
November 1st, 2011

The papers were scattered across the table. Eli Regev rested his head on his left hand and leaned his body into the desktop. A toothache had been tormenting him since early morning, and he could hardly focus on anything other than the pain, at one point thinking there was nothing worse than that feeling. The unexpected death of Shmulik Sade also tormented and distracted him. He needed to solve the riddle of the two "brothers" and find these young people as soon as possible. The papers on his desk showed many curious facts, and he really wanted to solve the death of Shmulik Sade. He was almost certain the accident was caused not by a madman who didn't stop, as the police had said, but by an assassin. He also preferred to investigate this case on his own, because everything seemed connected. There was a higher hand in it, of that he had no doubt, but the question was, whose?

Regarding his current mission, if this project was organized by the Ministry of Defense and executed by the Mossad or Shabak, why had the Ministry of Defense now given him free rein to ask around about the two young men? And who would be trying to interrupt this work? Among his table full of documents there were reports of the murder of Rachel Mizrachi, the nurse who had participated in the births of the switched children, and other reports on the attack against the young Leonel and Moshe Cohen in the Jerusalem cafe, and even more on the recent death of Sade. He had to calm down and examine the threads to understand the implications and connections of these events. Plus, there was something that added intrigue to everything: someone wanted to get rid of Leonel and in France had tried again. The young man had already escaped three assassination attempts.

The worst thing was that nobody knew anything. It had been many days since the footsteps of the pair had vanished. The Arabic, who in fact wasn't so by birth, had fallen off the radar since getting to Iran. His arrival in Persian territory had already been confirmed by the Mossad. He knew of a possible plot that worried the highest levels of government and had already reached the table of the prime minister and the president himself. The other young man was lost in Scandinavia. His GPS device hadn't logged a signal for several days and there was no sign of his whereabouts. It seemed he had also vanished.

Eli scratched his head and turned back to the papers. His personal problems disappeared for a moment. For quite some time, his life hadn't been normal. His wife, who had mistreated him for years, had died a while back of cancer. He had always loved her, but never felt reciprocity. They had two daughters, both living in the United States and both of whom maintained little contact with their father. He had become addicted to work, and could spend whole days in his office, or lying on the old sofa in his apartment in north Tel Aviv, reading whatever he had on hand that was related to his job.

His roles in the areas of government and the Mossad itself were somewhat confusing to people who knew him. Now he was independent. As an army general, he had gone on to serve in the Defense Ministry, where he handled different functions in different government offices, always in the area of secret investigations. Ten years before, the Defense Ministry had fired him suddenly, and no one knew why. A week after his dismissal, the defense minister himself invited him to his office in Tel Aviv HaKirya, where he had prepared an office for him. Eli found he had been reinstated, but in a new role. The defense minister explained to him that he would no longer be working with the government, but would become a liaison between the Ministry of Defense, the Mossad, and Shabak. He would be accountable to no one other than the minister himself or one of his envoys. At first, it was a rather confusing situation. It made it quite difficult for him to adjust to his new position, but he eventually understood the forces at hand: the government needed more control over the two agencies, the Shabak and Mossad; they wanted him to double-check that everything was being done as it should be, that orders were being followed, and he needed to make sure any problems or events were kept from the press or other dangerous hands.

Eli knew that of all the cases he had handled up until that day, what he was now working on was the most important of them all and would define his career for better or worse. Data existed that pointed to the Mossad having covered up something, and the defense minister wanted to know what it was. The young men had to appear, right? That's what the minister himself had said, and he promised to provide full support and all the resources needed. But at the same time, the government was very concerned with rumors of a "cyberwar." The most curious fact found in the heap of documents on the table was the name of Moshe Cohen. He wasn't sure how someone with Moshe's profile was involved in all of this, or what his relationship was with the young Jew. Why had they tried to kill him? Or perhaps the bullets in the cafe in Jerusalem had been meant only for the young man?

He realized he would need to work a little more on that mystery and then try to contact Cohen. He needed a little more information and data, so he devoted himself to going over everything that was on his messy desk. A police report drew his attention, and again, after the murder of Rachel Mizrachi, appeared the name of Moshe Cohen. The old man had been in the house late the night before, and had even shared a bed with the victim moments before her death. Go figure, he thought. The report didn't mention Moshe as a suspect because he had an alibi that placed him elsewhere at the time of slaying. The information was very convincing. He didn't believe that Moshe Cohen had killed Rachel Mizrachi, but who had perpetrated this murder? He closed the door and turned on his laptop. In his database he quickly found the phone number for Moshe Cohen. The code was in Jerusalem. For a moment he tried to get into Moshe's mind. If it had been him, he would have had to move very quickly to leave this place and move as soon as possible from the first attack and the others that followed. The conclusion was that Moshe Cohen certainly no longer lived in Jerusalem. This was confirmed when he telephoned 02-88612345, and a recorded female voice said the number had been disconnected.

41

Metzuba Kibbutz - Northern Israel
November 1st, 2011

Moshe counted the money again. A close nephew had withdrawn all funds from his account, as he had entrusted. A few days before he had signed a power of attorney authorizing his nephew to handle all of his belongings. Now, with the money in hand, he was just sitting in his blue Subaru, watching the coast of Rishon LeZion where he had spent the last few days. After Rachel's death, he had left Jerusalem and had hid at his nephew's place. He started the car and took the Hayarkon route, going North. It was 3 p.m. and he knew this would be a good way to travel, as traffic was relatively mild. He had three hours to get to Metsuba, a kibbutz[39] located in the north very close to the perimeter of Lebanon, where a good friend lived who would let him stay until all this blew past. He knew that even there he couldn't feel entirely safe. He didn't yet understand the events that had unfolded. Who killed Rachel, and why? Who tried to kill Leonel in Jerusalem, or was the attack for him and not Leonel? There were too many coincidences, too many questions, and not one answer.

So he decided to disconnect from the world for a few days in the north, far away from the heat. His name had appeared in the newspapers. In the police, everyone knew him, and, although he hadn't made any enemies, he also hadn't made many friends, and it was very clear that more than one wouldn't hesitate to use a rumor to destroy him. To crush him like a fly. This was the world he knew, where everyone jockeyed for the best position.

---

39 Kibbutz: An Israeli collective community.

He was already far from that game. While he was thinking of the recent events, a cold sweat trickled down his forehead. He thought of Rachel and her life, all that she had sacrificed, and he relived the memory of that night that was his, as whole as it had always been. He still had her naked figure before him, her lips, her arms. Suddenly, a white Fiat cut him off and jolted his thoughts back to reality. He gave the finger to the driver and decided to concentrate on the road.

At 6 p.m. he arrived in Nahariya, and stopped to buy a falafel[40] at a place beside the road, because he was hungry. He filled a pita with the falafel and devoured it, dribbling some hummus down his shirt as he gobbled it up. He wiped up a bit and, as he was doing so, happened to notice that the same Fiat that had cut him off a few hours before was now driving into the parking lot. He hesitated, but the significance failed to register. He got out of his car and went into a bar next to the restaurant, hoping to find a cold beverage to wash down the falafel. He ordered a Macabbi beer and sat on one of the bar stools, watching the news on an old TV. When he heard about the death of Rachel again, he went out, threw down and furiously stamped on his cell phone; now, he felt free without it. He asked for a phone in the bar and called his friend's kibbutz, announcing that he would arrive in an hour, as they had agreed.

He headed north along the path by the sea. As he watched the waves lap against the coast along the highway, he thought about the whereabouts of Leonel and how he could contact him now. He felt like a fugitive, even though he didn't know who had been involved or even what had really happened. He needed time to study the equation and find out who was behind all this. He thought of changing his identity to help him operate more freely.

By the time his Subaru arrived at the kibbutz, it was 7 p.m. At the gate, a soldier with a shotgun in his arms asked for his documents and marked the visitor register. Then he manually opened the fence.

Moshe knew the place. When he stopped the car, he watched the pines sway in the wind and began to feel a hint of peace. But his friend surprised him from behind in a bear hug that alarmed him. Startled and without having seen his face, Moshe made a split decision that he had

---

40 Falafel: A deep-fried ball, made from ground chickpeas or fava beans. It's a very popular dish in the Middle East.

learned in the police — he threw his friend over his shoulder. As he slammed into the ground, his friend shouted, "What are you doing, you bastard? Are you crazy?"

"Forgive me, Niv! You scared me!"

Niv had good stature and the muscles of a man who clearly toiled on his farm, so he wasn't hurt.

"What have you been up to?" he asked as he rose to his feet.

"Forgive me again; I'll tell you," Moshe said, as he grabbed his stuff from the car, "but first I need to rest."

"You won't find trouble here. Come, I prepared the room overlooking the pool. You have the entire balcony for yourself, as you always liked."

Moshe went up to his room, left the bag on the bed, and went to the balcony. He took a deep breath and stared at the hills of Lebanon. After a moment he wondered if Ahmed would be found in that country.

42

Metzuba Kibbutz - Northern Israel
November 1st, 2011

The murderer waited a few hours in his car. It had been a long trip and his Fiat Uno was overheated. Once the car had begun to steam, he made a pit stop in Shlomi, a small town close to the Lebanese border. He had decided to find a mechanic, because he couldn't continue. Time was his worst enemy. At 8 p.m., the possibility of finding someone to help him with his vehicle in this tiny city was a fantasy. Despite the odds, he walked the dark streets and stopped at a bar to ask for a mechanic or someone who could help him with the car. The shop's employee winced, indicating that he knew no one. An old man who was enjoying his beer at a table near the counter overheard his query and spoke to him.

"I know someone who can help you; he lives four blocks from here," he said.

"Take me there, please."

"Buy me a beer for the road," said the old man, who had already drunk way too much.

The murderer paid for the beer and left with the old man, who was finishing off his bottle. They began driving until they reached a deserted street with a garage that had a sign that read "Shuki the Mechanic" on its closed door. The old man went to look for the mechanic, who came out in his pajamas, saying that he couldn't help so late at night.

"It's too late!" he complained.

"Please at least give me a diagnosis," the murderer asked him.

Shuki shook his head, but said, "It'll be 150 shekels just to take a look."

"No problem. I promise to pay."

The murderer retrieved his vehicle and the mechanic began examining the engine. He soon had found the problem.

"It has a hole in the radiator," he told the murderer.

"Can you fix it now?"

"Now? Are you crazy? I told you I would just have a look to see what the problem was."

"I need it now," said the murderer, raising his voice.

"There is no way I can fix it for you now. It's almost 9 p.m.! Leave the car, get a room at the motel, and I'll fix it tomorrow."

The murderer was losing his patience. He demanded that the mechanic do the work immediately, explaining that he couldn't waste any more time. During this exchange, the old man stood to the side drinking his beer. Then the murderer moved quickly, drawing a gun with a huge silencer attached and placed it against the mechanic's temple.

"I need this now, I told you!

"Hey ... relax. Lower the gun," Shuki said, scared.

"I'll lower it when you begin working."

When he saw the gun, the old drunkard started running. The murderer didn't hesitate a second: he quickly aimed and pulled the trigger. The bullet pierced the old man's back without a sound and he collapsed onto the sidewalk next to a sewer. The assassin made the mechanic help and together they pulled the body into the garage.

"I don't have a replacement radiator for you, but I can weld the hole in this one so you can get back on the road."

"Perfect, do it quickly. It shouldn't have come to this," he said angrily.

They looked at each other strangely. The mechanic put a blanket on the floor, leaned back, lit the welder flame and began to patch the hole in the radiator. In half an hour the car was ready. The garage floor was wet with blood coming from the hole in the back of the old man. The assassin, standing with the gun in his hand, considered the mechanic, unsure of what to do. In the end, he tossed 500 shekels on the counter, got into his car, reversed, and then accelerated forward out of the shop and onto the highway, traveling at full speed.

He took the road leading south and after eight kilometers found himself at the entrance to Metzuba kibbutz. He was frustrated by the night's events, and especially by his car, which had disappointed him for the first time at the worst moment possible.

He left the Fiat on the side of the road and pulled a pair of large, steel shears from the trunk. The main entrance was about two kilometers away, at the end of a steep hill, but he preferred to cut the fence and climb up from there to avoid the security gate. He waited until 10 p.m. to start making the hole, because he knew that the security patrol made its rounds every half hour. He had it all noted down. The next round would be at 9:50 p.m. He knelt between some bushes and the fence and got to work. Within 10 minutes, he had completed the hole, slipped underneath, and begun to climb. In the hustle and bustle, he tripped and hit the same leg he had hurt while coming down from Rachel Mizrachi's house only a few days earlier. The wound was fresh, and he began to limp. These setbacks made him think that he had failed in scoping out this job. He had found Rachel's murder extremely easy, but this was getting too complicated.

After 20 minutes of walking, he was below the balcony of Niv Rozen's house. He made sure the gun was loaded properly and screwed on the silencer. He looked for ways to climb up to the balcony, which was not very high, but he didn't think his leg could handle it. So he decided to knock on the front door.

Gaby, Niv's wife, didn't hesitate for a second when she heard the knock. Her friends from the kibbutz often visited her at night, looking to borrow something from the kitchen or coming over to have some of her sacred tea. When she opened the door, the murderer barged inside, covered her mouth, and took her to the kitchen as he pushed the gun between her third and fourth vertebrae.

"Silence," he said, quietly. Nothing more.

Niv and Moshe were sitting out on the balcony on the top floor. They hadn't heard the knock on the door or Gaby opening it. They were drinking chamomile tea that Niv grew in his private garden. The night was damp, the treetops barely moved. They talked a lot about the past and very little about the present. Moshe dodged questions about his current life; Niv could sense there was something odd about his old friend, but didn't want to subject him to any harsh line of questioning. They had met in the army when they both were tank drivers and a few years later they were in the same division of the Jerusalem police. Niv detested city life, prompting him to drop everything and move to the kibbutz. This was his thirty-fifth anniversary in Metzuba.

The murderer decided to wait in the kitchen until his victim came down. He had no Plan B. He had taped Gaby's mouth closed with some duct tape he had found in a drawer so she wouldn't make any noise.

Moshe got up from his hammock and said, "I want to rest. Maybe we can continue this tomorrow."

"No problem, good night," Niv replied, and started down the stairs that led directly to the living room. The murderer heard the steps and Gaby fidgeted nervously. When he was very close to the kitchen, Niv called for Gaby. The murderer went to meet him as he dragged the woman with him.

"What's happening here?" Niv said when he saw the murderer with his wife.

"Shut up or you both die!" the murderer whispered. "Go find your friend and bring him to me. If you make a wrong step, I'll kill her. If you say something about me, I'll end her life."

He was nervous and confused. Everything had gotten complicated. He had his finger on the trigger and when he saw that Niv was about to climb the stairs, he said softly, "Don't go upstairs! Call him down from here!"

Niv did not know what to do, but he had no time to think, so he started calling Moshe. He shouted again and again, but the old man didn't come down. Then they suddenly heard a noise, like a heavy object falling down.

The murderer realized that Moshe had jumped from the balcony. He quickly hobbled outside. Niv tried to stop him by sticking his foot out, but the murderer dodged it and shot him in the stomach. Niv collapsed while the murderer hurried to the door. When he got outside, he circled around the house and looked towards the forest. Then he turned toward the path that led to the exit. He huffed in a moment of despair. He thought it would be very easy to hide in this place and that his escape would be simple. He hadn't planned properly. In seconds, he heard a powerful siren and was blinded as harsh lights pointed at him. It was the patrol — a soldier and a kibbutznik[41] aboard a 4x4 truck. They shouted at him to stop, but the murderer hastened his steps toward the hill. Following protocol, the soldier shouted at him to halt once again, fired in the air and then at his legs, but missed. The kibbutznik rose from his seat and, with a burst of bullets, stopped the murderer in his tracks.

Moshe Cohen had jumped nearly three meters; his leg was bleeding and his tailbone, which had always been an eternal problem for him, wouldn't let him walk now. After hitting the ground, he didn't have the strength to run, so he hid beneath shrubs, honeysuckles, and a huge bamboo tree. He stayed crouched down for 10 minutes without moving. He was well out of sight. All of a sudden he heard shots not far from his hiding place and thought the worst had happened. He regretted having entangled his old friend, Niv, in his problems. He began to move as quickly as possible away from the scene because he didn't want the police to question him. He reached the top of the hill. He knew there was a barbed-wire fence about 300 meters down and that he didn't have much time. He curled up, covered his head with his hands, and threw himself downwards. And just like that he slid like a snowball through the grass until he struck against the barbed wire. Now he could barely move. Both of his legs were bleeding, but he made one more effort and began to dig with his hands under the fence, which was pretty run down. When he made a hole big enough, he slid through it and crawled about 50 meters until he came upon the road that connected Metzuba with Nahariya. He heard the police from afar and saw the lights of the kibbutz. When he finally managed to get up, he tried to stop a car to pick him up; although several passed, none even slowed down. Finally, a Toyota pickup truck stopped when they saw him injured on the side of the road.

"What happened to you?" the driver asked.

"I fell and hurt myself trying to push my car from the ditch."

"And where is your car?"

"Two-hundred meters from here."

"I haven't seen any car on the road," the driver said, bewildered.

"No, of course it's not ... it fell into the ditch, which is why I'm so banged up."

---

41 Kibbutznik: A member of a kibbutz.

The driver of the Toyota wasn't entirely convinced of the truth in Moshe's words, but took the old man to the hospital in Nahariya anyway and left him there in the emergency room, waiting to be seen.

Moshe thanked him and told him not to worry, that he would manage it from there. When the man with the Toyota left, Moshe stayed in the hospital waiting room for a while, and then slipped away without anyone seeing him.

He found a motel near the place and spent the night there. He bought gauze and alcohol in a 24-hours pharmacy, cleaned his wounds, and stayed awake, trying to figure out what to do. He barely slept, but now things were a little bit more clear for him, and he decided to make a move. The next morning, he saw that his wounds were not all that bad after all. He went straight to the post office and sent a letter he had just written and addressed to:

Avi Lifshitz – Yedioth Ahronoth
Yigal Allon Street 127 Tel Aviv, 67433 Israel

43

LEONEL
Faroe Islands - Egypt - Gaza Strip
October 30th, 2011

I think that it was one of the coldest nights I had experienced in my entire life; not even on the open sea had I felt the sensation of such cold permeating my bones, although that might have been all the vodka we drank to keep from losing our heads on the open water. My captors had left me a white sheet and a pillow, blindfolded me, and tied my hands. I tried moving my body around to stay warm, but ended up falling out of bed, hurting one of my bound hands. I had no idea what time of day it was nor where I was — I couldn't see anything at all with the blindfold. Suddenly, the door opened and two men came in. They tore off the blindfold and untied my hands. A trickle of light from a high window blinded my eyes. When I managed to open them, I looked at my arm. The bandage was new; there was still some bleeding, but the wound seemed better. My head was spinning like a whirligig. The guy with the shaved head had a gun, and the bearded guy wasn't carrying anything, though he clearly had very powerful hands. Shaved head turned to me and handed me a bag.

"Today we travel by boat," he said. "I want to see you wearing the clothes in the bag, and put on the dark glasses. Don't try any strange movements; we won't hesitate to finish you off."

"Where are you taking me? They're wrong ... I don't know anything."

"Do not worry. We are aware of what you know and what you don't. Keep silent and stay as close to us as possible and nothing will happen."

"Where are we going?"

"You'll find out. Now change; we're leaving."

The bearded man left a plate on the table that had a pita with some butter and jelly, and I devoured what little there was in seconds. The place where we were, looked like a cellar. I dressed and went out; the bearded man was behind me and shaved head was in front. The street was deserted and the day was cloudy. A very fine rain managed to wet us completely. Suddenly, we stopped beside a gray Volkswagen, and the three of us got into the back seat. The driver was a young man with blond hair who appeared to be local. He didn't say a word the entire trip. I was sitting in the middle and I couldn't even consider escaping. The bearded guy was holding me with his hand, and I knew shaved head had his gun in his bag.

***

After 20 minutes, I glimpsed the sea and realized that we were approaching the port. A boat with an Egyptian flag was anchored on one side, somewhat away from the other ships. We passed through immigration control, but no one asked us for passports or identification. The driver passed an envelope to the immigration officer and that was that — no one bothered to inspect the car. In no time, we found ourselves next to the cabin of a small fishing boat. I didn't get to see any crew members. Right away I was locked inside one of the cabins with the band on my eyes and my hands tied once again. After a while, shaved head entered with the bearded guy. One of them grabbed my hand and jabbed in a needle. Then I remember nothing more.

I have no idea how long I slept, but I woke up with a strong headache. I remembered that we were on a boat — had we traveled to Egypt? I wondered about the origin of the flag I had seen while boarding the boat. Could I have been taken there? Eventually, I heard footsteps coming and realized it was the bearded man. He untied my hands and slipped the blindfold down so that I could see. He gave me a plate with food on it. The menu consisted of olives, cheese, tomato, a pita bread, and a cup of something that looked like coffee but had no flavor at all. I was so hungry that I ate it all, including drinking the horrible black liquid, which I assumed was coffee.

Then they took me outside to breathe the sea air. It was there I saw some sailors who spoke Arabic. No one addressed us. It was as if we were transparent or invisible. After 10 minutes watching the waves while exposed to the catatonic cold, I was returned to the cabin. I sat again in the chair, they blindfolded me again, and I once more felt a prick on my hand and fell asleep.

When I awoke, I heard a great buzz. The ship was steady in the water and the bearded guy ordered me to wear dark glasses. As I left the cabin, I saw the port, but didn't recognize where we were. Shaved head was more attached to me than ever. The place was crowded; I realized that we were walking through the space where the fishing boats were anchored, and as the sailors opened their nets, fresh fish were jumping, some still trying to escape. We walked about 100 meters until we reach a gray car that was waiting for us. Turning my head, I saw a sign in English saying "Port of Cairo." The car engine was running, and I was pushed roughly through the back door, again seated in the middle of my two companions. We traveled about four hours without stopping until we reached the Rafah crossing. There we stopped urgently because we all needed to use the bathroom. Even while my kidney fluids were discharging, I was subjected to intense vigilance. Finally, I began to receive instructions.

"I suppose you know where you are," shaved head said. "Take your Spanish passport; you have to go through as you are, a Spaniard. If they ask why you have come to the Gaza Strip, tell them you're a freelance journalist who is doing research on life in the occupied territories. If you try to escape, we'll kill you. We have people on both sides of the border, and you should know that the Egyptians don't care much what happens to you."

I nodded and got ready to go. There was an endless line of merchants who were trying to enter Gaza with their merchandise.

We headed towards a desk dedicated to business people. The bearded guy went first, followed by me in the middle, with the shaven one behind me. We had no problems at all; they stamped my passport without asking anything. A car was waiting for us on the other side. Clearly, everything was very well coordinated. The car had small curtains that prevented me from looking out, and another curtain separated the front of the car from the rear, so I had no vision outward in any direction. Also, I was quickly blindfolded with a white cloth and they tied me up again. Earlier, the shaven one had shown me his gun and, as he did so, I noticed the curtain move and I peered out. When the car finally stopped, I was left in the vehicle for quite a while and I could hear quite a commotion of noise all around. I quickly lost track of time.

Finally, they took me out of the car and, when we began to move, I remember we went down a ladder three or four floors. I felt a little dizzy. Finally, they untied me and removed my blindfold. I was seated and served a delicious meal of potatoes, rice, and meat. As I ate with relish, I looked the place over. The walls were cover with Arabic signs that I didn't understand, there was a small, closed window high up on the wall, a narrow bed, the table where I was eating, the chair, and nothing else.

The bearded one twisted his beard in his fingers as he watched me eat. When I finished, he picked up everything and left the room, leaving the door closed. Finally, I could make use of my eyes and my hands. What did they want from me? What was the point? At least for the moment I was relatively free ...

44

Tel Aviv
November 2nd, 2011

A rain of Grad type rockets had fallen in the morning close to Katzerin, in northern Israel. The newspaper was aware of the attack, so in an effort to stay ahead of the news, reporters ran from one place to another, frenetic after a piece of information. There were no casualties, but two houses were hit by Hezbollah mortars, air force aircraft bombed Tripoli and Southern Lebanon, and everything indicated that the situation was heating up in the north. The morning editor instructed Avi Lifshitz to write an article on the situation happening up there. Needing a strong impact cap, the photos were ready.

Sitting in front of his computer, Avi was trying to find the right words to introduce the news with a touch of sensationalism. While looking for ideas, he checked his mail and began reviewing the envelopes. One in particular caught his attention, because on the cover his name appeared in handwriting. When he turned it around, he saw that there wasn't a sender's name. Curious, he opened it and began to read. Suddenly, he froze, stood up, and began pacing in his small office. He looked all around and decided to re-read the letter, looking for some way to determine who had sent it. At the same time, he began to question the validity of its contents.

For the past 10 years, during which he had been working as a correspondent for the army and state security manager, writing for the most widely circulated newspaper in the country, he hadn't seen anything like this. In the written note were the explosive details of a huge scandal, and, apparently, someone who knew him wanted him to detonate this bomb. Needless to say, he knew he couldn't talk about this with Golan Toker, the morning editor. He'd have to wait for the evening to show it to his friend and confidant, Gabriel Pérez, the evening editor. Golan wasn't a problem, but Avi considered him too conservative; he'd want to do 100 laps before drawing conclusions.

He put the note in his back pocket and got to work, focusing on what was happening up north. He still didn't know which direction to take to write on the matter, when Golan approached to find out when they could publish something on the newspaper website. Avi was so confused that he began to stutter.

"What's the matter?" Golan asked nervously.

"Nothing; excuse me, I lost my concentration."

"Did something happen? Can I help you?"

Avi didn't know what to say and decided to invent an excuse.

"Trouble with my wife ... you know."

"Is there anything I can do for you?" Golan added.

"No, nothing, it's just routine, thanks. In 10 minutes I'll have everything ready for editing."

"OK, but please tell me if there will be any problem meeting the deadline; you know how it is, we have to be first. Ah, I did want to tell you that there is another story, but Moshe gave it to Yehudi London, because he didn't want to overwhelm you with so much work. Yours is more important."

"What is it, if I may know?"

"An assassin, apparently Israeli, killed an old man in Shlomi, then headed to Metzuba, where he entered the kibbutz and killed another man."

"Do you know why?"

"No, nothing yet, but security at the kibbutz killed him. We're finding out; I think that your article will be published first, because at least in your case we have clear facts and some pictures of the place. It is also much more important."

"Why would an Israeli murderer enter a kibbutz in the north, when everyone knows there is so much security?"

"Please don't stop with this; keep moving and put together your article."

Avi was disturbed. He returned to his computer, while leaving Golan mumbling something unintelligible. He finished the article in 15 minutes and immediately sent it to the layout, style, design, and literary correction departments. It had to appear on the web in 28 minutes; the attacks had been reported 44 minutes ago and the only thing that was on the newspaper's website was a banner that said "Rockets rain in the North, two wounded. IDF responds with an airstrike in Southern Lebanon." Maariv, the daily competition, had already had information published for around seven minutes. Golan was boiling; the newspaper was his life, and being first was very important to him. Once the article was posted, he called Avi to his office.

"Next time, let me know if you can't complete your work on time," he said. "We all have problems, but this is a daily. We need the first fruits, as you already well know. You're not a rookie."

Avi lowered his head and left. He knew he had something much bigger, something huge, perhaps the most important news story that had reached him so far. He had spent 20 years struggling to find an amazing story, and now he had it in his pants pocket. He needed to calm down and think, and the daily office wasn't the best place to do that, much less now, with all the hype that was moving north.

Citing problems with his wife, he asked Golan for and received permission to go home early. Avi left the building preparing to face the traffic in downtown Tel Aviv, but before getting into his Daihatsu, he called Gabriel on his mobile.

"I need to talk to you," he said.

"Can't you wait till tonight, when I start my shift? Today I start around 5 p.m."

"No, it can't wait. I'll meet you in 20 minutes in the parking lot of Ramat Gan stadium, where we met last time. Today I left early."

Gabriel sensed that this was important because he'd received the call at home while enjoying a little winter sun on his balcony. The last time they had met in the stadium parking lot was when Avi had received an anonymous note related to a case involving corruption in the army, news that had lasted for two weeks, until the accused naval general decided to resign. Since that incident, they had agreed that this would be the place to treat major news leads, because the publication of the article on corruption had increased enemies out there, although they knew that was part of the job.

At 12:25 p.m. they were both in the stadium parking lot in Ramat Gan. Avi had arrived first and waited for five minutes for Gabriel to arrive. In the meantime, he received a message from Golan asking if everything was OK and saying he regretted being a little hard on him in the morning. Avi replied that everything was in order, not to worry. He had a few minutes to look at his article published in the foreground on the web.

When Gabriel arrived, Avi handed him the letter. Gabriel took a while to react. When he finished reading it, he said, "Are you hungry?"

"Is that all that you can say after reading that?"

"Relax. Let's eat and talk."

Avi agreed with a nod of his head. He was very anxious. They went to Ramat Gan Mall, just steps from the parking lot, and sat at table in the Atikva restaurant, where they requested falafel, hummus, and shwarma. They loved typical Israeli food. While they pounced on the fresh pitas and hummus and falafel, Avi asked, "What are you thinking about?"

"I'm thinking that you have to take it easy and be very clear on what you intend to do."

"Take it easy?" Avi's face registered his surprise. "I receive a bomb of this type, which can change both our lives, and you suggest I take it easy!"

"There has to be an investigation first. For example, why did this letter come to you? Why would someone report something like this? And, you know, we have to confirm its veracity."

"Tell me something I don't know," Avi said, draining his beer in one gulp.

"Well, I would tell you that there is much to lose and no room for mistakes. A simple misstep and your wife will be taking flowers to the cemetery. Do you think that the Mossad is behind all these facts?" Gabriel asked, adding, "Do you think that the Mossad would play with the lives of two people alone to do an experiment and is now seeking to erase the traces?"

"Look, I don't know what I believe or do not believe," Avi said, "but in the letter they mention events that happened and have never been resolved. Think about the shooting in Jerusalem, the death of the woman, Rachel Mizrachi, and what happened last night in the kibbutz. Everything is written and detailed in this piece of paper, everything seems so true; well, the facts are real. Why was there a murderer in Metzuba? Don't you wonder who he was looking for?"

"That's a good question. How do you relate that to everything that has happened?"

"After receiving the message, I considered who could have written it. The only clue in the text is that they would have tried to murder him just a few hours ago in a kibbutz. I noticed all the reports we receive in the newspaper about killings and possible attacks. There was just one incident in a kibbutz last night. I think the murderer was looking for someone else, and really he killed the wrong person."

"And, maybe the person who wrote the letter," Gabriel said.

"Good point," Avi added, as he looked at it again. "Does the letter offer any suggestions?"

"First of all, this doesn't have to go past you and me," Gabriel said. "You already know it well. Second, I think we have to understand what happened last night in Metzuba. I feel that the writer of this letter is desperate and wants the issue to get out to the media. I think that if we find a clue there, we can decipher everything else."

"I'm going to the north. Can you cover for me at the newspaper?" Avi asked.

"What did you tell Golan?"

"I told him I had problems with my wife."

"Perfect. I'll tell the same story. You can leave and stay in touch. Don't speak a word of this to anyone."

"But, what can I do in Metzuba? How do I maintain the secrecy? That place is full of police and the army. I can't say I'm a journalist investigating with fellow-reporter Yedioth, because this article is being covered by him, and if he sees me there everything will be ruined; I'm sure that the dwarf is already on his way north."

"Let me fix this with Golan. I'll tell him you will travel north for the rockets, and along the way, you'll stop in at the kibbutz, to cut costs and what not, and help out Yedioth if he needs it."

"Then the story about my wife needs to be changed."

"Don't worry about it. I'll sort out Toker and the little guy. You just have to worry about the article on Metzuba."

"OK, that sounds good. I'm heading out now."

"Hey! You forgot to pay the bill again!" Gabriel said, showing it to Avi, who simply smiled and kept going.

"You have to communicate with London," he said, and hurried towards his car.

45

AHMED
Tel Aviv
November 3rd, 2011

During my stay in Iran, I followed the insistent admonition to learn English. I spent more than four hours a day studying in my room and two more hours in class. After nearly 13 days with that routine, I had managed to become a competent user of the language — not native, but good enough to express myself like a tourist.

Upon returning to the room, I packed my things quickly, then wordlessly, before the astonished gaze of the receptionist, I paid my account and went outside, stopped a taxi, and sat in the back seat. Now, I thought wryly, I'm in a taxi circulating in Tel Aviv conversing in English with the driver on the situation in the country and the conflict with the Palestinians. When I got to my apartment on Arlozorov Street it was very late. I had to walk up four floors. I put the key in the lock, turned it to the left, and fortunately, was already inside when suddenly a cat came over to me. It gave me a shock that nearly left me paralyzed. What was a cat doing there? Who had let him in? With what goal?

I was exhausted and didn't want more unanswerable questions, at least not that night. Yes, I did have a voracious curiosity about the program I had in my hands. I had had contact with parts of the program but not with its entire contents; I didn't have access to complete sections and the material of the USB key was an enigma to me. So I turned on my computer and inserted the CD. When I opened the program, I couldn't believe my eyes. I needed time to understand, but soon realized I was dealing with something huge; everything appeared very detailed. Four parts infected the computer, and worked in an infinite loop until the memory and the network connecting the invaded computer was filled; websites, communication programs, instant messengers, and everything else found along the way was removed. I had 347,000 lines of well-armed and compiled code. I remembered that a special group had worked 21 days and 16 hours in the testing of each of these lines. Now everything was in front of me. The program in the USB memory neutralized the port of the affected mother and activated the program. I had the task of copying the contents of the CD to the USB device before my mission; but first, I had to try it all together. I still had to receive the other parts of the program, because what I had now would only manage half the task.

I started to read the sheet that my contact had given me, detailing the instructions to execute the software. The note told me that in the closet I could find equipment consisting of a server, two laptops with the program that would run on different platforms, and a couple of CAT5[42] ethernet port connected to a router[43] connected to a socket in the wall, which would quickly and safely facilitate a DSL internet connection. Glued to the router were its username and password combination.

I went to the kitchen with the cat walking between my legs. The fridge had plenty of high-end food, including an enormous jar of hummus, many pita breads, and several dishes I had never tried in my life. I figured I would have food for around two months. How long would I be there, though? I went to sleep with a salad of uncertainties in my head.

Early the next day, I followed the instructions. I began to assemble the system and create the network simulator. I had a server with an access control bar, a very sophisticated firewall system, a computer running Windows and another running Linux with no graphical user interface. The two computers had all access to external ports and other interfaces blocked, such as the camera, HDMI port, and the printer. I connected the computers to the server, creating a closed loop (a peer to peer network). The router possessed a very basic interface and was the

---

42 CAT5: Type of Ethernet connection, wired connection
43 Router: A device which connects multiple clients to a network.

only connection to the Internet. Three websites were configured and exposed only to the private network to test the penetration with the virus. The system was not accessible from outside the closed network, which was necessary to test whether the program would block these sites from running.

Three hours later I had configured the entire system. It took a long time to set up and verify the network security and the web sites. When I finally completed the checks ensuring me that all USB ports were blocked, I prepared to insert the USB stick. And just at that moment, the doorbell rang. I threw my hands up in exasperation. Right now! Who would it be? The clock said it was 12:30 p.m. I hadn't eaten or even seen the sunlight yet. I waited a while, but my persistent visitor pressed the bell twice again. I went to the door and looked through the view finder: A large woman was on the other side. I had no other choice but to open the door. I suddenly remembered that my language had to be English.

"What do you want, lady?" I asked.

"I saw you're new to the building and came to welcome you," replied the well-mannered neighbor.

I noticed something covered in her hands that raised the hairs on my neck.

"I brought some empanadas I made yesterday, so you feel more at ease. I live in the apartment across the hall. My name is Sara. And you?"

"I'm Enzo," I replied.

"Oh! And where are you from? You speak English very well."

"I am Belgian; I am here for work issues."

As we talked I watched her. She more or less had my height, around 182 cm, was well built, with nice curves and a large bust. She clearly took good care of herself. I estimated that she was in her forties, or perhaps a little more.

She handed me the pies and we touched hands.

"Thank you," I said.

"If you have any questions about living here in this crazy country, don't think twice, just knock on my door. OK, I won't bother you anymore. Ciao, Enzo."

And she left. When she turned, I saw her pretty butt swaying provocatively, perhaps more than usual, which created invisible forms in the air. I stayed a few seconds contemplating this sensual movement until she opened the door to her place. Then I closed my door. For a moment I had forgotten what point in the process I was, and that my religion forbade me those carnal desires.

It took me a while to relax and regain concentration. I recalled that the program had been tested at least five times on platforms with more than 100 computers and various physical and virtual networks, servers, and high-tech websites of different formats. Nevertheless, it was the first time I would test it, and I had never seen the full code or compiled assemblies and systems working together. In Iran there had been a special group working alongside ours that was in charge of testing the program, analyzing errors, and giving feedback to the programmers. But now, here I was, alone against all, with a front-row seat and the honor of witnessing a trial run of what was to occur in just a few days.

All I had to do was insert the USB stick into a computer and wait for it to spread across the network. Then I remembered to set the monitoring system to record the results. One of the components of the auxiliary system was a physical scanner, a sniffer that was connected to the router. This device detected and visualized all the different parts and packets circulating throughout the network. I connected the sniffer and configured it. Now, everything was ready. A monitor showed me everything that was happening on the network, the servers and computers in real time, with its parameters on the screen of my laptop. I had software that showed me how the entire system was running, part by part. I could see how each section of code impacted simultaneously each part of the system. In the control panel, I was able to control the TCPIP traffic settings, the state of the broadband connection, the processors of both the servers and computers, and memory usage. Next, I included along one side of the panel the status of the firewall for every step of the code's progression.

To better help me see the indicators, I turned off the light in the room. Then I inserted the USB memory into the computer with the Windows operating system, ran the program with the password, and watched as my laptop screen began to display what was happening. The lines ran quickly across the screen, much faster than the human mind could process. First, it neutralized the security system of the USB ports and the other accessories; then it launched the DDoS worm, as fast as it was deadly. The physical tracker screen began to fill with different types of traffic, coming from all number of IPs and protocols, including UDP, TCP, and HTTP. Everything happened as planned in Phase 1. When the program went into Phase 2, the websites were no longer responding and the Windows computer could barely run a process or a simple application. In the midst of Phase 2, the Windows computer reset itself and the Linux system took 15 seconds to do the same. At the beginning of Phase 3, the powerful server no longer worked, and any contact between the PC and the server no longer existed. They had been completely disconnected. Phase 4 terminated with complete system collapse. The router failed and was no longer able to handle traffic. The computer and the server were now in Phase 4, resetting themselves every 20 seconds. This phase ended with chaos; the router had dropped completely, the network was silent, the computers had overheated, and their chips had burned up. Finally, the server and the network router had been completely wiped out. Even the tracker stopped working because it couldn't store so much traffic. Suddenly, everything went out as if there had been a power outage. A very sharp whistle blew in my ears. After just three minutes and 43 seconds, the systems had stopped working altogether.

I sat down to digest the situation. It was the first time I had seen something like that. I was silent and stunned. I went to the window to breathe some air and looked down. Some kids returning from school played with a ball. The world out there was normal. My levels of adrenaline were in the roof.

A blonde girl crossed the street and I focused on her. I remembered, as usual, Mariana — my Mariana — who was still alive inside me.

46

LEONEL
Gaza Strip
November 2nd, 2011

Four days had passed without me going outside or seeing the sun. Like the schedule of a prisoner, I had scratched each day with a cross on the wall above the nightstand. The routine was boring. The three daily meals always contained the same ingredients: pitas, hummus, two olives, and rice. The third day I got a piece of chicken. The drink was always water, and on the fourth day, they brought me tea without sugar. This was followed by a session of physical activity, in which I walked around a completely closed-in, dark courtyard. They took me to the Heder[44], as they called it, a tiny room with no windows, a small gray door, two chairs and a two-by-two old table. It was the place where they performed interrogations. The questions were always the same, and came in the same order: what was I doing in Gaza working with the Red Cross, who had sent me, what did I do in Pakistan, and above all, why? The strangest thing was that there was never any violence in any of these interrogations. Occasionally, one of my guards, or security agents as they called them, might push me, but that was it.

For the first couple of days, I was extremely anxious, fearing what was to come. I thought they were going to torture or kill me. I had no idea what they wanted from me or why I had been kidnapped. Eventually, as days passed fast, and with the constant daily routine, I star-

---

44 Heder: A small room or cubicle.

ted to calm down a little. But at night, I couldn't sleep. A combination of anxiety and the sweltering heat gave me chronic insomnia. I never swayed with my answers to the questions of my captors. My script never changed: I was studying medicine and I wanted to work in a place where I could expand my knowledge. The Red Cross and Gaza allowed me to do so, and no one had sent me to Pakistan. I was looking for my girlfriend, who I had met at the Red Cross in Gaza. We moved to Denmark after she was held captive by the Taliban. When asked what I was doing in Faroe Island, I said I was escaping from the Taliban themselves, who were chasing me for having carried Mariana from Afghanistan. Almost all the answers were very close to reality. I knew I couldn't mention that I was evading the Mossad and had gone to Pakistan in search of Ahmed.

I eventually realized that my captors knew the whole truth, and were holding me there to perhaps later do a trade for a contingent of Palestinians. That's probably why they were treating me so well. They weren't going to get useful information from me. I think they understood that immediately.

Early one morning after breakfast, which surprisingly included coffee with sugar, croissants, and orange juice, they brought a camera and a microphone and began to arrange the room so that it became a bright and lively study. They opened the small window, focused white light, and covered the wall with a picture of the same color, to avoid any trace that could identify the place where I was being held captive. They brought me new clothes — brown trousers and a white shirt — and allowed me to bathe unsupervised, something I hadn't been allowed to do since the fifth day. They also brought a razor and one of the security officers shaved me perfectly. Soon I was spic and span wearing neat, clean clothes. On the table was an Arabic newspaper with the current date and a note inside indicating what I had to say. They ordered me to read it aloud as I held open the newspaper. The camera focused on my face and especially on the date of the newspaper; I was ordered to hide my emotions and to remain calm, always looking at the camera. It took four takes to get it just right.

I, Leonel Cohen, am captive of the Hamas. I am being treated very well, and I have been given good food and clean clothes. I ask the Israeli government to do everything possible to get me free and end this. Please do everything that Hamas asks.

"Cut!" said the camera operator, a pale man with dark skin and long hair. "Congrats. It was perfect."

Soon the setting was dismantled and the atmosphere was again dark, as always. I went to bed and hoped that maybe this ordeal would soon end. How much longer would I be able to stand this situation?

47

Northern Israel - Metzuba Kibbutz
November 2nd, 2011

Avi Lifshitz pressed the accelerator until it bottomed out, speeding along the sea route that connected Tel Aviv to Haifa. He knew he was risking being caught by a speed camera or by the police themselves, but the letter he had received was explosive enough that he could transgress any law that got in his way. After two hours and 45 minutes, he was at the entrance of the Metzuba kibbutz, probably a speed record. It had been one day and 15 hours since the incident with the intruder, and the site was still swarming with people — journalists, security, army, and even some onlookers who had no business being there.

He knew it was going to be very difficult to overcome the wall of security and harder still to get information. With all this, his experience was evident. He knew the procedures in these cases: shut down everything from anyone who had no business in the area until the army or the police, according to the offense committed and who was suspected, establishes what happened after having made all the necessary confirmations. The only people who had access to the place were the spokesmen of the army and police, but they also let in direct relatives of those involved. At the end there was almost always a contingent of outsiders hanging around.

Avi had kept his old army journalist card, which, although it had expired nearly 15 years before, was nevertheless real. He had doctored the due date and changed the picture. Now he was willing to risk using it. A tall police officer with an enormous belly took the card in his hand

and examined it. In the other hand, he held his cell phone, which suddenly rang, distracting the fat guy enough that Avi could get through.

Once inside, it wasn't hard to guess where the events had occurred. A kind of corral formed by red ribbons indicated the space where the murderer had been killed. There were still bloodstains on the spot and three forensic experts working to collect trace. Avi decided to leave the site and search the home of the widow Rozen.

In the doorway was a huge gathering of people, many from the kibbutz and lots of others. Apparently, Yehudi London had done his work and left. He was nowehere to be seen. Avi managed to go unnoticed in the fuss. He wanted to interview Gaby Rozen for details about her husband's slaying. When he tried entering her room, he was stopped by her uncle, who told him that the widow didn't want to see anyone and that she was suffering a stress crisis. The doctors had medicated her and indicated she shouldn't be interviewed. The authorities had also recommended that she not discuss anything about the tragedy.

Avi felt there was not much to be done there, so he hung around the house and tried to imagine what had happened. Data was needed from someone who at that time had no connection to the family. He knew that if he discovered the identity of the letter writer, the police wouldn't let him keep it to himself. He had to do his work quietly, almost secretly.

As he was leaving, a slight, red-haired man approached him. His boots were muddy, as if having just returned from working in the field.

"Who are you?" he asked.

"I'm a correspondent with the army."

"And what do you have to do here? Don't you know everything already?"

Avi found the opportunity to take advantage of the question.

"Yes, you're right, we know a lot, but there is a rumor that someone was in the house when this happened to Rozen, a person other than the murderer."

"Oh ... you mean old Moshe Cohen. I think the police already know. You didn't speak with them? He was a good friend of Niv's."

Moshe Cohen. Avi couldn't believe it; he would never have imagined it. He put on a face that was at once both innocent and surprised, quickly said thanks, and went in search of his car.

Again he pressed the gas pedal hard while thinking about his next steps. He knew the police had already won their hand. At the intersection of Haifa and the Ayalon highway, he made a sharp left to head to Jerusalem. He clicked on the radio and tuned in to the news, where he heard that Hamas had released a video of a young Israeli captive somewhere in the Gaza Strip and demanded 1,000 Palestinian detainees in Israeli jails in exchange for the freedom of the boy, whose name was Leonel Cohen. Avi slammed the steering wheel with rage and shouted, "Again! These damned terrorists have screwed us again!"

He had no idea that this young man was the same one referred to in the note he had received just a few hours earlier.

48

Jerusalem
November 2nd, 2011

Rain was falling in the streets of Jerusalem. From his position, Eli Regev could see that the Wailing Wall was soaked, and the only ones saved from getting their heads wet were the orthodox wearing their big, black hats. Eli watched everything from his car parked in one of the highest places of the Ben Yehuda market. Now and then he took a sip of his muddy Turkish coffee. He had a wood-colored carpet bag, full of papers, and an egg sandwich from which he had taken only one small bite.

In 10 minutes he would meet with the minister of police. When it came to the case that he was in charge of, he realized he had the potential to reach the highest ranks. That day he had received a message from a police officer in the northern zone, informing him that they had found Moshe Cohen in a hotel in Nahariya. Eli immediately requested an audience with the minister of police, who canceled two appointments to meet with him at his offices in the center of Jerusalem. His persistence and influence with the upper echelons prevailed. Five minutes before the scheduled time, the staff invited him to go straight to the office of the minister, a man in his sixties with an outstanding reputation in various positions in the police and army. Regev knew him and recognized him as someone one could trust. They greeted coldly. To Eli it seemed that the minister appeared quite a bit older than the last time he had seen him. Between the two of them, there was no need for formalities; they both knew each other well. The minister called his secretary and asked him to bring Yosi to his office, too. A few hours before Regev was to arrive, the minister had sent an urgent message to Yosi to take charge of the trouble that Eli had brought him. He also knew that Yosi was investigating two cases in which he could supposedly collaborate with Regev.

Eli thought about who this Yosi was that the minister had appointed, and when he saw him enter, he recognized him immediately. His hair was a little silver, but with the same amount of hair gel as ever; even the smell of the famous gel was familiar to him. In a moment, Regev wondered if it might not be beneficial to find Yosi here on his path.

"It's been so long!" Regev cried as he entered.

"The same to you," said Yosi, fixing his hair.

"Did Moshe Cohen say anything?" Eli asked directly, not wanting to waste time.

"Not much; rather, not what we expected."

"What did he say?"

"That he doesn't understand why they wanted to kill him."

"He doesn't understand? He knows full well that one plus one is two," Eli said, sarcastically.

"We can't do much with him; if you think about it, he hasn't done anything. I don't really think we can hold him."

"And what excuse did you find to keep him close?"

"I proposed security; we have two agents watching him."

"And he didn't object?"

"Surprisingly not. I thought the same as you — I assumed he wouldn't accept them."

"The old man is a fox, you know; he knows all the tricks," Eli said.

"I have no card to play against him at this moment," Yosi said, motioning to the minister of police, who did not intervene.

"You know what I think?" Eli asked, worried and resting his hands on the table.

"What?" the minster said.

"That he knows a lot, and that is the only clue we have. I want to talk to Cohen."

The minister was surprised. "How? And how will you appear?"

"Like a police investigator; I still have my license." He took it out of his wallet and flashed a smile. "We've known each other for a long time. Perhaps we could find out some history of the 'brothers,' which is so important for everyone."

"Well, I'm not going to oppose this," the minister said. "I'll give you the phone number of one of the officers guarding Cohen; ask the man where he is. Look, better yet, I will contact them and I'll send you the details."

"Good. Thank you. I'll be urgently awaiting the information."

Already nervous about the situation, the minister said impatiently, "Everything is urgent! Everyone needs something now, this minute."

That said, the minister stood, held out his hand and sent him away.

"Go now. I have other matters to attend to," he said.

Eli wasn't offended; he knew the politics of these people. But something bothered him about the minister's attitude, although that did not surprise him. The police did not like anyone getting in their way.

"Where are you going?" Yosi asked as Eli was leaving.

"Tel Aviv."

"I'm going to Tel Aviv, too. Do you have time for a coffee before leaving?"

"Yeah, come on."

They sat in Roladina, a cafe located one block away from the police headquarters.

"What do you think about this?" Yosi asked.

"That there's something fishy here; everything is very secret and mysterious," Eli said.

"Who wanted to kill Rachel Mizrachi?" Yosi pushed a little further.

"I have no idea," Eli replied. "I just heard about that a few hours ago."

"You know that Cohen had fingerprints all over the house. I was in the place." Yosi showed that he had some data.

"The old man was the boyfriend?" Regev said, trying for more information.

"I don't know, but he has an alibi; he was in the Rishon Letzion police station renewing his police investigator license. Check it out."

Eli thought for a few seconds about Yosi's words.

"This matter was planned by a professional," he said.

"Yes, I think so, too," Yosi replied.

"Well, I have to go."

"Can I ask you a favor?" Yosi asked as he took the last sip of his coffee.

"What do you want?"

"Can we work together on this?" Yosi realized they could be useful to one another.

Eli paused. "Look, I don't know. Let me think about it," he said.

"I'm not looking for justice; my assignment is confidential, secret," Yosi said.

"Maybe we can exchange some information. Now I have to go."

"OK, take care of yourself."

Yosi stayed in the cafe, somewhat puzzled. He knew that with Regev at his side he could open any door and, at that moment, he needed him.

Eli quickly left the cafe and went to the Ben Yehuda market. He knew he could wait a long time until he received information on the whereabouts of Moshe Cohen. If he were in Jerusalem, the comings and goings would be avoided. But he knew that the police minister would act urgently in this case. Even though he liked the position of having such power and authority over all these people, he was still a bureaucrat. The prime minister himself had ordered all the ministers to help Regev solve this case.

After about 20 minutes, as he was finishing a cutlet sandwich, Eli received a message from the minister's secretary. All it said was, "Arohe Street 29 Ramat Gan, first floor, apartment number two."

He pulled the siren out of his trunk, put it on the roof of the car, and shot toward the center of the country, trying for full speed.

In one hour and five minutes, Eli was standing before an old building on Arohe Street, a populated central avenue, with construction from the sixties that started at Bialik Street, a main road in the city, and went all the way to the University of Bar-Ilan.

The police had mounted a 24-hour security operation at Moshe's house, and the patrol was there, waiting. The building, like other old structures in the area, was built with huge wooden beams that supported its entire weight. Eli greeted the guards from afar. They responded with nods. He looked around, carefully inspecting the area, then went upstairs.

When he knocked on the door, Moshe took his time answering. A camera had been installed on the ceiling of the corridor and was focused exactly on the entrance to the apartment. After two minutes, Moshe finally opened the double-lock-secured, armored door, and greeted his visitor gently, not at all surprised by his arrival.

"What's up? It's been so long!"

"Oh, you know, this and that," Eli said as he surveyed the room with a quick glance.

"Sit down, make yourself comfortable," Moshe invited, pointing to the sofa. "Do you want to drink something?"

"Only if you take one."

"You know what? Let's have whiskey today, like in the good times; I need to lift my spirits."

Eli didn't understand the comment.

"What's going on? Why do you need to lift your spirits?"

"Ah, again. Eli, we've known each other for such a long time; do you really think I don't know why you're here? You know that there are secrets that can't be hidden from the police."

"What exactly are you talking about?" Eli continued to act, showing a look of surprise.

"Wait," Moshe said, and went into the kitchen, shuffling in his slippers. He returned with a bottle of Johnny Walker Double Black. "This is the good stuff!" he said, pouring the alcoholic beverage in two glasses with ice. "I know everything, but what about you? What are you doing here?"

Eli sipped his drink and said, "Who wants to kill you, Moshe? And why?"

"You think if I knew I wouldn't have already solved it? You know I have all the contacts for that. This time I'm really in trouble."

"Why would anyone want to get rid of you?"

"I don't know."

Eli was beginning to lose patience. He was sure the old man was hiding his cards, but also recognized that there was a bigger problem here.

"Listen, if you don't speak, we'll have to put you into custody. Is that what you want?"

The old man sighed and visually relaxed. It was his second glass of whiskey. He lifted his heavy body and walked towards the window.

"Look, Eli, I have almost nothing. I lost the woman I had wanted all my life. She shared a secret with me that it is not for you, it's of the children who were switched at birth, the story you already know. Rachel was aware that this had happened, but never knew who had planned or executed it. What's more, she thought it was her fault in a day of great commotion and a lot of work in the hospital. She just wanted these young people to know the truth, but she left this world without success."

Eli felt he was on the right track. Cohen, a little less on his guard because of the booze, seemed willing to continue talking about the case.

"Tell me, how do you explain why it took nearly 30 years to kill her? Why didn't they do it right away?"

"Good question," Moshe replied. "Perhaps the people who organized everything thought that no one knew what had happened that day."

"And so how did they suddenly learn that Rachel had that information?"

"It's probably because, once she offered a million shekels to find the other boy, all kinds of things started breaking loose."

Eli was amazed that he didn't know that part of the story. He went to the window and stood a short distance from Moshe, wanting to see his face closely.

"And now what?" he asked.

The old man moved away from the window and returned to his chair.

"The problem isn't me," he said. "It's not important whether they kill me or not. The young man who appeared today in the Hamas video is one of the two boys. Do you understand that?

Eli couldn't believe what he was hearing. He was aware of the video that Moshe was referring to, but he hadn't had the faintest idea that this young man was one of the two boys. He remained by the window, not knowing what to say.

Moshe rose with his third glass of whiskey in his hand, took Eli's arm, faced him, and said, "You have to help those guys; Leonel must be rescued immediately." His eyes were glazed.

"And the other?" Eli asked. "Where is he?"

"I have no idea. The last thing I heard of him was that he was in Pakistan. I am sure, the Mossad knows everything."

"The Mossad knows everything. Thank you, Moshe, I have to go work on this right away. Your help is priceless. We will watch out for your life, I promise."

He squeezed his hand and quickly left the apartment. As he exited the building, he didn't see the guards, so he called directly to the police official in Tel Aviv who was assigned the task of watching Cohen. When told the news, the official also didn't understand what was happening.

"Wait on the line," he told Eli. After two minutes he came back, and said, "I've been informed that Tel Aviv headquarters ordered the guards to leave. No one knows who gave the order, but don't worry, in half an hour, another patrol will be there."

"What's going on?" Eli asked, confused.

"I don't know, I don't understand," the official said, mournfully. "And I can't find the guards who were supposed to be watching over him."

"Well, try to send someone immediately. It has to be before half an hour. This is all very strange."

"I'll do my best, yes."

Eli headed to his home in north Tel Aviv, and on the road began to think he should have stayed until security arrived on the scene. It was 6:15 p.m. and traffic was moving slowly, like an eyedropper. He was on the Ayalon highway, at the height of Ramat Aviv. His head was programming the next steps. He figured he would have to meet the chief of Shin Bet[45] and then, with more information in his possession, he would establish contact with his colleague in Mossad. They would have to cooperate to untangle this web. He was still concerned about the issue of the guards, although he knew that irregularities were common in the police force — orders were often given and then rescinded and given again. It was all part of the mess in the police deparment. He checked his watch and saw it was already 7 p.m.; he had barely moved in 45 minutes, blocked by the gridlock. As he was leaving the highway, he turned on the radio to hear the latest news:

A man around 65 years old was found dead this evening with two bullets in his chest. The murder occurred on Ramat Gan, Arohe street, just half an hour

---

45 Shin Bet: Israeli Internal Security Service, equivalent of the FBI in USA.

ago, and the police are on the scene investigating the crime. The traffic is cut. No shots were heard in the building, so it's likely that the weapon had a silencer. No witnesses have been found. Police have completely closed off the area.

Eli abruptly began to slow his car and turned quickly toward the shoulder. The dangerous maneuver prompted a chorus of honking. He stopped the car and hit his head furiously against the steering wheel.

"Why did I leave him alone? Why? Shit! By God, I'm going to expose whoever is creating this chaos, the Mossad, the government, or the holy police. They're not going to get away with this!"

He took five minutes with his head lowered to compose himself, then re-entered traffic. He thought to himself, "Likely the only clues to be found will be in the room where the two boys were born." At the exit for Ayalon-Ramat Aviv, instead of going right to his house, he turned abruptly left and took the highway up the road to Jerusalem. Again Jerusalem...

49

Jerusalem
November 2nd, 2011

The rain had stopped in Jerusalem; it had been storming all day and had finally returned to normal. It was 7:30 p.m. when Avi Lifshitz got through the traffic and entered the city. He placed his car in first gear and began climbing the route to Mount Scopus, where the Sharei Tzedek Hospital was located. When he arrived, he parked the car two blocks from the hospital. Just as he opened the door, the sky cracked open and a torrential rain began to fall again. In seconds, there was a veritable flood, so he decided to stay in the car and wait a bit. He turned on the interior light, opened the letter, and read it a second time, to see if there were any details that had escaped him before:

Dear Avi:

I have chosen you because I always thought you were the best in your profession. I want to tell you a story that will seem implausible, but it is real.

On October 22nd, 1982, two newborn babies were switched in the Sharei Tzedek hospital in Jerusalem. A Jewish family recei-ved a Muslim boy and the Muslim parents received the Jewish boy. With the exception of a nurse named Rachel Mizrachi, no one else noticed the mistake. The next day, Rachel tried to repair the error, but the Muslim family had already left the hospital and it was impossible to find them.

She lived with this secret for nearly 28 years, until she decided to try to bring the two boys together. The one who was in Israel wasn't difficult to find; I helped on that task. But locating the other was a much more complicated matter. More than anything in the world, she wanted these young people to be brought together as brothers to learn the truth, so she gathered together her life savings along with an inheritance she had received from a widowed man in New York, whom she considered her uncle. In total, she offered a million shekels to whoever could locate the missing Muslim boy.

Since then, a string of attacks have begun against anyone involved in the secret. They tried killing Leonel, the young Israeli man, by spraying poison gas into his home. Unsuccessful, they tried again, this time with bullets in a cafe in Talpiot, Jerusalem. Later, they tried again to kill the Jewish boy, this time while he was in Paris, and it was at this point that my Paris contact was killed. All this information came to me from a friend who is a retired Mossad agent. He also passed me the news of a certain Eli Regev, who was appointed by the government to investigate the events, since the news of the switched brothers broke through the halls of parliament. Next, they killed Shmulik Sade, by running him down with a vehicle after a meeting at HaKirya, in Tel Aviv, with the same Eli Regev.

At the same time, the government assigned Regev the task of keeping an eye on the Mossad. The fact that the Muslim child works for Hamas on the "viral bomb" and has become a threat to the country, opens many questions about the functioning of that organization. All this causes havoc; however, in high places, they prefer to keep this a secret, since they admit that there is nothing concrete yet.

Of this entire list of dark events, what has affected me the most was the murder of Rachel Mizrachi a few days ago; if there was one person who had suffered through all this and didn't at all deserve such an end, it was her.

Personally, my life is in danger, like everyone else who knows something of this puzzle. In fact, just a handful of hours ago,

in the Metzuba Kibbutz, they tried to kill me, but instead they
killed a faithful friend of mine who had allowed me to stay at
his home.

If you can find out who organized the switch, the origin of
the whole story, which could well be the Mossad or Shabak,
you will probably have one of the most important articles of
your life (or maybe two at once, if you consider the danger of
a cyberattack). And who knows what will come out once all
this craziness finishes.

Kind Regards.

The letter was anonymous, and it wasn't signed. Avi still couldn't
believe what he had in his hands. His editor friend had hoped to unveil
the whole plot that had so much news potential, but at the same time
posed a great risk.

The rain didn't stop; on the contrary, it intensified. Avi realized he
would have to get out and get soaked if he were to continue on his quest.
However, he waited a little longer, listening instead to the 8 p.m. news.
Galei Tzahal, the official radio station of the army, reported:

*Murder in Ramat Gan. They gave the name of the victim: Moshe Cohen, a
retired police officer. The murderer forced the door and fired two shots into the
victim's chest. However, no one heard gunfire, so it is presumed the gun had
a silencer. Ramat Gan police are in charge of the case. They have closed the
entrances to the city in an effort to find the murderer.*

Avi lifted his hand and smashed it violently against the steering
wheel in anger. Then, rain be damned, he left the car and ran to the
hospital.

Once inside, he realized he needed some authority to obtain information. He verified that in the back pocket of his pants he had his old army
journalist card. It was 8:30 p.m. and the receptionist escorted Avi to an
office where a secretary said that there wasn't anyone in Archives at that
time. Then she told him that records older than 20 years were kept in a
storage room on the seventh floor, that it was open from 8:30 a.m. to
4:30 p.m. daily, and that she recommended he return the next day.

Not content with a "no" from a shift worker who probably didn't have the authority to say "yes," he showed the card with the emblem of the army. The secretary, a blonde with a Russian accent, looked at the card, shook her head, and said, "I'm sorry, but I can't help you right now."

"OK, call your boss, or the archive administrator."

"At this time?"

"Yes. This is an urgent matter. I need some data."

"What data?"

"Among other things, the names of some guys who were born here about 28 years ago, and also those of their mothers."

"I'll call the manager, but I don't think that information will be available to just anyone."

Avi raised his voice; he felt he could assert himself better this way.

"What do you mean, 'anyone?' I'm coming from the army and I have been assigned a mission for which I urgently require data."

The secretary, realizing this issue was above her head, called her superior. They had a brief, quiet conversation, after which the young, golden-haired girl handed the phone to Avi.

A man with a shrill voice was on the other end of the line.

"What do you need?"

"I need the birth records for 22 October 1982."

"What do you want that for? Do you have any relationship with any of the children born that day?"

"No. Right now, the information is of vital importance to the military."

"Do you have a signed document certifying that the army sent you for that data?"

Avi again used his power of conviction, throwing everything he could into it. He had to know now!

"What is this signed document thing? I have a membership card from the army, which is an official document. I'm coming from the IDF (Tzahal). Do you think I would be here at 9 p.m. at night, in this pouring rain, if this wasn't an urgent situation?"

"That information is confidential," the administrator replied.

"I'll have you know that for the army, nothing is confidential. Would you like me to connect you with the headquarters in Tel Aviv HaKirya so you can talk to the chief of the army?"

After a pause, the administrator said, "Give the phone to the girl."

They talked for a while. Avi couldn't understand the conversation; it was almost a whisper. Suddenly, she hung up the phone and said, "Follow me."

They went to the seventh floor. She opened a door through which he could see endless rows of shelves with cardboard boxes packed tight with folders.

"Stay here and wait," the blonde said.

After 10 minutes, she returned with a pink folder. They went back down to the first floor where there was an enormous photocopier. She began feeding the machine, sheet by sheet. There were 15 in all. Each sheet was a recounting of all information pertaining to the births for a given day and hour with details on whether it was a normal or caesarean section, or if there was any abnormal surgery. Another sheet of signatures and stamps included the names of the children, families, doctor and head nurse, the midwife, and the shift secretary.

When she finished photocopying the documents, she handed the copies to Avi and asked him to sign a form to record what he had taken. She asked for his identity card and he realized he had no choice but to use his real name. He left happy, like someone who receives a gift without it being their birthday.

He began examining the sheets, looking for the two babies born at the same time. It didn't take long to find them. Sheets four and five were very clear; they had recorded the same time of birth: "Leonel Cohen and Ahmed Asad, midwife Rachel Mizrachi, attending physician Dr. David Levi."

MALWARE
0101010101010
10 1000011
01 MALWARE 10
01001 010101
1010 1010
010101010101
1010101010101010
100 1010

0 0
10
10
1010
1111
0101
10 1
0180

POLICIA

50

Jerusalem
November 2nd, 2011

With the greatest effort, Eli Regev arrived at Abu Gosh. It was 10:20 p.m. and he was hungry and exhausted. He greeted the restaurant owner affectionately, an Israeli Arab who had known him for many years. The man knew what his preferences were, so he prepared a shwarma and a plate of hummus with a boiled egg, olive oil and paprika, a dish he liked. He ate savoring the hummus with hot pitas, taken fresh from the stone oven; in the end he devoured a baklava[46], which left a pleasant, sweet taste in his mouth. Finally, he took a muddy black coffee and quickly got back on the road to Jerusalem.

He arrived at the hospital on Mount Scopus at 10:50 p.m., and the rain, which had been coming down in buckets for the past 15 minutes, let up for just a moment. The central receptionist led him to the same blond girl who had attended Avi Lifshitz just a few hours previously.

When he asked for the birth registrations for October 22nd, 1982, the blonde thought he was making a joke; she couldn't believe it.

"This is a joke, isn't it?" she asked, confused, then added, "two hours ago someone asked for the exact same records."

"Who?" Eli demanded.

"Someone from the army."

"Someone from the army?" Eli repeated, astonished. "Who was it?"

"Excuse me," said the blonde, now thoroughly perplexed. "I have to call my superior. This isn't normal."

---

46 Baklava: cake made with nut paste and topped with syrup.

"Yes, call him now." At that moment Eli was more interested in who was after the information than the information itself.

The blonde, now totally lost, spoke with her manager, who had surely been awakened. The shouting was heard from afar.

"Don't you dare say that to me!" the girl said into the phone. "I don't know what is happening today. They are all crazy!"

She pulled the receiver from her ear after listening to her boss and said to Eli, "You should come back tomorrow."

Eli showed her the letter from the government and his ID card, and the girl went back to the phone.

"He has a document on government letterhead and an identification card just like a minister."

Eli raised his voice and said irritably, "Tell him I have no time for bureaucracy."

The blonde repeated his words, waited a few seconds, cut the call, and annoyed, said, "Follow me."

They went to the seventh floor. Already chagrined, and knowing where to find what she had come for, she quickly grabbed the report of all that had happened that day in the delivery room. She took him back down to the photocopier and left him there. Eli photocopied the folder items, and a little more than he needed. When he finished, he took the documents with both hands, like someone holding a priceless treasure.

"Who is the person who was here? I have to know."

The blonde thought for a moment, but was too tired to resist; and she wouldn't do anything in that moment to annoy her boss again, so she was happy to give the info.

"Avi Lifshitz," she replied. "Here is his signature."

And she showed him the register.

Eli left the office, noting the deterioration of the hospital, and at the same time thought about the name she had given him. When he was just about at the main entrance, the blonde shouted, "Hey! You have to sign before taking that material."

Eli turned and approached the girl.

"Photocopy the note I showed you when I came in and call the number that appears there if you want to know about me."

"Go away!" said the blonde, turning away to her office and leaving the receptionist staring after her.

In his car, Eli began reviewing the sheets until he found the records he had come for. He checked everything he knew; there wasn't much new data, but he had to examine everything. The names were clear. There were three files, a report of everything that had happened that day and a birth summary for each of the babies. Starting with the families was something he had discarded some time ago, considering that it was pointless after so much damage had already been done.

The name of Rachel Mizrachi was there, as old Cohen had told him, but what caught his attention most was that the pediatrician on duty that day, a man named Rafi Segal, who had joined the hospital just a week before, had a new assistant who was also admitted to the hospital just a few days previously; and that same October 22, the assistant marked his work card manually and left long before finishing his shift. Why is it that on such a busy day in pediatrics, a novice in the hospital had left before finishing his shift? Rafi and his assistant were the ones who made the identification of babies that day, but the assistant name was not on the record of babies with his signature; it only appeared in the summary of the day.

So who was Rafi Segal? And who was his assistant? How was it possible that the hospital didn't have that man's data in such an important report? Everything seemed so strange. The reports of the maternity ward were very detailed, but clearly were missing something.

Eli felt he had to investigate further what had happened that day. Perhaps the doctor or his assistant were the missing piece of the puzzle.

He knew Avi Lifshitz. The Yedioth Ahronoth newspaper reporter was very popular for his controversial articles, all of them detailed and well-edited. He knew Avi wasn't a sensationalist and wouldn't write anything baseless, but how did he find out about this matter? Eli knew that if Avi were to publish something, it could destroy Eli's entire investigation. Moreover, it could cause a lot of damage to the system — the last thing the government or any other institution involved needed at this time.

Perhaps the priority now was to talk to Avi or his editor.

51

Tel Aviv
November 2nd, 2011

Avi calculated that by driving at full speed, respecting the maximum speed limit, he could reach Tel Aviv at around 10 p.m. and meet with Gabriel. So, at the exit from Jerusalem, as the car began descending between the hills, he sent a text to alert him that he wanted to see him soon. Gabriel was in the newsroom, covering his shift; he said they'd meet in a cafe, a block down from the newspaper, to avoid suspicion. Avi knew that rival journalists in the newsroom had no qualms when there was a story in play; there were always a few lurking around, trying to eavesdrop. Many times he had to be part of that game, though. Whenever possible, he preferred sanity, truth, and honesty. He also knew that Gabriel was very much like him and was tuned into the same values, which is why they worked very well together.

While driving at full speed toward Tel Aviv, he began to string together the pieces of the enigma of the two young men exchanged at birth. He still didn't have the material he needed to put together an article and he knew that Gabriel wasn't into scandal; he would only use cold, hard facts. After reading the lists from the hospital, it struck him that the name Leonel Cohen was the same name he had heard on the radio just three hours before. Could it possibly be the same person? If so, events had taken a very dangerous turn; perhaps a horror movie, he thought.

He arrived in Tel Aviv as he had planned, and was outside the newspaper's offices by 10:05 p.m. Gabriel was already sitting in the cafe.

They greeted each other and Gabriel said he had only 10 minutes. They got right to the point.

"What did you bring?" Gabriel asked, a little anxious as he ordered a black coffee.

"I am thinking too much and too little at the same time," he replied. "First, the one who sent me the anonymous letter was old Moshe Cohen."

"You know that's who was killed today?" Gabriel interrupted him, amazed.

"Yes, I heard it on the radio on my way to Jerusalem."

"This is heavier than I thought!" Gabriel said. "And I imagine you went to the hospital in Jerusalem to inquire about the children." Gabriel knew very well how Avi managed those situations.

"Yeah, that's true," said Avi, "but look, there's something else — everything written by old Cohen is true. Mizrachi Rachel's name is listed on the birth records of the babies, but what worries me most is the Jewish child, Leonel Cohen."

"What are you worried about?" Gabriel asked.

"Didn't you hear on the news that the Hamas captured a civilian?"

"Yes, yes, we published that two hours ago and the name is exact to the letter, Leonel Cohen! Are you perhaps thinking it's the same person?"

"Look, I don't think there are many people with the same name and age. Leonel isn't a common name; his family is Argentinian. The moment I first heard the news, I was confused and it took me a moment to associate them."

"Now I realize why I like working with you," Gabriel said with a smile, "but we're also nowhere near writing an article, I don't think."

"Yeah, you're right. We need concrete and verifiable data," Avi said.

"I agree; you know I'm never interested in overstatements."

"You think we'll be in danger if we run with this?" Avi asked.

"Well, now that Moshe Cohen is dead, perhaps the only one who knows the truth is you. Or perhaps someone else behind the scenes," Gabriel said.

"We'll have to be very careful," Avi added, worried.

"Well, friend, on that we're agreed. We'll just have to keep our eyes peeled," Gabriel said as he finished his coffee.

"Look I have an idea," Gabriel said, "try to find out whether the data on our Leonel Cohen matches that of the kidnapped young man. I'll try to find out if there is someone else who is aware of all this and I'll reach out to my contact in the Shabak to learn who planned the baby exchange in the first place. We need money, you know that, right?"

"OK. I'll take care of the information on the kidnapped youth and I'll get some money. How much will that bastard charge?"

"A few months ago, the minimum was $3,000 American," Gabriel said.

"Well, let's not make trouble for ourselves. It isn't worth it to deal with all the paperwork the newspaper will require to get this information, because then there'd be too many questions to answer. We'll have to manage it between us. I'll contribute with $1,000 you know my situation; you try to get the other two thousand."

Avi saluted, left 20 shekels, and stood up. From the door of the cafe, smiling, he said, "You see that I didn't forget to pay."

"Bla bla bla, what about the five hundred that you owe me?"

52

Mossad Headquarters - Tel Aviv
November 3rd, 2011

Just as on every workday morning, the head of Mossad parked his car in his reserved space on the first underground floor in front of the elevators. Today, his secretary had been waiting there for 20 minutes. She wanted to give him the news before he got to his office. As she accompanied him into the elevator, she spoke quietly into his ear, summarizing the night's events.

The Mossad had a general system for receiving investigation notes; everything they received from the different types of agents, Kaza or Sayanim[47], was filtered from the lowest ranks up. As it was received, a note would be affixed to it, highlighting its importance. From there, it filtered through the various ranks until, if necessary, it reached the head of the Mossad. Also important were the scale and urgency of the information received, and whether it was arriving domestically or from abroad. Regardless, everything was subjected to the filtering system.

The news the secretary was now sharing had circulated up through all levels of the organization and had been seen by the heads of all the different sections. It had been deemed important enough to grace the desk of the "kingpin" of the Mossad, but it had been decided that it wasn't so important that they had to wake him from his sleep.

The chief, on the other hand, was furious that he hadn't been awakened immediately. He wanted to know why they had waited to give him

---

47 Sayanim: Mossad agent who acts voluntarily and lives outside of Israel.

the news. He immediately ordered a meeting in his office with the heads of each department, even those who weren't directly involved in the issue. Once the agenda had been passed and all were seated, he stood in front of the whiteboard and wrote: "The Hiat is here in Israel." Then he started talking in his hoarse and stern voice.

"As almost all of you know, this has been brewing for quite a while right under our noses. The time we lost following the paths of Hamas and that young Ahmed in Pakistan was the time the Iranians needed to develop this cyber program. What they planned in Pakistan was just a cover; Hamas cooked up a huge lie and we ate it up like idiots. Then they took Ahmed and Reza to Iran." As he spoke, he recorded everything on the board with a red marker.

"I want the head of Unit 8200 here in half an hour, to see how we can protect ourselves from all this," he went on. "At noon I will have an emergency cabinet meeting behind closed doors; I need to be prepared."

Those present at the meeting were aware of the news and knew very well the details of the " El Hiat"; it was no wonder that no one asked for clarifications. The room stayed silent.

Then one of the people in charge of Internal Affairs stood.

"What we do with the issue of the two children?" he asked. "We're fucking up too much with that."

Irritated, the Mossad chief barked, "I want Eli Regev here before noon!"

His secretary noted the order.

The meeting ended earlier than expected. The secretary tried to erase the board, but the chief stopped her.

"We're not deleting anything until this damn thing is taken care of once and for all!"

At 10:30 a.m., Eli Regev arrived at the Mossad's offices. He had received a call to present himself within half an hour; otherwise, they would go looking for him. Eli didn't even hesitate. He knew well enough to take orders from the top very seriously, even if they came from a friend. As he stood before his old acquaintance, he thought back to when they had worked together in the army. They had both held the rank of general at the time. Eli was in charge of the forces along the southern borders of the country, whereas the other had been in charge in the north.

They had had their differences, but they respected each other. Eli sat without being invited to do so.

"It's a good thing you called me. I wanted to talk to you."

"I don't think it's about the same subject, or is it?" the chief said. "Listen to me: I don't want to hear about those two boys or anything to do with that matter. I also don't want anyone in this organization participating in any interrogations, at least for now. I know you were given the liberty and support to conduct your research as you see fit, but we're experiencing difficult times right now, and as you know, anything that distracts us can lead to serious implications for the integrity of our state."

Eli took a breath and asked,

"What's going on?"

"I can't give you details, but we're facing an immediate threat of a cyberattack that could paralyze this country!"

"Is it from Hamas?"

"I'm sorry; I can't give you any details. I've already said too much. I want you to stop your research and leave us alone for now. On the other hand, we have the Hamas trying to bribe us with that young man who was captured."

"Look," Eli said solemnly, "you know that I appreciate and respect you very much, but I'm not sure I can do as you ask. I've come quite far in this. They're actually killing people out there and, frankly, I also think my research has to do with both this possible cyber threat and the kidnapped young man. Also, remember that I was assigned to monitor what you're supposedly trying to hide from me now!"

The old chief didn't want to hear more. His skin was crawling; he was so angry. He wasn't used to hearing answers such as Eli's and he didn't much care for Eli's final statement.

"Well, you can leave now; make your own choices. You know what I think. I respect you very much, and, supposedly, we both want the best for this country."

"Listen to me," Eli said. "I want to be aware of everything that is happening, do you understand?"

"All right, we know that Ahmed, one of the youths, is here in Israel with the computer virus in his possession. We're looking all over the place for him. Today, I have a cabinet meeting. I don't know more than that ... is that OK for you?"

"Yes, that's fine. Thanks for everything. I'll try not to bother any more of your people, but I have to be informed about what's happening at all times."

As Eli left the office, he realized he needed to relax for a few moments and think. Was everything that was said in that conversation negative for his mission? Not at all, he thought; now he had more data, more information, more pieces of the puzzle. Listening to the chief trying to convince him by alluding to patriotic issues wasn't that surprising to Eli; both were experienced players and both were already into their sixties. Eli well knew the different characters in this game; he could stay out and let them do their jobs.

He had no doubt the other man had told the truth, but he nevertheless felt that solving the riddle of the boys could help with the possible worm crisis.

Eli lacked depth with the chief when it came to Leonel, captive in the hands of Hamas, although he knew that these types of cases passed quite quickly from the Mossad to the government cabinet, especially when the victim was a citizen and not a soldier. He also wanted to know once and for all whether the Mossad was behind the latest developments. He was sure that the head of Mossad would deny any involvement of his organization in the recent killings. He would have to show facts to blame anyone, especially if everything had been their responsibility.

What bothered him most, mainly because he didn't understand it, was the death of Shmulik Sade. Surely, Shmulik knew the story of the boys, how they had grown up and how they had changed over the years, but the work had come to him through an intermediary who was never identified, and the money, from an anonymous account at Bank Leumi, in Israel. He saw the guy once a month to get reports, and Eli had learned after Shmulik's death that although the guy called himself Mark, it was a pseudonym.

Six years ago, Mark had told Shmulik that the job he had been doing for the organization had been terminated. This time they had left a very fat check in his locker, much higher than the not inconsiderable sums he had been receiving in cash for years. They had also given him a final warning to never discuss the matter with anyone, ever. Did the government know that Shmulik Sade was engaged in this? Why had they chosen him and then forced him not to talk? Perhaps the government was trying to get "clean" by laying blame on the Mossad or on another agency. These ideas were floating around in Eli's head as he processed the possibilities. After his dialogue with the Mossad boss, he formed a question that possibly only Moshe Cohen could answer, if the old man weren't already dead.

53

Cabinet meeting in HaKirya - Tel Aviv
November 3rd, 2011

A short, red-haired and well-groomed young woman was preparing the long table in the cabinet room. There was room for 25 people, and the staff had confirmed the presence of 20 cabinet members. The Ministers of Sports, Health, Economics, Religious Affairs and Infrastructure weren't attending. Those who would be on hand were there very early. It was a well-known strategy for hearing rumors and building alliances. The woman went in and out bringing pies and orders of all kinds, plus jugs of water, lemon and orange juice. The coffee would be served a little later, when the atmosphere was "warmer."

They all sat. The prime minister was seated at the center, while on either side, the ministers of defense and interior were located. In addition to all the ministers, several special guests were seated at the table, including the head of Mossad, the Shin Bet director, the general of the police and the head of Unit 8200. The IDF general functioned as a minister in these hearings, and was located at the head of the table.

The news about the possible cyberattack and the kidnapping of the Jewish citizen at the hands of Hamas were the first items on the agenda to be addressed. The Mossad chief rose from his seat to walk the group through the information that had been obtained so far about the possibility of a cyber event. With a quiet albeit leering tone and while looking at the defense minister, he began his presentation:

"We have proof that a massive cyber threat is imminent and that the Iranians are responsible. One of their agents has already entered the country with foreign passports. We think he's in Tel Aviv, but we haven't yet been able to determine his exact whereabouts. Our agents are working around the clock to locate him. We are permanently connected with the Shin Bet, the Shabak, and police across the country. The subject entered Israel with a Belgian passport under a false identity. His fake name is Enzo Shiles."

The head of Unit 8200 then stood up; he was accountable for national technology security.

"We know that the attack will be a combination of DDoS (denial of service) and Payload (the damage the virus load detonates). We are predicting that the attack will be against private networks, especially those that are extremely important and essential to the country's institutions, but we don't have details yet on what type of worm will be introduced, what it will do, or where it will target. In recent days, we have been working to install a special system to detect the majority of the worms and block them. We've already implemented it in the police offices in the Shabak, and today and tomorrow we'll do the same in the Mossad offices in Tel Aviv, Mossad facilities in Herzliya and HaKirya. Meanwhile, yesterday, the army began installing the program on their most exposed units. At this point, all we can do is cover our most strategic locations across the country. I think that in two days this will all be over."

They all stared with wide eyes at the gestures of the prime minister, who evidenced great agitation while listening to the reports.

Next up was the head of Shabak, who rose and went to a map located in the center of the room.

"I don't have anything to add in relation to cyber issues. As it has been noted, we are in permanent contact with the Mossad to find the individual who entered the country. We have some clues, but still nothing concrete. So far we have all the paperwork that was generated at the airport during that period of time and we know he is in Tel Aviv. In relation to the recording by Hamas on the capture of the Israeli man, we've checked every detail, and we are confident that the video is genuine; the newspaper is legitimate and it shows the actual date it was published. The recording environment was very well prepared, so we were unable to distinguish any features which would have helped us locate the place. However, I have good news, too. Our spies in Gaza have

managed to locate the place by paying a mashtap[48]. The place is here."
And he showed a point on the map.

At that moment, the IDF general stood up and walked to the map where he began to mark the different options.

"I educated myself on the case of the kidnapped citizen," he said. "We've asked the general of Special Forces to plan a rescue. I received a report from him this morning in which he explains that there are two options. One is to go in by sea, as the place is very close to the beach. The other is via helicopter, which would land near the beach. There is a problem in both variants: the place is full of people, civilians. The young man is being held in an old house that has three underground floors. He is located on the lowest floor, in a room with a small window that has no strategic value for us. Furthermore, the door is reinforced, so we'll need to blow it in. Obviously, doing so carries many risks, not to mention the danger to our own forces. The place is crowded, and there are always a lot of people there. To clarify my point: the building right next door has six floors and houses, in this little square live more than 250 people. It would be impossible not to injure civilians. Our recommendation is to negotiate for the moment and wait; perhaps they will move to another location where conditions are more suitable for an operation to take place. Right now, we are evaluating the list of prisoners they have requested we release. Some are impossible — they still have fresh blood on their hands. For the others, we'll get more information and see what we can do."

The defense minister stood up and said, "We have to be very careful not to confuse these two events. If we turn around, our enemies can take advantage."

The prime minister was fuming. That's all he had to say? he thought. For quite a long time now they had had serious disagreements between them.

The minister of labor requested the floor. He was a man in whom the cabinet had great confidence. He faced the guests of the Mossad and Unit 8200.

"What would be the consequences if the cyberattack you are suggesting is successful?"

The head of Unit 8200 responded. He was relatively new in his job, although he was well recognized for his long career in the military.

---

48 Mashtap: Arabs in Gaza collaborating with Israel.

"It depends on the epicenter and also what the pre target will be for the worm that, according to trusted sources, they will try to inject. When a virus attacks, the first thing it does is reproduce itself over and over again in the shortest possible time without the owner noticing that it has entered the affected system. Once it has attained a critical mass, it will start wreaking havoc. For example, it will steal files and credit cards, or it could implant itself in the system and extract secret information. Eventually, it could hinder or even destroy entire systems. If the target were the army, it could interrupt the communications and planning systems, preventing units in the field from contacting each other, effectively cutting them off from resupply and aid. We have many systems that could fall apart, but, as I noted, it's very difficult to pinpoint the exact results without first knowing the type of worm, the epicenter, and the target."

The labor minister adjusted his shirt and asked, "Can you give us probabilities?"

"The main probability, based on current information, is 50-50," the Unit 8200 head replied. "I think the systems we are installing, plus the extra layer of firewalls, can block the worm and keep our systems online while we hunt for the ultimate solution. In addition, I have a hunch that they will be performing a manual injection of the virus into our network; otherwise, they wouldn't have sent someone here with the malware. What's more, the Iranians know very well that no virus can penetrate our external defenses."

The prime minister finished his second meat pie, took a sip of his coffee, and approached the microphone.

"I want all police, Mossad, Shin Bet, Shabak, and any other unit or security person who has not already been assigned, outside around the clock to find this cyber terrorist and his contacts, because obviously he isn't acting alone," he said. "We need to know who he is, where he comes from, where he was born and when. Right now we need everything — completely everything — that we can find out about this guy. If the Iranians are really behind this plan to destroy us, I will host a news conference to alert the media. We also need an initiative — by that, I mean we should formalize a plan between the Mossad and Unit 8200 to graft one of the worms they are developing and use it before

the Iranians do. I want to know if that's possible. Regarding the kidnapped man, I agree that we can't do anything to rescue him right now.
It would be a dream to emerge unscathed from something like that. We
need to buy time to keep him alive, so we should start negotiations with
another country as collateral.

"The Germans are always ready ...

"We will revisit the list of Muslims whose release has been requested.
I designate the minister of labor to negotiate with the Hamas and the
Mossad chief to take ownership over the possible cyberattack. Within
two days, I expect us to be back here, in this room. Needless to say, I do
not want a word on this computer attack to leak to the media. Thank
you everyone."

The room was filled with murmurs. The ministers dispersed as they
left. The defense minister had not been chosen to deal with any of the
situations and that, surely, would bring political consequences.

The concern about the virus was obvious in the faces of the crowd.

The minister of labor asked the Mossad chief for the exact information about Leonel Cohen, curious to know who he was and why he had
been chosen by Hamas.

54

AHMED
Tel Aviv
November 4th, 2011

The expected call came while I was in the bathroom looking in the mirror and wondering from what part of the family these chestnut roots came from. I couldn't remember anyone in my family with this hair color. The cat was playing with a ball of paper I had made last night, when my cell phone rang. A voice I knew was on the other end of the line.

"Meet me today at 2:30 p.m. at the Ramat Gan train station, next to the ticket counter," it said. "Tell that to the taxi driver. I'll be waiting by the ticket office. You don't know me, so to help you locate me easily, I have a green-colored bag. Bring all your belongings and your laptop. Leave the cat, the computers, and all the other electronic devices."

I had no time to react or say anything. As I opened my mouth to speak, I heard the phone disconnect in my ear. Making short calls was part of the tradecraft, I knew. No call should ever last longer than 15 seconds. Any longer than that and a call can be traced. In the same way, they had a special process for hook-ups.

It was 1:37 p.m. I searched the Internet for how long it would take to get to the ticket booth. The internet told me 20 minutes, so I added 10 more for traffic. My bag was always ready to go. All I did was pick up my toothbrush and a few other small things, my laptop, and at 1:55 p.m. I left the house. I felt like someone was watching me and I thought it was my neighbor, the one with the pies. I quickly walked down the street to the taxi stand and took the first available cab. At that time there were many available. At 2:26 p.m., I was at the station.

As I got out of the taxi, I saw that there were policemen and soldiers posted in front of the ticket office, examining passengers. My heart started thumping and my stomach began to show signs of a revolution. Why did they choose this place? I wondered. The station wasn't too crowded, but there were plenty of bystanders, many of them soldiers. It was the first time I had seen so many people together, all of them well-armed, all very green, with boots and faces challenging — or so it seemed to me. I realized that I felt no hatred toward them or anything like that, and that bothered me, because repudiating the army had been a feeling that had been instilled in me from when I was small. Now I had them in front of me and I didn't feel that way at all. My eyes flitted around like radar. I felt completely unprotected, like standing in the middle of nowhere. My contact touched my shoulder, and I immediately saw the green bag on his back, dark glasses, a mustache, and a kippah[49] on his head. With all this outfit I didn't recognize him, and I felt some fear, but he began speaking in Arabic and I recognized his voice.

We walked under the Ayalon Bridge, away from the cars and noise. There he placed a key in my hand.

"You've got to change places," he said. "The Zionists already know you're here. The country is on alert. Take this bag; you will have everything you need. You will find a USB stick with the final program code. You have to compile everything as instructed. In the memory, you'll also find an encrypted code that will protect the main algorithm. Of that, you're quite familiar. Now you must go. As soon as you can, read the note in your bag. Tomorrow afternoon will be zero day. I wish you luck."

With that, he took off his black shades and, for the first time, I saw his eyes. Then he put the glasses back on and left. As soon as I could, I read the note. My new refuge was located in 115 Alia Street in South Tel Aviv, on the first basement floor. The note stated that I should immediately go to the site. I took a taxi and in half an hour I arrived. The building was old and run down, and had three floors. It was surroun-

---

49 Kippah: is a brimless cap, usually made of cloth, worn by Jews to fulfill the customary requirement held by orthodox halachic authorities that the head be covered. It is usually worn by men in Conservative and Reform communities at all times.

ded by shops selling clothing, mainly fabrics. The street was one of the city's main corridors; in fact, according to my map, this was a central vertebra of the city. It cut across the city, from south to north, starting off as Allenby and then becoming Ben Yehuda, finally ending at the sea.

I opened the apartment and found there my companion, the same cat that I had left two hours before in the kitchen of Arlozorov. He began spinning between my feet, as was his custom.

On the table was all the equipment that I had left it in the other house: a server, two laptop computers, a router and a tracker (sniffer), all plugged into an intact network. To this they had added two very sophisticated firewall systems, which were still unconnected.

55

Prime Minister's Residence
Herzliya Pituach
November 4th, 2011 - 11:50 p.m.

A vehicle festooned with the flags and plates of an army general's staff car burst through the gates of the prime minister's house a few minutes before midnight. Stuffed inside were five people: the minister of defense, the first general, the commander of the Southern Zone of the Army, the chief of Mossad, and the driver.

The prime minister, trailing his security team, came out to meet the visitors, and together they all made their way quickly into the house. A member of the presidential guard stood outside, while the driver parked the car a block away from the home.

They sat at a table, in the central room of the house, large enough to accommodate more than 20 people. Without preamble, the first general opened the meeting. He sounded euphoric.

"We have an opportunity to rescue the young man!" he said.

"How?" asked the prime minister placating, trying to keep things calm.

"Our mashtaf in Gaza informed us that today there is a very important Hamas event in Haniounes, 12 kilometers from where they're holding him captive. Two, or at most three, guards will remain on site. Plus, there is a place nearby that's partially obscured, so we can land a helicopter there. Two mashtafim will wait there and accompany the special squad to the house, located less than a kilometer from the landing space. We have a plan to get inside, too; one of the guards invited a couple of women to have some fun and we expect them to arrive at 1 a.m. When they enter, our team will seize the opportunity to attack with silenced guns. They'll kill the guards and break down the door on the third basement floor. If all goes well, in 17 minutes we'll be out. We calculated five minutes to reach the site on foot, three minutes to go in and remove the guards, three more to knock down the armored door, then six minutes to get back to the helicopter. We'll bring the mashtafim back with us, because we'll have to evacuate them after completing the operation."

"Are you telling me that you're going to do all of this in an hour? It's crazy! We need to plan better than this."

The prime minister was seething.

"We don't improvise," the first general replied. "We don't act without thinking carefully about the details. What are the risks?"

The Southern Army commander took the floor.

"Sir, we received this information at 4:30 p.m. Our special forces have been preparing since then. The helicopter is ready — just one call and it will be good to go. The risks aren't great this time, but as we are going in we could lose lives, as it is with any operation; our men will be a little exposed returning in the helicopter, but everything will be done with silencers. We think that given the hour of the operation, there won't be any losses. Our forces will go in completely camouflaged, simulating Hamas fighters. The event in Haniounes ends at 2 a.m., so we have to finish the operation quickly. Honestly, I think this is our best opportunity."

While the prime minister was examining a map spread on the table, which had the points of arrival and departure marked on it, the house where the youth was being held captive, and some surrounding reference points, the defense minister took the opportunity to speak up.

"This operation could be very favorable for us," he said. "We would recover the confidence of our people, and that's what this government needs most right now."

The Mossad chief backed up the minister of defense.

"This is the best time, prime minister — and we don't have to be accountable for this to the Americans."

The prime minister was fuming. Throughout his career, he had always liked to take the initiative, "take the reins," as he often said. But this time, he felt that they had prepared everything without him and he had no choice but to agree to the proposal. He put his head in his hands and thought carefully about the plan. He knew he had no alternative, because if he faltered on this, the media, the opposition, and the people would crucify him. In addition, deep down, he was much more concerned about the cyberattack.

"And what about the cyberattack and its operative?" he asked, combatively. "Have you found anything yet?"

"We're working on it," the Mossad chief replied. "We think by tomorrow we'll have our prey."

The prime minister stood, looked toward the vaulted ceiling of his home in Herzliya Pituach for a few seconds, then touched one of the marble walls of his beautiful mansion. The air was shrouded in silence.

Finally, he said, "Let's do it!"

56

The blades of the Bell AH-1 Tzefa had been thumping the air for several minutes on the deserted airstrip with 10 Special Forces soldiers waiting to board. The colonel went over their orders and made sure that each and every one of them was ready for what was to come. The operation would also involve a doctor, two nurses, and a specialist helicopter mechanic. Four stretchers and various other medical instruments had been prepared.

Two Apache helicopters, loaded with bombs and heavy weapons, would be in the air five minutes after the Tzefa and would remain prepared for any eventuality. After 10 minutes, an ambulance helicopter would take off to deal with any contingencies. These three aircraft would remain in the air just six minutes flying time from the Tzefa's rescue site, flying almost over the coastal city of Ashkelon in southern Israel.

At 12:38 a.m., the helicopter took off from Palmachim Air Base in Rishon Letzion. The estimated time of arrival at the landing site was 12:52 a.m. The helicopter hugged the coastline of the Mediterranean Sea to avoid suspicion, and at 12:49 a.m. turned towards the target, about two kilometers from the beach. The colonel's order sounded loud and clear: "Prepare for descent."

The Tzefa maneuvered sharply 35 degrees to the right, and its nose pointed directly toward the coast. The pilots began their descent, heads swivelling, looking for the mashtaf, who was supposed to illuminate the precise landing site. At 12:53 a.m., the pilots spotted the lights and descended rapidly. As soon as they landed, the engines fell silent.

The two mashtafim led the unit to the target house. The walk lasted about five minutes, and at 1:01 a.m., the soldiers were in front of the building. There they divided into two groups of six, with a medic in each and two snipers providing cover. One group hid behind a 50-centimeter-high shrub, their bodies pressed to the ground. The other group waited crouched off to one side. The two groups were communicating by closed-circuit radio.

Everyone watched the entrance and waited for the arrival of the girls. At 1:04 a.m., the two prostitutes arrived in a taxi and sauntered up to the door, their high heels clicking loudly against the tile path. They knocked on the door and it swung open almost immediately. As the women entered the house, a terrorist came outside for a quick look around. He watched the taxi depart and turned around to go back inside.

The order to advance was given, and the two groups of soldiers moved quickly from their positions and ran toward the house. The colonel was leading. As they moved forward, one of the snipers took out the terrorist at the door with a single silenced shot to the back of his head. With the house standing wide open, eight soldiers entered immediately, while two remained out front. The women were screaming, and two terrorists appeared and began to exchange fire. The attack ended with two wounded soldiers, one hit in the leg and the other in the chest, and both terrorists dead. One of the women was also injured. First-aid officers set about treating the wounded, while the rest of the group quickly descended to the third floor underground, looking for the prisoner. They came up against a security door, but as they had planned, they warned Leonel to get back and take cover, and then detonated explosives they had been carrying, blowing the door to pieces.

Two soldiers lifted Leonel, who was in shock, and struggling to rise. Above them, the injured woman was being seen to, while the other was already bound and gagged to prevent her from making any noise.

Quickly, without wasting a single second, the soldiers left the place behind, running toward the helicopter. Along the way, they met with a burst of gunfire from terrorists who lived in a neighboring house, but no members of the rescue mission were hit. At 1:17 a.m., the helicopter took off amid a hail of bullets. At 1:21 a.m., it was already far from the coast of Gaza. Then, after checking on the wounded, the colonel contacted the prime minister's house directly, where everyone was waiting for news of the operation.

"The package is in hand," he said.

"Losses? Wounded?" the Army general asked.

"No losses. Two minor injuries."

The prime minister couldn't hide his joy.

"Put the young man on the line," he ordered

The colonel passed the handset to Leonel, who was still in shock.

"Baruch a Shabim!"[50]

"Thank you for everything you've done! I have no words with which to thank you!" the young man stammered.

The prime minister resumed his political tone.

"We have a responsibility to our citizens. We have only done our duty," he said.

The Tzefa landed in Palmachim and there the festivities began. Leonel's parents were on the landing strip and they all embraced emotionally.

Suddenly, another smaller helicopter landed, and the prime minister and his entourage disembarked. There, on the helipad, he started the media party: photos of the leader with Leonel, hugs with his parents, and, minutes later, the press conference.

"This operation has shown that we never forget our soldiers or our citizens," the prime minister said. "We have a responsibility to protect everyone, no matter where or in what conditions they are in."

The nation's top politician had an enormous smile; it clearly was his night.

---

50 Baruch a Shabim!: Welcome back!

57

Tel Aviv
November 5th, 2011

It was 1:48 a.m. when Avi Lifshitz received the latest photos and material from the rescue. There were statements from the prime minister and the army general, and brief sentences expressing gratitude from Leonel and his parents. He put everything together and sent it off to be printed in the morning. He also sent another version to the newspaper's website.

There wasn't much to add or comment on. The government had acted strategically at the best possible time, when there was a lot of political turbulence. It had been a fast and accurate operation — everyone agreed there was no room for criticism. It was a time for celebration.

Avi thought about Leonel and his mistaken identity. Did the government know about it? Had they launched the operation because of it? Was there another motivation for the rescue? Why the rush? He estimated that the Hamas video had been broadcast only a few days ago. Why not let matters cool down as they had done on other occasions?

Gabriel Perez was pleased with the article. It appeared in huge letters on the cover and first two pages of the newspaper, as well as occupying the central section of the website. The two colleagues took to the streets to breathe some fresh air.

"Today I delivered the money to our contact," Perez said.

"Ah, that's good. Did you explain that it's urgent?"

"Yes, of course, but because of the urgency he wanted another $1,500."

"Where did you get the money?" Avi asked, worriedly.

"I said that when he has the information, I would give him the rest."

"And he accepted that?"

Avi knew that their contact always wanted all the money before starting his work.

"Yes, it's rare, I know, but he says the issue intrigues him. He wasn't sure if he could get the information quickly."

"And what do you think?" Avi asked.

"I think we have something very big on our hands — perhaps bigger than we think. He also said something very interesting."

"What? Tell me." Avi was extremely intrigued.

"And he told me this for free," added Pérez, only increasing the curiosity of his friend.

"Come on, tell me!" Avi was getting impatient.

"All of the state emergency systems are on red alert."

"OK. Why?"

"Apparently there's a terrorist in the country, and his mission is to run a cyberattack with a deadly virus," Perez said, enjoying the scoop.

"That's huge news!" Avi said, excitedly. "Why don't we spill the beans on this?"

"Because the government censored it, claiming the state is in danger."

Avi was confused and shocked at the same time by the news. He knew that any secret information had to pass government censorship, especially when it endangered the state. Newspapers and other media were required to communicate with an official government spokesman before posting an article like that.

After thinking about the rule for a moment, he said, "And the news about the two brothers — you don't think it will be censored, too?"

"No, I don't think so. But just in case, we'll risk it and go ahead without consulting the spokesman."

"What exactly are you talking about?" Avi said anxiously.

"I've thought about it," Perez said. "We're going into this unchecked; we can't stop, or we'll mess everything up."

"I agree 100 percent. I was always convinced we had to risk everything, and I'm pleased to hear you think the same."

"Well, now you know I'm with you on this matter, my friend. But get ready. The next few days will be very hectic. Come on, let's go."

Pérez's smile ended the conversation.

"Hold on a minute!" Avi said. "That young man — don't you realize who he is? He's the 'brother' of the Muslim! Do you remember the letter from old Cohen? He's referring to him ..."

58

Tel Aviv
November 5th, 2011 - 7 a.m.

The Air Finland flight landed half an hour late. It was 7:05 a.m., and it had originally been scheduled to arrive at 6:35 a.m. Shaul, a Mossad agent, was waiting impatiently. His contact would appear at any moment. He had already arranged everything so that she would enter the country via a private area, designated for ministers and Mossad agents.

Mariana, real name Shlomit Barak, hurried into the waiting area with her Israeli passport in hand. She was gaunt. She had been in a special clinic in Denmark for almost week and a half, and had managed to recover under the Mossad's zealous vigilance and care. She was relieved to reach Israel. Her blond hair had been trimmed tidily, but her beautiful body had lost its shape in recent months. She was pale and very thin, to the point that he could see the bones and veins in her hands.

She hugged Shaul, and he took her bags.

"How are you, Princess?" Shaul said, using the familiar name he had for her.

"I'm afraid I've been better," she said with a wry grimace.

"How are you feeling now? How was the trip?"

"As you know, I was in a very bad way, but I received the best medical care and I feel much more like myself now. I do have to continue psychiatric treatment, though. I have a whole collection of pills in my bag that I have to take daily."

"Have you heard the news?"

"What happened?" she asked.

"Earlier today, the army rescued Leonel in Gaza."

"For real? You're not lying to me, right? Tell me the truth — I can't believe it!"

For the first time, Shlomit smiled, and her features looked beautiful again.

"It's true," Shaul said. "Even I'm a little amazed. I thought they were going to leave him there and forget about him. I think it was a very political move; they saw an opportunity, and went for it. Now, everyone is euphoric and the government is celebrating, although ..."

"Although what?" Shlomit said, seeing the worry in Shaul's face.

Shaul was recognized as one of the agents who had advanced the most in Mossad in recent years. A very smart and clever man, he came from a family of army generals. He was muscular, dark, and had exotic, dark-green eyes. On top of that, he was 185cm tall and had a shaved head. He was always well-dressed and drew the eyes of all the women he passed. He had two kazas and four sayanim under his command, operating in Europe. While dragging Shlomit's luggage, he told her about the situation.

"There's a state of red alert for government forces across the country," he said. "We have information that there is a terrorist now in Israel who intends to launch a cyberattack."

"A cyberattack?" Shlomit repeated, hesitantly.

"Yes, on computers, something like a virus. You're lucky you're on leave now; if not, you too would be asked to take to the streets to find him."

"And tell me ... have you had any news about Ahmed, any information about what has happened to him since they lost him in Egypt?" she asked.

"Yes, we suspect that Ahmed is the terrorist we're talking about. We lost focus on him for awhile; we knew that he had left Egypt for Iran, but our agents failed to detect him there. They didn't know what to do, or how to act, and now, apparently he's here. He entered the country with a European passport."

"Is there any particular evidence? Where will they start? Are you sure it's him?" Shlomit was becoming intrigued and anxious at the same time.

"All I have right now are suspicions and theories. We think Ahmed is the terrorist, but we can't be certain. We know he studied cryptography and hacking. The photo from the airport when he arrived isn't much use, because he has whiskers and a different haircut. We're not 100 percent sure, but there are many probabilities."

Shlomit began to concentrate. They got in the car, Shaul started the engine, and they set off for Tel Aviv. Lost in thought, she didn't speak. A revolution was going on in her head. Shaul noticed that she was acting strangely.

"What's wrong?" he said.

"I'm wondering if … no, it can't be."

"What? Tell me. You have always been good with hunches."

"The terrorist is Ahmed. I'm sure of it."

Shaul swerved and pulled the car to the side of the road.

"Sure of it? How can you be so certain? How do you know that this is Ahmed?"

"If you're talking about a cyberattack, given that he's a genius in this area, he is absolutely the right person for the job. The Iranians always prefer to send a Palestinian so they can avoid the blame. Think about it — a Palestinian from the territories would not want to get involved. An Iranian would be too obvious. Even though Israel knows that it was the Iranians who organized this, in front of the rest of the world it'd look bad and create problems."

Shaul was impressed.

"I hadn't thought about that," he said as he maneuvered the car back into the stream of traffic. "Even if what you are saying is true, though, we still have no clue as to where he's hiding. We know he isn't working alone."

"You're right," Shlomit said. "Where do you think he might be? Do you know what the target of the attack is?"

"We have some idea of his whereabouts. We're working on it. As for the target, different hypotheses are being considered. One of them is an attack on an army base, perhaps HaKirya in Tel Aviv. Another possibility is the Hadera Power Station, and yet another is the Mossad secret database. If any of these organizations or targets are affected, it would be a disaster. Now, if you can put yourself into the mind of our enemies, what would you attack?" Shaul asked, as he stopped for the traffic light at an intersection.

"I wouldn't hesitate for even a second to attack the Mossad database first," Shlomit said. "Although it would be the most difficult to infiltrate, if they succeed, it would be a victory of enormous magnitude. In the more than 60 years this nation has existed, they have never managed to steal information from us. In this institution, there are many state secrets. An attack on Mossad would leave us highly vulnerable. Ahmed is the right person for that. When he makes a decision to act and feels completely convinced of it, he won't stop until he achieves his goal. You know that I know him well, too well.."

59

Tel Aviv
November 5th, 2011 - 9:30 a.m.

At 9:30 in the morning, Eli Regev noticed all of the reports organized into an endless line on his desk. Emma, his forever diligent secretary, had arranged them alphabetically. Regev thought of what a pleasure it was, having her at his side. They had been working together for 22 years, almost a lifetime. He was worried because, lately, she had begun to broach the subject of her possible retirement, as she was approaching 65 years of age.

In the stack were the profiles of all the people who had been working in the maternity ward on October 22, 1982, with precise information that even included their current activities. The doctor who had been in charge that day had worked in the same hospital for years, and nothing in his records drew any attention. Dr. David Levi had been partially retired now for only two years and now worked as a consultant at the Kfar Saba Hospital. Rachel Mizrachi was dead. Two other nurses still worked at the hospital, but one would retire the following week.

Interestingly, the pediatrician's assistant listed on that day had a blank space where his name should have been. Thanks to Emma's superb research skills, she had found the name of the missing man: Tal Elad, a nursing student who had never finished his studies. On October 30, 1982, he had left the hospital suddenly without explanation. Five months later he was drafted into the army after the outbreak of war in Lebanon, and had died five months after that when the army invaded Beirut. In the file there was a picture of him in a Merkava[51] tank. The same vehicle had been blown up in an ambush, and no one in the tank could have survived. Tal Elad's short stay in the hospital, and the fact that he had transferred to work with babies in the nursery, made him the prime suspect for making the switch.

As he was reflecting on these facts, Emma came in with more papers in her hand.

"This young man passed the Mossad exams before starting his nursing studies," she said, "and two months after leaving the hospital, he worked for Shabak until he entered the reserve army to fight in Lebanon. In nursing school, they say he was a normal student, and at the hospital, nobody understood why he suddenly quit his job."

"And what do we know about his family?" Eli asked.

"His parents are separated. His father still works at the University of Tel Aviv, as dean in the Department of Medicine. There's no information on his mother. One day she disappeared and never returned."

"Brothers and sisters?"

"He had no siblings."

"Hmmm. This is something of a puzzle. Where do we start?"

Eli couldn't decide if it was worth going further with the investigation into Tal Elad.

"Maybe we'll question the father a little. Do you have his details?"

"Yes, here they are. Dr. Jacob Lachman."

"Hmmm. Apparently Tal changed his surname."

"Yes, it seems that he never got along that well with his parents — at least that's what they told me at the nursing school," Emma said.

"I'll stop by the university. It's on the way home," Eli said. "Perhaps I'll leave a little early today, I need a break. You know that yesterday I got home at 12:30 a.m.?"

Emma looked at him, then turned and grimaced in annoyance, while muttering to herself, "Of course I know. You woke me up and ordered me to get everything ready for today."

Out loud, she said, "Are you going to arrange a meeting with Dr. Lachman?"

"No, I'd better not. Given the circumstances, I think it's better to surprise him."

---

51 Merkava: a tank of Israeli origin and production.

60

LEONEL
Bat Yam
November 5th, 2011 – Early morning

I was in the place where I had grown up, lying in the same bed I had occupied in my teens. The night hadn't been easy. We got home at about 3 a.m. after the media festival, which had been just as jarring as the previous events. I still had the sound of gunfire ringing in my ears. I'd had a hard time falling asleep — my mind was a whirlwind of images, emotions, and unanswered questions. Only a few days ago, Hamas had been recording the video of their demands in exchange for my release, and now I was in my old bedroom. Those 15 minutes of action in Gaza had passed so quickly that they resembled one of those silent films where the characters never stop running, without uttering a sound.

I hadn't been too surprised to see the prime minister and his entourage greeting me, but I was deeply touched when I saw my parents there on the landing strip. It had been so long since I had been with them, living at home! I realized how much I missed them.

When I arose and moved to the living-room window overlooking the street and looked out, I saw a crowd waiting for me by the door of the house. There were many photographers with their equipment all set up, and several neighbors, some of whom didn't even know me. Everyone wanted to see, and if possible touch, the young man who had returned from hell. What impressed me most was that two guards were blocking the door of the building and refusing to let anyone in.

My father hadn't gone to work and had been following me around, hoping for a conversation, a few words, a sign; my mother, however, had taken the approach of offering food. Everything seemed strange, even the taste of food. I was supposed to feel happy and elated, but I felt down and embarrassed. I retreated to my bedroom to try and find a little peace and quiet. I closed the door, lay down, and stared at the ceiling for a while, trying to organize my thoughts. Now what? What happens next? My identity had been exposed completely. Although the morning papers said Hamas had captured me in Egypt, none explained how I got there. Perhaps the fact that I had really been grabbed in the Faroe Islands was censured, since I was Mossad's responsibility, and they had been looking for me there.

Several photos of me hugging my parents, greeting the prime minister, and embracing the minister of defense, were highlighted on the front pages of all the newspapers. As politicians, they hadn't lost this coveted chance to win votes.

I didn't have the slightest doubt that Mossad knew everything. From Paris to Pakistan and even in Denmark, they had been following in my footsteps. I still had the wound from the GPS device they had implanted in me, which had later been brutally extracted by Hamas. Mariana also appeared in my mind. I still had the image of her in the hospital, completely out of it, imprinted in my memory. I didn't know if I would ever see her again. It was all still very fresh — and I cared about her, I still had feelings for her.

I thought about getting in touch with Jacob, and going back to university. I guessed that I could now afford it, without needing to work, at least for a while. The last time I had checked my bank statement, I had 10,000 shekels in my account, but I felt I should return the money because I hadn't found Ahmed and had no idea where he was. I had thought about just charging my expenses and returning the rest to Rachel. I connected to the Internet to check my account again and decide how much I should return. When the page finally opened, I couldn't believe it. The balance was 978,000 shekels. The money had been deposited two weeks ago. I didn't understand why Rachel had given me all the money, seeing as I hadn't fulfilled my end of the bargain. As well as that, I hadn't had any news from her since leaving Israel. I grabbed my cell phone and called her number, but it was disconnected. I tried to call Moshe Cohen next, but had no luck there, either. What had happened? Then I tried to speak to Jacob, but his secretary said he was busy, so I left a message asking him to call me as soon as possible at my parents' house. I was paralyzed and couldn't stop looking at the figure in my account. Perhaps it was a mistake on behalf of the bank. I was resolute that I should return the money. Then I heard my mother speaking to me through the door. Suddenly it opened and she came into my room.

"Someone wants to talk to you," she said.

"How did they get past security?" I asked.

"They're with Mossad; the man showed me his ID."

"I don't want to talk to anyone right now."

"Look, Leonel, they told me that it's urgent and you can't avoid this meeting. They asked that your father and I to go out for a walk while they talk with you. They want complete privacy. Leonel, I don't like this — I don't like this at all." She looked worried.

"Don't worry," I said, trying to reassure her, "now go."

I heard the front door open and close and knew my parents had left the house. Then I heard the voices of two people — a man and a woman — and I was surprised. I was sure my mom had said it was only a man. I left my bedroom and headed downstairs, and as I walked through the dining room, I froze. I couldn't believe my eyes.

Mariana was standing there in my kitchen, like a graceful statue, accompanied by the agent. As she looked into my eyes, a tear slid down her cheek. Her companion stood up, extended his hand, and introduced himself, mentioning only his name, Shaul. Mariana didn't need to introduce herself.

61

Tel Aviv
November 5th, 2011 – 11:20 a.m.

It had been a long time since they had worked overnight at the news-paper. It was heading toward noon and the troop of journalists was still giddy. There was so much happening, and more news happening every second, so they couldn't stop to rest. As well as Leonel's rescue in Gaza, the sirens had gone off in the north last night. Two Sager rockets had fallen in open fields in Galilee, although they hadn't caused any major damage to people or property. That kept Avi awake for another two hours, because he needed to know to who would take the credit for the attack. It always happened like this: first the incident and then the recognition of those responsible. Finally, Hez-bollah claimed responsibility for the attack, and he was able to finish the article.

Avi felt that the north was a furnace whose temperature had risen in recent times. The Iranians were behind a lot of the attacks, as they manipulated Hezbollah's actions, and then hid behind the organization so they couldn't be held directly responsible for events. They seemed to be trying to bring the area to the boil. Something had to happen soon to change the current situation. He saw the country as a seesaw, with moments of high tension alternating with brief periods of calm, which lasted until the enemy regrouped and attacked again. The Iranians were trying to set the northern border on fire — there was no doubt about it. As he was walking to his car, his cell phone rang.

"Avi, how've you been?"

"Who's speaking, please?"

"It's me, your old friend, Eli Regev."

"Eli Regev? Ah, Eli. How are you?"

"I'm fine, and you? You must be busy with the news."

"Yeah, you know how it is. I had to work all night to get the job done."

"So, you must have gone to the rescue media party as well?"

"That's right, but not live, because I was in the newsroom."

"I need to talk to you right away," Eli said, all preliminaries aside.

"Look, Eli, I'm a little busy right now. And I've got to get some sleep. Can't it wait until next week?"

"No! There isn't time to wait until next week. We're after the same thing — I can help you, and you me."

"What do you mean?" Avi asked.

"I know that a few days ago you were in the Shaare Zedek hospital in Jerusalem."

"Ahhh — so what?"

"Don't play dumb. You went looking for information about what happened on October 22, 1982. You're investigating the case of the swapped children."

Avi was surprised. He supposed that there was no point in trying to hide the truth.

"Correct," he said.

"Let's have a coffee together. In half an hour. I'll wait for you in the center of Ramat Aviv Gimmel."

"Why there?"

"Afterwards, I have to meet someone important at the University of Tel Aviv, which is not far from there."

"OK. I'll be there in half an hour."

Eli arrived first. He went into the Zanzibar cafe, a nice restaurant that overlooked the Ramat Aviv Country Club. He sat next to the window, his favorite place, from where he could see the tennis courts and the Olympic swimming pool. Avi arrived five minutes later and, as he was walking in, Eli examined his acquaintance carefully. He had dark circles under his eyes, suggesting that he hadn't slept for several nights, not just since yesterday. He wore sneakers and jeans, and he carried a leather satchel.

He was thinner than the last time Avi had seen him.

"How are things at Yedioth?" Eli asked, casually.

"There's a lot of pressure now. Ever since the news website became so popular, we have to work twice as hard. Before, we produced one edition per day; now we're working around the clock."

"They should pay you more," Eli said.

"Tell that to your friend Shalev," Avi remarked. Shalev was the owner of the newspaper.

"It's been a long time since I talked to him, but if I see him, I'll throw in a compliment for you," Eli said with a laugh.

"Well, let's get on with it then. What is it you're looking for?" Avi said, wanting to cut to the chase.

"I want to know the same thing you do. Who switched those babies. And why."

"Right — that's exactly what I want to know."

"And how did you get information on this case?" Eli asked.

"That I can't tell you."

Eli hadn't expected this response. He had assumed that with Avi he would not have to enforce the government's authority. But he didn't want to lose time or patience, so he took out the document with the prime minister's signature and put it on the table. At that moment the coffees arrived.

Seeing the paper, Avi realized that the government was also anxious to discover the truth about what happened.

"Honestly, I don't owe the government anything, and your letter won't work with me, but I'll tell you anyway. Moshe Cohen sent me an unsigned letter before he was assassinated."

"And how did you realize it was him who sent it?"

"The day I received the letter, I had traveled to the Metzuba Kibbutz and discovered that he had been there the night the kibbutznik was shot and the murderer killed."

"Very good move," Eli said. "You're one of the most astute journalists of our time, but what I like about you is your decency, something quite rare in your profession."

"Thank you. And you? Have you found something, or rather, something you're willing to share?" Avi asked.

"Nothing. We have the information from the hospital, but so far I've failed to find the connection between the different parts of this story. Do you think that the person who switched the babies might also be responsible for the deaths of Moshe Cohen and Rachel Mizrachi?"

"I think you might be right — there is a common thread here, that's for sure. But I still have no idea why."

Neither gave their game away and let slip clues to the other. The only thing that Eli Regev got out of the meeting was that old Cohen had sent a message to Avi Lifshitz. Meanwhile, Avi learned that the government also wanted to know of those involved in the children's story.

Eli thought he had wasted his time. He paid for their coffee and stood up. As he was leaving, he told Avi, "You know very well you can't publish any of this. Before you did, you would have to pass censorship. This subject has a 'national security' classification."

"Yes, I know. Don't worry."

Avi left mumbling obscenities. The situation was getting very complicated. It would be impossible to go unnoticed if something were published, and now he had received his first warning.

62

Tel Aviv
November 5th, 2011 - 12:49 p.m.

As they had on other occasions, they met in the parking lot of Tel Aviv's Metzitzim Beach. It was around one in the afternoon on a wintry day, and the beach was totally deserted. It was no accident that both men were wearing dark glasses. They had never seen each other's eyes and neither of them were interested in the other's identity.

One of them, who had a scar on his forehead, asked, "What do you want now?"

"I need you to eliminate three more."

"You still haven't paid me for the Metzuba kibbutz. I told you that you have to pay me first. Without payment, I won't work with you anymore. Plus, this is getting too risky."

"How much are you expecting me to pay you?"

"I told you — 10,000 shekels. That's half of what I charge for others, because my man failed. He paid for that with his life."

"OK, fine, here you go." And he handed over a wad of cash.

"Who are the three you want to make disappear?" Scar-head asked

"First, you have to get rid of Gabriel Perez and Avi Lifshitz. They are often seen together because they're colleagues. You could take care of both of them at the same time, like you tried in Talpiot with Cohen and the young guy, even though you failed there."

"I know those two. They're journalists. This will have a big backlash. I don't like this sort of thing. I'll have to think about it."

"I don't care what you like."

"And the third?"

"The other one is Eli Regev."

"Who? Hey! He's a politician, and killing a politician will cost a lot of money! It's not easy to find the right person to do it."

"Tell me how much."

"My fee is 150,000 shekels."

"What? Are you crazy?!"

"Look, these are not ordinary people, like before. You're talking about nothing less than killing two journalists and a man involved in politics and in current events."

"You have to give me a special price! These will be the last jobs I'll ask of you."

Nervously, the man with the scarred forehead, who was eager to end the meeting, shook his head.

"There is no special price for this," he said. "In this game, there is no supply and demand. This is not the market, where you buy potatoes. Lives are at risk here and people die. As I said before, this time the risk is huge. Listen, I don't have time to negotiate. If you want to go, ahead, then leave me the half money at the usual spot. When do you need the work done?"

"Today. I need it done today."

"You're insane! You know I need more time than that!"

"Well, I'll carry out my part of the deal. I'll leave the money in the agreed-upon place this evening. If you can do this, call me before 6 p.m."

"I'll say it again, that's not the way we work. I need time to plan things, to get it right."

"You've got until six. If you don't call me, I'll look for an alternative."

They didn't say goodbye. Both departed in opposite directions.

63

LEONEL
Bat Yam - Israel
November 5th, 2011 – morning

I sat in front of Mariana at the kitchen table. Her eyes were still watery, and she didn't open her mouth, but her look said it all — the tension in her eyebrows and the focus of her sky-blue irises showed deep sadness.

Shaul gave us a moment in which we simply looked at each other, and although he was there, we had moved to another galaxy. Suddenly, Shaul interrupted our almost mystical state.

"I'm here on behalf of the Mossad," he said.

Always the Mossad. What did they want from me now?

"You could have given me a day off," it occurred to me to say sarcastically.

"We don't have time. The country is in a really dangerous situation and we need you badly."

"What situation are you talking about?"

"We need to find Ahmed."

"Ahmed? Count me out! I don't want anything to do with that case anymore!"

"Do you know anything about him?" Shaul insisted.

"The truth is, I never got to see him. I looked for him in Pakistan until what happened there, which you know full well."

"We need more information. Who asked you to look for him? Why did you decide to go after him?" Shaul said.

"You must already know all that. You saved my life in Paris."

"We received anonymous information indicating you were in Paris and that you were going to Pakistan to find Ahmed, so we alerted our agents in Paris, who began searching for you."

"Anonymous information? What are you talking about?"

"That's what I said. We got anonymous information about your whereabouts and your destination on the same day you left Israel."

I was confused — only Moshe Cohen knew where I was headed. Why would he have told them? For what purpose? Was there another party involved I didn't know about? I didn't think the old man would have done it.

"I can't tell you who sent me to look for Ahmed or why; in fact, I didn't really accomplish anything on that trip. I've just gone through some incredibly rough times since I started this whole thing," I said.

I couldn't reveal any trace that would lead them back to Rachel Mizrachi. She had placed all her trust in me, in addition to promising me a million shekels.

"Why, all of a sudden, is Ahmed a national danger?" I asked, feeling somewhat curious in light of this new piece of information.

Shaul seemed impatient at my question. Mariana remained silent.

"We believe Ahmed is in the country and will soon set in motion a cyberattack of great impact. Something they call the 'viral bomb,' " he said.

"I don't know anything about that — that's entirely new to me," I said. "Unfortunately, I can't help you out, and I don't think learning who entrusted this mission to me will contribute to the cause at all."

Shaul got up abruptly. "I'll leave you two alone. I imagine you have to talk," he said, and headed for the living room to smoke a cigarette.

When he was gone, Mariana's hand touched mine.

"How are you?" I asked her.

"Better than that Mariana you left at that hospital."

"I'm sorry ... I had to escape. They were after me."

"I know," Mariana said while looking down.

"What do you mean, you know?"

"Listen, Leonel. I must tell you the truth. I am a kaza from the Mossad. I was assigned the mission to follow in Ahmed's footsteps.

What happened between us in Gaza and then in Pakistan was a mistake. I got carried away; I felt something for you, and now I'm very confused. Since I'm not completely recovered, I can't seem to clear my thoughts. You have to forgive me for not being the person you thought I was and for not telling you. We were both playing the same game. My stay in Gaza and my transfer to Pakistan were all motivated by Ahmed's situation, and the rest, you already know. I've suffered a lot; I'm still sick and heavily medicated."

"I can't believe what you're saying!" I told her, astonished. "I didn't play any games with you. I risked my life and left everything behind for you. I even stopped looking for Ahmed to take care of you!"

"And I will be forever grateful," she said, starting to cry. "You saved me from certain death, and the Mossad will take care of you all your life, if they have to."

That made me furious.

"I don't need any shit from the Mossad! I did it all because I love you! Do you even understand what it's like to love someone? I don't belong to Mossad; they intercepted me and used me. Do you understand?"

"Leonel, there's no time for this. Israel needs you. I'm in no condition to decide anything about myself right now. At least tell us who sent you on this mission so that we can put the pieces of this puzzle together and come up with an idea, a clue to find him. Ahmed is here, and if he's not stopped, he will soon cause a national disaster!"

For a moment, I thought I should reveal the secret. After all, sooner or later, if the Mossad really wanted to, they would get that information, the easy way or the hard way. Rachel Mizrachi would be interrogated, and she would be forced to tell the truth. Actually, I thought she hadn't committed any crime. Even though she'd noticed the babies had been switched, it hadn't been her fault. I still couldn't understand how this information could be of use to the Mossad. How could learning the details about Rachel Mizrachi, or even Moshe Cohen, help them with anything?

"I don't understand why knowing who sent me to find Ahmed is useful to the Mossad," I said.

"Leonel, when you were in Jerusalem with Moshe Cohen, they tried to kill you, do you remember? And maybe Moshe Cohen, too. Do you think that attack was a coincidence that had nothing to do with you? Cohen was killed three days ago, and about a week ago, Rachel Mizrachi, who was also allegedly involved in this case, was also murdered."

At this shocking news, my heart began beating so hard that my arms and legs began to tremble. I put my head in my arms on the table and tried to digest what I had just been told. I needed to get the Mossad out of my way and gather my thoughts. These people didn't care the slightest about the fact that only a day ago — only one day! — I had been going through a living hell.

But now that I knew Rachel was dead, it soon became clear to me that there was no reason to keep hiding her identity. And now I understood why there was so much money in my bank account.

"Rachel Mizrachi was the one who offered me this job, and a significant amount of money in exchange," I said.

"And why did she do that? Why would that woman be interested in finding a Palestine terrorist, a member of Hamas?" Mariana asked.

"I don't know; she didn't tell me," I replied.

"Yes, you do," Mariana insisted. "She came, offered you money, and you practically went to the ends of the world to search for this person? Leonel, look, I'm not going to question how much money she offered you, but you need to help me with this — it's the last thing I'm asking for."

I sighed and decided to tell her what she wanted to know.

"Rachel told me about an accidental switch of babies she had been involved with back when she was an assistant labor nurse," I said. "She felt horribly guilty and wanted to find Ahmed to let him know about his true identity. Later, she planned to do the same with the other boy. She seemed to have suffered a lot because of that. It was a pain that didn't let her truly live."

I decided to wrap things up with that, so I stood and said, "No more questions."

"Thank you so much, Leonel. I won't torture you anymore. One last thing I have to tell you, though. My real name is Shlomit Barak. But please, please — give me time about us. I'm broken. Only you know what I went through," she said, standing and putting her arms around me. "Like you, I also want to take a break and disconnect from this world, but the country needs me. It needs us both!"

"How urgent is all this? What kind of danger are we talking about?" I asked, disconcerted further by finding out her real name.

"Immediate and extreme," she replied.

Shaul, who obviously had been listening, walked in and interrupted our intimate moment, when once again, and after so much time, I was able to feel her body next to mine.

"Thank you, Leonel. We'll keep in touch," he said. "I think we'll see each other very soon."

"I hope not," I said.

As they were leaving, Marianna/Shlomit softly kissed me on my mouth. I recognized the texture of her lips, and they had the same taste as in my memories. Everything we had lived together in Gaza suddenly came back to me. Then I went back to my bedroom and threw myself on the bed, and the ceiling was suddenly full of images of her, my beautiful Mariana. I looked at them and had the weird feeling something very bad was about to happen. At some point, I finally fell asleep.

64

Tel Aviv – Ramat Aviv
November 5th, 2011 – 1:25 PM

For a moment, strolling across the campus, Eli Regev felt like a student on a spring day; being around so many youngsters had taken him back to his youth. There, at this same university, he had met his first love, Rebecca Tashbi, whom he had married after a year. At 32 years old, after 12 years in the military, he had entered the university, while Rebecca was only 25 when she met him. They went to live in a small apartment in Shenkin, in the heart of Tel Aviv. After obtaining a degree in politics and international studies, he was offered a position at the Ministry of Defense, and then came the children. He thought about all of this in the blink of an eye while viewing the beautiful gardens of the university. Just like in one of Chaplin's movies, it all had happened so fast — after being together for 27 years, they had gotten divorced, and since then, he had decided to fill his loneliness with work, work, and more work.

He felt somewhat nostalgic while entering the School of Medicine offices. At 66, he already had two grandchildren and a lot of free time and, although his children didn't visit him much, he didn't resent them. Nor did he ever regret divorcing Rebecca. It had been by mutual agreement, since they both understood that their relationship was long gone, and because they had always been so practical, they decided to go on with their lives separately.

Jacob Lachman's friendly secretary welcomed him, and, since he didn't have an appointment with the professor, he decided not to linger and pulled out his ID. However, Jacob showed up after half an hour, even though his secretary had told him about the urgency of this visit.

They said a formal hello and spoke almost at the same time.

"How can I help you?" Jacob asked.

"I apologize for taking some of your time, but I'm doing highly confidential research and I need some data, which I think only you can give me."

"What do you need?"

Before launching into his questions, Eli reflected on how he had a lot of experience when it came to interrogating people, and he had done it frequently. In the not-too-distant past, he had performed grillings as a member of the Shabak. Back then, he had been in contact with all kinds of individuals, most of them terrorists who would often refuse to talk.

The night before, he had been up for hours trying to work out the story of the babies who had been swapped. All the details and the dates confirmed that Leonel, the young man rescued by the Israeli forces, was one of those babies.

Going by that theory, he traced Leonel's footsteps from the moment he had left his parent's house in Bat Yam, and his record showed a relatively normal life: army Unit 8200, an invitation to join the Mossad, medical studies at the university and an internship at the Ichilov hospital in Tel Aviv, a busy life in the same city, and a job as a security guard at a bank to pay for his studies. One thing worth highlighting was that in the last month and a half, he had put off his studies and quit his job for no reason. Eli had recently learned that Jacob Lachman had given him a special break, which wasn't given very often, especially at the School of Medicine, and that was precisely the time surrounding the lack of information regarding the last 40 days. In the face of this situation, that morning before going to his office, Eli decided to enforce his authority and contacted the chief of the Mossad, who happened to be in his car at 8:45 a.m., and asked him if the Mossad was involved in anything related to the young man who had been rescued, or if he had any information regarding Leonel Cohen's whereabouts in the last two months. The chief was preoccupied with all the problems concerning the cyberattack, and so his head refused to deal with anything else.

"Look, I have no time for this now. I told you that the last time we spoke," he said.

"You do know I have authorization to make you give me all the information you have," Eli said.

"I've already heard all that, don't repeat it," the chief said furiously. "Look, I'll get in touch with Shaul — you know him, talk to him. I'll give him a call and ask him to give you the information you need. Wait for half an hour and get in touch with him."

"Thanks, have a good day," Eli said, ironically.

At 9:15 a.m., he called Shaul, just as they had agreed.

"How are you doing, buddy?" he said.

"Oh, hello, Eli ... how are you?" Shaul replied. "I was expecting your call. So why is this topic so urgent for you?"

Eli was considering the idea that the Mossad was trying to buy time, but he still couldn't get why, which made the organization more than suspicious; nevertheless, he still needed concrete facts, actual evidence.

"I have a rather important appointment today," Eli said, "and I need to know what has happened to Leonel in the last two months, why he was kidnapped, how he got to Egypt, and why the Hamas would have any interest in this kid."

Shaul seemed prepared to tell the story, but for a moment there was silence. Eli thought they had gotten disconnected, when suddenly Shaul started talking non-stop, as if he were reading from a script:

"Less than a month ago, we got an anonymous tip informing us about a young Israeli in Paris who was looking for a Palestinian terrorist we were also after, so we decided to investigate and corroborate how truthful this information was, and that is how we found and started following Leonel's lead. The man's description totally matched the information we had received. A hooker from downtown Paris tried to murder him, but we got there just in time to save his life; however, we never found out who sent that woman to kill him, and so as not to lose track of him, we put a GPS chip in his arm. We also assigned a contact person in Pakistan, given we had decided to support him. Once there, we started to follow him, but at one point we lost him, because the wireless signal got blocked. Later, we found out he had been in Afghanistan, and, after being blocked for a while, the GPS started sending signals again, but this time from Denmark. We decided to send our agents there to watch him more closely, but it was too late, he was no longer there. We believe that from Denmark, or some island nearby, he headed for Egypt, but since then, we hadn't gotten any other tip concerning him. The last time we heard from him was when the Hamas released the video, and now, as you well know, he's here, safe and free."

Eli listened closely to his story, without missing a detail.

"Is there anything else?" he asked.

"Don't you think that's enough? Shaul said.

"Why was the Hamas interested in this young man?"

"We don't know, but we think that they were somehow tipped off that he was looking for the Palestinian terrorist."

"Hmmm … but who could have possibly given them that information?"

"We have no idea," Shaul replied.

"And you weren't interested in finding that out? That's very strange…"

"Yes, the thing is that when he got to Egypt, we lost track of him."

"No, you didn't answer my question. Why didn't you try to find out who told the Hamas Leonel's whereabouts in Denmark?

Shaul didn't have an answer, and at that moment was sitting next to Shmolit and couldn't talk further. It was clear, though, that Eli had cast doubt on the situation and he decided to remain silent. He could remember losing track of Leonel, but he couldn't understand how the Hamas had gotten the details of his location in Denmark.

"Shaul, are you there?"

"Yes, look, I'm sorry. I have nothing else to say to you."

"Are you sure?" Eli persisted.

"Yes, that's all. I have to hang up now."

"Wait, one more question. Have you ever tried to find out why an ordinary young man would just jump on a mission such as this one? Do you know who sent him?"

"That's what we are still investigating," Shaul added, trying to get rid of Regev once and for all.

"Thanks for everything, Shaul. I would have told you to go for a coffee, but I know you're too busy."

"That's right," Shaul said and hung up.

Eli was a big pain for the Mossad, Shaul knew. The whole thing was like a fire that kept getting bigger and bigger that could get the organization in serious trouble. The chief of the Mossad had put him in charge of this case, but there was also the imminent danger of the cyberattack threatening the country, and that had become the priority.

Eli, because of this exchange with Shaul, had dispelled a few of his doubts. Now, he was at the university about to confront Jacob Lachman and finally confirm that Leonel Cohen was indeed one of the babies. He was impressed by the figure of this old man, with his gray hair and wearing a vest as professors used to do back in the seventies.

"Do you know a student named Leonel Cohen?" he started by asking.

"Yes, of course I know him … and now everyone does," Jacob replied without hesitating.

"He left the university a month and a half ago. What were his reasons for doing this? Why did the university give him the break that he could come back when there are so few spots in the School of Medicine?"

"It wasn't easy to achieve," Jacob said. "Leonel was a very good student. He's had a really tough life, and he was working as a security guard in a bank to pay for his studies and taking shifts at the hospital. I care about him."

"But what was the reason he gave you to ask you to hold his place?"

"That he was going to receive an inheritance, and to do so, he would need to make some investigations abroad; he needed free time."

"And you believed him?"

"Not really, but … what could I have said? It seemed to me as though he was going through a rough time, and so I decided to support him. I think this boy is a computer genius and very good at medicine, too. I still don't understand why he chose medicine over computing. I thought that supporting him would be the only way to keep him at the university; I even ran this by the provost."

"Tell me about your son. I know he was lost during the Lebanon war."

"Look, I don't want to talk about that. Forgive me — and respect my wish." Jacob looked down at his clenched fists on the table.

Eli felt he had affected him; that he had touched his weak point, but without losing sight of his goal, he continued.

"I understand and respect you," he said. "I know very well what it's like to lose a person you love, but I have a mission and a document that compels you to cooperate, so tell me, did your son work at the Sharei Tzedek Hospital in October 1982? Do you remember anything about that time?"

"I remember he was studying nursing and was at the hospital for a short time, but we didn't really get along back then, and I don't know the details as to why he quit. Then, he was called up by the army to fight in the Lebanon war. Of course, you know about the tragedy."

Eli had so much experience with interrogations that he immediately knew Jacob Lachman was telling the truth. But he made one last attempt to try to get some more details.

"Do you know anything about Tal Elad's time in the Shabak?"

"No, the truth is I don't know anything."

"What about the Mossad, his tests?"

"I found out about them after he died."

Jacob got up from his chair and came over to Eli.

"I have nothing to hide," he said, "and I believe I can't help you. I don't know what you're after, either, but I'm convinced I don't have what you want."

Eli felt that from that point on, he would only be wasting his time, but he decided to keep Jacob in his agenda.

He thanked him for his cooperation and gave a polite goodbye. As he was about to leave, Jacob stopped him.

"Tell me, did my son do something bad?" he asked.

"I don't know, doctor, I'm trying to figure out this puzzle, and your son's name happens to be in it."

"Look, Mr. Regev, I don't know if this piece of information will be of any use, but I remember that the person who offered him a job at the hospital was some doctor named David Levi."

"And how do you know that?"

"After my son quit the hospital, someone called me and asked me if I knew where he was. It was a rather mysterious call. I felt worried about him, so I decided to hire a private investigator to find out what had happened to him, why he had suddenly left the hospital."

"And what was the result of your investigation?"

"None. We never got an answer. The only thing the investigator was able to find out was that some doctor named David Levi had become acquainted with my son and offered him a job. It all happened rather fast until he left the hospital."

"Did the investigator ever try to interrogate Dr. Levi?"

"Yes, when my son went missing, he spoke to the doctor, but he gave absolutely no clue."

Eli thanked him again for his help and promised to keep him in the loop should he find out anything new related to his son.

Jacob told him he would also like to know about Leonel, so Eli Regev nodded in the affirmative. In that distinguished educator, he could see a very noble and long-suffering person. After this, he decided Dr. David Levi deserved a visit, too.

65

Jerusalem
November 5, 2011 - 3 p.m.

Shouting in the halls of the Knesset parliament, at 3 p.m. the prime minister ordered his entire retinue to meet urgently in the main hall. The minister of defense, the chief of the army, the head of Unit 8200, the heads of the Shabak and the Mossad, who had arrived together, were all present. The prime minister couldn't hide his anger.

"How is it possible that we haven't yet found the cyber terrorist?" he bellowed.

Half an hour earlier, with his advisers and the minister of defense, he had decided on a plan which they called Operation "Hod Arie." At the meeting it was decided to communicate the details of the operation, which included:

- Recruitment of reserves to strengthen the northern border.
- Recruitment of reserves to strengthen Unit 8200.
- Contact universities and companies to solicit help from experts in security, who would subsequently be under the command of Unit 8200.
- A state of red alert across the country, excluding the press and civilians at this stage. This would apply only to the army and government.
- Distribution of Unit 8200 in four nerve centers: the Mossad offices, Hadera Central Electric Energy power plant, army divisions stationed in the north, and HaKirya in Tel Aviv.

The retinue members left the meeting dazed and the prime minister went to his office after giving his orders, all of them without explanation.

At 3:40 p.m., he decided to talk with his counterpart in the United States to seek help from NSA, which established an immediate connection with Unit 8200. The country was in arms and he had decided to do everything necessary to counter the enemy, was the answer the prime minister had given the Mossad chief when he questioned the call to Washington.

At 4 p.m., the whole party left, heading to their respective offices and barracks, almost all on their way to Tel Aviv. The Unit 8200 chief, on his way to Tel Aviv by chauffeured car, made himself busy summoning specific reserve soldiers; he wanted them all at HaKirya in Tel Aviv by 6 p.m.

Israeli reserve soldiers are summoned once or twice a year and remain active for a period of two to four weeks. In situations of national emergency, the government can make the decision to call them up, and when that happens they generally return to perform in the same positions they held during their compulsory service. This was one of those times when the country needed them.

The core of Unit 8200 belongs to the army; thousands of soldiers serve in it. Its facilities are located at the Urim base in Negev, southern Israel, about 30 kilometers from Beersheba. As a result, the reserves usually gather on that base when they are called for a mission, but this time there was no time for that, as they were needed in the center and north of the country.

At 4:30 p.m., the Unit 8200 chief received the confirmation he had been waiting for — 90 percent of the reserve soldiers he wanted had been reached by telephone and had confirmed their arrival. He himself had taken care of the task of talking to some of them. But he had in mind someone special, one more person who still hadn't been contacted yet.

66

Daniel Brodsky had been working all morning long trying unsuccessfully to track down an error in a computer program. After several hours of trying different options, everything suddenly started working as it should. He smiled to himself, pleased. Mossad was developing special software for the security of mobile devices and he had been assigned to validate it all.

As he was scanning along the lines of code, his cell phone rang. He ignored it at first because he wanted to see the program completed without interruptions, but the phone rang again, so he decided to answer it. A woman's voice informed him that he had to present himself urgently at HaKirya in Tel Aviv at 6 p.m.

"6 p.m. today?" he asked.

"Yes, today at 6 p.m. at HaKirya, by the north entrance. It is urgent. You will receive an email with the details in five minutes. Please confirm."

In his seven years as a reservist, he had never been called upon so urgently. Normally, he was informed of duty at least a week in advance, so he figured there must be something extreme going on. He forwarded the email to his boss and also telephoned him. His boss expressed some displeasure, but he had no choice. In some situations, even Mossad had to defer to the army.

This was not a normal situation, though, because in the army, Daniel had belonged to Unit 8200 and in this section, the rules were different. His boss asked him to forward the work he had done so far and wished him luck.

Daniel grabbed his bag, sent his program without checking to see if it worked properly, closed the computer, and went to his house to pick up his uniform and some personal articles, since he had no idea how long he would be gone.

On the way, he decided to do something that he had been planning to do since early that morning — talk to his friend, Leonel. He knew he might not take the call, but he wanted to try. He hadn't called the night before so as not to add to Leonel's stress, but he had been following the events closely and wanted to check in with him. He missed him and was anxious to know in more detail what had happened.

The phone was answered by Leonel's mother, who greeted him warmly. He had known her since he was a boy. She explained that Leonel was lying down and asked not to wake him up for anything in the world, he told him to wait; she will do an special exception for Daniel. She went to the bedroom, knocked on the door, and entered. Leonel had been asleep for about four hours. When she entered the room, she whispered his name to see if he was sleeping.

"Leonel! Leonel!" she said, softly.

67

LEONEL
Bat Yam
November 5th, 2011 - 4:15 p.m.

I was deep in a dream. I was lying naked in a strawberry field under a clear blue sky and bright sunshine. Mariana was wearing a transparent white dress, and as she began to take it off, I heard my name and smiled, thinking it was her. Trying unsuccessfully to retain the scene, I clenched my eyelids shut, but the sound of the voice calling me became stronger and I eventually opened them. There, at the door, I could see the outline of my mother.

"What's up?" I managed to say.

"Nothing important. I just wanted to know if you were sleeping."

"Obviously, I'm not now," I grumbled.

"Well, Daniel's on the phone. Do you feel like talking to him?"

Drowsiness and sleep instantly wore off, and I thought that chatting with my old friend would be a good way to bring myself back to reality.

"How are you, Leonel?" Daniel said when I got to the phone. It did me good to finally hear a kind and friendly voice.

"Well, I've been better," I replied.

"Always the cynic."

"It's the only way I know how to be."

"I heard that you went traveling around the world and now at least you know Gaza pretty well," Daniel said, tongue-in-cheek. "What was that all about?"

"This calls for a get-together," I said, chuckling at his sense of humor.

"Ugh — I don't think I'll have time until next week," Daniel replied.

"What's up? Some woman?"

"Yes, you could say it's a 'love interest.' I've been called urgently back to the Unit."

"Urgently? What do you mean?"

"They called at about 4 p.m. to let me know I had to report at 6 p.m. at HaKirya."

"What? Are we at war? Does it have something to do with my rescue?"

"I don't know," Daniel replied. "Something urgent and top secret is going on. I told you about the meeting because I assumed that you would also have been called up. Keep quiet about this. You know we can't discuss these things."

"Don't worry," I reassured him. "I thought you had a higher opinion of me than that."

"Well, as soon as I'm done with this I'll call you and we'll catch up," Daniel promised and said goodbye.

I returned to my room to go back to sleep. I wanted to jump back into the same scene with Mariana in a field, alone. As I was settling into bed, I heard the phone ring again. I covered my ears, but I heard my mother speak and understood it was for me. My mom came back into the room with the phone in her hand.

"What now?" I asked, in a bad mood.

"It's a man. He says it's urgent and can't wait."

Urgent again? Damn! This time I stayed in my room, lying down and staring at the ceiling as I took the phone.

"Who is it?" I said, curtly.

"Leonel, how are you?" said the voice on the other end of the line.

I recognized him immediately; he had one of those voices that you don't forget. It was the chief of Unit 8200. I'd met him a year ago during my annual reserve duty. He was relatively new in his role, but very approachable and flexible, and an eminent person in all matters relating to system security, especially cryptography.

"Fine. And how are you?" I replied, actually excited to hear his voice again.

"Do you recognize me?"

"Yes, of course," I said.

"I've heard about everything that happened to you and, believe me, I'm sorry. Look, I don't have much time to talk now, but I wanted to propose something. You can accept or decline it, but I hope you'll say yes."

"What do you need?"

"I want you to step up as a reserve soldier today. We have an emergency. If you say no, I'll understand, but if you feel you have the strength, I would be glad of your help. If you decide to come, I'll send my personal driver to pick you up. I think being with us at this time will help you recover."

A couple of images passed through my head — my heart needed a distraction, my mind needed a break, and at home I would get neither of those things.

"When do you need me?"

"I'll send my driver in half an hour. Be ready then."

"Very well, I'll get ready now."

"You don't know how much I appreciate this," he said and hung up.

As I began to prepare my bag to stay for a few days, I heard my father and mother muttering. They finally plucked up their courage and entered my room.

"Where are you going?" my father asked.

"I have an urgent matter to deal with. The army called me."

"What?" my mother said. "They have no respect whatsoever — it feels like you got back less than 20 minutes ago!"

My mom loves to exaggerate things.

"Look ... they didn't force me, they asked me. But I feel as if they need me, and if I don't go, I'll never have peace. It is a delicate and secret situation."

My father was sad. He had thought we were going to spend a few days together and had even taken a few days off work. When I was leaving with the bag in my hand, Mom cried.

"Don't make a tragedy out of this," I said. "Everything will be fine. I need to clear my head, and taking part in a mission will be the best thing for that. You know I'm not going to the front."

"Yes, but ..."

"Mom, relax. See you soon!" I called back to them.

As I approached the elevator, my dad followed me and took me by the shoulder.

"Take care of yourself, son," he said. "Life is not a game; you have already seen that. With everything that has already happened to you, do you need more of this?"

I felt he wanted to say something else, but he stopped and let me go.

68

Tel Aviv
November 5th, 2011 - 4:15 p.m.

Shaul left Shlomit at the Hotel Panorama on Hayarkon Street in the heart of Tel Aviv. On the way, they had sat down to eat at an Italian restaurant in the Opera gallery, a triangle-shaped, 23-story building that had stunning views of the coast and is a few blocks from the hotel. While he enjoyed his pasta Bolognese, and she ate without much appetite, he went over the exact details of his conversation with Leonel. Eli Regev's words were still fresh in Shaul's mind: Mossad had never figured out who had betrayed Leonel when he was in the Faroe Islands, who had provided information to Hamas so that they could kidnap him. Who could it have been? The organization had no one in that country, and he doubted that Hamas had a representative there.

The only person who had been posted relatively close at that time was Shlomit, but he also knew that she was in no condition to be questioned, to explain herself; moreover, she had been confined to a hospital in Denmark. Besides, she was one of the Mossad's most faithful spies, and she had been responsible for multiple secret operations. Shlomit had been reporting to Shaul for three years already; he had never had any suspicions about her, nor had she caused any problems. She had been in Gaza, Iraq, Syria, Pakistan, and all over Europe. He had never thought he would suspect her of anything, but now he was in a bind: the protocol stated that Mossad should trust no one, without exception.

There was something else that had caught his attention. Mossad had proposed that she remain on vacation until next month and she had decided to come back 20 days before without having even been officially discharged from the hospital.

"Why now?" he asked himself.

He stopped his car in front of the Hilton Hotel, about 200 meters from Panorama. The hotel was near the coast. He tried to breathe some fresh air while watching the sea. He spotted the red flags which indicated a dangerously turbulent sea. Two attractive young women in bikinis braved the cool weather and strolled along the beach. He took out his mobile phone and called the office. A few days before, his boss had assigned him an American agent who was in the country on training. His name was Gavin and he was young, new, and had very little experience, but he was very ambitious and eager to learn. That was what he needed now, someone hungry for glory. Gavin picked up on the first ring.

"I want Shlomit's mobile phone and the phone in her hotel room tapped," Shaul said. "In addition, I want two agents following her 24/7."

"Are you sure?" Gavin asked.

"I don't like it, but I have to do this."

"Look, we don't have many people available right now. Almost all of them are out looking for the terrorist," Gavin said.

"Consider it part of the alert. We have to address this now," explained Shaul, amazed that the young man was questioning his decision.

"What do you mean by that?"

"I need the information; afterwards, I can explain to you why, or you will understand on your own. Gavin, if there is no one else, take your car and wait outside the Panorama Hotel in Tel Aviv."

"No problem, Shaul. I'll talk to the boys in communications and then I'll head down there. I hope you're onto something concrete."

"Contact me immediately if you hear or see anything strange."

Shaul went to HaKirya. He wanted to be as close as possible to the Mossad chief. He had to let him know the details of his meeting with Leonel and his conversation with Eli Regev, although he wouldn't tell him about his suspicions regarding Shlomit just yet, not until he had solid evidence. The idea of not being able to trust her caused a sharp pain in his stomach.

69

Gavin parked his blue Toyota Corolla in a paid parking lot opposite the Hotel Panorama. He focused his gaze on the door to the reception area, and after 10 minutes, called the Mossad telecommunications unit to ask if they had already tapped Shlomit's mobile and room phone. They answered affirmatively, confirming that for five minutes now they had been recording everything on those lines.

At 5 p.m., Shlomit left the hotel. Gavin, startled, got out and followed her, walking along the sidewalk as well but keeping a distance of about 30 meters between them. As Hayarkon Street was crowded with tourists, it was easy to blend in with other people. Shlomit walked for two blocks, and at the intersection of Hayarkon and Mapu, she turned and made her way to number five Mapu Street. From a pay phone located there, she made a call that lasted two-and-a-half minutes, and then returned to the hotel.

Gavin immediately reported what had happened to Shaul, and his boss gave the order to intercept all public telephones located around the hotel.

"If she called once, she'll call again," Shaul said.

Gavin opened a digital map on his iPad tablet, which showed the locations of all public phones nearby, and marked those located within about three kilometers. They couldn't afford to miss the next call. With a digital pen he wrote on the touchscreen, marking the cardinal points and creating a plan of where all the pay phones in the area could be found. He turned the record into a document, saved it, and sent it to the telecommunications department with instructions to intercept calls from all of them urgently. Gavin knew that tapping into these phones took longer than with private land lines or mobiles, but he asked them to proceed as quickly as possible.

After half an hour, he received confirmation that the seven pay phones near the hotel were being monitored by Mossad.

At 5:49 p.m., Shlomit left the hotel again. This time she went in the direction of the sea, the opposite path to the one she had chosen the first time. Gavin didn't miss a beat. With a black briefcase slung over his shoulder, he followed her for nearly two-and-a-half kilometers, walking toward the Tel Aviv marina. They were headed to a place called Little Tel Aviv, which was famous for its restaurants and night-life. Before reaching the coast, she stopped at a pay phone next to a kiosk. Gavin had been praying that Shlomit would not walk much far-ther, as the next phone box was outside the three kilometers he had initially marked out, and he feared that once again the call would not be intercepted.

Shlomit looked around and, satisfied that no-one was watching, placed a call. The conversation lasted 15 seconds, according to Gavin's stopwatch. After looking at his iPad, he called telecommunications.

"Cardinal point 333 bar 42, call made about two minutes ago," was all that he said.

"Wait a moment," came the reply.

After a few minutes that seemed like an eternity, he heard, "Here's the recording."

"I'm listening," Gavin said, anxiously. Immediately, he heard Shlo-mit's recorded voice saying, "Activate the 'el Hiat' at 11 p.m.; I repeat, activate today at 11 p.m."

Gavin urgently contacted Shaul, exultant with his find. "Finally, an important piece of information," he thought.

"Shaul, you were right. Shlomit placed a call 10 minutes ago and told someone to run the viral bomb today at 11 p.m. She's working for the enemy!"

"Any idea as to where it will be done?"

"No, nothing."

"Follow her. Don't lose sight of her for a minute. I'm on my way there. Go into the hotel reception, make sure she doesn't see you, and wait there until I arrive."

Shlomit entered the hotel lobby and went up to her room. Gavin entered just after her, and 20 minutes later Shaul came running in, looking agitated. The two immediately went to reception. The two employees there were attending to some French tourists. Shaul took out his ID card and Gavin moved the people away from the counter, ignoring the complaints from the French people.

"I need the key to Shlomit Barak's room! Now!" Shaul said.

The receptionist was terrified. Her hands shook as she looked at the screen, searching for the room number. At last she said, "There is no one here with that name."

"Then look for 'Mariana.' "

The girl went back to searching on her computer.

"There's no one here under that name, either."

"Think of all the people who checked in at around 9 a.m. today. The woman I am looking for is blond and traveling alone. Perhaps you remember someone fitting that description?" Shaul said.

"Only one woman checked in at that time, a German woman named Sheila Kuntz."

"Sheila Kuntz? Give me the key to her room, fast!"

The receptionist instantly handed over the key to Room 9 on the 24th floor.

When Shaul and Gavin got to the room, they knocked on the door, but nobody answered, so Shaul decided to use the key and enter. Before opening the door, they drew their pistols. They didn't see anyone in the room, so Shaul headed toward the bathroom.

"Look!" Gavin shouted. "On the balcony!"

Shlomit was standing on a chair outside on the balcony, one foot on the seat and the other on the railing. Shaul approached and shouted, "Don't do it!"

She didn't hesitate, she just plunged straight into space. Gavin and Shaul immediately looked over the railing to see the chilling fall, and watched her slender body pick up speed as gravity grabbed hold of her. The impact finally came and her body was dashed onto the pavement next to the pool. The water quickly turned red.

On the table on the balcony was a note:

> "Forgive me; what's done is done. I never thought I could be
> so cruel."

Shaul was incandescent with rage, Gavin was pallid.
"Who would have thought she was a double agent?" he said to Gavin. "Remember what I told you on your first day — 'trust no one, not even your own shadow.' "

70

LEONEL
HaKirya - Tel Aviv
November 5th, 2011 - 6:00 PM

At 6:06 p.m. the barrier to HaKirya's northern entrance opened. Our driver steered the light-brown Peugeot 204 across the road to the military base's parking lot. Before passing through the gate, the car was subjected to a very thorough security check. From there we headed to the conference room bearing the name of the hero David Ben Gurion, located in basement number 2. I had presumed that all of my reservist colleagues would be there, and I was right. When I entered the room they began to clap, an act which moved me. On the board was written "Welcome Leonel."

The head of Unit 8200 gave me a hug in front of everyone.

"Another day we will have time to celebrate your return; you know I won't forget it," he said.

First Officer Ronen, subordinate to the Unit 8200 chief, began to speak. In front of him was a laptop connected to a projector.

"Welcome, everybody," he said. "I'll try to be brief, because we have very little time. You were summoned here today because there has been a very serious warning indicating that we will be subjected to a cyberattack, and we want to be prepared to definitively prevent and if possible eliminate the attack before it occurs. We hope that the existing protection and firewall systems, which were recently hardened, can block this menace. We need everyone operational if the attack does go ahead. We will split up into four forces that will be distributed at strategic areas where the soldiers of this unit are already stationed. The intention is to reinforce our presence with experienced computer people like you. Throughout the day, we have been strengthening the program that alerts us to any event that threatens security. One officer will be in charge of each group. When you hear your name, please stand behind the corresponding officer in charge."

Near Ronen were four officers holding signs.

1. Officer Gaby. Electric power plant - Hadera
2. Officer Yair. Ramón IDF central base - Galil Alto
3. Officer Alon. HaKirya IDF central base - Tel Aviv
4. Officer Tomer. Mossad offices - Herzliya

As the names were being read out, Daniel came over and gave me a hug, and many others patted my back — I was in good spirits; I felt a sense of belonging. These were my people. I knew my decision to come had been the right one. Both my name and Daniel's were mentioned at the end. We would position ourselves behind Officer Tomer in command of the Mossad Central Department in Herzliya. I counted eight other reservists there with us.

After 20 minutes, everyone started filing out of the room and we were last. We got into a military truck and traveled to Herzliya, half an hour from Tel Aviv. We were escorted by a police patrol, which cleared the way for us because traffic was heavy. We were supposed to arrive at 7 p.m. The group that had left for the north had done so in a cargo helicopter belonging to the army, as they were also short on time.

When we arrived at the Mossad offices, we were subjected to a thorough inspection. A tactile image was taken of each person's hand; that was to be the code used to enter the building and various other offices. In addition, a cubic machine recorded our retinas. The entry system to the central server sector and the secret database was a combination of tactile image and retina. They explained to us that we would be accompanied when we entered the site.

The whole process was quick and efficient, authorizing our entry into the spaces where we would be operating. Daniel; Ruben, another one of the reserve soldiers, and me headed to the central computer room. We aligned our eyes and hands with the corresponding devices and the doors opened. Five minutes later, Tomer, the officer, arrived. Our five other colleagues were distributed in different offices across the security department. Inside we discerned four nodes where Mossad operators and Unit 8200's reinforcement soldiers were stationed. We were assigned to node 4, which was empty. We each had a computer. Tomer immediately guided us to review the firewalls layer by layer and to connect ourselves to the sniffers and monitor them constantly. They gave us a sheet of paper that had system authentication keys written on it. Tomer showed us the software and infrastructure installed a few days ago by our unit, and we added an extra layer of security to the firewall, which brought the total number to six, a level I had never seen before. To violate the security of the installed systems, a virus would have to be of extraordinary magnitude.

Behind the nodes was the main computer. They explained that it was one of the most powerful in the Middle East and Europe. It possessed a processor with unimaginable force, surpassed only by the NSA in America. The computer was covered with a steel dome. I examined it from the window. We had no access to the space, as it could only fit two people. One of those two people appeared in our node. He was a thin man with glasses and white beard who walked slowly everywhere he went. He jerked his head, indicating the epicenter in which the great dome reigned, and said with a smile, "Come with me. I'll show you what you came to protect."

He entered a code on a numerical device, then reached into a wooden groove and focused his eye on a small hole in the wall. The door opened. There was no sound at all; not even the computer noise was audible. Two electrical generators on the ground were connected to the two-meter-high dome. The only thing that was visible was a great fingerless glove that was used to manually open the dome. Our guide explained that it was almost never used; it was installed as an emergency measure if something extraordinary happened. All control of the main computer happened at node 1, which was equipped with many display screens that supported many different controls, alarms, and performance parameters of the host machine. The operator controlling the security systems was located at node 2. The monitors showed tracking and security-system status; and six different screens allowed for the observation of the state of each layer of the firewall. Node 3 contained the control system of the entire internal Mossad network, and six operators worked there using nine 40-inch screens. Node 4 had been dedicated to cryptography. They had moved their operators elsewhere, and the place had been reassigned to us. Our computers were connected to tracking devices so that we could constantly monitor the status of the firewalls and traffic flow on the network. All of the equipment there was much more advanced than that of Unit 8200. And it made sense, because this was the center of the country's most confidential and secret information. Standing in front of all that computer equipment, I felt my body shudder.

At 8 p.m., we received a report stating that all the reservists had reached their bases and were ready. Tomer gave us a special code to enter into a closed-circuit system that would allow us to interact with other groups and with Unit 8200 in Uber, which was our headquarters located in the south of the country.

Everything was ready. At 8:30 p.m., we received the news that the attack would be at 11 p.m. At 9:30 p.m., they began debating whether to interrupt the network connections of all systems, especially the Internet.

Daniel and I looked at each other. We couldn't believe it. This was what we had worked so hard for since high school, for all those years, and finally we were in the eye of the storm. If the reports were true, in two-and-a-half hours we would be facing the greatest test of our lives.

71

Tel Aviv
November 5th, 2011 - 4:30 p.m.

At almost 4:30 p.m., Eli Regev called Emma at the office from his car, ready to set off to his next destination.

"I need urgent information about Dr. David Levi," he said.

Emma seethed with anger. She had been planning to leave the office in 15 minutes because it was the day she picked up her grandson from kindergarten. The call had come at the worst time; she had already turned off her computer and prepared her purse.

"David Levi?" she said in a controlled voice. "The information is in the folder I gave you this morning."

"Forgive me, Emma. I didn't notice it. I need to know what he does now and where he lives. I don't have the folder with me."

Emma gritted her teeth forcefully to contain her anger, and went in search of the information.

"It says here that he is still practicing medicine, but only works twice a week at Meir Hospital in Kfar Saba. He also lives in that city and is married without children."

"Thank you, Emma. Please send me a message with his current address."

As he had many times in the past, Eli thanked God that he had Emma by his side. What would he do without her, he wondered. When he received the message with the address, he sped off towards Kfar Saba. He knew it was the worst time to travel — with the heavy traffic it could take up to an hour-and-a-half to reach the city. However, his job afforded him some privileges, so he reached under his seat and took out a flashing light that the police had provided him with when he had been working for Shabak. He put it up on the dash, behind the windshield, and activated his siren, which immediately began blasting a high-pitched wail. Within seconds, the other cars began to move aside, and he was able to push ahead, unhindered. He reached Kfar Saba in 30 minutes.

As he approached the entrance to the city, his phone started to vibrate. He looked at the message on the screen: *"I have to meet you urgently. Yosi."*

He tried to ignore the message. Everyone wanted something "urgently," he thought. Even he had used that strategy, more so in the last two weeks. When he stopped at the first traffic light, his cell phone starting to ring. Yosi's name appeared on the touch screen, indicating a call rather than just a message. Given the caller's insistence, he considered that perhaps it was worth listening to him. He recalled the proposal that had been put to him in Jerusalem that they work together. "Who knows?" Eli thought, as he answered the phone. "He might have some valuable information for me."

"How are you?" Yosi asked above some kind of commotion in the background.

"Fine. What is urgent enough for you to call me twice?"

"I need to talk to you. Indeed, it is urgent."

"Urgent? Well, how about tomorrow in my office?"

"Where are you now?"

"At the entrance of Kfar Saba."

"Oh," Yosi said. "Well, I'm 20 minutes away, at the Ramat Hasha-ron exit. I can meet you at 5:40 p.m. in the new gallery, in the north entryway, which is the main entrance."

"I can't now."

"As I said, I'll be there in 20 minutes. You should really hear what I have to say. I know who committed the murders, and one of them will surprise you. You're going to be the first to know, but only if you're willing to work with me on this."

Eli tried to say something else, but the line went dead. Yosi hadn't given him a chance to dodge the meeting.

The gallery was packed with people, and whole families were waiting in line at the food outlets. Eli settled in a cafe, where he ordered a cappuccino with no sugar. Time passed and Yosi didn't appear. "He probably got stuck in rush-hour traffic," he thought. He waited until 5:50 p.m., then he called him but got no answer. After a few minutes he tried again, but still didn't get an answer, so he left a voice message explaining that he couldn't wait any longer. It seemed odd that Yosi hadn't contacted him. He had been very insistent on this meeting, one that he had labeled as "urgent," and he was not a man to pass up an interview that could be potentially useful.

Eli left the gallery and focused on what he had come to do. He found himself facing a newly constructed building, with eight floors, located in Arlozorov 178. The facade was a combination of Jerusalem type stones and dark-brown wood, a strange but pleasing mixture. The apartment that he was after was one of the three penthouses that were on the eighth floor. Eli studied the entrance for a few minutes, then decided to push the buzzer on the intercom. A woman answered.

"I need to talk to Dr. David Levi," Eli said.

"Who is looking for him?" she asked.

"I'm Eli Regev, a government agent, and I need to ask him a few questions."

"The doctor is working at the hospital today. He will return home in about 20 minutes."

"OK, I'll wait for him here."

"Is it important?"

"Yes, it is, but don't worry."

Eli decided not to wait. At no point had it occurred to him to think that the woman was lying, because she had acted very naturally. He was five minutes from Meir Hospital, so he went straight to the hospital to ask for Dr. Levi. The surprise factor was essential in the strategy he had planned. When he asked at reception desk for the doctor, he was informed that his office was on the fifth floor in Obstetrics.

He went and talked to the secretary there, who informed him that Dr. Levi had left a little earlier than usual that day.

"What time did he leave?" Eli asked.

"About five minutes ago," the woman replied.

"Did he have any appointments, any patients he had to attend to?"

"Who are you?" the secretary asked.

"I'm from the police," Eli declared, to keep things simple.

Nervous, the secretary blurted, "He had to attend to a patient, but he canceled that visit himself at the last minute."

"Thank you." Eli ended the conversation.

He decided not to return to the doctor's house. Obviously, the doctor had escaped, maybe after receiving a call from his wife, which indicated that he was hiding something. Back in his car, he accelerated and headed for the highway, en route to Tel Aviv. In the rear-view mirror he could see a black Polo Volkswagen that had been following him for at least five minutes. He began to get suspicious. He turned to make sure that they were really following him, and sure enough, the black Polo stayed behind him. He decided that he had to get to the highway as soon as possible. It was well-lit there, so he would feel safer. Far down the street, he could see the entrance to the motorway, and pressed the accelerator to the floor. He calculated there were three more cross streets until he got there. He had just passed the second corner when a white Subaru truck pulled out in front of him and blocked the road. Eli slammed on the brakes and came to a stop just meters from the truck. He stole a look in the rear-view mirror and saw that the black Polo was gone. Suddenly, a hooded man got out of the truck in front of him with a handgun, walked up to his car, and fired three shots at point-blank range. Bullets slammed into the windshield. Then the guy quickly got back in the truck and escaped.

Terrified, Eli felt each impact. Fortunately, the bulletproof glass that had been installed a few days before saved his life. He wondered if it had been intuition or fate that had driven him to make the car bulletproof. After Shmulik's death, he had requested protection from the government, and it had been granted. His head had struck the steering wheel violently when he braked to avoid hitting the Subaru, and the impact had opened up a small gash on his forehead. The car's engine was still running, but he realized that he couldn't continue driving. People began to gather around and help him. Soon the police arrived. Everyone was surprised that nothing serious had happened. The glass showed three bullet marks, although it remained intact. Eli was in shock. The police began asking questions and an ambulance transferred him to Meir Hospital in Kfar Saba.

Explaining that he worked for the government, and that he was on a special mission, Eli asked the police officer to let him go. He also promised to collaborate with the police in the investigation into the shooting, giving his credentials as he showed the document with the government seal. A doctor examined him and suggested that he remain under observation for half an hour. Then they authorized him to leave. Eli thanked the officer who took him to his home in Ramat Aviv.

Along the way, the officer tried to obtain more information about what had happened.

"Why would anyone want to kill you?" he asked Eli, after introducing himself as Ronen Rotem.

Eli decided to say he didn't know. He figured the police couldn't do much against hired murderers, and he needed time to think about what he had learned. He had no doubt that the attack was the work of a professional. He also knew he needed to find David Levi as soon as possible, because he sensed the doctor might have had something to do with it.

72

Ramat Gan
November 5, 2011 - 5:45 p.m.

Gabriel Perez arrived at the Ramat Gan stadium parking lot at 5:45 p.m. He was due to start his night shift at the newspaper at 8 p.m. He was distressed and troubled after the meeting with his contact, who, as usual, had fulfilled his mission in an exemplary fashion. Perez had invested almost all of his savings to obtain the information. He knew that Avi was having problems with his divorce, but he had no doubt that when he had money, he would repay the debt. Now, as he waited for his friend, he leaned on the hood of his new car, a Fiat that had been provided by his employer. It was considered a privilege at the newspaper.

Avi arrived late, at 5:55 p.m., complaining about the traffic at the HaKirya exit in Tel Aviv. It was strange that it had been so heavy there, because while there were always a lot of cars in that area, traffic rarely ever came to a standstill. Something big must be going on.

"What happened?" Gabriel asked.

"Traffic was horrendous at HaKirya. It was moving at a snail's pace. There was a huge amount of security there, too, cars bulldozing their way through with sirens, and two helicopters landing at the same time. Is there something going on in this country that its own journalists don't know about?"

"Yes, something is happening. I have good news!" Gabriel said.

"Tell me."

"Well, my contact came through — he told me everything."

"Just tell me!" Avi raised his voice, almost losing his patience.

"It's true that the two children were switched and that the two are involved in everything that is happening here now. Leonel, who was rescued yesterday, is the child who was born Muslim and handed over to the Jewish family. The other is Ahmed. His story is a scandalous one, just like they said. You know that the government ordered a red alert across all units, and especially in Unit 8200, because Iran is allegedly preparing a cyberattack. You know that, right? Well, Ahmed is here to carry out the attack, to make sure it goes ahead. He entered the country under the identity of a Belgian businessman, an Enzo ... something. I have it written here ..."

"And? Do I need to tell you again to keep talking?" Avi interjected.

"All of the security cabinets, Mossad, Shabak, Shin Bet, the police, army, and others, are looking for this man right now. They know he's in Tel Aviv and apparently the cyberattack program will be activated today."

"Aha! So that was what the whole mess at HaKirya was about. Perhaps they were calling up and assigning reservists."

"Nobody knows anything; it's all top secret. They don't want people to panic. If I understood correctly, they are only calling up the reservists for Unit 8200. But, as you know, this won't be publishable news, and they will censor us," Gabriel said.

"Who switched the children? Did your contact have any information on that?"

"Come on, let's go to my car," said Gabriel.

When they were seated in the car, Gabriel handed an envelope to Avi.

"This has everything we wanted. It was worth all the time we have spent doing this damned, thankless job. At last we have a major news report. It's better if you just read it for yourself. It's well-told and very detailed; it will make for an incredible article. It won't be good for much here — it probably won't pass censorship, so even if we wanted to, we couldn't publish it. But think of the New York Times! I did some research, and they could potentially pay millions for a story like this. Now read it."

Avi pulled out three sheets of paper and his eyes began to dart from side to side as they moved down line by line. He was absorbed in his reading. After the first page, he smiled and looked at Gabriel as if he had discovered an unknown dimension. He continued eagerly with the second page. He was elated, jubilant. All their lives they had striven for what they now held in their hands.

Suddenly, the abrupt sound of a motorcycle interrupted them. They didn't see where it came from or paid it much attention, until the noise grew louder and they saw the motorbike right in front of them. Two men, their faces covered, were astride it. The one on the back drew an Uzi and took aim at the Fiat at point-blank range, without getting off the bike. He fired 18 bullets directly into the windshield and the engine. The bike sped off, and neither of its riders looked back as the car burst into flames.

When the police and firefighters arrived, they found the remains of two charred men, holding each other.

73

Ramat Aviv
November 5th, 2011 -7: 30 PM

Eli Regev sat on his favorite sofa, one of the ones that doubled as a rocker. He was rocking gently back and forth as he watched television. The shocking noise of the bullets hitting his windshield still echoed in his head. "Breaking news," a young journalist with well-groomed hair announced very seriously on the TV. Behind him appeared graphic images of a burning car.

Two journalists were killed today at around 6 p.m. in the parking lot of the Ramat Gan Stadium. The victims have been identified as Gabriel Perez and Avi Lifshitz, both of whom worked at the daily newspaper, Yedioth Ahronoth. The journalists were shot at in their car from close range, resulting in a fire and causing their instant death. The shooting suspects were driving a motorcycle, and have yet to be located. The motives behind this fatal incident are not known. Police are investigating. Meanwhile, Yedioth Ahronoth has ordered the closure of its offices, joining the victims' families in their grief. Gabriel Perez was a shift editor manager at the newspaper. He lived with his wife and daughter. Avi Lifshitz was a journalist covering stories related to security issues. In the past he worked as a spokesman for the army. He lived with his wife and two children.

And we go now to another incident that happened today. A vehicle traveling the Ramat Hasharon - Raanana highway careered off the road and crashed into a tree. The only occupant of the vehicle was Yosi Rechter, a high-ranking police officer. He died instantly. The details of this accident have still not been clarified. Hasharon police are investigating, and we have no further information so far.

Eli could not believe what he had just heard. He sat frozen in his rocker. At almost the same time he had been attacked, they had killed Avi Lifshitz, his partner Gabriel, and also Yosi. They all knew about the switching of the babies. In addition, Yosi had pressing information that he had promised to tell him. All of these attacks and deaths had something in common. Someone was trying to block the investigation.

He got up and went to the kitchen. He needed a coffee. He prepared himself an espresso, and while he was drinking it, he patted his pockets and found the card from the policeman who had brought him home after hospital, Officer Ronen Rotem. He felt very lonely and insecure right then, so he thought it would be a good idea to contact this man, who had been so kind and accommodating. He had nothing to lose; he knew his life was in danger and he needed to trust someone.

He thought suddenly that maybe he should contact the government. After considering it, though, he decided that he had no facts to convey, only theories, and politicians only wanted to hear information backed up by concrete evidence. Although the recent killings and his own attack were very real, he decided that, for now, he would not involve the government. It would leave him more breathing room in which to work.

He finished his coffee and decided to call Rotem.

"Hello, Officer Rotem? It's Eli Regev. Do you remember me?"

"Yes, how could I forget, it was only an hour ago that I dropped you off at your house. You're lucky, did you know that?

"Why do you say that?" Eli asked, intrigued.

"I'm right outside your building. I came to see you. You told me in the hospital you would help the police with their inquiries. And please call me Ronen."

"Perfect, Ronen. Come on up, room Nine A."

Eli heated water for his second coffee. Ronen came in and sat in the living room, glancing at the television. The walls were adorned with old paintings, some well-known copies and others less so. Ronen saw no family photos or evidence of children in the house.

"Where should we begin?" the officer asked, looking intently at Eli.

Eli switched off the TV. He held back at first, waiting to see how the conversation unfolded before telling the whole story.

"Well, let's start with the fact that someone tried to kill me," he said.

"Why?"

"I don't know."

"What were you doing in Kfar Saba?"

"I was looking for Dr. David Levi."

"Did you have an appointment with him?"

"No, I just wanted to ask him some questions."

"Had you spoken with him before? Did you find him at home?"

"No, I didn't. His wife said he would be at work for another 20 minutes, so I went straight to Meir Hospital."

"And you found him there?"

"No, he was gone."

"I imagine that when you spoke to his wife she would have wondered who you were ... "

"Right."

"And what did you say?"

"I told her my name and explained that I was there on behalf of the Israeli government. I also said that I was waiting for him outside his home."

"Why did you go directly to the hospital?"

"Because I thought that his wife would call him and he wouldn't come home."

"Why did you think he wouldn't return home? Does he have something to hide?"

"Maybe."

"What?" Ronen insisted.

"I'm not sure, but it's possible that Levi is behind this attack, and some murders, too."

"Murders? What the hell! What is the meaning of all this? Look, Eli, I'm sorry for speaking so frankly, but we could talk all night, and if you don't want to collaborate with me, we won't get anywhere. You work for the government, and you should know that. If someone is trying to kill you, they will keep trying until you disappear. Don't you agree? You saw today that assassins went after two journalists from Yedioth Ahronoth, and they were less fortunate than you and were burned to death."

Eli got up and paced to the window and back. He had made his decision.

"What I am going to tell you is strictly confidential, top secret," he said. "If anything is leaked, this could all go very wrong and many people would die."

The officer nodded his understanding.

Eli poured himself a whiskey and also offered one to Ronen, but he declined. After the first sip, Eli began to reveal the whole story, from October 22, 1982, up until the events of that day. He spoke of his suspicions regarding Mossad and Dr. Levi. Then Eli listed the attacks that were probably associated with what happened on that momentous date in 1982:

- Gun attack at the Talpiot café in Jerusalem. Moshe Cohen and Leonel were inside and were uninjured.
- Assassination attempt by a prostitute on Leonel in a hotel in Paris.
- Murder of Rachel Mizrachi in Jerusalem.
- Shmulik Sade run down by a hit-run driver in the center of Tel Aviv after being in my office a few minutes before.
- Attempted murder of Moshe Cohen at the Metzuba Kibbutz.
- Moshe Cohen murdered in his home despite being in protective custody, a few minutes before I questioned him.
- Attempt on my life in Kfar Saba.
- Murder today in Ramat Gan of two journalists who knew something about what happened on October 22, 1982.
- Yosi's accident en route to Kfar Saba, Raanana. Yosi had urgent information to share with me.

After speaking, Eli felt as if a bag of cement had been lifted from his shoulders. Now it was Ronen's turn to get up and walk to the window. The officer needed time; he was shocked by what he had just heard.

"If there is any logic in what you have told me ... does that mean you're next?" he said.

"It would seem so, although I hope not," Eli replied.

"It's so difficult to investigate when it comes to hired murderers," Ronen said. "They leave no trace; they're professionals. I was, in one way or another, involved in four of the events you listed, and not a single shred of evidence was found at any of them. And since we are speaking of secrets, today a woman committed suicide in a hotel near the beach in Tel Aviv as two Mossad agents entered her room.

"How?"

"She jumped from the 24th floor."

"Who was she? What was her name?"

"Shlomit Barak."

"No, I don't recognize the name." Eli furrowed his brow and searched his memory.

"Look, Mossad seems a bit untouchable, and if they are the brains behind all this, it will be very difficult to prove. We'll have to burn bridges and destroy myths to uncover the truth," said Ronen, implying he wasn't keen on that option.

"We have to find Dr. Levi," Eli said. "I strongly suspect that he is involved in all of this."

"If the doctor is involved in this case, by now he will already be deep in hiding," Ronen replied.

"Well, luckily, we have the best police in the country working with us," Eli said, smiling.

Ronen also smiled. It was the first time the two felt comfortable together.

"Come with me," Ronen invited, "you won't get any sleep tonight, either.

"Where will we go?"

"To the Central Police Station in Tel Aviv."

"I hope you're not going to book me," Eli joked.

"If you stay home, you'll miss out on the action," Ronen said with a laugh

"No kidding," Eli said.

"I have a hunch that nobody is going to get any sleep tonight."

"Let's go, then," said Eli as he grabbed his jacket and bag.

74

AHMED
South Tel Aviv
November 5th, 2011 - 6 p.m.

The call came at the agreed time. The voice on the phone seemed familiar somehow, but I was in a public phone booth, and the noise from the street nearly drowned her out, so I was unable to confirm who it was. By the time it occurred to me to ask a question, the woman had already disconnected. The rules dictated that calls should not last more than 15 seconds. The time she had given me was 11 p.m. I checked my watch; there were still at least five hours to go. I started thinking about ways I could kill time without doing anything that would make me more anxious than I already was — or more conspicuous. According to the instructions, I still needed to receive information that would let me know whether the program or worm was already in the systems targeted in the attack. I should receive that information in half an hour. On the way back, I saw a police car, so I ducked into a fabric store. When I walked in, the owner asked me what I wanted, and I said I was looking for something for my wife. When the wail of the police siren had disappeared, I fled back to my refuge. I walked quickly into the apartment and sat down at my computer to wait.

The last message specified that the main target was the Mossad main computer in Herzliya. This wasn't a surprise, because rumors that this would be the target had been tossed around back in Iran. While going over the plan again for how the virus was to be inserted, my astonishment increased. The Iranian spy in Israel had been following a Mossad agent who worked in Herzliya. The woman, named Hanna Ben-youn, worked as a computer systems operator for Mossad. She worked different shifts: three days in the morning, two beginning at noon, and one at night. Usually, when she had finished the afternoon shift she went with her friends to a bar in Ramat Hasharon, which was about 15 minutes from the Mossad offices. She always went straight from work and took her laptop. The days in which she worked a morning, afternoon, or evening shift varied during the week, but after following her for two months, the spy realized that there was a regular routine. If one week she worked on a Monday afternoon, the next week it was Tuesday afternoon, and thus her shifts changed every week. One Wednesday that Hanna was scheduled to work an afternoon shift, the spy decided to go ahead with the operation. He knew she would arrive at about 7:30 p.m. at the Sisro bar in Ramat Hasharon.

On one of his frequent visits a few weeks before, while loitering around the bar, the spy had managed to strike up a conversation with one of the Arab servers working there. He had made an agreement with him, promising to pay 1,000 shekels for a photo of Hanna's bag. After a week, the Iranian spy had the photograph in his possession. Then he bought a bag that was exactly the same, and a week after that, he returned to the bar with the bag and a laptop inside it. He instructed the waiter to exchange the bags when he took her order. The spy would wait outside, inject the virus via the USB key into Hanna's computer, and the boy would change bags again when he delivered dessert. The boy was reluctant at first, but in the end he couldn't resist the 10,000 additional shekels that the Iranian was offering.

I estimated that according to the plan, the virus must have been installed the day before and therefore was already in the woman's computer. Today, the day of the attack, was Thursday. As per her usual routine, Hanna had to work at night, and she would come in at 6:30 p.m. sharp. When Hanna connected to the network, I would receive a signal from the virus on my screen. I would wait for it to spread silently through the network and would activate it precisely at 11 p.m.

At 6:20 p.m., I heard a noise coming from the hallway. Alarmed, I ran to the door. A white envelope had been slipped underneath it. I opened it and found another surprise. I immediately recognized the handwriting; it was my Iranian counterpart. He was letting me know that the attack had another target: the Hadera Electrical Plant, and subsequently, the electricity grid of the entire country. The virus had already been there for a week. Why had I not been informed of this before? Everything was designed and executed so that each member of the plot knew a part of the plan, but very few knew everything, the "A to Z," so to speak. The Iranian spy was one of them; he knew what the goals were. When it came to the virus, the Egyptian in Iran, and a group of three who had carried out the principal testing of the malware, understood the code and each of its lines in full. Now, supposedly, I knew the target and in a few moments I would understand the program in its entirety.

The spy explained in the note how the virus had been grafted into the power plant. He had used a system to capture RFID[52] signals. These systems have a very small electronic device with a wireless connection, like those used on the cards that open the doors of restricted-access areas in some workplaces or parking lots. The entire RFID system consists of a base interrogator that reads and writes data on the devices, and a transmitter that responds to the interrogator. The Iranian had tracked one of the janitors as he left his shift at the Hadera Power Station and had approached him in the bus. In his bag he had a device for capturing RFID that read the employee's card via a wireless connection. He had then used an RFID card-copying system to reproduce the worker's card. One morning, when the man was working, the spy entered the factory as well, dressed as a cleaning employee and using the cloned card. He inserted a USB memory stick into one of the computers in the power plant, and after a few minutes the virus spread throughout the whole system. After reading this I was amazed at how everything technology-related was so easily violated. I knew that the human factor was always the weakest link in any IT security system.

The virus was designed to remain dormant for a week. During that time it would study the industrial control systems of the power plant, and then intercept them and introduce erroneous commands. To me it didn't seem too extensive; the code would alter the speed of the turbines and the actions of the valves and piping, and the entire operation would

---

52 RFID: A system of wireless radio-frequency identification.

radically change after the systems had been penetrated. At 6:40 p.m. today, the virus would have to create a report and it would be activated at nearly the same time as the other, at 11:02 p.m., just two minutes after the Mossad malware.

"Wow, everything's in place to make this operation a success," I thought.

75

Herzliya
November 5th, 2011 - 6:30 p.m.

Hanna Benyoun stopped her car outside the Mossad offices in Herzliya; it was 6:20 p.m. and her shift started at 6:30. Her colleagues, who were also due to start work, had formed a long line of cars as they waited to get inside the building. She had never seen this happen before. She got out of her car to see what was happening and saw that the security checkpoint had changed. Normally, two security officers oversaw people entering the offices, but on that day five guards stood at the entrance with an additional two policemen backing them up. One security guard was checking all of the cars; as usual, another was doing a full–body check, and two more guards were examining everyone's computers, something unusual. Luckily, one of the guards was her friend. She beckoned him over and he explained that everyone's computers had to be checked by a new program, before authorizing entry. This program controlled an antivirus and could supposedly detect if the computer had been accessed by any person other than its owner, or if any port had been compromised.

When Hanna's turn came, the guards proceeded as they had with all of the other employees. They checked her car, her person, and her computer. The security check didn't turn up anything suspicious, so she was allowed through. She entered the parking garage of the building, still a little surprised, parked her car and went straight to the basement, where she worked. Her task was to operate the main computer and take care of its safety and functionality. She sat at node 1. She asked her coworkers if they knew what was going on. They told her that a red alert had been put out due to a possible cyberattack. Adding to that, a friend explained, "Today we had three visitors to node 4, all of them members of Unit 8200."

Hanna, who was in her thirties and single, joked, "I'm going to put my good manners and feminine wiles to use and go and introduce myself as soon as I've logged in. You never know ..." And she laughed as her hands started whirring over her keyboard.

After settling in and chatting to her companions, she connected her laptop to the network and accessed the central system by entering the appropriate passwords. She noted that after inserting the numeric password that was part of the two-step authentication process (the first step was to enter a one-time pin code from a little device), the computer took longer than usual to grant access.

"What's up with the network today?" she asked her friend.

"I really don't know. I logged in right away, no problems." Her friend said.

Hanna thought it must have been because of the programs they had been using at the security checkpoint. Finally, after two minutes staring at her screen, she read: *access authorized*. And finally she could begin her shift.

76

Central Police - Tel Aviv
November 5th, 2011 - 8:30 p.m.

A nightmarish cacophony of people shouting and yelling reigned in Tel Aviv's Central Police Station. Prostitutes, junkies, and pickpockets were crawling all throughout the corridors, each one of them handcuffed and being escorted by a police officer. Ronen looked at Eli's face and smiled.

"What? Haven't you been here before?" he said.

"Yes, but clearly I had forgotten what a mess it is. This looks like a madhouse."

"Come on, don't act all sophisticated. It's not all roses where you come from."

They went to level two, where the Special Investigations Unit was located.

"Sit down," Ronen said, upon entering his office. Inside, it was nearly empty. On his desk he had what looked like a picture of his family, a computer, and a stack of papers. Two simple chairs were the only other furnishings. On one wall, near the window, he had pasted a huge black-and-white photograph of the nation's founding father, David Ben Gurion.

"I admire him, too," Eli said, referring to the picture.

"To be honest, it was here when I moved into this office. I never got around to taking it down, or even deciding if I like it."

Just then, an excited officer entered the office without knocking.

"We found a suspicious motorcycle, similar to the one in the incident with the journalists in Ramat Gan" he said. "The two riders left the vehicle at the Raanana exit, but someone who saw them called the local police. They found them heading north along the old route, in a cream-colored '82 Subaru."

"Are they sure it's them?"

"Yes, when police tried to stop them, they tried to escape. They followed them for three kilometers and cornered them between three patrolmen."

"Where are they now?"

"They'll arrive in 10 minutes."

"Thank you. Bring them here as soon as they get here."

Ronen smiled, looked at Eli, and said, "I told you, no one's going to get any sleep today."

"Why? What are you thinking?" Eli replied.

"I'm thinking that if everything is as you say it is, these two will give us the information we need."

"Maybe … but do you really think they'll talk so easily? These types almost never 'sing.' "

"Who knows? Surely they'll speak when instead of going to prison for life we offer them 10 years."

"Ten years?" Eli was amazed.

"Think about it," Ronen said. "We can close five or six cases in one go. Do you know what that means for the police? It's worth more than two fools rotting in jail for life, when you and I have to pay to keep them there. Maybe you can get some insight into your case as well."

"If so, it's worth it. You have my full support."

Accompanied by four policemen, shackled hand and foot, the alleged murderers were ushered into the office. One was young, about 20; the other seemed a little older. Strangely, they had no criminal records and that made the process more difficult. The weapon they had used had not yet been found.

The prosecutor on duty was called and he and Ronen locked themselves in an interrogation room with the suspects. First, they questioned them alone, and then together for almost an hour. The alleged offenders had no experience with this and were duly terrified.

Half-an-hour after the interrogation started, they discovered evidence that implicated both of them. One had torn his pants and shreds of it were found near the bike; the other had a bloody wound on his elbow, which matched the blood found on the back seat of the motorbike. At 9:50 p.m., after difficult negotiations, they gave up the name of the person who had hired them. In return, they were promised a 35 percent reduction in prison time. When offered this bait, they "sang" almost simultaneously.

The contractor's name was Hanan Jalfón, a mobster who had a file full of run-ins with the police. He had been free for eight years, after having been in prison for 10 for drug smuggling and his involvement in the death of another Ramat Gan gangster. He had been released early for good behavior.

Ronen immediately ordered the police to alert all airports and border posts about Jalfón. At the same time, he distributed his latest picture to all of the country's border crossings. At 10:15 p.m., they received an emergency call from Ben Gurion Airport in Lod. Jalfón had been arrested with a false passport while trying to leave the country on a flight to Rome.

He was transferred with a special security squad to Tel Aviv's Central Unit, where they awaited Ronen and the prosecutor on duty for questioning. At 10:42 p.m., the police van arrived with Hanan Jalfón on board. Ronen knew him, or rather, he was aware of his extensive record. Jalfón was a short man with completely white hair. He was about 50. He looked calm; he didn't raise his voice or behave in an agitated way. He seemed experienced in situations like this one. His appearance was that of a man who was about to do business, and not one who would spend the rest of his life behind bars.

"This is going to be harder," Ronen told Eli Regev. He was elated after the string of events.

"Would you like me to go in with you?" Eli asked. "I have a lot of experience in this type of thing."

"No, better to wait outside for now."

At the same time, other agents began preparing material on the attacks mentioned by Eli, trying to find a connection to Jalfón. Eli went out for a while to get some fresh air and coffee. It was 10:45 p.m. and he was losing his battle with fatigue, but he felt that Ronen was right when he said that no one would be getting any sleep tonight. They had gotten hold of the facts so fast and now they had the most solid evidence in the case, the man who had apparently been sent to kill him just a few hours ago. If he decided to talk and they found out who had paid him, perhaps his mission would be over soon.

He thought Mossad probably wouldn't need to hire the services of a man with such a long police record, although he had heard stories saying that in the past they had done so. He decided to call Emma, his secretary, at home. He knew it was not a good time, but as always, he needed her.

"Emma? How are you?"

"Have you seen what time it is?" she replied.

"I'm sorry, I know it's not working hours, but I urgently need more information about Dr. Levi."

"At this time of the night?"

"Yes. I need to know if he has had any problems with the law, or if there is anything shady in his career, or whatever it was that made him leave the hospital in Jerusalem."

"Can't this wait until tomorrow?"

"No, it can't. Look, if you get this information for me now, you can take the day off tomorrow."

The line went quiet. Emma always loved the idea of a day off.

"I'll call you back in a few minutes," she said.

77

Seated comfortably in the basement under the Mossad offices, the security manager and the head of systems were satisfied because the shift change had been fluid and smooth. After reviewing every computer that entered the building, it had been decided to intensively monitor the network for half an hour, all the traffic that went through the wire, packet by packet. When the sniffer had finally finished, it threw up a message on the central monitor, a 40-inch screen in the center of node 1: no anomalies detected.

The firewalls were also checked and found to be in perfect condition; internal and external traffic, the latter from the Internet to the private network inside, flowed smoothly, and all TCP / UDP protocols examined (the language that the computers used to talk with each other) were intact, with no signs of possible malware or other abnormality.

The central authorities met in HaKirya. The minister of defense, the general manager of Unit 8200, the First Army general, and the heads of Mossad and Shabak were among those present. The systems chief informed them that everything was normal following the shift change. The same was reported from the Hadera power plant, from HaKirya, and also from the North Army Base. The defense minister wanted to know if there was any sign of Ahmed. Shabak and Mossad both responded negatively. The police also didn't have any information about the terrorist.

They decided to intensify operations and security forces were sent from other cities to the center of Tel Aviv. It was 8:50 p.m. when Shaul received an urgent call while driving to the Mossad offices in Tel Aviv. The call came from the organization's telecommunications unit.

"We've managed to identify the public phone that received the call from Shlomit today at 6 p.m.," a spokesman said.

Shaul knew that was difficult to achieve if both phones had not been tapped.

"How did you do it?" he asked.

"We work in conjunction with Bezek, the national telephone company. We took the full list of calls that were made at that time from all public booths in Tel Aviv, and after analyzing the combinations and possibilities, the list was reduced to a single number."

"Where is that phone?"

"In Southern Tel Aviv, at 180 HaAlya street, to be precise," the spokesman said.

Shaul immediately called his bosses in HaKirya and reported the news. They decided to search all the homes in the area and to block traffic there. Special police forces were sent to the scene, and an army contingent also made its way to the site.

78

AHMED
South Tel Aviv
November 5th, 2011 - 6:49 p.m.

At 6:49 p.m., I woke up. Without even thinking about it, I had fallen into a doze on the couch. The first thing I felt upon awakening was hunger; I needed to eat. I checked my monitor. Nearly 35 minutes had passed and there was no sign of the worm. My computer was connected to the Internet tethering via my mobile phone, so I decided to turn the screen 180 degrees so it faced the kitchen, and went to make myself a sandwich. I slathered two pitas with hummus and began to devour them. The refrigerator was full of food I wasn't familiar with and wasn't willing to try. I glanced at the computer screen, but there was still nothing. I began to get impatient. I should have received the signal an hour ago. When I went to grab a third pita, I heard a sound come from the computer and saw that the monitor had changed color. It was 7:06 p.m. Three dots appeared, then a few more, and after two minutes, there was a whole line of dots. A new command came through, and on the monitor appeared the words:

```
Mossad connection established
```

I waited a little longer for the signal from the Hadera Power Plant. The screen filled with dots and spaces, which was weird. My impatience grew. Suddenly, the laptop screen went white and I thought it was damaged or frozen, or maybe it had been infected. I was just about to restart it, when a message finally appeared:

```
Hadera connection established
```

I felt excited and nervous at the same time. According to the instructions, I was supposed to receive another password which would indicate that the virus was ready to be activated, but that message didn't appear. I left the hummus and pitas and went to the computer. The screen was once again covered with dots. The lines were completed quickly, as if something was interfering with the communication. I checked my watch; it had already been six minutes since the first message. "Patience," I told myself. Different possibilities started running through my mind. I tried to stay calm. I thought again about restarting the computer; perhaps the delay was due to a PC malfunction, but I hesitated. Suddenly, the dots stopped, the screen color changed, and the message I had been waiting for emerged:

```
Worm inserted, pending activation, Mossad and Hadera
```

I took a deep breath. Everything was in place. I was relieved that the time to deliver the mortal blow to the Zionist enemy was finally approaching. After so many months of work and effort, I felt it was all worth it. For a moment, I considered myself privileged to be there, responsible for the execution. I felt as if I could touch the sky with my hands.

Soon, though, I began to worry. What if someone barged in and tried to stop me? I decided that it was no longer safe for me to be there. I put my laptop in my bag, because the activation could be done from anywhere, and I no longer needed the testing equipment. I opened the refrigerator and left a feast for the cat. Then I went outside and headed toward the coast. With the help of GPS on my mobile phone, I discovered I was only 18 minutes' walk from the sea. I decided I needed to relax a little, and stretch my legs. Seeing the water and waves while walking would help calm me. Besides, being in the apartment I felt like prey; I could be easily trapped. I chose to walk through the narrow streets of southern Tel Aviv so I would go unnoticed. I had put on my hat and my sunglasses.

When I activated the program, I wanted to be facing the open ocean. I wanted to see heaven, earth, and water all at once in that ruinous moment. At 11 p.m., I would be ready to end it all.

79

LEONEL
Herzliya
November 5th, 2011 - 9 p.m.

At 9 p.m., a young woman approached our node. She was wearing a black blouse with a respectable neckline, and her perfect curves were emphasized by her tight trousers. She wore her dark, brown hair pulled tidily back. Her green eyes contrasted with her black shirt. She looked very pretty. Finally, I thought: a fresh, bold presence, full of life in the middle of this pressure cooker.

She introduced herself with a beautiful smile. Ruben and Daniel were also impressed and abandoned what they were doing for a moment.

"Hey, guys, how are you? I come to introduce myself. I'm Hanna Benyoun and I work in node 1."

Ruben and Daniel began to babble, so I decided to take the initiative.

"And how are you? It's nice to meet you, even though this is a bit of an unusual situation. Let me introduce you to my friends, Ruben and Daniel. And I'm Leonel Cohen."

"Leonel Cohen? Weren't you the one who was rescued from Gaza?"

"That's me," I said with a shrug.

"And now you're here?" she asked, smiling. "This country won't leave you alone for a minute, will it?"

"That's right," I said, "but this was my choice."

"You chose to come and stare at screens and complicated codes instead of resting at home with your girlfriend or wife?"

"Oh, no — no girlfriend, no wife, I'm free as a bird. Between you and me, at home with my parents, I felt the need to distract myself. After spending half a day with them, I couldn't stand it anymore," I said with a smile.

After this exchange of words and smiles, she began touching her hair. I felt like I had established a good vibe between us. I liked her presence; it was nice to be near her. We spent 10 minutes talking about nothing. Then we had coffee together in the kitchen and she told me a little about her life. Finally, I said, "I have a proposal: If we make it out of this alive, I'll take you out to dinner."

She laughed and replied, "You know that there will probably be nothing left after 11 p.m."

"That's why I'm asking you out now," I said, trying to bring some humor to the situation.

"I've never had any luck with men," she said with a sweet grin, "and when I finally find someone I like, who appears to be intelligent ... the end of the world happens."

We laughed together for a moment. Although it was short, the time we shared was very pleasant, like an oasis in the midst of those weeks that had been charged with fright and physical challenges. We said goodbye to each other and returned to our nodes.

At 10 p.m., a meeting was held in one of the conference rooms. The five of us from Unit 8200 had been summoned, along with Mossad internal security agents and two experts from the Department of Cryptography. The meeting aimed to assess different response options if the attack we had been warned of actually happened. I asked the first question: "What are the implications of disconnecting the main computer from the internal network?"

The security chief stood in front of the blackboard and began to explain.

"The Mossad network mesh supplies about 1,000 ISDN connections and more than 688 direct Internet connections, point-to-point or private virtual networks. The data center is constructed in such a way that the power supply is guaranteed, in case of an accident or a cyberattack. You've seen the dome; the many security systems protecting the Internet and telephone connections, and the power supply itself, is buried in underground, in reinforced steel containers that feed interior systems. Now, specifically answering the question, to disconnect the central computer that contains one of the largest databases in this country, well, that involves a complex series of confirmations and protocols. Comparatively, it's more complicated than organizing the launch of nuclear missiles from across the country. It is also necessary to understand that to reactivate all the connectivity would take more than eight hours. We would have to confirm all connections and protocols again and make sure everything is functioning normally. There are more than 300 procedural commands to follow."

I didn't quite understand if what this guy was saying was real, or if he was exaggerating, but his comparison made me realize that turning off this machine was our last resort.

"What if we only disconnected Internet and IDSN connections?" I asked.

"That is no less complicated. That would involve fully disconnecting from our agents in the field. Some military systems are connected to the Internet via the central computer. Panic would be complete. The two options you suggested have almost the same consequences."

I realized it was very difficult to receive an objective opinion from someone who had so much passion for this bunch of computers, but I tried anyway.

"I understand what you're saying, but which of the two would have less of an impact?"

"I think disconnecting the Internet connection, although that wouldn't solve the problem if the virus is already installed on the private network. In that case, the malware would also infect the central computer."

"You mean that we would have to perform both procedures?"

"Correct," he said.

"Do we have people in this building who can run the process?" I asked.

"I think so ..." he said, hesitantly.

"What do you mean you 'think so?' " I asked, emphasizing the "think." "We need these people here and now!" I exclaimed in alarm.

"We can't cause panic for no reason."

"Panic? More than 60 reservists were called up to Unit 8200 within two hours, the entire cabinet is assembled, military systems are on red alert ... and you say we can't cause panic? Please call the people who have the ability to execute the commands to carry this out if necessary."

"All right, maybe you're right. I'll do it."

"How soon can they be here?"

"In 45 minutes," said the security chief.

"Try to make it in 30," I said. We ended the meeting there.

Daniel asked me if I hadn't been too harsh; I said no, we had to be prepared for every eventuality and emergency, and one of them was to disconnect the systems in their entirety. If we were attacked and the virus was activated and managed to spread, what would we do? We wouldn't have time to respond to that emergency or to create a program that would counteract the virus. We had to have provisions that allowed for quick decisions if necessary.

"Let's hope for a quiet night," Ruben said as he yawned.

"I'll say," I agreed.

At 10:27 p.m., Ofer, one of the reservists assigned to the Hadera Power Plant, contacted node 4. He wanted to talk to us. He wasn't overly worried, but he wanted to ask our advice. Ofer was something of a "wunderkind," a phenomenon. We had been in the army together and he never ceased to amaze me. He worked for Symantec, a company dedicated to the security of personal and business systems; he specialized in viruses of all kinds. He loved "Zero Day" type viruses for their complexity, and he was one of the few in the country who almost always found a way around them, or at the very least, an alternative. Unit 8200 had sought to have him in their ranks for life, but like others, myself included, Ofer found that army life didn't quite suit him.

When he contacted me, I sensed he had found something. We were put on conference call.

"How are things over there?" Ofer said.

"We're taking it easy around here. I even met a pretty girl," I said.

"Lucky for you! Here they're all men, and they aren't even cute ..."

"Did you find something abnormal, Mr. Zero Day?'"

"Look, I don't know if it's serious, but there is a very strange routine that has been running on almost all of the computers here for two hours. It's not doing anything and it doesn't leave any tracks behind, but it's rather weird."

"What's weird about it?"

"Right now the people who work here are executing a process where they send commands to the turbines to convert the gas into electricity."

"Yes ... what's the problem?"

"I started to compare the commands sent yesterday and last week, in everything relating to the management of the industrial control systems, and I saw that a very small code has been added to this torrent. It seems that other commands have crept in there somehow. The problem is that I can't detect this traffic. I think it's hiding behind a DLL and getting straight into the memory. I'm 100 percent sure that it doesn't work in the application layer, making it much more difficult to detect."

"Have you asked if they are operating the same routine as normal today?"

"Yes, I already checked with the systems manager. Wednesday, Thursday, Friday, Saturday, and Sunday they produce energy from gas. The remaining days they do so with coal. The programs and machinery used are completely different in each case. Fifty-five percent of the energy is produced with natural gas, and the rest with coal. The most worrisome thing is that all the power plants are connected to the same network and process the same programs. The only thing that's different is the production. In Haifa, for example, they produce electricity with gas and coal daily; in Riding in Tel Aviv they use almost exclusively gas."

"Do you think it's a virus, Ofer?"

"I don't know. Getting all the details takes time. I just got here two hours ago, and those are industrial system, something than I not very experience on. It's not showing any characteristics of a virus, though that's almost always the case in the beginning: at first it shows no signs, but then it ends up being one anyway. It might be nothing, but I'm not completely sure. That's why I'm calling. I want you to check if there's a program running right now in Mossad that has increased traffic in the private network. Try focusing on routine processes, programs that extract information."

"OK, no problem," I said. "I'll have a look and call you back in 10 minutes."

I had no doubt that Ofer was onto something big. Daniel began tracking the volume of network traffic, Ruben began to analyze it, and I went to node 1 to get a report or an estimate on the amount of network traffic for this time of day. I went straight to Hanna's desk, and she greeted me with a huge smile.

"Did you miss me?" she said.

"Yes, what can I do. It's not all the time that one falls in love at first sight. I need some statistical data, though."

"Detailing what?"

"Network traffic. Is there a program that is operating now that we can compare with yesterday's or last week's program?"

"Right now we're compiling and analyzing the information that has come to us from outside the country. It's complicated, because the traffic is not linear or uniform. Data volumes change from day to day, and on top of that there are the processes of compression and duplication."

"What a job! Have you noticed anything different, especially today?"

"I've noticed you." And she flashed her beautiful smile again. "But, no; in all seriousness, the truth is no. Although ... ah ... wait ... I don't think it's anything important, but today when I arrived, after the security check at the entrance, logging in to access the network took me more than two minutes, when usually it's almost instantaneous."

"Have you asked anyone else if the same thing had happened to them?"

"I asked my colleagues in this node, and they told me that logging in had been normal for them. Do you think my computer is infected?"

"I don't know."

I said goodbye to her and left quickly, as she followed me with her gaze. Meanwhile, Daniel and Ruben had found nothing unusual or strange in the network traffic. We called Ofer. This time he seemed more anxious.

"Did you find something?" he asked, nervously.

"No, it's actually very difficult to find any repetition in the traffic that's processed here. They compile all sorts of computer data and texts, which are then stored, but this information varies from day to day. The only strange thing one of the operations employees noticed is that her computer took longer than usual to log on to the system, but it only happened to her."

"Maybe her computer is infected."

"But it was checked today when she entered."

"I don't think that a common screening can detect a worm like the one we've been threatened with."

"Now you're calling it a worm?" I said, curious.

"I'm sure there's something; the computer that was slow getting authentication could be another piece of information to support my theory. In the identification process, many DLL commands are invoked. If the virus works like I think it does, it apparently rides through a process that looks normal; then, after being activated, it infiltrates the memory and spreads to other systems."

"And what can we do?"

"The entire Symantec Antivirus Unit has been working on it for 10 minutes now. We need to find what weaknesses it exploits and what it actually does."

"Do they have any clues?"

"Clues? No ... but they have a hunch. I think the worm is 'asleep,' that it's spreading and just awaiting activation."

"But the activation will have to be done online, via the Internet," I guessed.

"Yes, I know what you're thinking," interrupted Ofer. "We can't disconnect the Internet here because that would leave the entire country without electricity."

"Are you saying that there is nothing we can do?"

"We need to know more. It usually takes us days, even weeks, to neutralize different types of viruses. We have to wait until it's activated and see how the internal firewall and other security systems respond."

What? I couldn't believe what I was hearing. It was true that there was no evidence, nothing was certain ... but wait!

"We have to notify the directors," I said.

"And what shall we say? That we think something is happening but we have no concrete evidence to prove it? That maybe there's someone who can solve this better than us? Better leave the people who make decisions out of it until there is real and visible danger."

"But we have to anticipate the real danger," I protested.

"Leonel, listen. We need to understand what's happening to be able to fight it. You know something else?"

"What now, master?"

"I think if it really exists, the virus is the type that has a RootKit, as it's designed to hide the fact that an operating system has been compromised. I'm pretty sure of that, because it works like Stuxnet."

"What do you mean?"

"That what we are seeing in our networks would indicate that it may have been inserted via a USB memory stick. It's extremely unlikely that with all the systems we have in place that it would have come from the Internet. Our external firewalls are the safest systems I've seen, and the security policies are also very strict."

"Are you saying, Ofer, that you think a computer was affected and the virus has since spread to the entire network?"

"Right. I think so. You told me yourself that the young woman brought her laptop from outside and it took a long time to connect to the system. That's a symptom of this type of virus. Hey, look! There is a small thing we can do that's not too difficult and, who knows, maybe it'll help, although I don't have high hopes."

"Tell me," I asked, curiously.

"We can block the Internet traffic that connects us with the rest of the world in two places, here and in your location. Not physically, but in a different way. It's not very complicated. All we have to do is blacklist everything coming from sites outside the country, or only allow traffic that comes from within the country. For example, blocking all '.com' addresses and allowing only '.co.il.' Symantec will create something more sophisticated than that, though."

"But there are a lot of websites and domains within the country that use '.com.'"

"We can launch a more intelligent strategy that tracks users by their IP addresses, proximity and other parameters." Ofer said. "That way, at least we can block whoever is running the program from outside the country."

"You're right; we need to do that. It's the least we can do. We should pass this message on to everyone else. I'll talk to the head of the unit so that he can handle it, I know it will not be easy as it will require changes of many rules. We'll wait until 11 p.m., as agreed. Stay in touch, and stay where you are."

"I can assure you that there is no way I'm going anywhere tonight..."

80

South Tel Aviv
November 5th, 2011 - 9:20 p.m.

Shaul headed to the south of Tel Aviv. He knew he had to be there, keeping on top of things. He had never had much confidence in the police. Officer Shuki Ben Hamo was waiting for him, a tall, thin man who had been in the police force for 30 years. He was in charge of the operation. Shuki's police career had been characterized by honesty and commitment, but he had never been responsible for any extraordinary mission.

The 50 agents under his command spread out over an area of five kilometers and began entering every house, asking arrogantly if anyone had seen anybody new in the neighborhood. Every officer had a photo of Ahmed. Shaul spoke to Shuki, to let him know that he would be hanging around, and asked him to contact him if they found what they were looking for. They decided not to distribute posters with the terrorist's image, in order to avoid panic in the general population.

South Tel Aviv was a very old area that had never taken off from an architectural point of view; it was characterized by old buildings and businesses of all kinds. A lot of young people lived in the area, along with illegal immigrants, gangsters, and prostitutes. After visiting every building along an entire street with no success, Shuki came to number 115 HaAlía street. It was a four-story building. He knocked on the door. A Russian woman, about 30 years old, opened it in her nightgown. He thought she must be one of the women who worked there. She covered her chest and looked scared at the sight of Shuki and three policemen at her door. Shuki told her he hadn't come for her and managed to calm her down. He began asking her questions.

"Have you seen anyone new in the building lately?"

"No, no," said the girl quickly, trying to get rid of them. Then she reconsidered. "On second thought, yes, there is someone. I think a new tenant arrived yesterday. He's on the underground floor, next to the cellar."

"You've seen him? Is this him?" And he showed her the photograph of Ahmed.

"The truth is, I only saw him once, but he does kind of look like that."

"Who owns the house?"

"An Arabic guy from Jaffa; he's a nice man."

"Have you got the owner's address, telephone number, or name?"

"No, I don't have anything like that. I've just seen him a couple of times, and he seemed very cordial and friendly."

"Did he use your services?" asked one of the young policemen standing behind Shuki.

"No," said the girl. "Anything else?"

"No, thank you," Shuki said.

The four of them went downstairs. There was no time now to ask for keys or to find out who and where the owner was. They knocked on the door and there was no answer. The place seemed deserted. There were no lights on and no indication that anyone was at home. Shuki decided to call Shaul before entering the apartment. He didn't want to create problems with Mossad, but, then again, the woman said the new tenant may have been their man. Shaul turned up five minutes later and asked why they hadn't already opened the door, then told the police to step aside, took a short run up and kicked the door open. When they entered, he saw a cat vomiting in the corner and an open refrigerator. Turning his head, he took in everything that was on the table: computers, servers, routers. Everything was connected to two screens. He left everything intact. He thought about it, then said, "The terrorist was here."

He ordered Shuki and his unit to extend their search to the whole of downtown Tel Aviv.

"We need a special permit and more agents for that," Shuki said.

Shaul lost his temper when he heard that comment.

"Give me the phone. Who do I have to talk to? Dial the number now! Don't you understand that the whole country is in danger? Does 'Red Alert' mean nothing to you? And you're talking to me about paperwork?"

Shuki stepped back and spoke to his boss, who ordered him to continue searching. He promised that in 15 minutes a special force would come to join the task force. The instructions were to strategically move from the south to the center. Someone called and told them that special army patrols were already in the area. Shaul proposed focusing on the hotel zone near the coast. Shuki muttered that it was like looking for a needle in a haystack. Shaul, whose anger and nervousness were growing, turned and approached the officer until their noses were almost touching.

"Let's get to work!" he said.

81

LEONEL
Herzliya - Mossad Offices
November 5th, 2011 - 9:50 p.m.

I immediately called the head of Unit 8200, who was meeting with the other leaders in HaKirya. I explained that we thought it would be a good idea to disconnect the Internet and block all traffic coming from sites outside the country, by identifying their IP addresses and other variables. By doing this, we could at least avoid the possible activation of the virus from a remote site. The chief accepted the proposal and sent his trusted deputy to communicate the agreed-upon actions to the four risk points.

"Are you suggesting this move because you found something?" he asked me.

"We haven't found anything concrete. We'll have to wait until 11 p.m. to find out more. For now, we just have to take preventative actions."

"What are you thinking?"

He didn't let it go. I decided there was no point in trying to hide anything.

"We found strange traffic at one of the sites, but still do not have a trace on it. We don't understand the routine, so we passed it on to Symantec Israel so they can analyze it."

"Where is this happening?"

"At the Hadera Power Plant."

His silence showed he was analyzing the consequences.

"They can disrupt the electricity supply throughout the entire country. Can you imagine what that would mean?" he said, sounding concerned.

"Yes, I know, or at least I can imagine."

"What's the routine? What is it doing? How is it affecting the systems?"

"We're seeing added commands, which at this time have no influence on the functionality of the industrial infrastructure, but we're afraid that for now it's just dormant, waiting to be activated."

"Everything you're describing to me sounds like a mutation of Stuxnet."

"Apparently, it is something similar. We assume that the virus was physically introduced and is hiding behind DLL system files. We think that it attacked a weakness and lodged itself in the computer memory rather than the operating system; but, as I said before, nothing is certain, we are still studying it. And it will be extremely difficult to decipher anything before it is activated."

"Well, I'll organize a video conference between all of the sites," the Unit 8200 chief said. "Let's see ... at 10:55 p.m. I want them all connected. The activation is supposedly scheduled for 11 p.m. All of the leaders will also be present, of course. We'll see how it all unfolds."

I tried to relax for a while. I went online and opened the Yedioth Ahronoth website. The home page showed the grisly murder of the two journalists that had occurred in the stadium parking lot in Ramat Gan. There was a picture of a charred car and a report stating that the two men had suffered the same fate. That was the last thing the newspaper had published. Since then, the workers had begun a strike and a demonstration against the attack. The world is crazy, I thought.

I kept scrolling down, and then I saw her. The article read:

> Suspicious death at a hotel in Tel Aviv. A woman committed suicide by jumping from the balcony of a room on the 24th floor. Police are investigating.

The woman had been identified, with a German name. They had published two photos along with the text. The first showed the woman after the fall, in a puddle of blood next to the hotel pool. The other was of Mariana, or Shlomit Barak, the same woman who had been with me just a few hours ago. I shuddered at the sight. I knew she had been suffering psychiatric problems after the events in Afghanistan, but I had thought she would be better by now. We'd just seen each other! It was hard to see those photos and read what was said about her. I was especially surprised that the newspaper article went on to claim the victim was a Mossad agent, as this violated censorship rules. I was nonetheless deeply affected; I still felt something for this woman, something that until now had been difficult to define. I felt pain and grief, but more than anything, rage. The article didn't explain the details of the event; nothing else was mentioned other than that police were investigating. That seemed strange, but I thought that as she had been with the Mossad, they wouldn't release any more information.

I took a deep breath and went to the bathroom. I was heartbroken. I couldn't believe it. I hadn't cried in a long time, but there, in front of the mirror, I couldn't stop my tears. I promised to find out what had happened. I took another deep breath, washed my face, and went back to node 4.

"Is everything all right, man?" asked Daniel, seeing my anguish.

"Yes, yes — everything's fine."

"Really? Are you sure nothing's wrong? I'm your friend. You know you can trust me."

"I know, but don't worry. I'm just still a little traumatized from the kidnapping. It was only one day ago ... it's not easy to forget."

"Yes, of course, I understand. Despite your ordeal, we're very glad you decided to come and work through this crisis with us."

82

AHMED
South Tel Aviv
November 5th, 2011 - 8:10 p.m.

The streets were dark, and a shudder of fear rippled through my body every time a car passed me. With the help of the GPS on my mobile and my hurried steps, I made it to the Jaffa coast in 25 minutes. I was walking down Jerusalem Street, one of Jaffa's main streets, according to the map. There were crowds of pedestrians and heavy traffic, with many buses and cars clogging up the street. I spotted the police in the distance and quickened my pace. I ran the last two blocks to the beach. The GPS indicated that I was on the border between Jaffa and Tel Aviv.

There was only one small group of four people on the coast. The winter chill wasn't ideal for walking along the beach. I went to the marina and looked for a place where I could feel safe. I was far away from the street and far enough from the shore. I found an old, abandoned building called Dolfinarium. The poster with the name was still on the wall, curled and about to fall. Inside was a series of tiered seats. A large window faced the sea, stained by time and neglect. In the center of the seats was a large pool, home to dolphins — those poor, captive sea creatures forced to perform — in better times. I remembered the place immediately, because a Hamas terrorist had sacrificed himself there a few years ago, killing some young Jewish Russians at the same time. I scanned the room and went in a little deeper. The further inside I went, the safer it seemed.

I turned on my computer, logged on to the Internet via my phone and went to the Al Jazeera website to learn a little of what was happening in the world. On the homepage was Mariana's face, and in the same article was another photo showing a woman lying in a pool of blood. The headline read:

I couldn't keep reading. There was no doubt that the photo was Mariana, my Mariana, the woman I hadn't forgotten, who I still loved. My hands were shaking as I continued reading. Haziza Malem, an Egyptian journalist, recounted her version of events:

At around 6:30 p.m. today at the Hotel Panorama, located on Hayarkon Street in central Tel Aviv, Shlomit Barak, alias "Mariana," committed suicide by jumping from the 24th floor, when two Mossad agents entered her room. Reliable sources have confirmed that Barak was a double agent who served Mossad and Hamas simultaneously. She was the daughter of Danish parents of Arab origin. Barak had worked for Mossad in Europe for more than five years. In the last two years, she began to cooperate with Hamas in the struggle for the liberation of Palestine. It is said that Barak was the one who leaked the information to Hamas which led to the capture of Leonel Cohen, who was rescued yesterday in a surprise operation carried out by Israeli Special Forces. A member of Hamas confirmed that Barak had been following Ahmed Asad, a computer expert in the organization, while he was in Pakistan carrying out a secret mission. The same source confirmed that at that time Barak had informed Mossad of Asad's whereabouts.

As I read, I felt a tightness in my chest which made it hard to breathe. When I managed to calm down a little, a tear rolled down my cheek, and though I wanted to, I couldn't stop it. I couldn't remember the last time I had cried. I felt great pain for her death, and great sadness because I loved her. The little time I had spent with her were some of the best moments of my life. Mariana was the only woman I had ever been in love with. I never doubted her honesty. At the same time, anger came over me and I started to feel sick. I shut the computer and tried to concentrate on my mission. It suddenly occurred to me that the voice that had contacted me from the pay phone had been her, and I realized they must have discovered her and that had led to her suicide. Perhaps the Israelis knew the time of the attack, but it would be useless to them. The worm malware was already installed deep in the systems; in a few hours, I would bring it to life and everything would end. If I could speed up time, I would execute the attack on the spot.

And then what? I thought. I had to wait for instructions and hide until I could return to the territories and, perhaps, to Iran again. I didn't like that idea at all. Thoughts ran through my head and made the pounding in my chest worse. I came to question my own decision, and I wondered if this was really the life I wanted, a life where I was alone, waiting, suffering in the cold and about to commit an attack. Maybe I should quit, get out. But, no, it was already too late for that.

I heard the distant sound of sirens growing increasingly louder as they drew closer and closer to me. I was being hunted and I had only one weapon: the activation code.

83

When Emma had heard the promise of a day off, she didn't hesitate. She immediately started working on Dr. David Levi's file. She had almost everything organized from earlier that day. She only needed to make two urgent calls to obtain references which would complete the records. Her efficiency and contacts meant that in eight minutes she had all the material she needed, and she sent everything to Eli by email. After doing so, she called him. It was 10:56 p.m.

"Eli, I sent you everything you asked for. It's in your email."

"Ah ... Emma! Thank you so much! Wait a second, I'll just check I received it. Could you give me a quick summary?"

It annoyed Emma that Eli always wanted information broken down for him, but that evening it was worth the effort, because it meant she would be able to visit her grandson next day and that was invaluable to her. So she politely complied.

"Yes, no problem. What I think will interest you most is that the same year the two children were born, Levi spent two months in psychiatric treatment because of an emotional crisis and, because of this, left the hospital briefly — this was in April 1982. That's confidential information, so it's not common knowledge. He returned to the hospital on May 30 the same year. During those two months, he spent two weeks in a psychiatric hospital in Jerusalem, where he was prescribed large doses of Lithium and powerful antidepressants."

"And all that for an emotional crisis? Really?" Eli asked, amazed.

"It seems so, but I couldn't get more details on the cause of his illness. Without a doubt, something big happened to him. The strange thing is that in November 1982, unexpectedly and without advance notice, he took 24 days of vacation and returned to work in late December that year. An important part of his story is that in February 1980 he started a relationship with a nurse who worked for him, and married her a year later. He was 36 years old, and she was five years younger. They never had children. Two-and-a-half months ago, he left Jerusalem, the city where he had lived all his life, and moved to Kfar Saba, where he bought an apartment in Arlozorov in the city center. He began working at the Meir Hospital for only a few days a week."

"How did he leave things at the Sharei Tzedek Hospital? Is there any information on that?"

"I'm told he left voluntarily, no problems whatsoever. At the hospital everyone was very surprised, because it was believed would finish his career there. He was always very professional, had maintained an excellent relationship with staff, and had an unblemished reputation. With that resume he didn't have any trouble getting work at the Kfar Saba hospital."

"There's something odd about all this. Help me out and tell me what you think," Eli asked her.

"What I think is weird is the emotional crisis, and the fact that he left Jerusalem after a lifetime in that city, especially because he could have finished his career at the hospital where he'd worked for so long. It's not often that people who've spent their whole lives in Jerusalem just change cities for no reason."

"I noticed a few other inconsistencies, Emma, besides those you mentioned. The crisis took place in mid-April '82. From January to October, when the babies were born, is nine months, the gestation time of a normal pregnancy. Then he returns to the hospital and takes a vacation in November, a week after the birth of the children. Hospitals are sticklers when it comes to authorizing holidays. You need to plan them a long time in advance, because patients need to be covered by substitutes, and in this case that didn't happen. Perhaps there was some emergency or unexpected event. What is also striking is that two months ago he moved to Kfar Saba, which happens to coincide with the string of attacks, and Rachel Mizrachi asking Leonel Cohen to find Ahmed, for which she promised to pay him a million shekels."

"Yes, you're right — there are too many coincidences. Are you saying that you suspect Dr. Levi is involved in this story?"

"Perhaps more than just a little involved, Emma. Well, I have to go now. I have to find out what's going on with the police. It seems they've found the person responsible for the attacks. Remember, you have the day off tomorrow."

"Thank you, Eli," Emma said, although she didn't need to be reminded that she had the next day free.

It was 11 p.m. Eli went upstairs. He wanted to know more details of what had happened with Jalfón. Perhaps the criminal would join forces with the police, providing the missing information needed to solve the riddle.

He found Ronen on the stairs. He was surprised; it was the first time he had seen him smoking.

"What's up?" Eli asked.

"As always, he doesn't want to talk. He's asked for his lawyer. He's laid down a million conditions."

"And what do you think?"

"That it will be hard to get anything out of him — this is not a man who's going to fold at the promise of a few less years. He's not a novice in the prison or judiciary systems."

"And do you have a strategy?"

"We have to find his weak point, Eli. There are some options that we can still use; for example, we can propose that he works for the state."

"But you know that this is urgent. Who can make the decision today?"

"We need a judge to issue the arrest warrant. It's on its way; the magistrate on duty is bringing it."

"Look, if you need a hand up there, I'm available," offered Eli.

"Thank you, but I'm fine for now. We have the whole night ahead and, if I don't smoke a quiet cigarette now, I'm done for."

"Sorry, Ronen, but we don't have all night. Do you know what time it is? It's 11 p.m.!

84

AHMED
South Tel Aviv
November 5th, 2011 - 10:50 p.m.

The shriek of sirens and shrill whistles were all that I could hear. The police were so close I could sense their movement in the area. Hebrew words sliced through the air of my hiding place. I peered out. On Hayarkon Street, parallel to the Dolfinarium, I saw a row of police cars. The street was closed to civilians. Security forces were approximately 500 meters from where I was hiding.

I decided to go a little deeper into my den and curled up in front of the abandoned pool. This place once housed dolphins, but now it was only an empty pool holding a few puddles of stagnant water. I heard waves in the distance, and concentrated on the sound of the sea to calm my fear. At 10:51 p.m., I opened my laptop again and connected to the Internet via my phone. I checked the battery of both devices: the computer had 60 percent left and the phone 41 percent. I had to act quickly and effectively. Suddenly I received an anonymous email with instructions what to do the day after, I didn't open it, but in the preview I saw some names, addresses and phones numbers, I decided to save it in a memory stick.

I opened the application with the activation program and then immediately monitored the communication with the sites. The data received by the program went to the website www.hiatligthson.com, where it was redirected by DNS to a local site in case external traffic was blocked. This site had the same name, but used acronyms and local IP addresses. I opened the website and on the screen appeared:

Hadera Central Electricity – communication established
Mossad Headquarters – communication established

The malware spread without needing an Internet connection, using a P2P (peer to peer) mechanism, where information is shared between computers without requiring a central server. I decided to get up to date on what was happening in each of the target attack sites, to find out exactly how many computers had already been infected by the virus.

Hadera Central Electricity – 346 computers, 49 servers
Mossad Headquarters – 183 computers, 29 servers

Fantastic! With these statistics the program could not fail and the activation of the virus would destroy the infrastructure and paralyze those places. The volume of traffic that the program would produce after being activated would be very difficult to neutralize.

The only option left for the Zionists was to disconnect the private network and the central computer. The malware was sleeping deeply in the memories of computers and servers, waiting for activation to wake up and demolish everything. My estimate was that in facilities such as Hadera, once activated, it would take 30 or 40 minutes to raze the system. It might take less time to work in Mossad, although the network there would be more difficult to breach, so I concluded that times would be the same for both systems. I figured that, at the latest, at around 11:50 p.m. the two powerhouses of Israel would be paralyzed. The consequences: intermittent power outages and disconnection of electricity supply in most of the country, especially at strategic points. The last report from the Iranian spy said that, according to the odds analyzed in Iran, northern Israel would remain without power for more than 15 minutes, the time it would take for the generators to kick in. I had no knowledge of the ultimate goal, but I assumed that Iran and Hezbollah would take advantage of this time to launch a massive rocket attack and maybe to launch ground attacks as well.

Mossad's central database would be unprotected and would be expo-sed to any hacker with a simple modem or Internet connection. The files and greatest secrets of the country would be completely vulnerable, since when the program finished its run, there would be no internal firewall, no security at all.

The same program would begin downloading the data stored in the central computer, and would load them onto the website www.hiatlig-thson.com, until the machine was switched off, if that happened. Again, because I didn't know the whole plan, I had to make assumptions. I thought that Mossad weren't fools, and as soon as they detected a virus threatening the private network and jeopardizing their central database, they would immediately disconnect the Internet and the entire site.

Some dogs began to bark. I looked out and saw them. They were police dogs. I lay down on the floor and began to slowly crawl toward what had once been a functions room. I reasoned it would be safer. I was afraid I would be found before I could activate the attack. My instinct was telling me not to wait, to awaken the virus now; in the end, I thou-ght, what difference did a few minutes make? But then I remembered that the last message I had received had emphasized the importance of the timing.

Everything was ready for activation; I just needed a bit of luck, and to enter the secret code.

85

The communications technician was sweating. He had spent five minutes trying to connect the video-conferencing system without success. The audience was composed of none other than the minister of defense, the chief of Unit 8200, and the chiefs of both Mossad and Shabak. The First Army general had told them he would come at 11 p.m. At 10:52 p.m., the techie finally figured it out, and one by one, the sites connected themselves to the system and the cameras started recording the faces of those at the conference. As soon as they saw each other, they shared greetings and introduced themselves. There were four people plus the technicians representing each of the four sites involved. In the Central Mossad Office were the head of Unit 8200, Tomer, Daniel, Leonel, and the information security manager for Mossad. At the other sites, the pattern was the same: the person in charge, two reservists, and the security manager were present at each one. The giant screen embraced them all. Each site had also added the status of their security systems to the conference, which meant that the main screen that everyone saw had eight windows.

The head of Unit 8200 stood and directed his question to all those present.

"Anything to report?"

"We're waiting for the exact moment, at 11 p.m.," Tomer replied.

The others gave the same answer.

"In five minutes, I want you to give me the options you've thought of in case of an attack, starting with the base of the north," the Unit 8200 head said.

Then they heard a deep voice. It was Officer Yair, from the Ramon Base in Galil.

"The private network is connected to the IDF Defense Force's network, but our central computer has a specific shutdown routine and can operate independently. That's our first option. The second is to cut off the power supply to all systems. It would take longer and would have different consequences, so it is definitely our number two choice."

Officer Alon, head of Unit 8200 in Tel Aviv, stepped forward to compare their options with Yair.

"Currently, we have almost the same options here in HaKirya IDF base, although there is the fact that disconnecting from the central network is more complicated, since the central servers are in the Bor[53]. We would have to activate the 'disaster recovery' program, a path which would decouple the network and pass it to a data center in the south of the country. This could take two to three hours."

It didn't sit well with the leadership that the process of disaster recovery (DR) took so long. Disconnecting the IDF network was one of the options that everyone was seriously considering as the most appropriate.

It was Gaby's turn. He was a tall official in his thirties, whose appearance showed advanced fatigue. With a delicate and rather high-pitched voice, he spoke of the implications and measures to be taken in the energy sector.

"Any process here is critical," he explained. "We can use the two options noted by our peers, but both could bring serious problems for electricity disconnections because generators would not support the production of electricity for the whole country. If the virus has entered the network, it will spread to the other power plants as well. After Hadera, the most critical are the Haifa and Tel Aviv. A power outage at Central Haifa for more than half an hour would trigger darkness throughout the North, and would become extremely critical. Cutting the communication network is, perhaps, a more feasible option, but this

---

53 Bor: One of the army's best kept secrets, the location of the central network.

would also affect electricity production. As you can see, the situation here is very complex."

The defense minister was very nervous. Time and indecision bothered him. He looked into the eyes of the Unit 8200 chief, who was seated in front of him.

Tomer, a young man still completing his compulsory service but who was seen as a promising member of the organization, approached the microphone.

"The same options exist here in the Mossad, although disconnecting the central computer, one of the more important in the country, could have a strong impact that could stretch for hours. We could lose contact with agents across the world who need continued support. On the other hand, isolate the network is possible, but recovering it would take more than six hours, since it would have to reconnect with more than 2,000 lines, and thousands of programs would have to be tested. The most feasible action we have discussed with our Hadera peers would be to disconnect Internet connections based on IP addresses. This could prevent data theft if the virus manages to penetrate security and reach the central computer."

The defense minister stood and looked at everyone in the room. Then he turned his eyes to the camera and began his impromptu speech in a loud, clear voice.

"What is it you're telling me? After everything that is happening in today's world, with all the advances in technology and our supposed cyber potential, with leading defense organizations such as the revered Unit 8200 and the Mossad, we find ourselves on a day in 2011 completely exposed. Is this what you mean to tell me? That everything is so complicated? That the possible preventive processes take hours to run?"

Nearly everyone lowered their heads and no one dared to answer. The minister was exploding with rage, his face contorted.

"If something happens, how will you explain to the prime minister that nothing had been done, that the country was not prepared for this eventuality?"

At 10:58 p.m., he left the video-conferencing room to smoke. Everyone looked on. The wall screen showed long faces, worried that the systems weren't revealing any sort of active virus or malware ... yet.

86

AHMED
South of Tel Aviv
November 5th, 2011 - 10:58 p.m.

The minutes seemed like decades, and by 10:58 p.m. the cold had me shaking. The dogs were close, and each time I heard their barking it was progressively closer. I decided to move back and down the stairs to get to an environment that was more secure. Mice and rats paraded before my eyes, unfazed by my presence, and all I could see was grime and dirt, the latter of which prevailed in that small space with its cracked concrete wals. I checked my cell phone reception and found that it was the same as on the surface.

I opened my computer. It was 10:59 p.m. The program was running as I had left it, in terminal mode, checking the Internet connection. The terminal glowed green, and so I began to enter commands.

```
Admin > Connection
Admin > Connection Established
Admin > Activation
Admin > Activation Code
```

I checked the time on the computer and on my watch: 23:00:05 p.m. My hands were shaking and slipped across the keyboard; for a moment, I thought I couldn't control them. I set my eyes on the monitor:

```
Admin > XXXXXXXXXXXX
```

Every character I wrote seemed like torture, but the decision had
already been made. Now I had only to wait for confirmation, and the
process would come into action. The noise intensified on the surface,
and I waited as it shook the damn signal.

```
Admin > Activation Authorized
Admin > Program Activated
Admin > .........................................................
..................................................................
..................................................................
..................................................................
..................................................................
Admin > Program initialized at Hadera Power Plant
Admin > .........................................................
..................................................................
..................................................................
..................................................................
..................................................................
Admin > Program initialized at Mossad Headquarters
```

It was done. I breathed deeply. Now I only had to wait. I heard the
sound of a panting dog, who had come from the surface; obviously,
someone was near the place I was hiding. The rats fled in fright and I
stood there, with nowhere else to go. Under these conditions, the only
thing I could do was pray. My mission was already accomplished.

87

Tel Aviv - Central Police Station
November 5th, 2011 - 11:07 p.m.

At 11:07 p.m. they urgently called Ronen, who was smoking and drinking coffee at the bar located opposite the police station. That was the place where the police force gathered and spent their free time. It was one of the few places in the area where smoking was allowed. When the owner of the place called out his name, Ronen left quickly, as if burning out in a cloud of smoke. At the station, he ran straight into the room where they were interrogating Jalfón. Upon arrival, he saw the presiding judge sitting by the prosecutor. He was pleased with the judge; he was a very daring young man who was not afraid of anything. He liked to close cases and hated stretching out matters longer than necessary. Eli Regev also knew him and said a few words in his ear before entering. The young judge had glasses, a black suit, a white shirt, and a blue tie. He wore well-polished shoes. His black hair was very neat considering the time. He looked shy, but was efficient and fast.

Jalfón was smoking, even though such a thing wasn't allowed in that chamber. He looked as calm as if he were in the garden of his house.

"Why was I called in so urgently?" Ronen asked softly.

"Jalfón is ready to confess."

At the request of Ronen, he, the prosecutor, and the judge left the room to talk.

"How is it that he suddenly decided to sing?" Ronen asked.

The judge had in his hand a bundle of typewritten sheets.

"Jalfón has an enormous record, from here to China," he said. "Among other crimes, he was found leaving the country illegally and is accused of having perpetrated a few attacks in which he was ordered to kill for money."

"But ... so suddenly? Before I left to smoke, he said he wanted to see a lawyer. How come he changed his position?"

"We're offering him a lot," said the prosecutor. "The Mossad ordered us to close the case as soon as possible, regardless of the cost."

"And the Mossad, what do they want to see?" Ronen was furious.

"I don't know," said the judge. "What I do know is that we have to finish this. They made it very clear to us that this is a matter of great importance, a national security case. I myself spoke with the head of Mossad."

"What does Jalfón receive in exchange for his confession?"

"Eight years in prison, and with luck and good behavior he'll be out after five," the prosecutor explained.

"That was the offer? Only eight years?" Ronen persisted.

"Look, work with us."

"Ah! It's just as I feared," Ronen said. "Well, let's go; I want to know who ordered all the attacks."

They returned to the interrogation room. Jalfón was still smoking like a toad. He crossed his feet and asked, "What do you want to know?"

"We want to know who sent you to kill all those people."

"Above all," declared Jalfón, "I want to see the document containing everything I was offered and I want my lawyer and the judge to confirm its validity. I'm in no hurry."

"Did you call your lawyer?" asked the prosecutor.

"Yes, he's about to arrive."

Ronen left the room again and told Eli Regev that Jalfón was about to confess.

"I knew that this judge was very efficient," Eli said.

"This was not accomplished by the judge, Eli. The Mossad made Jalfón an incredible proposal in exchange for information."

"The Mossad? How they are stuck in this? How do they know we're here? Have you spoken with them?" Eli asked angrily, looking straight into his eyes.

"Easy, Eli. I didn't talk to anyone. I don't understand it, either, and I'd like to have the answers to those questions as much as you. The important thing now is that he's going to speak. Come, let's go."

At 11:19 p.m., Jalfón's lawyer came in, an old man of 65 years. He was disheveled and looked like someone who had been pulled out of bed by smacking. He had a brown leather briefcase.

The lawyer donned huge glasses and began to read the contract. At 11:23 p.m., he said, "Let's sign it. It's all good."

Jalfón and his lawyer both signed, and eventually, so did the judge, who legalized and sealed it.

"Who sent you to kill so many people, Jalfón?" Ronen asked anxiously.

Jalfón looked again at the paper in front of him. He had never signed such a good deal in his life. Were it not for this document, he would have had to serve two life sentences and would have ended his days rotting in prison. But now he could see a future ahead.

"We don't have time, Jalfón," Ronen tried to push him. "Who paid you for all those crimes?" he asked, pointing a finger at the second sheet of paper.

"It was Dr. David Levi."

"I knew it!" Eli said exultantly.

Ronen left the room accompanied by Eli and immediately called the Hasharon area police. He ordered a unit of the Tel Aviv special brigade to urgently find Dr. David Levi. Then he contacted Shaul, since that was the contact he had been given by the head of Mossad.

"Shaul, this is Ronen, of the Tel Aviv police department."

"Yes, what's up?"

"We have the name of the person who ordered all the attacks."

"Who was it?"

"It was Dr. David Levi."

"Have you issued orders to look for him? Where do you think he is?"

"The last time anyone saw him was in Kfar Saba."

As Ronen was about to end the call, Eli Regev abruptly seized the phone.

"Hey, Shaul, how are you?"

"Who's talking?"

"Your friend, Eli."

"Ah ... what do you want?"

"Tell me, how it is it that the Mossad arranged for this mafioso to confess?"

"You know, Eli, I don't have time for that now. The country is in danger, you know? Incredible danger!" he shouted and hung up.

88

LEONEL
Mossad offices - Herzliya
November 5th, 2011 - 11:08 p.m.

Tripping over a trash can and without knocking, Hanna entered the video-conferencing room, visibly shaken. She was pale, and could barely control her breathing.

"There's a huge flow of traffic on the internal network," she said to everyone present.

"What kind of traffic?" Daniel asked.

"It's a combination of TCP / IP and UDP. It occurred to me that it's a Distributed Denial of Service (DDoS) attack. I don't understand how it can expand, though, because we have strict protection against all types and variations of this virus. The internal websites are falling apart and there are all kinds of processes running on the network: http, https, eximd, ftp... Almost all of them are being affected. Those are the ones I've recognized so far."

Ofer abruptly interrupted.

"We have the same thing here in Hadera. The internal network is being bombarded and websites are falling one after another. Look at the wall screen."

As he spoke the screen displayed the workings of one of the attacked servers sending two commands "Netstat."

```
netstat -ntu | awk '{print $ 5}' | cut -d: -f1 | sort | uniq -c
```

```
| sort -nr

netstat np | grep SYN_RECV | awk '{print $ 5}' | cut -d. -f1-4
| cut -d: -f1 | sort -n | uniq -c | sort -n

IP Server: IP 192.168.0.3
Attacker: 192.168.0.5

tcp 0 0 192.168.0.3:80 192.168.0.5:60808 SYN_RECV
tcp 0 0 192.168.0.3:80 192.168.0.5:60761 SYN_RECV
tcp 0 0 192.168.0.3:80 192.168.0.5:60876 SYN_RECV
tcp 0 0 192.168.0.3:80 192.168.0.5:60946 SYN_RECV
tcp 0 0 192.168.0.3:80 192.168.0.5:60763 SYN_RECV
tcp 0 0 192.168.0.3:80 192.168.0.5:60955 SYN_RECV
tcp 0 0 192.168.0.3:80 192.168.0.5:60765 SYN_RECV
tcp 0 0 192.168.0.3:80 192.168.0.5:60961 SYN_RECV
tcp 0 0 192.168.0.3:80 192.168.0.5:60923 SYN_RECV
tcp 0 0 192.168.0.3:80 192.168.0.5:61336 SYN_RECV
tcp 0 0 192.168.0.3:80 192.168.0.5:61011 SYN_RECV
tcp 0 0 192.168.0.3:80 192.168.0.5:60911 SYN_RECV
tcp 0 0 192.168.0.3:80 192.168.0.5:60758 SYN_RECV
```

The head of Unit 8200 asked if there were any anomaly at the Ramon Base or at the HaKirya in Tel Aviv.

"No anomaly here," said Yair.

"Nor here," Alon added.

The army chief asked his assistant to investigate in all the IDF bases if they had spotted malicious traffic in their networks. After seven minutes, the emissary returned with a negative answer. The head of Shabak also reported negatively. It was decided to continue calling strategic locations, among which were the Bezeq Telecommunications Center, the Gas Reserves and the State Water Company.

"We have to isolate the infection," the defense minister said.

At 23:20 military time it was confirmed that the only places affected up to that point were the Power Station in Hadera and the Mossad offices. The official, Gaby, also added in this report that the Reading

Power Plant in Tel Aviv, and Haifa, were infected as they were connected to the internal network and were victims of the same harmful traffic flow.

"Ofer will present an overview of what is happening," Gaby said.

Ofer stood and began drawing on the blackboard; the camera followed him and all participants in the video-conference room watched him intently. Ofer had spoken with Symantec technicians to fully understand how things were affecting the systems. He combined the data obtained from Symantec with what he had found.

Also, the head of Unit 8200 had communicated with the general manager of Symantec, ordering that nothing was to leave the country via the Internet for now, and he made it very clear that if he did not obey the sanction there would be consequences. Ofer, as he finished presenting the variables of the malware, began to explain the details of the situation. Before starting, he clarified that all the information they now had, had been acquired in the short time they had been managing the issue and, in reality, it amounted to an unconfirmed thesis. Normally, he said, it took weeks to discover this kind of worm.

"As we thought, the virus appears to have been physically inserted into a computer that connects to the network," Ofer said. "It is very feasible that it was introduced via USB memory, even though the USB ports are blocked for any use, to avoid a virus. It shouldn't be able to run 'autorun.exe' programs nor DLL files, especially not programs that use DLLs of the operating system, in this case Windows. Next, it detects a weakness in a driver and stays in the memory of the computer. Therefore, resetting the system is useless because the virus will be cleared but will act as if it is a rootkit.

"After being housed in the computer memory, the virus was activated and began to launch a Distributed Denial of Service (DDoS), as we can see, in three routines.

"One is the attack using the TCP / IP connection: the virus sends requests via the TCP / IP connection from falsified or nonexistent addresses. The server accepts the connection and waits for a response, but as the IP address does not exist, it does not receive any. When making thousands of requests at once all its resources are consumed, locking the service.

"Another is volumetric attack, or ICMP Flood: the virus sends mass data packets requiring the return of a response packet, consuming all the bandwidth of the service.

"And the third is the UDP Flood attack by fragmentation: the virus fragments send UDP messages to the victim, making it difficult to re-assemble and making the system slow down or crash."

The defense minister had been listening, too, and shook his head nervously.

"How can that be?" he burst out, then he asked, "How long would it take to clean that virus?"

For the first time, I got angry; there was no time for such expressions. I got up from my seat with the intention of leaving the place, but a gesture of Hanna brought me back to reality. So I decided to intervene.

"Here is not the place to talk about cleaning the virus. In an infection of the magnitude we have, it's impossible to do so promptly, it will take days. The question here is how to deactivate it before it gets to the central computer here in Hertzlia and the industrial system in Hadera, and thus prevent the power generation systems from stopping. This virus is a program that contains an activation code and the same code disables it. Deactivation would stop everything instantly."

"But how do we get that password?" asked the Unit 8200 chief.

"The only way is to find the person who activated it. Activation was done online from somewhere within the country. This virus was injected under our noses, and took out our guts. The code was asleep in our systems for several hours here in the offices of the Mossad until it was executed. The malware dodged detection systems and is now headed directly to the central computer. Right now, it's invading computers, servers and routers. In my opinion, the next step will be to devour each of the inner firewall layers, one after the other. You should see how they react. We should cut all private network connections to prevent our data from escaping the country. Imagine the consequences this would bring.

"We have to cut the connections. There is no choice. We'll have to do it all at once, not by procedures. If we do it the proper way, it'll take hours that we don't have."

The Mossad security manager moved his hands, expressing his discontent.

"That's suicide. To reconnect each line will take days, maybe weeks," he said.

"If we don't, the result will be that we risk losing all of the classified information this country has compiled over the last 50 years," I explained.

The Mossad chief interrupted my argument.

"Cut the Internet now! Call the Bezeq telecom engineers and do it with them. We can't worry about the agents right now. This data cannot be violated; it's worth more than anything else!"

The defense minister looked at him and nodded. He didn't have much sympathy, because in the not-too-distant past, they had had many differences that had led to public fights. This time the minister felt he had to take his side. That precious data belonged to the whole country; it was not time to think about retaliations and reprisals. All agreed, and the order was given. Regarding the Hadera Power Plant, it was decided that there was no reason to disconnect the Internet from the private network, since it wasn't used to preserve any secrets.

In an instant, everyone turned their eyes to the wall screen to see the status of the firewall system. The virus was destroying the first layer of protection in both places at once. It had taken just three minutes to raze; it was the firewall layer that protected the FTP protocol, with almost no resistance to the voracious malware.

"We have a very serious problem," the head of Unit 8200 said.

"How much time do we have?" I asked.

Ofer, who had been silent and was looking at his computer trying to ascertain what else the demon was doing to destroy everything, was the one who answered.

"If we're lucky, and my calculations haven't failed me, no more than half an hour. The virus here has another objective, we calling it 'the Payload': files that have been analyzed show that it was inserted into the system a week ago and has been asleep for the last seven days. I think what it was doing was studying industrial system routines. I think once the firewall can no longer resist it, it will start sending erroneous commands to the turbines, valves, and pipes to stop electricity production. Again, these are my speculations, but there's something about this virus that's very familiar. If it's what I think it is, then the problem is huge. I have nothing else to say."

89

Tel Aviv - Central Police Station
November 5th, 2011 - 11:20 p.m.

At 11:20 p.m., police in the Hasharon area were distributed across Kfar Saba, Raanana, and Ramat Hasharon in search of Dr. Levi. Reinforcements had come from both Mossad and Shabak forces.

Around 11:25 p.m., his photo was distributed throughout the area. The operation was coordinated along all sides with everyone reporting to the Tel Aviv Central Station. Every five minutes, Shaul, who was in the center of Tel Aviv looking for the terrorist, was in contact with Ronen.

Meanwhile, Eli Regev received an emergency call from a highly placed government official who asked him to stop the investigation for the moment.

"What do you mean?" Eli asked, annoyed.

"You have to leave everything. The country is in a very difficult situation."

"What's happening?"

"A terrorist inserted a lethal virus into the networks for both the Mossad offices and the central electrical grid."

"And do we know who it was?"

"The terrorist is Ahmed."

"What Ahmed?"

"Ahmed, the youth from your story."

"Why do I have to suspend my duty?"

"Because you're becoming an obstacle. Now leave all that, leave the police and the Mossad in peace. These orders come from above."

Knowing Regev's obstinacy, the official reiterated his government's request.

"Promise me, Eli. If you keep going, everything will go to hell."

"I promise," Eli said, still disturbed by what he had heard.

At 11:29 p.m., an old man out walking his dog called the Herzliya police and reported that he had seen David Levi walking near the Herzliya Central Station.

At 11:33 p.m., the police took the doctor off a micro bus he had recently boarded, destined for Haifa. The bus was about to leave and Levi didn't resist. He was arrested with his dirty clothes and in shock, and he was immediately taken to the central police station in Tel Aviv.

Ronen got the call.

"We got him," said the first officer of Herzliya Central. "We're about to leave."

"Great. Thanks. Hurry up, we need him here as soon as possible. If you want, we can open a corridor."

"No, that's not necessary. I have two patrolmen. We'll be there in 13 minutes."

Ronen was exhausted; he turned, looked at Eli, smiled, and said, "We've found the doctor!"

90

AHMED
South Tel Aviv
November 5th, 2011 - 11:28 p.m.

The noises continued, the voices began to approach, and dogs were barking incessantly now. At one point, I clearly saw the lights of the flashlights forming shapes across me. Police were on the surface. The only thing that separated me from them was a wall and a staircase. If they decided to go down to my shelter, I wouldn't be able to exit. I could only stay in place and pray that nothing happened. I looked at my phone and saw that it no longer had battery power, and at the same time realized that no one could help me. The police were now in the area of the pool adjoining the ballroom. How ironic, I thought. Before this had been a luxury place and now it was all completely destroyed.

"We can go, there's nobody here," I heard someone say.

The sounds began to move away and with them went my fear, but my hands were still shaking. Soon I couldn't hear any more voices, so I thought it was safe. But then my cell phone began broadcasting the low battery indicator noise, and instantly I heard a barking sound that frightened me. A dog came downstairs and started harassing me. It growled loudly, like a hungry tiger. I managed to cover my face, and the dog dug it's mouth in my pants leg. Shaking it furiously without releasing it while I desperately kicked out, hitting it with my other leg. With each kick, the animal began to howl with more intensity. Before officers arrived, I found a deep crack in the wall and quickly hid the USB key, which contained the main program, another piece of software that they never disclosed to me, and the email what to do the day after.

Soon two soldiers had grabbed me by the shoulders and calmed the dog, while a third handcuffed me. Then he picked up the computer and my bag, and took my phone. They were satisfied. They had captured their prey.

"We have him!" one of them radioed. "We are in the Dolfinarium. Let Shaul know ASAP!"

Shaul arrived at the scene just five minutes later. He was elated. He introduced himself as a Mossad agent and asked me my name. If I got caught, I had been instructed to be quiet and to not reveal anything, and so I did just that.

Shaul looked me in the eyes. His face was contorted.

"Do not do anything. We need you; we know who you are and what you have done," he said.

I remained silent. It was strange. I had stopped shaking and no longer felt fear. I felt that I was safe, that the worst was behind me. I looked and saw that my pants were stained with blood, but nothing seemed to be hurt.

They shackled my feet, checked my handcuffs, and shoved me into a patrol car.

Shaul gave the order to take me to the Central Police Station Tel Aviv.

"Go quickly. Don't stop for anything. We have to be there as soon as possible," he said.

In the car, as I watched the pretty lights of Tel Aviv, my body was a swirl of feelings, and my head for a moment forgot about the virus and began to think about what would become of me now.

91

HaKirya - Tel Aviv
November 5th, 2011 - 11:54 p.m.

At 11:30 p.m., the prime minister arrived at the video-conferencing room in HaKirya Tel Aviv. The defense minister had decided to call him urgently, because he felt that someone would eventually have to make some important decisions that night.

When he sat down, the prime minister was instantly immersed in a troubled environment. The wall screen displayed the failing status of the firewall systems. The virus had no trouble overcoming the second layer of protection at the offices of Mossad, and there was no way to stop it. The network was flooded with traffic, servers were resetting one after another, and the routers had overheated and stopped working. Apparently the payload of the malware started to work. Energy production at the Hadera Central plant began to decline, and the same was true in Haifa and Tel Aviv. The chief of the Central plant said that in 10 minutes they would have to connect generators to stabilize the power supply.

The prime minister asked what the choices were. He didn't like the answers he received from the defense minister. Then, in a sudden rage, he shouted, "How can it be that in 2011 we are so exposed? A country like Israel!". This phrase sounded familiar to the defense minister.

Nobody said anything and the room fell silent. They'd heard a very similar complaint quite recently.

The Mossad chief tried to calm things down. He got up and said, "We're disconnecting all the cables for the internal networks and hoping that no files escape from the country."

Just then, he received an urgent call and left the conference room to take it.

"We have Ahmed with us! We have the terrorist!" he announced when he rejoined the group, telephone still in his hand.

"That's the best news I've heard in a long time!" the prime minister said. "Where is he now?"

"On the way to the Central Police Station in Tel Aviv."

Then, speaking into the phone, the Mossad chief said, "Shaul, we need him to clear the virus."

"For now, he isn't talking," Shaul said.

"Look, Shaul, he has to talk. We need the key to deactivate the virus. He is the only one who can help us. I leave it in your hands. Call me when you get to the station. We have less than half an hour."

Shaul said nothing and hung up. His mind had begun focusing on the strategy to speak to Ahmed, to get him to give them the key. Time was playing against them. They had less than half an hour before complete disaster. It seemed like an impossible mission.

In his experience, he could guess how the young man would behave: he'd be silent and try to extend the time as long as possible. If only he knew Ahmed's sensitive side, something that he could use to touch his heart, maybe they'd have a chance. He put the siren on his private car and drove at top speed towards the Central Police Station.

On the way, he thought of Eli Regev's story. Ahmed was one of the babies who had been switched at birth. Perhaps Eli Regev had an idea how to convince the young man.

92

LEONEL
Mossad offices - Herzliya - Hadera Central Energy
November 5th, 2011 - 11:39 p.m.

At 11:39 p.m. we were sitting in the video-conferencing room when we were joined by an expert cryptographer from Mossad, an authority on secret keys who belonged to our group, and Hanna, who specialized in monitoring systems. The same technicians were incorporated into the Hadera Power Plant. All infrastructure-related equipment was checked thoroughly along with the data backups stored on site and in other locations. All copies were in order and protected elsewhere more than 50 kilometers away. There was routine in place to take the backups to a distant facility every day. Yet the main fear was not losing the data, as there were copies, but instead that data could be downloaded and fall into enemy hands.

The main concern was that nobody had an accurate idea of what payload the virus had. The market was full of malwares and different viruses whose main objective was to steal identities and credit cards, do fraudulent banking, or just show up and create panic. But in this case, all we had seen was an infinite amount of DDoS traffic destined to tear down everything that was in its way and whose special mission was to destroy the compute defenses. We didn't know what else was to come.

The first impact occurred when, at about 11:42 p.m., gas turbines at Hadera, which were used to generate electricity, began to diminish significantly in speed and production. When industrial systems technicians began investigating the reason, they found that control systems were sending erroneous commands. In some cases, the turbine rotors had begun to spin faster with much higher RPMs (revolutions per minute) than normal, and in others, the temperature had changed to abnormal levels. Added to that, some valves began to function erratically, opening and closing at the wrong times. Together, these changes caused the turbines to burn out and to cease functioning totally. In other cases, the destructive process was somewhat slower.

The Hadera plant had six giant turbines, two of which were no longer working and, indeed, were in flames. Firefighters were on their way. In Tel Aviv, blackouts began when one of the turbines of Central Reading site went offline and the outage also affected the Hasharon area and the area of East Jerusalem. The South remained "lights on" because only a single turbine had suffered damage at the Hasharon Plant. Power outages were intermittent and expanded to areas of Eilat, the Galilee, and the Golan.

Once Haifa in the north joined the wave of blackouts after two turbines went offline and another caught fire, the cabinet made the decision to operate emergency generators that would provide constant electricity for the next half hour. It was 11:44 p.m., and an energy expert said that the emergency generators along with the turbines that still worked, could sustain the electricity supply until 12:24 a.m. Then the whole country would be dark and exposed. The tension grew. The final decision was that of the prime minister.

Hanna began to show me on her screen that the virus was already breaking down the third layer of the firewall without slowing down at all. The antivirus system and the traffic protective platform were having no effect. Her face had lost the glow that I had seen just a few hours ago; she was anxious and very upset.

The cryptographers gave the opinion that the program was full of private keys and that the secrets could be found in the program itself. They were clearly amazed with the program's structure and quality. Ruben, on his own, began trying to decipher the activation code, but it was impossible, and after much calculating and comparison with probability algorithms the system pushed out an answer which wasn't what we had wanted.

"There are more than 60 million possible variations in this code," Ruben said.

The defense minister instructed the IDF general in 20 minutes to give the order to put into action two squadrons, 30 aircraft in all, to patrol the country's airspace. He also ordered that helicopters be ready to light up the northern skies with flares.

There was a deep concern about what could happen in that area, with the tension caused by Hezbollah and Iran. There was no time now to find out who the instigator of the attack was, but everything pointed to Iran being involved.

The prime minister left the room for a moment to consult via the red phone with his counterpart in the United States, and this made NSA experts available to Israel, now working directly, not just for consultation.

At 11:47 p.m., a copy of the malware was sent to IT departments at the NSA in Texas. The prime minister returned to the meeting and announced that at 12:07 a.m. they would issue a special bulletin to the public to be broadcast nationally by all media.

Suddenly, Hanna called my attention to her computer screen.

"Look, it's beginning to take over the fourth layer of the firewall," she said. "There are only two left and then the central computer will be at the mercy of anyone."

Ruben was infatuated with the key, and had lowered the odds to 53 million, while the cryptographers were still trying to figure out how this virtual monster was armed and were increasingly more amazed with the perfection of algorithms and commands they were discovering.

It was hard for me to believe what I was living through. On all sides I could feel fear and helplessness. Incredibly, in 24 hours, I had passed from one ordeal to another.

93

Tel Aviv - Central Police Station
November 5th, 2011 - 11:49 p.m.

It was strange to see two policemen of relatively short stature bringing in Dr. David Levi, who stood a full two meters tall. They led him directly to the second floor of the Central Police Department in Tel Aviv. It was 11:49 p.m. when he poked his white hair into Ronen's office. At the moment he was going in, he passed Jalfón coming out of the interrogation room with a winning smile. The accomplices glanced at each other and Jalfón said, "I warned you that it was too much."

A policeman grabbed the mobster and said, "Let's go!"

The doctor said nothing and chewed on his anger. Jalfón had betrayed him and probably would have gotten a good deal, he thought. He knew from the beginning that he couldn't trust the likes of Jalfón.

Ronen knew that time was not in their favor and had contacted the on-call defense attorney 10 minutes before Levi's arrival, assuming the doctor would request one before confessing. Ronen was introduced to Levi and they moved into the interrogation room. Inside were the defense counsel, the presiding judge, the prosecutor, and Eli Regev.

David Levi sat next to his legal representative. When he saw Regev, he shuddered, because he was not aware that the assassination attempt had failed.

Everyone in the room identified themselves. When Eli's turn came, he said, "I am the one who you tried to kill a few hours ago."

The doctor, who knew him from his picture, looked defeated and remained silent. He lowered his head and nodded. He rested his hands on the table. He felt so weak, so exhausted.

"Doctor, can you tell us why you killed or tried to kill all these people?" Ronen asked, showing him a document containing the list of all the attacks in recent months.

The defense attorney whispered in his ear and Levi nodded quickly. Then he stood up and said, "I want to talk to the judge and the prosecutor alone."

Grouchy, Ronen and Eli Regev stood up and left the room.

"This is a night of business," Ronen whispered.

"What do you mean?" Eli asked, although he well knew the answer.

"That doctor will only speak if his conditions are accepted, as happened with Jalfón and with so many other murderers."

"I get it," Regev said. "And I think he's obviously going to give up, but with everything he's done ..."

"Look, we're here to enforce the law, but more than anything to resolve and close cases. There are facts that he is charged with, but if he remains silent it won't benefit anybody."

"I think this man is keeping a big secret," Eli said.

"I hope you are right and soon we can clarify this mess once and for all."

Just then, Shaul came hastily down the hall. When he saw Ronen, he asked, "Where is he?"

"The doctor is here, negotiating his statement."

"No, Ahmed! Where is Ahmed?"

"He isn't here. Has he been found?"

"Yes, it's urgent! Call patrol 323 and ask where they are ... we need him now!"

Ronen connected to the patrol by radio.

"In three minutes they'll be here," he said.

While they waited, Shaul chose to speak to Eli and Ronen at the same time.

"Listen to me well," he said. "In a moment the terrorist will arrive. An hour ago he triggered a virus that is affecting power plants across the country and the computers of the Mossad. In less than half an hour, the entire country will be plunged into darkness and the most secret state data will be exposed to everyone. The only one who can stop this is Ahmed! He activated it and he has the code to disable it. Obviously, with him there will be no business to do, we have to force him to talk. There's no time to torture him or anything like that. We need to find his sensitive side, something that moves his heart, his feelings. I was thinking that maybe we could use the story of the swapped children to move him. We know that Ahmed is one of them and the other is Leonel, who is in the Mossad offices right now fighting the virus. What do you think?"

For Regev, it was like playing head games, because now the nation needed him.

"Look, I still think the key is Dr. David Levi," he said. "I'm sure he knows things that can help untangle everything."

"Like what?" Shaul asked.

"If he was responsible for switching these children and then began a string of attacks, he must have some reason. If he did it because he went mad, surely there is something that sparked such madness. Think for a moment about Ahmed's family."

At 11:51 p.m. the young judge left with the prosecutor and the two had a smile on their faces. Shaul pounced on them.

"Yes? Is he going to talk?"

"What does it look like to you?" the prosecutor asked, sarcastically.

"Look, I have no time for bullshit!"

"Yes, he will confess," interjected the judge.

Shaul turned to Eli Regev.

"You will be in charge of interrogating him. Don't waste time; go straight to the point. We only have until 12:05 a.m. to act."

"Don't worry, they're here with Ahmed," Ronen said as he got off his phone.

Indeed, as he spoke Patrol 323 geared down, climbed the sidewalk, and stopped at the gates of the police station. Two officers got out of the car holding Ahmed handcuffed between them. They went directly to the second floor. Shaul saw him and asked for a room on the third floor to separate him from the other terrorist, Dr. Levi.

"What was the deal you gave the doctor?" Eli asked the judge.

The judge, who wanted to get it over with, looked at his watch and said, "It was not difficult. He wants to clear his name and clarify the story. He prefers not to go to trial and, instead, to be sentenced and treated with dignity. The defense attorney was impressed, as he had been prepared to take advantage of a better deal, but the doctor is sorry and wants to end it all. His name is very important to him. One of his conditions is that the media not be involved. He further requested consideration when the verdict is read."

"How much prison time did you give him?"

"I promised that he would not receive a life sentence, and that, with good behavior, he could be free after serving between 12 and 15 years."

"There is something fishy here," Eli thought. "How is it possible that a man who murdered so many people gets so little time in prison?"

At 11:52 p.m., the prosecutor, the judge, and Eli Regev returned to the room to take Dr. David Levi's statement. Inside, the sound system was ready and everything had been prepared for recording. Eli looked around the very old, gray chamber and knew he was about to hear something that would change everything.

94

LEONEL
Mossad offices - Herzliya
November 5th, 2011 - 11:53 p.m.

I went out to get some air. The atmosphere of tension in the video-conferencing room was increasing the pressure. Inside that room I found it hard to concentrate as I tried to fully understand the impact that this virus was having. My colleagues were experiencing the same thing. It was one of those situations where impatient managers and bosses demand quick and efficient solutions without understanding anything about how to accomplish them.

When I returned to the room, I asked Tomer if Ruben, Daniel, and I could leave the video-conference to look more closely at how the beast worked. He gave the order, so we got together and left

All three of us were in agreement that the virus had been physically inserted via a USB memory stick, or key, which was not acting as it normally, would. In a regular case, it would create an "autorun.inf" file, but in this case, it had created three new, encrypted ".lnkl" files, and we had no idea what they were for. We also remembered that the private keys were in the same program, which was not linear, so the keys could be hidden in another command that could run another process.

This collection of files streamed via an operating system DLL and then attacked a vulnerability in one of the Windows drivers. Symantec's team was able to confirm that the virus operated via mouse drivers and this produced a "Zero Day," which sat in the computer memory. At the same time, after manual activation, the virus sent a systematic denial of service, not only to bring down the websites but to drown the net and everything that was in the way. Their actions resulted in an end to the protective layers of the internal firewall.

The three looked at each other and together they all realized the same thing at the same time — a similar occurrence had happened not so long ago. They simultaneously exclaimed, "Stuxnet." It had almost the same features, including these ".lnkl" files and the Stuxnet ".lnk." We had to study and review all the lines of code, but we were certain that there was a similarity, even though the current attack was unleashing a fierce DDoS onslaught, something which Stuxnet didn't have. Stuxnet affected only Siemens PLC systems and, although the virus was on other computers, it hadn't done anything.

Ofer in Hadera listened to our explanation and said he thought the same, but added that this mutation had two goals or payloads. One was to attack the Mossad central computer, a goal which would be fulfilled once it had gotten rid of the firewall system that protected it. Then it would be exposed and open to the world; the files would be completely exposed and anyone who wanted to download them could do so. Ofer also suspected that the program itself would try to download the secret information somehow. The second objective was power plants. The program attacked the Electra Inc. system which managed the TR11 and TR12 turbines in a way we had yet to decipher. The code increased and decreased rotational speed until the movements caused the system to self-destruct.

Something was clear to the group: the Iranians had learned a lot from Stuxnet, perhaps too much, and had hired — or coerced — the best professionals in the Middle East.

Hanna came out of the conference room. Her face was as white as milk. She looked at us and said, "The prime minister wants everyone inside. The virus is accelerating its attack. It has already destroyed four layers of the firewall and has begun to destroy the remaining two. It has also broken down 15 turbines across the country in the last seven minutes!"

With the entire team gathered again, the prime minister raised his voice and began:

"I want to use the option to disconnect the Mossad network," he said. "I do not understand computers, but we cannot allow all our classified information to be unprotected. There are reports and documents that are the foundation of this nation. I don't care how long it will take to put it back on line. The only thing I care about is keeping that data from the hands of our enemies. If they get hold of it, there could be a national disaster. When only one firewall layer is left, we need to disconnect."

I felt the prime minister was more concerned about data from the central computer than the lack of energy in the country. I got up and went to stand directly before the head of our government.

"I want to repeat," I said, "that in this situation the only thing that will help is to deactivate the virus,."

"I heard that the first time, Leonel," he addressed me curtly, using my first name, "but as a state we need other options. Yes, we've caught the terrorist now and are working to get the code. But it is my responsibility to protect the information that is housed in that computer. Everyone must be very clear. This is an order, not a request!"

95

THE CONFESSION
Central Police Station - Tel Aviv
November 5-6th, 2011 - 11:54 p.m.

Ronen took a jug of water with six glasses to the second-floor confe-rence room, where the walls were covered with vintage paintings, inclu-ding portraits of the founding father of Israel, Ben Gurion, Golda Meir, Shimon Peres, Yitzhak Rabin, and the current prime minister. The walls were painted, but the ceiling was peeling a little more each day and had lost its freshness.

It was 11:54 p.m. when Dr. David Levi took a sip of water and said he was ready. Ronen checked recording system. "Ready!" he said.

The prosecutor began the interrogation.

"Name?"

"David Levi."

"Birthdate?"

"5 January 1945."

"Profession?"

"Medical Obstetrician."

"Current address?"

"189 Arlozorov Kfar Saba."

"And between 1978 and 1984?"

"Armon Trumpeldor -76 Anatzib Jerusalem."

"Work and address working between '78-'84?"

"Obstetrician, Sharei Tzedek Hospital in Jerusalem, zip code 878923."

Shaul entered the room with a chair and sat to one side. The prosecutor went on with the questions.

"What is your license number, doctor?"

"One moment, I have it here, it should be this … it's here: 35M98B2333."

Shaul began to lose patience quickly.

"Eli, can you start with your questions? We aren't fortunate enough to have time for the preliminaries," he said.

Eli took over.

"Doctor, can you tell me what happened on October 22, 1982? Start at the time you were in the hospital delivery room, at about 10 a.m.," he said.

Levi took another sip of water, cleared his throat, and began his story.

"Around 10 a.m. I think, the nurse, Rachel Mizrachi, entered the room where I was waiting. She was agitated, because I remember that day we were short-handed and the delivery room was filled with women in labor. Rachel told me I was urgently needed because the obstetrician on duty had to attend a cesarean section in the operating theater. When I entered the delivery room, I observed there were three women with full dilation. Almost simultaneously, two women began giving birth, a Muslim and a Jewish woman. He could see the heads of those two children peeking at the same time. I put on gloves and began to help the Muslim, who seemed to be having a little more difficulty; I asked Rachel to take care of the Jewish birth. In short, the two gave birth at exactly the same instant, something completely unusual."

He stopped, finished his glass of water, and put his hands on his forehead. He could hardly continue.

"What happened then, Dr. Levi?" Eli insisted.

"As I said, the women gave birth at the same time. I knew that whatever happened outside the delivery room would be monitored first by Tal Elad, the pediatrics doctor's assistant with whom I had previously reached a monetary agreement. From the beginning, the young man was fearful, but lacking money. I remember having taken the Muslim and Rachel did the same with the Jew. Rachel was the one who usually took care to identify the babies with bracelets that bore their names, but given the state of emergency and haste, she did not, partly because the third woman immediately began to give birth — so fast I told her to attend her and I called the pediatrician room. The room where he was working was a few meters away, but that doctor was busy, so we left the two babies in cribs. Just then I saw the haunted eyes of Tal Elad already coming into the room, and I realized that my life would not be the same once the deed was consummated that I myself had planned. I turned quickly and, while attending the third woman in labor, I could see Elad taking away the babies. Rachel did not even notice. Poor wretch, from the beginning I realized that she felt terribly guilty. But no. Even if she had done her job and marked the names, everything would have happened anyway, because I had so decided. I was changed; yes, I definitely was. Tal Elad only met my orders and wrote the wrong names on the identity bracelets as he took the babies to the pediatrician. And that was it. Then I continued to work normally."

"But, why, doctor? Why would anyone decide to change the lives of two human beings, two families, two worlds? Did you not fear that someone was watching?"

The doctor asked for more water with a gesture, raising his glass. He moved in his chair like a caged cat. The water gave him a few seconds to think and recover, while in the room nobody took their eyes off him.

"In late November 1981, Ana Cohen came into my office in the Sharei Tzedek Hospital in Jerusalem for a routine check. I cannot explain it — there was an instant attraction and something started between us. With my help, she got a job as a volunteer nurse at the same hospital, while her husband, an Argentine immigrant who had come with her to this country, was employed at a hotel.

"By January, things began to change. We saw each other every day. I fell in love with this woman. We had a very intense romance that lasted four months. In March, she told me she was pregnant. She was sure that the child was mine. I suspected it, but arranged to confirm it by a special DNA analysis, for which I had to send samples to the United States, because, although here they recently had begun to do the tests, they were not reliable. In late May, I received the test result: the child was mine. I gave Ana this news and asked her to have an abortion, because I was married and held a very good position in the hospital. I did not want to ruin my marriage or my name. She refused. She wanted that baby and decided that she would raise it with her husband. That prompted frequent and strong fights and arguments, so that a month before delivery, she announced to me that our relationship was over. I could not be satisfied with the fact that the child would grow up without his real father, but also feared for what they would say about me in the hospital and my wife's reaction if they found out.

"In those days, I began to suffer bouts of anger and panic. I know what happened the day of deliveries was crazy; I know it well. But I was out of my mind with worry. A few weeks before the date I had estimated for the birth, I put together the plan. As I said, I offered a sum of money to the assistant pediatrician to make the switch. Although not very confident that it would work, I knew that the young man badly needed money. I also took advantage of the fact that the pediatrician, Rafi Segal, was a rookie in the hospital, and on a day of arduous tasks would not notice the change.

"When I saw the child born, the husband of Ana, and such joy on their faces, I could not think; I was disturbed, paranoid, and went ahead with the plan. I gave the child to a Muslim so that it was as far from me as possible. After that, I became almost crazy. I was admitted to a psychiatric clinic and managed to rehabilitate myself, but I could never forget that day. It was embedded in my mind, in my bones. Every morning, I woke up seeing the image of that day."

"Why give orders to kill so many people?" Eli asked, bringing the probe full circle.

"Many years passed and I always knew that the only one who saw everything that happened was Rachel Mizrachi. I also knew that Tal Elad had been killed in the war in Lebanon. I always kept abreast of what the nurse did and, when she retired, hired a private investigator to keep tabs on her. His research showed that Rachel had met with one of the switched babies, now an adult, and offered him a large sum of money to find the other, Ahmed. In the opinion of the investigator, she had revealed to Leonel the entire episode. Leonel, the Muslim woman's child, also began to be a danger in my life, so I tried to remove him at his home in Tel Aviv. The investigator recommended Jalfón's services to me, and thereafter, he was in charge of erasing from my life people that investigations showed were dangerous to me. It was as if a demon had possessed me. It had sprung a circle that never closed. So it was that I had Rachel Mizrachi and Moshe Cohen killed.

"Later, things started to get complicated. The journalists appeared on the scene, and you also started investigating me. All this was starting to cost me too much money. I got into debt and ruined my life completely. My wife never knew anything. She wanted children and could not have any. Also, I was always faithful and, to this day, she is still with me."

Eli was stunned after hearing this testimony. The story had been completed and had filled most of the empty holes. However, when mentally reviewing his list of questions, he found that it lacked some important details.

"Why kill Shmulik Sade, professor at the Weitzmann Institute?" he asked.

"I never heard that name. I do not know who you're talking about."

"So ... who killed him?"

"I do not know. I told you I never heard that name."

"And police officer Yosi. You never heard of him?"

"No, I do not know who that is."

Shaul impatiently interrupted the conversation.

"Do you have anything else to declare?"

"No, that's all."

"Do you know how we can find these two women, both mothers?"

"I have no idea. Since that day, I have had no contact with either."

One of the police detectives got out of the third floor elevator, entered the room, and asked to speak with Shaul. He said it was urgent. Eli, invited by Shaul, accompanied them into the hallway.

"Ahmed will not talk to the constable," the detective said. "Except for violence, we tried all our methods. He's locked in his own mental world, absent. He seems to have prepared well to face this situation."

It was 11:59 p.m. In a few minutes, Shaul should give the head of Mossad the results of the investigation. Shaul shut himself in Ronen's office with the detective and Eli.

"I figure there is only one way out," Shaul said.

"What?" Eli asked.

"We must bring the two mothers here. Children always listen to their mothers in extreme situations. We will tell the truth. We have nothing to lose. It may be our only chance."

"But ... is there time for that?"

"We're going to have to do this no matter what time is left." Turning to the detective, he said, "Find out now where these women live. I hope the Muslim is still alive in the occupied territories and has not migrated elsewhere. Get going! We have to take advantage of every minute!"

The detective rushed to comply.

As Shaul sat in the swivel chair, he glanced at the picture of Ben Gurion, then gazed out the window.

"Which of the two mothers do you think will help us?" Eli asked.

"The best question of the night. If I were Ahmed, I'd talk with the person with whom I grew up. The other he does not know."

"Then is it worthwhile to bring the two? It may not be useful to disclose the secret."

"We must end all these intrigues," Shaul said.

Within five minutes, the detective returned with the information. He had found the locations of both women and determined that both were now in their homes. The problem was that the Muslim lived in Bethlehem, a territory that Israel did not control.

Shaul immediately communicated with the head of Mossad and told him the news. After a consultation with the IDF first general, it was decided to send a command helicopter to fetch the Muslim mother. The clock read 12:03 a.m. and there could be no margin for error.

At 12:06 a.m., Ana Cohen was already in a police patrol car on the road to Tel Aviv Central Station. When they told her it was a matter related to her son, Leonel, she did not hesitate a moment and got into the car.

At 12:11 a.m., a Tornado helicopter landed in a vacant lot on a closed street 200 meters from the house of the Asad family. A brigade headed for house number 30. The darkness was absolute, and though the agents had infrared lights, it was very difficult to clearly see the numbers. The houses were low and were grouped one after another. The commander had a special satellite navigator by which he managed to locate the place. It was decided to enter by force, because otherwise it would take longer and the operation would be at risk.

They found Fatima Asad in bed. There was no man in the house. The voice of a young person screaming was heard, but the troops swiftly captured Ahmed's mother and quickly left the room. At 12:16 a.m., the brigade took off for Tel Aviv, amid a firefight started by some neighbors.

A bullet hit the helicopter, but did not cause it to malfunction.

96

LEONEL
Mossad Offices – Herzliya
November 6th, 2011 – 12:15 a.m.

At 12:15 a.m., the virus had crushed the final firewall layer. Hanna's hand shook as she showed me the screen. Ruben had dismissed the idea of cracking the code after reducing the total number of chances to 45 million. He was using a special program he had created himself. According to my estimates, based on the threat security monitor (SIEM), the virus would take between six and eight minutes to get to the central computer. Yoel, Mossad's security chief, approached our node and motioned for the three of us to follow him.

"Come with me," he said.

"Where to?" Daniel and I asked in chorus.

"We have to prepare to disconnect the machine."

"Are you sure we're going to do it?"

"Didn't you hear anything the prime minister said? His orders were clear."

Yoel was a very serious person who had grown up with the organization. He treated each object in the place where he worked as if it were his personal property, characteristic of many who had started their careers in the Mossad and had always worked there.

We were directly in front of the big computer, which until then had only been visible through a large window. Yoel put his hand on a magnetic platform, then put his retina to an infrared lens, and finally typed a password. The heavy door that separated us from the great beast slowly opened. When we entered, a cold wave slammed into my body. The cooling system maintained a constant temperature of 12 degrees Celsius. Yoel offered us special jackets to enter the place.

The dome that housed the central computer was lit up. It was an impressive spectacle that resembled a scene from a movie of distant galaxies and spacecraft. The surface was so clearly mirrored that we could see our faces in it. I still didn't quite understand where the access was. From a hidden panel next to the door, Yoel grabbed what appeared to be a giant suction cup and used it to pull up a huge floor tile, around a meter square. He then put a key into a hole in the floor and turned it twice. The lock creaked and gave way to a staircase of five steps. We quickly descended to the underground floor. The landing was occupied by racks of connecting fiber-optic cables, and in the middle was a rack packed with computer equipment. I figured it measured about two meters high and one meter wide. A panel of lights that continually changed color from green to yellow to red was installed above the rack. The space was completely closed off by a white wall with a door in the middle. On the door was a gigantic butterfly lock, far too big for our hands to manipulate. The cold was more intense down there. Mobile phones were blocked in that area, so Yoel carried a radio to connect with our colleagues on the surface.

To our surprise, Yoel opened yet another hidden panel and, from within, extracted what appeared to be an enormous oven mitt, which he used to twist the butterfly clamp two, three, and then five times from left to right. I lost track of how many twists he made. When the door finally opened, we were stunned. I looked at Ruben and Daniel. Their astonishment was identical to mine. I had never seen so much equipment working simultaneously. Now that the metal door had been opened, the noise was deafening. It was amazing how the compartment's exterior could muffle all that din. We covered our ears while Yoel showed us the central computer. He explained that the compartment was opened only once a month for maintenance, and clarified that only three people had access to it.

"I think this is a mistake; we shouldn't do it," he said.

I realized that I, too, had developed feelings for this machine.

"I think the same thing," I said to console him, "but there is no choice."

"It will take us more than a week to revive it, to reconnect the whole system, and even then, we'll have to pray that everything will work properly."

The radio blasted and Yoel pounced on it. While listening to the message, his expression changed — his brow furrowed and frown lines marked his face.

"Three minutes to turn off the central computer!" he said. He set the radio aside as all our eyes focused on the fateful switch.

97

HaKirya - Tel Aviv
November 6th, 2011 - 12:20 a.m.

Having decided to disconnect the Mossad main computer without consulting anyone, the prime minister now took the reins to involve Israel's allies. He called the president of the United States, as he still lacked an alternative plan to solve the energy problem. After much consultation and discussion, a solution was found for the dilemma.

The governments of Greece and Germany offered electrical generators, which unfortunately had different systems to those used in Israel. The hookups would be made with the help of a specialized technical team that would come from outside the country. The process would take about three hours. It was decided to accept Greece's proposal because they were capable of executing the equipment transfer in much less time. The United States would provide two Hercules aircraft for the move, and would ensure an aircraft carrier was located just off the coast in the Mediterranean. The independent generators would arrive in Israel in about two hours. One would be installed in Central Haifa in the north and the other in Ashkelon in the south. They analyzed how soon the entire operation could be executed, and estimated about six hours after leaving the port of Piraeus.

Two Hercules took off from a base in the Negev, where they had located seven huge spotlights with their own generators, which would be strategically installed. One would be placed in the Golan; another on the border with Syria; two on the Galil, on the border with Lebanon; one where Allenby gate linked with Jordan; one facing the Gaza Strip, and the final one in West Jerusalem, near the Wailing Wall.

NSA's Department of Informatics reported a new problem they had found indicating that the virus was programmed to do more than just initiate a "Zero Day" attack. The experts had concluded that the virus injected into the offices of the Mossad and the Electric Center were the same, but attacked in different ways, depending on the characteristics of the systems. In short, they needed more time to find an antidote for this malware, and even more to unravel it completely. They explained that understanding Stuxnet had taken the team more than three months.

It was 12:20 a.m. when the prime minister met with reporters and got ready to make an announcement on national television. Before beginning, he told those present that his speech would be short and that there wouldn't be time for questions afterward.

Then he lowered the microphone and began speaking to the nation:

I want to address the people of Israel in these difficult hours. My intention is to inform you that we have been victims of a cyberattack affecting the supply of energy and other secondary systems. Our best people are working to counter this onslaught. Fortunately, we have the help of both the United States and Greece, which have provided generators and lighting to help alleviate the problem. I want to publicly thank all the nations that offered assistance, including Germany.

I have great confidence in our experts and I hope everything is resolved in the coming hours. We do not yet have precise information on how this attack was perpetrated, but we know that the Iranians are involved. I want to make it very clear that anyone who tries to invade our nation and violate our autonomy will pay dearly.

Thank you.

The journalists responded like hyenas pouncing on prey, asking a thousand questions at once, thrusting out microphones, iPhones, and other recording devices, but the prime minister ignored them all and quickly withdrew from the enclosure.

98

AHMED
Central Police Station - Tel Aviv
November 6th, 2011 - 12:22 a.m.

As a pretty, red-haired nurse with beautiful curves cut my trousers leg to attend to my wound, two agents peppered me with questions. The Zionists were desperately demanding the deactivation password, which obviously meant that the program was causing havoc on the chosen targets. The room I was in was equipped with audio systems and cameras, as well as a bed, a table, and two chairs. At one point, they left me alone, although a policeman stood in the doorway, watching me. Then I was alone with the nurse, while the guard stood with one foot inside and one foot outside the room. My hands were still cuffed; this clearly wasn't the place for heroics.

The wound from the dog's bite, which I'd hardly felt, turned out to be significant. "This is going to hurt a little now," the nurse told me.

As she said that, she began to massage the wound area with a pink cream. Then she bandaged me, and afterward, pulled out a syringe and prepared an injection, extracting a clear liquid from a small bottle.

"Turn around and drop your pants, please."

"What are you going to do?" I asked.

"You must be vaccinated against rabies."

After the procedure, she asked me in a warm voice, "How do you feel?"

"Fine."

"Did it hurt?"

"What?" I asked.

"The injection I gave you. I tried to be gentle."

"I didn't even notice it," I said.

She smiled, took her bag, and as she headed to the door, she turned back and waved.

"Good luck!" she said.

"What is your name?" I countered. I really wanted to know.

"Aliza," she said, smiled again, and left the room.

Her presence had been like a wave of calm after so many days of agitation, fear, flight, and nerves. While I was with her, I got carried away by that image, as her brown eyes lingered on mine. I felt OK; I was well away from the nightmare I had been living in, and I even forgot I still had my hands restrained.

When the detectives returned, I flipped back to reality.

I had received a lot of training in Iran. I was trained to deal with situations like this. Silence was my only answer to all their questions. The first ones referred to my family, my contacts in Hamas, my travels in Iran, and my false identity. Afterward, they wanted to know all about the program, the virus, and its structure. One officer threatened that if I didn't speak, I'd spend my life behind bars, under the worst conditions imaginable. The other played the role of the good cop and told me that if I talked and helped with the password, I could be free very soon. My answer: silence accompanied by a gesture of denial by shaking my head.

Suddenly, the room dropped into darkness; the lights had dramatically gone out, leaving us almost completely in the dark except for an emergency globe in the ceiling. After a few seconds, the power came back up, but then fell again after only a minute. I looked at the clock on the wall. It was 12:22 a.m., so this meant the turbines and generators were beginning to fail.

I could hear the detectives speaking and then there was a knock on the door. When it opened, I just about fainted at what I saw. Had I not been sitting down, I probably would have collapsed to the floor. I could not believe what I was seeing. It had been a very long time since I had last cried, and now I couldn't hold back my tears.

99

At 12:17 a.m., the police car with Ana Cohen on board arrived. On the second floor, Eli Regev and Shaul were waiting. They had agreed to tell the truth to the two women and introduce them to Dr. David Levi, who was responsible for this atrocity. They hoped to convince the Muslim to help save her son. They would offer to forgive Ahmed's offenses and keep him out of prison, with a new identity and continuous protection.

Ronen called a translator to communicate with the Muslim. To save time, they invited Ana to enter the room where Dr. Levi was. Eli and Shaul accompanied her. The prosecutor and the judge were gone. When Ana and Levi's eyes connected, they both began shaking with emotion.

"What's going on?" Ana began to shout. "I was told that I would see Leonel!"

The doctor stood still as if frozen and couldn't open his mouth. Eli took the initiative.

"Yes, you will see Leonel in a little while. But we brought you here so you could know the truth about your son."

"I already know that that man there is the father, but I will never recognize him! His true father, the one who took care of Leonel since birth, is now in Bat Yam."

The doctor got up from the chair. His hands had been immobilized with handcuffs.

"Ana, listen, I do not consider myself the father of that child and I have no wish that you attempt to recognize me as such. The fact is that

I have committed a serious crime that involves you, and you and Leonel deserve to know the truth."

"What are you talking about?" Ana snapped.

"I ... I changed your son that day."

"How? What are you saying?"

"Yes ... I switched him with a baby from a Muslim woman. You raised the Muslim's child, not your own."

Ana went into shock, and she would have fallen had a police officer not been there to grab her.

"That is not true! It's not! It can't be true!" she repeated. "Liar! You were always a liar, and this is another of your lies! What do you mean by this?"

Eli stood back from the disraught mother and nodded.

"It's true, Ana," he said in a soft tone of voice, hoping to calm her down.

"Criminal! You're a criminal!" she began to scream, lunging against the doctor as Regev fought to restrain her.

"Criminal! You son of a bitch! How could you do that? You've ruined my life!" she cried as she tried to hold back her tears.

Shaul, Eli, and Ronen tried to stop her, but she was livid. She began shaking uncontrollably. Together, they pulled her out of the room. The on-site nurse, Aliza, attempted to soothe her and checked her blood pressure. Fearing a severe attack, she put a pill under Ana's tongue and injected her with a sedative.

At 12:20 a.m., the helicopter landed on the roof of the police department. Two officers stepped out and descended to the second floor with Fatima. Immediately, they led her to the room where Dr. Levi was being held. Eli also came in, along with Shaul, Ronen, and a translator.

Fatima was a typical big-hearted mother who had diligently raised five children almost totally alone. Her body had lost the form of youth and her face was lined with wrinkles, especially under her eyes. She wore her gray-streaked black hair under a gray scarf. Her whole life had been dedicated exclusively to raising their clan and managing the home. Her children were everything to her, and for most of her life, she had missed her son. Her husband had died seven years ago of a heart attack. He had spent his days working as a laborer in Israel for a contractor, and alternately migrated to Jordan when things got complicated between Israelis and Palestinians. Since her husband had passed away, she had been cooking for other people to survive, although periodically she also received some money from her sister living in Dubai. There were still three daughters living with her in the house. They were 16, 18, and 20 years old. Her eldest daughter, who was 32 years old, had married and was now living in Nablus.

When she entered the room, Fatima found it hard to recognize the doctor, but when she did, surprised, she went to him.

"What are you doing here?" she asked.

The doctor was nearly speechless. His gaunt face showed traces of the terrible day that he was living. He was touched, affected by what had come to pass. He wanted to finish everything once and for all, even his life, if it were possible.

"I'm here to tell you something," he said through the translator.

"What?" Fatima asked, becoming increasingly apprehensive.

"Your son, who you actually gave birth to, isn't the baby you raised. The baby you got was switched with yours just after they were born."

"What are you saying?" Fatima said, shaking her head in disbelief. "Where is my Ahmed?"

"When your baby was born, he was changed with a Jewish baby born at the same time as yours."

"What? But ... how is that possible?" she cried, and added something that the translator didn't care to repeat.

"It was my responsibility. I changed them. I was mad, crazy. I had fallen in love with the other mother — Ahmed is my biological son. Yours is now named Leonel Cohen, and was raised as a Jew."

"No, this is not possible! It's a lie! A dirty lie! A great lie by you Zionists!" Fatima shouted while the translator tried to calm her, but without success.

"Why has this been done to me? How were you able to ...?"

She was still screaming as she began to chase after Levi in an attempt to reach him with her hands. In plain view of everyone, she grabbed a stainless steel pen that was on the table, made a quick turn, and suddenly leaped forward, thrusting the pen with incredible force deep into Levi's larynx. Stunned and clutching at his throat, the doctor fell to his knees, choking and unable to get air into his lungs. When he fell over onto his back, Fatima jumped on his chest, stabbing him again and again in the side of his neck with the pen, puncturing the carotid artery in several places. Blood began to spurt everywhere. Ronen lunged forward and managed to pull her off Levi. He quickly bent to help the stricken doctor, but just as quickly realized there was little he could do. There were too many wounds — Levi was losing huge amounts of blood with every beat of his heart. Ronen shouted at the others to get help. Aliza came running into the room, yelping when she saw the bloody mess.

"What happened? Call a paramedic — now!" she shouted. She got down on her knees next to Levi, her pants immediately soaking up blood from the floor. She tore open a medi-kit and tried plugging the holes in his neck with gauze dressings, applying as much direct pressure as possible to slow the bleeding. It was largely ineffective. She saw that Levi was fading and shouted at him to stay awake. But he continued to choke for air and was losing far too much blood. There was little more she could do. The paramedics were on their way, but wouldn't arrive for at least a few minutes.

"He's lost too much blood! He's going into shock!" she shouted. She bent closer to check his breathing and started doing chest compressions and CPR, but it was to no avail. Finally, Eli grabbed her by the shoulders and lifted her to her feet.

"He's gone. You did all you could," he said. The paramedics soon arrived and could do nothing but confirm the doctor's death. Fatima, meanwhile, had withdrawn to a corner of the room. Her hands and clothing were covered in blood and she was clenching the pen in her fist as if it were a gun. Eli had to pry her fingers apart to get it away from her.

Shaul and Eli were paralyzed by the consequences of their plan, and Ronen was engrossed by what he had seen. There was blood spilled all over the room. Soon the medical examiner arrived to take the body.

Ana, who was in the corridor accompanied by a policeman, didn't understand anything.

"What happened? What happened?" she shouted.

The chaos was total. Nobody had expected an outcome like that.

Soon, though, Eli pulled himself together.

"What's next?" he asked Saul.

"We have no choice but to continue," Shaul said, looking at Ronen, who nodded in agreement

"Let's transfer the women to separate rooms while we clean up and get ourselves sorted out."

It was 12:24 a.m. when the lights suddenly flickered and went off, and the police station fell into emergency-lit shadow. Simultaneously, Shaul received a call from the head of Mossad.

"What's happening there? How are they? Anything new with Ahmed?"

"We're in the dark ..." began Shaul.

"Well, we're hitting the bottom of the barrel at this point. In two minutes the electricity supply will be briefly restored. At this point they're turning on the last row of generators. We'll have only about 10 more minutes of electricity. We need the key! There's no chance to stop this virus without that damned key password!"

"I'll call you in less than 10 minutes," Shaul said.

"Not 10 — we have exactly seven minutes!"

When the lighting came back on, Shaul didn't wait for even a second. He ordered the police to bring Fatima and Ana Cohen back to the interrogation room. The two women stood with three policemen, two very close to Fatima and one with Ana. Also present were the translator, Eli, and Ronen. Ana was still sedated and you could see it on her face. Fatima had also been injected with a tranquilizer. Her gray gown was completely covered in congealing blood. The two mothers looked numb.

Shaul stood between them.

"Listen! Both of you now know you've been the victims of a terrible crime. We know the baby switch happened — it has been proven beyond a doubt. I think that today, 29 years after this crime occurred, now that the boys have grown, there isn't much we can do. We can't change the past. But we believed that it was best that you and your children know this story. The only one who doesn't deserve any consideration, who is no longer among us, is the one who committed this crime, although his death was not the outcome we expected."

"What do you want from me now?" Fatima asked, addressing him through her translator. "You've already ruined my life ..."

"Fatima, listen; we have your son here. Ahmed is in this building."

"I want to see him!" Fatima's face brightened.

"And my Leonel? Where is my Leonel?" Ana raised her voice, trying to be heard, too.

Eli Regev soothed her.

"Leonel is fine, don't worry. We'll arrange a meeting for everyone to dispel all the deceptions and lies."

Shaul approached Fatima, who had the translator at her side.

"Your son, Ahmed, committed a terrible crime."

"No, this is not possible! My son is not a criminal!"

"Yes, Fatima, he did. And he could end his life behind bars. The only one who can help him is you. Plus, you just murdered a man. You could also go straight into a jail cell; you know that, right?"

As the translator spoke Shaul's words, Fatima's face changed colors like a chameleon. If she were in jail, how would their daughters cope, on their own? What would happen to them? Who would take care of them?

Shaul felt it was his time and he played his final card.

"But if you help us, we will give you immunity. Both of you will be free and you and your son will be protected forever by the State of Israel. Ah ... I almost forgot — and you will also be supported financially."

"What has my son done?" Fatima asked.

Shaul gave her a brief history and explained in simple words what had happened. When he finished speaking, and as the translator took over, he noticed that the clock showed 12:29 a.m. After hearing the story, Fatima opened her mouth and quickly covered it with her hand.

"We need the key to disable the attack, and we think you're the only person who can convince Ahmed to give it to us," Shaul said. "Explain to your child the consequences of refusal, and talk about your situation and what would happen to your family if you were imprisoned."

Shaul didn't want to waste any more precious time.

"Come on," Eli said. "Let's take the two women to the third floor." Turning to Fatima, he said, "When you see your child, you'll be able to fully understand all this."

As she entered the room where Ahmed was, it was 12:30 a.m. The second they saw each other, they ran forward and embraced, tears of joy and anguish streaming down their faces.

Given that image, Shaul immediately called the head of Mossad, who was with the cabinet in the Hakirya.

"I need Leonel Cohen on video conference in two or three minutes," he said. "Be prepared. I want him alone."

100

LEONEL
Mossad offices - Herzliya
November 6th, 2011 - 12:31 a.m.

Hanna's report indicated that the last firewall layer was still resisting, like a gladiator, and seemed to be offering more obstacles to the malware, but that it was gradually thinning. For us it was a surprise that the central computer was still protected. Yoel suggested we ask the leaders in HaKirya for an extension of time for the disconnection and nobody objected. The prime minister discussed the matter with the head of Mossad and allowed six minutes, which in the current situation seemed an eternity.

Yoel's radio sounded again, relaying the message that we were at 12:31 a.m. I was told that I was needed in the video-conferencing room immediately. One of the attendees came down to get me and led me to an empty room, in which a video-conferencing system had been hastily installed. He said that someone was going to establish a communication from a remote office. He didn't give me any more details and left me alone in the room.

Suddenly, the screen was filled with color and people. Shaul quickly identified himself and took the role of host. My mother appeared on the screen and, as soon as she saw me, she started to bawl. I didn't really understand what was happening. The camera rotated and stopped facing a young man who was handcuffed and was being guarded by a young policeman. I recognized him right away from the photos. I was looking at Ahmed, beside my mother. Shaul confirmed that reality by pronouncing his name. The camera then showed me an Arab woman, with a kind of blood-spattered nightgown, and Shaul introduced her as Fatima Asad. She also had her hands cuffed and was being watched by an agent.

At that moment all my suspicions were confirmed. I realized that for the first time, I was looking at my actual mother, an Arab woman, who was standing alongside the mother I knew and Ahmed. I understood immediately that we all had a lot in common. A great tightness in my chest, leaving me hardly able to breathe, finally made me realize that the circle had finally closed.

Shaul reassumed control of the conference and a man walked into the picture who introduced himself as Eli Regev, a sheliach[54] of the government.

"Twenty-nine years ago, something terrible happened," Eli said solemnly.

"Yes," said Shaul. "Everyone here, including you, Leonel, were involved unknowingly in the drama of a man who took advantage of his profession to put into reality his mad plan. That man was Dr. David Levi, the obstetrician who on October 22nd, 1982, helped two women — these two women — deliver their babies. This man, for reasons known only to him, switched the babies. We know this for a fact. Ahmed, you were actually born of a Jewish mother, and you, Leonel, a Muslim mother. I'm not here to solve anything that has to do with your personal lives or your families — surely you will sort that out on your own later. I'm here to tell you that this country desperately needs your help now!"

Shaul paused. Although I had considered the possibility since I'd met Rachel and had had some time to digest it, I was nevertheless paralyzed by the news. My ears simply weren't processing what they were hearing. My parents weren't really mine. My mother and the Muslim woman were dissolved in tears. Ahmed was staring into space, lost. Undoubtedly, this was causing internal ethnic turmoil at a critical time.

Shaul seized the moment and spoke again.

---

54 Sheliach: A very important person; a representative, messenger.

"Ahmed, your mother just killed Dr. David Levi in a rage upon hearing this secret from his own mouth. You well know that we need your help to clear the virus."

A deep silence fell over the meeting, only interrupted by the painful moaning of the mothers. I felt strange. I began to realize that I had lived my whole life wrapped under a blanket of lies. But I couldn't be angry with my mother — my mothers. They also had known nothing about this until now. Watching them cry, I couldn't help myself; a tear ran from my eye to my chin. Ahmed was locked in his own shell and refused to leave it. His mother was pushing him, trying to illicit a reaction. He shook his head from side to side, in denial.

Shaul, like an orchestra maestro, was playing with fire, juggling the right words to cause minimum damage and generate the maximum return.

"Ahmed, you and your mother could go to prison for life. You for your attempt against the state, her for the death of Dr. Levi. You can save her and save yourself. We will protect you both. But you have to answer now, before the program reaches its advanced stages. We'll disconnect the computers, replace the turbines and generate electricity in one way or another, but you and your mother will rot in a filthy prison."

I felt that Shaul had said it all. He had no more cartridges; he had used up all his ammunition and had run out of arguments. My mother looked at me and said, "We need to talk alone, son."

"Of course, relax, we will soon," I assured her.

Before leaving the place to Fatima and Ahmed, Shaul ordered me to go to the central room, where everyone was waiting, and then disconnected the video-conference call.

Shaul had given Fatima and Ahmed three minutes to talk alone. They also were left with an ultimatum: during that short time, they had to come up with a resolution.

101

AHMED
Central Police Station - Tel Aviv
November 6th, 2011 - 12:34 a.m.

The door closed. We were both handcuffed. How ironic to meet my mother in this situation, I thought. It hurt me to see my mom in that position where we couldn't even touch. I tried to repel Shaul's manipulation. Who knew if all that story was true or if he had invented it and that was the only way the Zionists had found to defeat me?

"Is it true that you killed that Dr. Levi?"

"Yes, son — yes, I did. When he told me the truth, I went into a rage. I couldn't think at all. I grabbed the closest thing to me, a metal pen, and stabbed him with it, over and over. I was so angry. I killed that son of a bitch. I don't know what came over me ... I've never felt like this in my life. I totally lost control. I killed him, yes. He didn't deserve to live."

"You know you're going to jail?"

"Yes."

"And who will take care of my sisters?"

My mom was speechless. She paused for a moment, composed herself, then asked, "Is it true what they say about this computer virus? Did you do that?"

"Yes, Mom, I'm responsible," I said.

"And so that's what you want? To end your days in prison?"

"I don't know what I want. I had a mission and I finished it."

"The mission to destroy your life!" My mom started wailing again. "I don't want that life for you. You must be free. The Zionists will protect you. Look at me, look at me — I'm your mother. Don't hesitate; it doesn't matter now what happened in the past. You've grown up and become a man with us. Don't hesitate. I don't mind going to prison if you decide to follow your ideals, but you well know that I never believed in terrorist organizations. They send others to sacrifice while they do nothing."

"I know that you are my only mother. Nothing has changed for me."

With that, Shaul entered the room and told us they had run out of time. They took my mother to another enclosure.

Strong emotions were coursing through my body and my nerves felt like they were all firing at once. I knew then and there that I was being offered a choice I had to take. I had to listen to my mother and do as she had asked. It was so simple, but so important — before me lay the tools to decide my fate.

Time was running out. According to my estimates, the country's electrical system was now probably working on generators, and possibly the Mossad's valuable data was already sitting at the mercy of anyone who wanted to violate it.

Shaul asked me for an answer now.

"I want to know the deactivation key."

"I'm going to give it to you, but I have my conditions."

"What are they?"

"First, my mother and I should be set free, and my family and I must receive protection and financial support. I want a new identity until I decide what to do."

Shaul looked at me nervously. I knew I was in a very good position to negotiate.

"Done," he said. "We'll connect you with Leonel so that you can turn off the programs. How long will it take?"

"It's immediate. I need an Internet connection and my computer."

It was 12:36 a.m. when, while standing beside me, Shaul called his boss to tell him the news. Suddenly there was another blackout, although the lights flickered back on. At 12:37, the power dropped off yet again, but this time it didn't come back on.

102

The video-conference room in Tel Aviv HaKirya looked like a battlefield. The wall screen showed the disastrous situation of the firewalls and other protection systems, and flashing numerals indicated that the power plants had had no protection for more than 13 minutes. Some turbines were completely damaged; some only rotated slightly. The virus had stalled 19 turbines across the country. The screen allowed us to see the disaster:

- Ashkelon Power Plant - 5 turbines out of operation and 1 decelerated, total production 6% - Time remaining on generators: 5 minutes.
- Coverage: South Zone Beersheva, Mishor Ahof, Ashkelon, Ashdod, Eilat, Yavne and Gaza Strip.
- Reading Power Station Tel Aviv - 4 turbines out of operation, total production 0% - Time remaining on generators: 4 minutes.
- Coverage: Gush Dan area, Rishon Letzion, Tel Aviv, Ramat Gan, Givataim, Bat Yam, Holon.
- Hadera Power Plant - 5 turbines out of operation and 1 decelerated, total production 6% - Time remaining on generators: 5 minutes.
- Coverage: Hadera, Netanya, Jerusalem, Jerusalem Zone, Central Zone, Kfar Saba, Raanana, Herzliya, Ramat Hasharon, Hod Hasharon, Samaria, Nablus and Mishor Ahof to Haifa.

- Ashkelon Power Plant – 5 turbines out of operation and 1 decelerated, total production 6% – Time remaining on generators: 5 minutes.
- Coverage: Zona Norte, Galil Elion, Galil Tachton, Haifa, Golan, Tiberias, Kriot, Carmel, Tzfat, West Bank, Jericho and much of the border with Jordan.

Tel Aviv was dark. In a few neighborhoods, electricity was still working, but services in most of city were no longer available. The same was happening in Jerusalem. HaKirya had been running on a generator for 25 minutes so far, and it had been estimated that it could run another 10 or 12 minutes, since it was serviced by a powerful and self-sufficient unit.

The prime minister came and went constantly listening to the reports. The defense minister discussed the state of negotiations with Ahmed with the head of Mossad. Finally, he received the good news that the terrorist would cooperate and, hopefully, the catastrophe would end soon.

The firewalls in the power plants finally crashed down around 12:16 a.m., since the payload of the virus was neutralizing turbine after turbine. The Mossad security system was somewhat stronger. Its last layer was still struggling to resist the attack, although according to the estimates by Yoel, it could only survive three to five minutes more.

The prime minister was informed that the first Hercules aircraft carrying the new turbines were already in the air and could land in the country in an hour.

At 12:38 a.m., there was a blackout in the north, and at 12:40 a.m. a shower of Katyusha rockets began to fall on the Galil north area. Never before had they seen so many rockets fired at the same time. Their origin was southern Lebanon, Syria, and Iran. The North seethed and the population was instructed to remain in shelters, which were dark.

Aircraft of the Israeli air force attacked Lebanon and lit up the sky of Beirut, while another squadron of planes flew over and attacked southern Syria.

The video-conferencing room was divided into two, and the War Cabinet began operations. The prime minister, defense minister, and chief of the IDF ordered tanks to approach the border with Lebanon and to be prepared to enter the south of that country.

The remaining leadership, consisting of the chiefs of the Mossad, Shabak, and their counterpart in Unit 8200, closely followed the impact of the virus and the progress made with Ahmed.

The prime minister decided to mobilize the populace, to activate the reservists. "The country is up in arms," he said.

103

LEONEL
Mossad offices – Herzliya
November 6th, 2011 - 12:40 a.m.

I was still very shocked and couldn't bear to see my mom crying. I felt so helpless. However, I became convinced that this pain we were living as a family would help us face the truth. In my head was the image of the Muslim woman who had dealt out justice with her own hands, for her son — for Ahmed.

When I returned to the video-conferencing room, there was complete pandemonium and people were moving from one place to another without any apparent purpose.

Shaul called and asked me to be ready in two minutes. That time was all that was left of the last firewall. The monitor clearly displayed the inevitable end, the tragic failure of it all.

"Ahmed has agreed to disable the malware and he needs a computer and an Internet connection," Shaul said. "He also needs to connect with the Mossad office system."

I warned him of the danger, because if we established the connection and Ahmed decided not to keep the agreement, he or his accomplices would be able to download the proprietary information, and that could have fatal consequences.

"Why are you so sure that he'll help defusing the virus?" I asked worriedly, as he ordered Yoel to focus on restoring the Internet connection in the private network.

"I don't think we have a choice. The country is entering war and is without electricity — didn't you hear what's happening up north?"

"No. What's going on?"

"We're bombarding targets from the north. It seems that the virus attackers had everything well planned. After the blackout, rockets began to fall like rain on all fronts."

"Since that's the case, I will take care of the connection right now. Give Ahmed back the computer we confiscated."

I thought about what I would do if I were in Ahmed's shoes. The man had a chance to be a hero or a villain, even if it meant that the latter option would find him spending his life in a cell and his mother suffering the same fate. Everything depended on the emotional "brainwashing" he had received. If I had a little humanity inside and cared about the future of my family and my own, I would deactivate the digital beast. But I was not Ahmed, so ... we would see.

"In a minute and a half we'll be ready," Yoel informed me. "We will prepare a chat connection and a direct link to the Central Police Station in Tel Aviv through a video conference, and you will see the console when he inserts his commands."

I spoke immediately with Shaul and I felt my hands shaking. He was in front of the computer. In another minute we would be observing either salvation or hell.

104

Mossad offices - Herzliya - Central Police Station Tel Aviv
November 6th, 2011 - 12:42 a.m.

Hanna announced that the firewall's last layer would cease to exist in about two minutes. The wall screen filled with white dots.

"I've never seen anything like it!" Hanna said. "According to page 213 in the firewall's manual, it says that this will happen when the network protection is about to be disconnected. It's a way to recognize impending doom!"

Yoel stayed with Leonel in the same room where they had had the video call just a few minutes before. He noted that the computer was already connected to the Internet, but had not yet been activated; they were waiting until the last minute to do so.

In the Central Police Station in Tel Aviv, a technical engineer established the direct Internet connection with the Mossad offices, and a policeman took off Ahmed's handcuffs. Shaul and a guard spoke with him. They connected his computer to the Internet and he began controlling it. After two minutes, everything was ready, and the technician said the connection was complete. Shaul asked him to be present to monitor the commands that Ahmed wrote.

The program would connect Leonel on the other side of the line, and the engineer showed him how to use it. The virus included a safety mechanism requiring the infected network connection to be disconnected. It was discussed whether Ahmed would be transported to the sites where the attacks had taken place, but this idea was quickly discarded, since to go from Tel Aviv to Herzliya would take 20 minutes and at least 15 to the others in Hadera.

In Herzliya, meanwhile, after receiving the signal from Tel Aviv, Yoel looked at Leonel and said, "Port enabled! Check your Internet."

Leonel replied:

"Internet activated."

"Connected to @PoliceTLV."

"Connected."

On Ahmed's screen appeared:

"Hey, there."

"Hello," typed Ahmed.

"Tell me what I have to do to disable the program."

"Check that you are connected to the private network."

Leonel executed a command / PING // Telnet and then answered:

"Verified."

"Telnet - Connect to ElHait !: @ # 84567."

"OK."

"User: Root"

"Password: @ElHait!#&?84567!J2W"

"Done."

Ahmed confirmed that Leonel was now inside the diabolical virus by saying, "Good, brother. Now you're in the program."

Hanna knocked on the door.

"There's almost no protection!" she announced. "The firewall is about to be detached."

Yoel calculated the time and monitored the Internet.

"They have already been connected for one minute. We have to finish this," he said.

"Pass me the deactivation command, brother," said Leonel.

Ahmed suddenly stopped. The engineer at his side looked at him and then turned his face desperately to Shaul.

Yoel, on the other side of the screen, yelled out that unknown traffic was trying to join the network, coming from an unknown source, and it was scanning all the local ports. Luckily, the security system was cha-llenging the requests, but only for another minute or so.

"Ahmed! Pass the command now!" Shaul ordered.

Ahmed closed his eyes and began to write in the messenger software. All eyes were on the screen as his fingers rapidly flew across the keyboard.

"Admin> Activate / d key code: RFR33D0M19NWAR48P3AC3"

"Are you sure? Activate?"

"Very sure."

Hanna and Yoel stood next to Leonel and watched the screen with a combination of hope and dread. Leonel's young hands trembled as he typed in what could be the last computer command of his life. When he finished, he pressed "enter" on the keyboard, closed his eyes, and then opened them again. The program wasn't showing the message that should be on the screen. They all spent 35 seemingly eternal seconds waiting with bated breath, when suddenly capital letters in bright red appeared:

```
PROGRAM DEACTIVATED
```

Hanna ran to the central video-conferencing room to see the results. Leonel was relieved but still didn't know with certainty whether the deactivation message was true. Yoel continued to control the Internet traffic on his laptop.

After a minute, Hanna returned, screaming happily, "The virus has been neutralized! The last layer firewall is recovering. DDoS traffic flow has stopped completely!"

Ahmed was still.

"What's happening there?" Shaul asked.

"The virus has stopped," Leonel replied, smiling.

"Brother," Ahmed said quietly, "do the same at the Hadera Power Plant."

"Brother, thank you!" exclaimed Leonel, who took a deep breath, sighed, and winked at Hanna.

Leonel contacted Ofer and together they defused the malware in the power plant systems.

At 12:52 a.m., the virus had been completely paralyzed. The turbines that had been restrained began to accelerate their operation, generating more and more electricity and, at the same time, the temporary generators were shutting down. At 1:02 a.m., every site was generating its own energy, and although some stations were producing less due to damaged equipment, they were creating enough electricity to keep the lights on in their regions. Three seconds later, a stable power supply returned to the entire country. In total, only four turbines had burned out and would need to be replaced.

The IDF tanks of Tzahal entered southern Lebanon at 1:22 a.m. and plowed through more than 200 terrorists, destroying their rockets and launchers all along the northern border. Meanwhile, the Air Force destroyed the terrorist bases in Quneitra, Syria. A massive bombardment of 25 minutes ripped through a system of rockets on the Jordan-Syria border.

At 2:30 a.m., the Americans, along with the Russians and Chinese, through diplomatic pressure, forced a ceasefire.

At 2:45 a.m., a Greek aircraft arrived with the promised turbines, now unneeded. The prime minister thanked his Greek counterpart and the Americans, and informed them that the cyberattack had been neutralized. At 2:50 a.m., he aborted the call-up of reservists.

Fifteen seconds later, he appeared in front of the press on national television to communicate again with the people of Israel. He publicly embraced the defense minister and began his speech:

We have lived through a very difficult day, but our people won, represented by our experts and our army. Unity and perseverance won the battle again. We will never let an enemy succeed.

The world must know that anyone who tries to undermine our state and our people will be severely punished. This is our duty and we will follow it again and again.

No technology or army in the world can make us betray our ideals.
Thank you.

105

Central Police Station - Tel Aviv
November 6th, 2011 - 2:45 a.m.

Shaul felt delirious with joy. His perseverance and his professional attitude had paid off. The Mossad chief called to congratulate him and schedule a meeting for noon the next day in his office. Very soon he realized that he had gotten what he always dreamed of. This operation would surely be worth a significant raise, probably a promotion. This time, no one was going to stop him.

Ahmed was taken by two policemen to a special cell, specifically for people of prominence, where he would spend the night. It wasn't the kind of place one would expect when thinking of a jail. He was promised that in the next day or so, he would be free. Before then, he would need to be interrogated and receive precise instructions on how to act in the future. He was also assigned a 24-hour protection force.

Fatima, his mother, was taken back to Bethlehem in one of the army's armored trucks.

Eli approached Shaul and patted him on the back.

"Good job, buddy," he said.

"Thanks. You helped me a lot. Thank you, too," Shaul replied.

"It's hard to believe what we experienced today."

"Yeah, that's true. It seems almost as if it was a dream — or a nightmare," Shaul agreed.

Eli also thanked Ronen for his contribution. Still, he wasn't entirely satisfied.

"I'm still worried, though, because I haven't been able to accomplish my mission," he said.

"What's bothering you?" Shaul asked.

"Shmulik Sade. I haven't yet closed the circle with him. When I interviewed him, he told me that he was constantly updating someone on the growth of the two children, but he wasn't sure who was receiving his reports. He even collected good amounts of cash every two weeks in his mailbox, in exchange for his absolute discretion on the subject, so someone was obviously following along. Who could have attacked him if not Dr. Levi?"

"As far as I know, we never discovered whether it was a crime or if someone accidentally ran over him and then fled."

"If it had been an accidental hit-run, it is rare they never found the driver. We have sufficient resources to do that. As you know full well, we have one of the best-equipped police forces in the world."

"I don't know what to tell you. Perhaps we can discuss this matter later and I can help if you want," Shaul said.

"Thank you for your offer. You know what? The death of the police officer, Yosi, was also very strange. His car crashed into an embankment when he was on his way to see me. No one, not even the police, talk about it."

"Well, get some sleep and think about all that tomorrow. Look at the hour!" Shaul exclaimed, anxiously showing his watch, which displayed 3:20 a.m. "Even the prime minister should be sleeping by now."

"OK, that's good advice. I'll call you tomorrow when I can think more clearly about all this stuff. See ya."

Eli left the room. Ronen followed and thanked him for his cooperation that night. Ronen had listened very carefully to the conversation Eli had just had with Shaul, and was also very worried. He asked about Shmulik Sade. He had heard about this guy a second time during the doctor's confession, when Eli asked David Levi about the professor. The first time had been when Eli had mentioned him in his home, just a few hours ago, while relating the sequence of murders, and now he wanted to understand what role the researcher had played. Ronen, too, was intrigued by this puzzle and also wanted to help solve it. Eli replied that he was too tired, but would call him to discuss the matter.

Two prostitutes and a drunkard were detained at the reception station. They were the same Eli had seen about seven hours earlier. He was exhausted, barely able to move. He walked down the street looking for a cab. As it was in Dizengoof 200, he knew he would find one quickly. At 3:24 a.m., a taxi approached and offered to take him.

He sat back, almost spilling himself on the seat and quickly fell asleep. The driver went straight through Dizengoof, heading north. He arrived at the Tel Baruch neighborhood, along the coast, turned onto a dark street, passed a roundabout packed with prostitutes, and went straight out to the sea on a dirt road. As the car bounced along the road, Eli woke up. When he looked out the window to see where he was, he realized something was wrong.

"Where are we?" he asked the driver.

"You're Eli Regev?" the driver responded.

"Yes. How did you know?"

Suddenly, in a lightning-quick move, the driver pulled out a .22-caliber Beretta pistol with a long silencer, whirled around, and fired two shots point blank into Eli's head. After stopping the car, he opened the door and dragged Eli up the dunes. He took a shovel from the trunk, dug a pit a meter-and-a-half deep, and threw the body into it. After filling in the hole, he hastily fled the scene.

106

LEONEL
Meeting - Ahmed & Leonel
Tel Aviv
January 10th, 2012

I chose my favorite restaurant, the same place where I often went with Jacob Lachman, in Iven Gabirol, Tel Aviv. The shwarma was spinning on its spit, wafting the aroma that always made me go back to that place. The kebabs were roasting on the fire and the hummus — ah, what a hummus! It was already on the table sprinkled with oil and paprika, waiting for the pita to be rolled up and turned into a great feast.

It's hard to believe that just two months before I was captive in Gaza, and one day after my release, I was dealing with both the biggest virus the country had ever seen and a vicious personal secret to boot. It was all pretty hard to digest. It's the kind of thing you expect to read about in a novel. Just like the weather, everything happened so quickly. Since those events, I had decided to leave the Faculty of Medicine to immerse myself fully in the world of computer security. In a year, I will earn my diploma. Following up on a great idea from Ofer, we got together with Ruben and Daniel to create a start-up company specializing in industrial system protection. The idea is still in development, seeking investors, and putting together programs and tools for the market.

That terrible day in Herzliya had ended almost perfectly — I say "almost," because after just 48 hours, Eli Regev's body was found on Tel Baruch beach, north of Tel Aviv. He had disappeared the same night of the attack, after we had disabled the virus. A couple of surfers had come across his hastily dug grave in the sand. Since then, I had thought a few times about it, but I decided to forget about it as much as possible for my own well-being. After all, he had to have known he was going up against forces he might not win against.

A few months ago, Jacob died of a massive heart attack just a few weeks after he found out about everything that had happened, including my betrayal of our trust and my plan to leave the university. He had become extremely depressed. He left me a very emotional letter asking forgiveness for what his son had done. What irony ... I had a great affection for Jacob, and I sensed after reading the letter that the feeling was mutual.

My mother also has had a very difficult time since the revelation of the secret. She had given birth to Ahmed and he was the son of Dr. David Levi. My father, as always, forgave her, and I did the same. There was no reason to look back. But she continues to suffer because of that; it is something that just must resolve itself over time; she needs to make peace with herself.

I was especially intrigued by my almost twin brother, Ahmed. I wanted to know what led him to commit such a crime, to get involved with terrorism, but what mostly interested me is how he was doing, what he felt that night, and why he gave us the key to deactivate the virus. I wanted to get to know the reason and the genius who helped to create the cyberattack program. I didn't know what to expect. Perhaps Ahmed had no intention of speaking with me or discussing his private matters. Perhaps he wouldn't feel comfortable. But I had a strong intuitive feeling that we could fit and share experiences. When I contacted him through Shaul and proposed that we meet, he accepted immediately. When I finally see him, I again refer to him as "brother," as it sounds just right.

AHMED

While traveling in the taxi en route to Tel Aviv, I opened the car window. I like to breathe the smells of the outdoors, even if it is winter. The freshness entered the pores of my skin. It felt good for my body. Still, I feel very detached after what happened only two months ago.

Since then, I have had to suffer through many interrogations and I've been in and out of the Mossad offices countless times. During these months, I have constantly been escorted by a security officer, sometimes two. I am relatively happy in Raanana, the city where I settled. I like the green areas, the parks, the squares, and there is a bit of everything for every interest.

I also have taken care to meet my mother a few times. For security reasons, we saw each other in my house, not in Bethlehem. Once she brought my sisters with her. We never spoke of that secret, that terrible night. I feel like there is no other mother for me. The one I have is the right one. I am proud of her — her courage and strength.

Through Mossad, I found a job at a security company, work that began just a week ago. My co-workers are very friendly, but we haven't yet established a close friendship or anything like that.

Everything seems fine with my life, but something is missing, and I can't quite explain what. I feel mostly free, but at the same time confused. The Mossad hired a psychologist for me and I've decided to give it time.

It is consistent with the crucial decision I made that critical day. If I had been alone, I would likely have reacted differently, but by imagining my mom behind bars, and my sisters abandoned forever, the world came crashing down and I did what I thought was best. I keep thinking it was for the good.

I don't know if I really ever had ideals; I think other people always decided for me. I haven't heard from anyone connected with my past, and I certainly haven't suffered any consequences from disabling the virus. I would assume my handlers from that event were more than angry with the outcome, but I have seen no sign of them. During these months, I have tried to erase that part of my life from my mind.

What shocked me the most was the revelation of the secret which had been under wraps for almost 30 years. Sometimes, when I let my mind wander, I think everything could have been so very different. But I always come back to earth with the realization that everything in our imagination is just speculation, imaginary ideas, and it is useless and too late to think about the past. But something in me wants to know more. Was only the doctor involved, or was there someone else, someone as yet unknown? When I heard about the fate of Eli Regev, I realized that my thoughts were distorted a bit, so I've started being more cautious about believing everything Mossad tells me.

As I watched through the window as we crossed the Hayarkon Bridge, I thought about Aliza, that sweet nurse who helped me at the police station. It seems like it was just days ago we had been navigating those rapids, laughing a lot. I remembered her warm hands and straight hair, so soft to the touch. Two weeks ago, I learned her phone number and we have started dating. Being with her is like a haven from such madness. Still I don't feel like I belong, and sometimes I miss my languish, my culture, my habits.

I like Tel Aviv, its streets, the places to eat, being able to live your life around the clock. As the taxi stopped and I saw Leonel seated at a table under the restaurant window facing the street, I experienced the feeling that we had known each other all our lives. His face is so familiar, and I want to know everything about him, his life, and what he thinks of the incidents that have marked us. For that I had accepted his proposal to meet. We have a lot in common, between what was the day of our birth and the events that unfolded following that date, October 22, 1982.

THE MEETING

Ahmed entered the restaurant and immediately felt at ease with the fragrance of the place. Leonel saw him and raised his hand to indicate where he was. When they got close and were preparing to greet, there were a few seconds of doubt that culminated in a long, emotional embrace that broke the ice between them. The two were hungry and ordered quickly. They ate with their hands, and Ahmed felt at home. Each time they stopped to put hummus in a pita, the two of them were grinning like two children. Then they started talking, and with a beer in hand, everything became warmer and pleasant.

"How are you feeling?" Leonel asked. "Are you going to be able to adapt?"

"I'm going step by step; I still need to learn some new habits, but I'm not in any rush and I'm going to take my time. You see that blue car parked out there in front?" Ahmed pointed with his hand to the street. "He's my companion."

"Great. Where else would you like me to take you, sir?" Leonel replied with a smile.

"No, not my driver; he follows me like a shadow, but we have no contact. Sometimes I think that their mission is more about spying on me than protecting me. It's not easy to live like this, with someone glued to your back."

"And where do you live?"

"In Raanana. It's very nice place. I love the outdoors; I'm not a city type. You won't find malls, galleries, and bustle on my agenda."

"How are things with your mother?" Leonel asked, wanting to know how she was coping after learning the story of their birth.

"We're fine," Ahmed said. "It would never have crossed my mind that she was not my biological mother. But I don't care that I was conceived in another belly. You understand me, right? And in your case? How did your family react?"

"I went through almost the same things you did. I was raised Jewish and still am. My mother suffers because she had to explain to my father how it was I wasn't his child. But he forgave her quickly, perhaps faster than she had expected. We've missed so many years!"

"And your plans? What do you do for a living?" Ahmed asked.

"I was studying medicine, but I decided to leave school and have started studying security systems. With some friends, we have the idea of starting a security company. If you want a job —" Leonel said and smiled. "By the way, that virus was a work of art. Two weeks ago I finalized understanding all the code, line by line — the commands, the programs, the encryption."

"Yes, I heard, and that it took two weeks to explain to the Mossad how the worm functioned."

"How was it created? What was the idea behind the malware? Can you talk about that?"

"I think I can tell you."

Ahmed took a sip of beer, looked into the street, and began to tell the story.

"The Iranians captured me in Pakistan and became my overseers. We — a friend of mine and I — were working on an interesting project. In Iran, we were taken directly to the Natanz Nuclear Base, where we stayed for a whole day. When we arrived, we didn't really understand why we were there. But I'll make a long story short: after Natanz, we spent a week studying Stuxnet, the virus that supposedly you and the Americans injected into the nuclear plants in Iran, which destroyed thousands of centrifuges. The Iranians wanted revenge, paying you back in the same currency. Before we arrived, they had compiled a group of cryptographers, programmers, and security experts from around the Middle East. They studied the virus very closely, took it apart, and spent months learning all about its structure. In an entire week, my boss and I weren't able to visualize the whole thing. The Iranians brought in two Russian engineers, experts in industrial automation, who devoted themselves to the PLC and SCADA systems which are used by the Israelis in their power plants.

"The virus was always one thing; there were never two varieties or mutations, as the Mossad experts thought. The program had a built-in command to detect if the local computers had PLC software. If such software was found, the payload was dropped in, a special program that caused the malfunction of the machines, itself hidden in one of the most important DLLs of the industrial software. When the Iranians found that DLL, they copied it and designed it to be able to change the speed and temperature of the turbines and the pressure of some of the valve systems. By having control over these mechanisms, they had everything they needed. By reducing and increasing the speed at a high frequency over a very short period of time, they could increase the temperature and cause the turbines to overheat and stop working."

Ahmed paused and took another sip of beer before continuing.

"Of course, before that, there was a phase called 'the worm,' in which the program inserted itself across several different objectives. The Iranians bought some 'Zero Day' programs from a European company. In the virus, there were three 'Zero Days,' which worked together to introduce the malware without problems. One attacked the mouse driver, another attacked a vulnerability in the USB port, and the last found a hole in the Internet browser.

"The systems were infected from the USB ports of two laptops that joined the local networks of both places, and the violation was not detected. The USB key didn't act like normal cases where an 'auto-run' would occur, but, instead, contained a '.lnk1' file, a large file that is shelled in a chain of DLLs that were part of the core program. All these files appeared encrypted, and private keys and codes were included in the program itself. When the virus attacked the 'Zero Day' vulnerabilities of the three 'holes,' the malware installed itself in the memory of that computer and from there sent an unusual DDoS attack that was intended to demolish the resistance of the firewall (any firewall), creating a huge traffic flow that not only collapsed the websites, but also sent millions of broadband requests that eventually brought about the disconnection of the private network. At the same time, it caused the firewalls to weaken, and the system became unable to address the high traffic flow.

"The Iranians knew there was not much chance that the virus would succeed in the Mossad offices, so they didn't bother to set a payload to fall there. They were concentrating on the electrical system, as they were planning a military attack on Israel when the country fell into darkness."

Ahmed finished his glass of beer and fixed his eyes on Leonel, who was fascinated with what he had just heard.

"And do you have any idea why they chose you to be the one to activate the program?" Leonel asked.

"I never found out," Ahmed said. "In fact, I was never in a position to ask questions. If you had doubts, the Iranians would liquidate you. My supervisor, who was my best friend, died at their hands. I always thought they picked us because we were Palestinians and they wouldn't want to be involved directly."

"It's amazing what you've lived through," Leonel said. "But tell me — how do you feel about this mission now?"

Ahmed paused before responding.

"I think I never understood the magnitude of this operation, and I never really became aware of what would happen to me personally. The Iranians never told me what would happen to me after the attack, nor did they show me how to escape from this country. In my situation, I couldn't say they weren't following me; I was being watched around the clock, just as I am here in Israel by the Mossad. The Iranians had an agent here who placed the virus on the computers. Now I realize that they left me alone, unprotected, and entirely on my own."

"Uffffffff! What stories of our lives, brother! Do you have plans? What will you do with your life now?"

"Well … as I told you, I started working, and I guess we'll see how it goes. I'll try to do a good job."

"That's the right attitude, brother."

It was time to pay the bill and go.

"Leave it and I'll pay this time," Leonel said.

"Thanks, brother!"

Leonel pulled out his wallet and handed his credit card to the waiter, then placed a check for 500,000 shekels on the table in front of Ahmed.

"What is this?" Ahmed asked, amazed by the amount.

"That's yours."

"What do you mean?"

"What I said. It's yours. It's a long story that maybe someday I'll tell you. But there is one condition. For the rest of your life, you need to remember one name: Rachel Mizrachi."

"No! I won't take it! Tell me now. Who is that woman?"

"Fine. She was one of the nurses who attended to our deliveries. She knew we had been switched, and she felt somehow at fault; but, though she tried, there was nothing she could do. She lived her entire life with great guilt and asked me to find you. In return, she offered me a million shekels. She never told me that I was one of those children, but I began to understand while researching more about you. And then she was murdered. I can't explain it all right now."

"I cannot accept this money. It's yours!" Ahmed cried.

"It's ours to share equally, brother. This is what she wanted, for us to get together."

They stared without speaking. Finally, Ahmed slowly picked up the check.

At just that moment, Hanna walked up to their table, smiled, and said, "Hello!"

Leonel quickly made the introductions. "Hanna, this is Ahmed. Ahmed, meet Hanna," he said.

"Nice to meet you," Ahmed said, extending his hand.

Hanna was surprised. She had been planning to meet Leonel there, but she hadn't expected Ahmed to be present as well.

"Brother, I have to thank you for introducing me to this beautiful flower," Leonel said. "Hanna works in the Mossad and was on the scene on that special night."

"Really!" Ahmed said, surprised. He paused, then asked, "What's your last name?"

"Benyoun — I'm Hanna Benyoun," she replied.

"Ahhhh!"

"What happened?" Leonel asked, amazed by Ahmed's reaction to her surname.

"Nothing," Ahmed said nervously, trying to deflect their interest.

"Come on, brother. Tell me what is," Leonel insisted.

"It was her computer that was infected with the virus."

"Noooo, really?" said Hanna. "How did it happen?"

"The truth is, I'm not exactly sure, because it wasn't me who did it, but I think it happened in a restaurant you go to often. Someone got access to your laptop somehow and inserted the virus."

"I can't believe it!" Hanna said. "I remember one day I met a friend for lunch, and probably I brought my laptop with me. I think it was the day before November 5th, because I remember on the day of the attack I had several problems when I connected to the network."

Everyone was silent as they left the restaurant and walked out into the street.

"Well, the issue is closed now," Leonel said, as he embraced Hanna, who appeared deeply troubled by the revelation. "Fortunately, everything worked out, thanks to Ahmed here. Don't feel bad, Hanna. Had it not been you, they would have simply inserted it into the system through another person."

"I suppose you're right," Hanna said, doubtfully. "I guess it's time we go."

"Brother, I'll say goodbye to you for now," Leonel said. "There's a protest being organized by a leftist group that will pass here in 15 or 20 minutes, so you'd better get out of here beforehand, otherwise you'll get stuck in the traffic." Then, smiling, he added, "Not to worry, though — they're pacifists."

The brothers melted together in a goodbye hug. Hanna noticed that as she shook Ahmed's hand, he did so somewhat coldly.

Once Leonel and Hanna had gone, Ahmed stared at the car from which an agent was eyeing him across the sidewalk and swiveled his head toward some shops, watching the comings and goings of the businesses without interest. Then his tail, who was beginning to lose patience, decided to leave the vehicle and stretch his legs.

Suddenly, two police cars began to block the street. A crowd came marching along, peacefully chanting choruses about peace. Israeli and Palestinian flags were being carried, and signs saying "One country! Two peoples!" were held high. Everyone was hugging or holding hands.

Taking advantage of the situation, Ahmed got lost in the crush of marchers. The agent began looking for him desperately, and he quickly called his partner, who was waiting just a few blocks away. The two began bobbing and weaving, frantically fighting for an opening in the human stream. They had lost their prey.

Ahmed ran for about five minutes in and out of the small streets of Tel Aviv. When he reached the corner of Rothschild and Marmorek, he entered a Leumi Bank to deposit the check. He knew they wouldn't give him that much money and, perhaps, they'd suspect him, so he decided to place all of it in his mother's account, which he had opened just a few weeks ago with the intention of sending her money each month. Afterwards, he went outside to the ATM and withdrew 10,000 shekels in cash.

Then he left the bank area and walked towards the ocean. When he reached the boulevard, he climbed up on a railing to better get his bearings. He turned his head toward the north and saw the Panorama hotel. He knew that was where his beloved Mariana had leaped to her death. If he did a 180-degree turn to the south, he would get to the Dolfinarium, where he had been caught on that fateful night in November. Those two places were like opposite poles in his life — on one side, the memory of love forever lost; on the other, the breakdown of everything he had been. He felt that he was caught somewhere between his traumatic past and a narrow, circumscribed future. Would he ever be truly free? Deep down, he was sure he knew the answer.

Ahmed soon decided to make his way south. He remembered feeling a kinship for the captive sea creatures that had once been made to perform in the now-abandoned building. He would retrieve the USB key he had stashed in the wall. If nothing else, he could pass the time trying to unravel the mysterious, extra codes that it contained.

107

Tel Aviv
January 10th, 2012

The agents were frantic, and couldn't understand what had happened. They requested reinforcements, and the force spread across the city. After two hours of searching, it was decided that it was time to let the boss know what had happened.

"Hello, Shaul?"

"Yes, how are you?"

"Not so good."

"What's going on?"

"We lost him."

"What?"

"Yes, we lost him."

Shaul grabbed his head in his hands. He couldn't believe what he had just heard. His promotion was planned for the coming week. Now he'd probably be kicked down to constable.

108

Jerusalem
12th of January, 2012 - 8:33 p.m.

GG arrived at the cinemateq, a beautiful place in Jerusalem a little later than what had been agreed upon. He was wearing a black beret that covered his baldness and that protected his scalp from the cold. It was 8:33 p.m. For the private nature of this conversation, S had asked that they meet outside the restaurant where they periodically went. S was wrapped up in a black, leather jacket and wore dark glasses that looked a little strange. G almost didn't recognize him. S led him for a walk, and as they as they sauntered along, they took in the towering walls enveloping the old city. Far off in the distance they could just make out the lights of the Wailing Wall.

G asked the reason for the urgency of their meeting. S removed the glasses and then answered.

"Everything needs to be eliminated," he said.

"What are you referring to?"

"All the material compiled by Shmulik Sade."

"But that's years of work — it's very relevant information."

"We must stop with all of that; I have orders and I intend to fulfill them. You complete your part."

"It's impossible. You know what that means — many people died, the risk is too high, and now, with all the effort we've made, you say we should throw it all to the wind ..."

"Listen to what I'm telling you and do it. We need to undo everything related to 'Achim.' Burn it, incinerate it, carbonize it, or whatever other synonym you need to hear!"

"Isn't there something else we can do? Lots of people have died, even if it was for the better good of the country."

"That issue has already passed. There are people here who are out to destroy us."

"I will never forget what happened."

"I recommend you do as I say, otherwise you will end up like Shmulik Sade and Eli Regev."

"And what about Yosi, the police officer? That issue will be very difficult to conceal completely. It's going to smell for sure."

S walked up to G, until their faces were nose to nose, then drew a Beretta from the small of his back, pointed it at G's head, and said through gritted teeth, "Forget everything. Eliminate whatever you've been up to. Nothing happened here. Remember that. Clean the gore until there are no traces whatsoever. Do you understand? Or do you need me to pull the trigger so you won't have to reconsider and return to reality?"

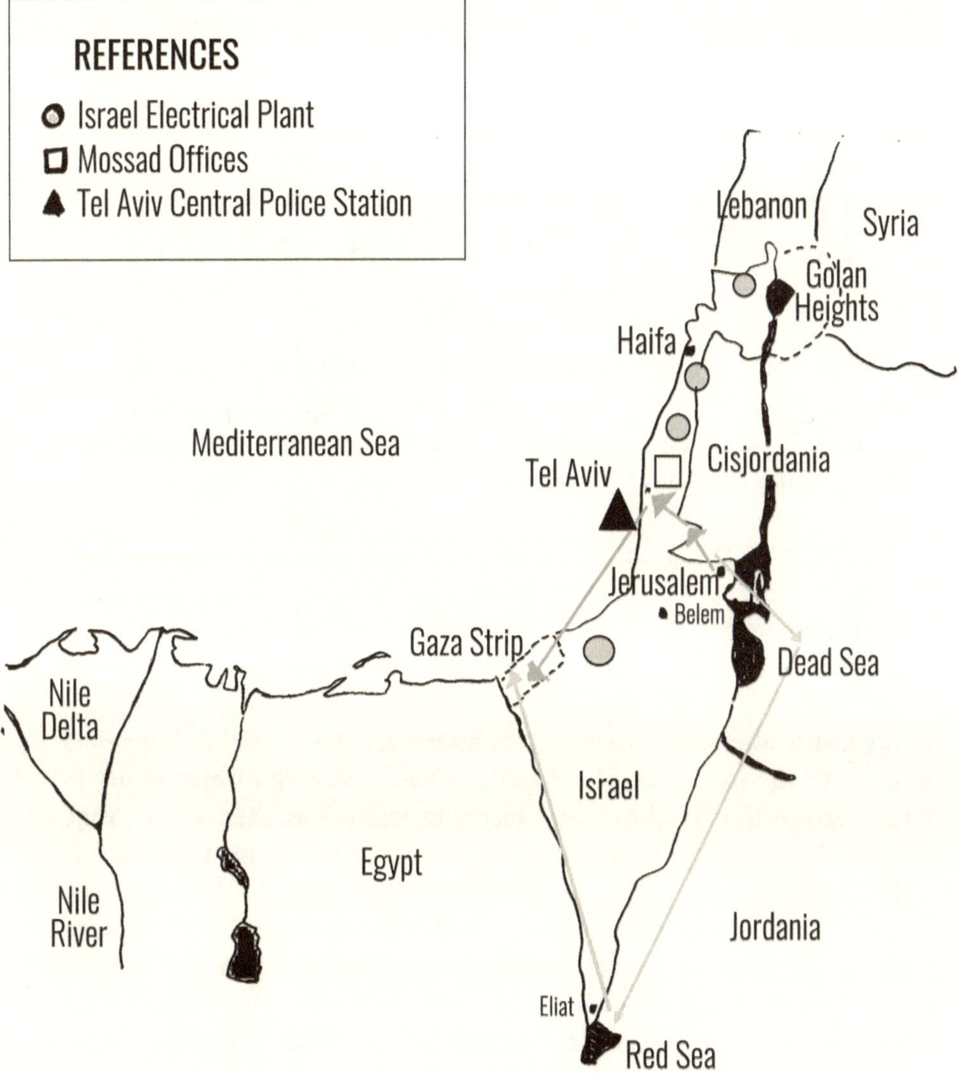

Brothers Paths:

Ahmed: Jerusalem, Belem, Amman, Aqaba (Jordania), Gaza Strip, Pakistan (Peshawar), Iran, Israel.

Leonel: Jerusalem, Tel Aviv, Gaza Strip, France (Paris), Pakistan (Peshawar), Denmark (Copenhagen), Faroe Islands (Denmark), Tel Aviv.

TECHNOLOGY GLOSSARY

Cybernetics: a transdisciplinary approach for exploring regulatory systems, their structures, constraints, and possibilities. In the 21st century, the term is often used in a rather loose way to imply "control of any system using technology."

Cybersecurity: Computer security, also known as cyber security or IT security, is the protection of computer systems from the theft or damage to the hardware, software or the information on them, as well as from disruption or misdirection of the services they provide.

Informatic war: the concept of computer war, digital war, or cyberwar; refers to the execution of a conflict where the field of operations is in cyberspace and information technologies. It has been shown that currently, in a war, you are most likely to defeat the enemy if you attack their infrastructure, rather than using any other type of physical attack. This strategy has been employed in various situations, either in military offensives from one country against another, an armed group against the government, or simply individual attacks by one or more hackers. It has been said that nowadays, weapons are special programs and computer viruses used to penetrate the security of computer systems, and that the new fighting soldiers are informatics and telecommunications experts. The targets of the attacks are usually financial, banking, and military systems, although there have been numerous cases where communication systems were affected.

Computer virus: a program or software that automatically runs and spreads itself by inserting copies of itself into another program or document. A computer virus is attached to a program or file so it can spread by itself, infecting computers by traveling from one to another. The insertion of the virus into a program is referred to as an infection and the infected files are referred to as hosts. Viruses are one of several types of malware or malicious software. Some viruses have a load-delay, which sometimes is called a bomb. For example, a virus may display a message on one day or wait for a specific time until it has infected a number of hosts. However, the most negative effect of viruses is their uncontrolled reproduction that overloads all the resources of the computer.

Malware: type of malicious (software) program.

RootKit: a program (software) designed to hide the fact that the operating system has been compromised, and which sometimes changes vital files. A RootKit allows a virus or malware to hide from the computer's protection system (antivirus). To install a RootKit, the attacker needs to obtain the system administrator's keys.

Zero Day attack: is an attack on an application or system that executes malicious code, thanks to the knowledge of vulnerabilities that are generally unknown to the public or the manufacturer of the product.

DDoS attack: A distributed denial-of-service (DDoS) attack is one in which a multitude of compromised systems attack a single target, thereby causing denial of service for users of the targeted system. The flood of incoming messages to the target system essentially forces it to shut down, thereby denying service by the system to legitimate users.

Firewall: part of a system or network that is designed to block unauthorized access while permitting authorized communications. It is a device, or set of devices, configured to allow, limit, encrypt, and decrypt traffic between the different areas on the basis of a set of rules and other criteria.

TCP/IP: is a set of protocols on which the Internet is based and which enables the transmission of data between computers. It is sometimes referred to as the TCP/IP protocol suite, in reference to the two most important protocols that compose it, which were the first to be defined, and which are the two most commonly used families of protocols:
 · Transmission Control Protocol
 · Internet Protocol

UDP: The User Datagram Protocol (UDP) is one of the core members of the Internet protocol suite. The protocol was designed by David P. Reed in 1980 and formally defined in RFC 768. With UDP, computer applications can send messages, in this case referred to as datagrams, to other hosts on an Internet Protocol (IP) network. Prior communications are not required to set up transmission channels or data paths.

FTP: a network protocol for transferring files between systems connected to a network TCP (Transmission Control Protocol), based on the client–server architecture. From a computer, a client can connect to a server to download files from it or to send you files, regardless of the operating system used on each computer.

HTTP: hypertext transfer protocol, which is very popular because it is used to access web pages.

Telnet: the name of a network protocol that allows you to connect to another machine to manage it remotely as if you were sitting in front of it.

RDS: a communications protocol that allows you to send small amounts of digital data, inaudible to the listener, with the signal of an FM radio station. The data is presented on a receiver's screen.

Cryptography: encryption techniques or coding to alter the linguistic representations of certain messages in order to make them unintelligible to unauthorized receivers. Cryptography is currently responsible for the study of algorithms, protocols, and systems that are used to provide security for communications, information, and the entities that communicate. Cryptography aims to design, implement, deploy, and make use of cryptographic systems to provide any form of security.

ISDN: a network from the evolution of the digital integrated network (RDI) that facilitates end-to-end digital connections to provide a wide range of services, through voice and other means, with standard access interfaces.

Private network: a network of computers that use specified IP addresses, which do not have access to the Internet. Computers or terminals can be assigned addresses from this space when they need to communicate with other terminals within the internal network, but not with the Internet directly.

Stuxnet: a computer worm that affects computers running Windows. It was discovered in June 2010 by VirusBlokAda, a Belarus-based security company. It is the first known worm that spies on and reprograms industrial systems, in particular SCADA systems, which are used for control and monitoring of processes, and it can affect critical infrastructure such as nuclear plants. Stuxnet attacks equipment running Windows using four Zero Days against operating system vulnerabilities. The worm has been expanding across different countries:

Country	Infected computers
Iran	62,867
Indonesia	13,336
India	6,552
United States of America	2,913
Australia	2,436

ABOUT THE AUTHOR

Ariel Mauricio Egber
(1969 – Present)

Bachelor's degree in computer science. Expert in virtual systems, cybersecurity, and infrastructure computing.

Born February 1, 1969, in the city of Buenos Aires, Argentina. Since he was a small child, he has developed an interest in literature, especially in story-telling. During adolescence, he distinguished himself with his literary productions and writing skills. His childhood was spent in Argentina, the country where he lived until the age of 15. In 1984, he immigrated with his family to Israel. There he finished high school and then studied aeronautical engineering. He then served three years in the Army Air Force. After completing his compulsory military service, he studied computers; immediately afterward, he began working in that field.

In 1998, he married Janett Warzawski, with whom he has two daughters, Joycee (16) and Hayley (14), and he currently resides in Melbourne, Australia.

His passions are writing, reading, cybersecurity and, of course, his family. Growing up in a multicultural environment, he became a citizen of the world with three different nationalities: Argentinian, Israeli, and Australian. His family is scattered across three continents. The combination of experiences, languages, and cultures infused in him the enthusiasm and the strength to express his ideas and give flight to his fruitful imagination.

www.ingramcontent.com/pod-product-compliance
Lightning Source LLC
Chambersburg PA
CBHW050608110726
47899CB00001B/28